# Green Monster

# Books by Rick Shefchik

*Amen Corner*
*Green Monster*

# Green Monster

## Rick Shefchik

Poisoned Pen Press

*Poisoned Pen Press*

Copyright © 2008 by Rick Shefchik

First Edition 2008

10 9 8 7 6 5 4 3 2 1

Library of Congress Catalog Card Number: 2008923137

ISBN: 978-1-59058-524-5  Hardcover

Poisoned Pen Press
6962 E. First Ave., Ste. 103
Scottsdale, AZ 85251
www.poisonedpenpress.com
info@poisonedpenpress.com

Printed in the United States of America

*For my mother and father*

# Acknowledgments

Thanks once again to Dan Kelly, a great friend and the best editor I know.

Thanks to Doug Britton for implanting the Red Sox habit, and sharing all the lows and highs since then.

Thanks to Claire Shefchik for her perceptive first reads.

Thanks to John Camp for the kickstart.

# Acknowledgments

Thanks once again to Dan Kelly, a great friend and the best editor I know.

Thanks to Doug Britton for implanting the Red Sox habit, and sharing all the lows and highs since then.

Thanks to Claire Shefchik for her perceptive first reads.

Thanks to John Camp for the kickstart.

# Chapter One

Lou Kenwood lowered the sports section of the Boston Globe and looked at the ocean through the back window of his Lincoln Town Car. A smile spread across his face.

Despite a string of recent losses, the sportswriters were still calling him "Lucky Louie." He never got tired of that.

Louis Albert Kenwood was seventy-eight years old. He was a billionaire. He had a thick mane of white hair, the constitution of a fifty-year-old, and a replica of the 2004 Major League Baseball World Championship trophy sitting on a glass-covered pedestal in his downtown Boston office.

Some men cured disease. Some won. Some put out fires, rescued drowning children, wrote beautiful music, designed magnificent buildings, gave millions to charity. Lucky Louie Kenwood had the good fortune to own the Boston Red Sox when they finally broke the eighty-six-year "Curse of the Bambino" and won the World Series for the first time since 1918. No scientist, soldier, firefighter, artist, engineer, or philanthropist had done nearly so much for the populace that lived between Connecticut and Quebec. Lucky Louie was the most beloved human being in New England—even among sportswriters.

Kenwood set the paper down next to him and stared out at King's Beach. He could see the peninsula community of Nahant from the road; he always wondered whether he and Katherine might have been better off buying an oceanfront home there instead of on Marblehead Neck. There was something more dramatic, and even romantic, about being surrounded by the ocean, but they hadn't been able to find a house that was big enough, and private enough, for their needs, so they'd gone farther up the shore. Their home on Marblehead Neck was huge, secluded, and provided spectacular views. The neighbors were similarly well-off, and respected the Kenwoods' privacy.

Kenwood instructed Paul, his driver, to take the same route into the city each day, detouring away from Route 1A to hug the beach on Lynn Shore Drive. Raised in western Massachusetts, Kenwood was still fascinated by the Atlantic; the sparkling blue ocean calmed him on sunny mornings and energized him on days like this, when the raw power of a storm surge swallowed the sand and crashed against the seawall.

Whatever the weather, it was always a great day to be Lucky Louie, the owner of the Boston Red Sox.

Ever since that glorious October evening when the Olde Towne Team beat the St. Louis Cardinals and took home their first World Championship since 1918, the turnstiles had not stopped whirling. When they repeated three years later, it was no longer considered a miracle, but the beginning of a new Red Sox dynasty. The Sox no longer needed to coast on the good will of its New England fan base; they had made the first steps toward replacing their hated rivals, the Yankees, as the dominant team in baseball. The charming, patched-over relic that was Fenway Park played to capacity crowds at every home date. Each time Kenwood glanced at the big trophy in his office, he could still feel the sting of champagne in his eyes and remember how it felt to be wearing a ruined $2500 suit and a dopey grin that lasted so long his face hurt the next morning. The replica trophy from 2007 sat in the club president's office; it looked identical, but Lucky Louie Kenwood—and everyone else in the organization—knew which one meant more to the team, the fans, and the region.

When he bought the club, Kenwood had been convinced that the Sox needed a new ballpark, just as all the other major league baseball teams were blackmailing their cities into building them new ballparks, in order to rake in more money to compete against each other in the game's murderous salary spiral. But that was before the Curse of the Bambino was broken, and the fans fell in love with the Sox in a way that surpassed all previous levels of obsession—and this was a town where the newspapers did a front-page story each February on the team's equipment truck leaving for spring training in Florida.

It wasn't just that the Sox had come back from a three-game deficit to defeat the hated Yankees 4-3 in the League Championship Series, or that they'd flexed their muscles and crushed the power-laden Cardinals in a four-game World Series rout. The astonishing and sustained outpouring of love occurred because this team had allowed every Red Sox fan in America to finally taste victory after generations of bitter disappointment. The eight dark decades had commenced after the Red Sox—then the most successful team in baseball, winners of five World Championships between 1912 and 1918—sold Babe Ruth to the Yankees in 1919. Ruth's departure to New York initiated the Yankees' run as the greatest dynasty in professional sports, and began two decades of total ineptitude by the once-proud Red Sox. The futility of those years turned to agony after Tom Yawkey bought the Sox in the late '30s and restored the team to respectability through lavish spending. The stage was then set for what writers eventually called The Curse of the Bambino—a litany of mistakes, failures, and misfortunes resulting in Red Sox losses: Pesky failing to throw out Slaughter in the '46 Series, McCarthy starting the washed-up Galehouse in the '48 playoff, Lonborg running out of gas in Game Seven of the '67 Series, Johnson going with Burton instead of Willoughby in the ninth inning of Game Seven in '75, Torrez giving up that homer to Bucky Dent in the '78 playoff, the ball going through Buckner's legs in '86, Little staying with Pedro too long in '03…

And as each season turned into the next, with Yankee championships piling up as fast as Red Sox failures, smug New York fans would hold up signs that simply said "1918"—reminding Boston fans how long it had been since the last World Series win by the Red Sox. The Yankees were not just envied rivals; they were the Evil Empire.

Kenwood had lived and died through every one of the famous disasters in Red Sox history, but he never believed the franchise was cursed. Like any right-thinking New Englander, he was a Sox fan from birth, saving money from his paper route in Pittsfield to attend a few games each summer at Fenway. From Ted Williams to Mo Vaughn, he'd seen them all, and seen them all fall short when it really mattered. While the Sox were failing with spectacular regularity, Kenwood was succeeding beyond even his most unrealistic dreams. He made a fortune in retailing, and turned it into a bigger fortune on Wall Street.

Then he bought the Boston Red Sox, and, miraculously, they won. They did what no Sox team since Babe Ruth's time—not the clubs with Teddy Ballgame, or Yaz, or the Rocket, or Nomar—had been able to do: They saved generations of Sox fans from going to their graves without seeing their beloved ballclub win a World Series.

Ever since that night, when church bells rang from Bangor to Hartford, Red Sox Nation had repaid Lou Kenwood many times over, with sellouts, astronomical television ratings, and souvenir and apparel sales second to no other team in the majors. For his part, Lou Kenwood had returned the favor by delivering another championship. Yes, the sweep against the Rockies had seemed something of an anti-climax, but now the Red Sox had something they could once have only fantasized about: taunting rights over the Yankees. And it felt good.

Kenwood had constructed a team that seemed destined to elbow the Yankees aside as kingpins of baseball. Boston—always known as The Hub—was being restored to its rightful place, abdicated for almost ninety years, as the center of the baseball universe. Sox fans now expected the team to win, expected management to outsmart the Yankees when it came to accumulating baseball's top talent, and expected Lucky Louie to outspend his mistakes, as the Yankees had always been able to do.

Lou Kenwood had no idea how long this stunning reversal of fortune could last, but he didn't expect to see the end of the love affair he was enjoying with New England. Fans still wanted to shake his hand, say thanks, and have him kiss their children; even the sportswriters, who were more comfortable tearing into local owners than celebrating them, kept the "Lucky Louie" name going, as though it were printed on his driver's license. And why shouldn't Kenwood feel lucky? At his last checkup, his physician told him he was in perfect health. He'd go another ten years, easily.

Not everyone in his life was so fortunate. There was Katherine's hopeless condition, of course. And Paul's father.

"How's your dad's health, Paul?" Kenwood asked his driver.

Paul O'Brien, wearing a black chauffeur's cap over his curly reddish-brown hair, took his eye off the constricted roadway that led through Revere and glanced in his rearview mirror without turning his head. Kenwood knew that Patrick O'Brien had been suffering from Alzheimer's disease, but Paul never spoke about his father unless asked.

"He's gettin' along, sir," O'Brien said. His South Boston accent was engaged in its never-ending struggle with the more appropriate diction of a billionaire's personal driver.

"Does he still watch the games?"

"Oh, he never misses the Sox. I have to remind him who they're playin' now and then. He remembers the Yanks, the Tigers, the White Sox...he doesn't too good...so well...with the Blue Jays or the Rays."

"Neither do I, sometimes," Kenwood said. "Remember, if there's anything your family needs...his care must be getting expensive."

"Thank you, sir, but, you know, like I've said...we manage," Paul said. His tone suggested the subject was closed.

Kenwood acceded to stubborn Southie pride, and turned to the Globe business section while Paul navigated the Lincoln onto the McClellan Highway in Chelsea, which slowly funneled them through the Sumner Tunnel and into downtown Boston. Kenwood always stopped at his offices in the One Financial Center tower before going out to the ballpark.

They parked in the underground lot and took the express elevator up to the 40$^{th}$ floor. Paul accompanied Kenwood into the office and then excused himself, waiting to be summoned for the drive out to Fenway later in the day.

"Good morning, Mr. Kenwood," his receptionist said as he passed her desk.

"Good morning, Ellie. Coffee and a blueberry scone this morning, please."

"Of course."

"Tough game last night, Louie," Bill Edmunds, his vice president of acquisitions, called to him from his open office door as Kenwood walked toward his office. "You ever seen a guy screw up an easier pop fly than the one Hurtado dropped in the twelfth?"

"It reminded me of that ball he dropped in the Series, when he was with the Cards."

"Yeah, you're right. So we're another game back in the loss column."

"There's still time, Bill," Kenwood said. "Two weeks left—the Yanks know we're not going to give up."

"Shouldn't we be looking at some kids?"

"That's what I want to talk to Joe about this afternoon. He says that right fielder at Pawtucket looks pretty good. We might sit Hurtado down for a couple of games and see what the kid can do up here. If Hurtado won't sign, we need options."

"Have you listened to the call-in shows lately? The fans are really dumping on Ivan. If we don't make the playoffs this year, I don't think they'd want him back."

"I never listen to those shows," Kenwood said. "We've got all the experts we need on our payroll."

Bill Edmunds' responsibility at the Kenwood Companies was looking for properties to purchase, but he was a Sox fan like everyone else, and was thrilled to have the opportunity to talk baseball with the owner every morning. Edmunds knew enough not to offer serious suggestions; that was better left to the hard-core callers to the talk shows and the baseball nuts who posted on the proliferation of Sox websites.

Kenwood walked into his office, a fifty-by-fifty corner suite with ten-foot windows that looked toward Fenway Park to the southwest and BMW Bay to the southeast. The replica of the World Championship trophy, with its thirty gold flags surrounding a silver baseball, rested atop a four-foot-high pedestal against the wall. Above it hung an oil painting of Fenway Park, looking from home plate toward the Green Monster.

The office walls were adorned with photos of himself, standing with the key players from the championship team, and with Sox greats from the past: standing next to Ted Williams' wheelchair and shaking his hand at the '99 All-Star Game; his arm around Yaz at an old-timers' day; sharing a joke with Pudge Fisk at a Jimmy Fund event; and standing between Bobby Doerr and Johnny Pesky at a Fenway ceremony honoring the old double-play tandem. There were framed stories and photos from the championship seasons, with LUCKY LOUIE and KENWOOD the prominent names in the headlines.

Kenwood picked up that morning's copy of the Herald. The headline on the sports page read:

"Sox feel the Big Hurt(ado)"

The sports desks never ran out of puns.

He dropped the paper on his desk, eased himself into his leather swivel chair, and picked up the stack of mail that Ellie had left for him. It was standard stuff except for a black envelope with his name and address spelled out in white ink. He slit it open with the commemorative letter opener presented to him by the Boston Chamber of Commerce at a banquet following the 2004 World Series. Inside was a piece of black stationery with more white writing:

*Lucky Louie,*

*The 2004 World Series was fixed. Unless you follow my exact instructions and pay me $50,000,000, a player will confess that he participated in throwing that Series to the Red Sox. He'll go to the press and to the Commissioner of Baseball no later than Oct. 1—just in time for the playoffs.*

*Think I'm joking? Don't bet on it. If this becomes public, no one will ever trust baseball again. The Red Sox will be the new Black Sox. The 2004 World Series—your proudest moment—will be remembered as a fraud. You'll go from hero to pariah overnight. Don't spoil all those precious memories for your fans. And don't go to the cops. I'm watching you.*

*I'll contact you again in a few days to tell you how to deliver the money.*

*Use your head,*

*Babe Ruth.*

# Chapter Two

*Minneapolis, Minnesota—*

Marcus Hargrove counted out "ONE! TWO! THREE! FOUR!" and Sam Skarda hit the first ringing C chord of the Temptations' "Ain't Too Proud to Beg" on his Fender Stratocaster. A half-dozen couples pushed their chairs back, got up from their tables around the dimly-lit Boom Boom Room bar and jostled for position on the dance floor as Hargrove belted out the first line of the Motown classic.

Sam loved the grainy texture to Hargrove's voice, and he loved the way Hargrove worked himself and the crowd into sweating ecstasy as he prowled back and forth in front of the band like a caged panther. A couple of nights a month, Hargrove shed his Minneapolis Police Department identity by putting on his Otis Redding suit and vest and singing with Night Beat, the oldies band Skarda had formed when he, too, had been a member of the MPD.

It was a warm Friday night in mid-September, and owner Ted Tollefson, a hulking figure with a shaggy walrus moustache, had propped open the front door to the Boom Boom Room to allow some fresh air to circulate. If somebody complained to the cops about the noise spilling out onto Hennepin Avenue—well, everybody in the band was, or had been, a cop. In addition to Sam and Marcus, drummer Stu Winstead patrolled a beat in Nordeast;

bassist Bear Olson was a vice cop; and keyboard player/singer Jean Dubrovna was an investigator with the juvenile unit.

Sam had been their colleague until resigning as a homicide detective in April. Thanks to a generous payment he'd received for some emergency detective work at Augusta National Golf Club in Georgia, he'd applied for a private investigator's license and opened a practice in White Bear Lake, an old-money beach town just north of St. Paul. There was no reason to ask clients to find a place to park in Minneapolis just so they could visit him in an overpriced downtown office building. Besides, most of the detective work people seemed willing to pay for was happening out in the suburbs.

He had some money now, but he still played the same '59 Strat through the same Deluxe Reverb amp, and he still lived in the same bungalow in South Minneapolis. Sometimes old things were better things. But after furnishing his office, he allowed himself two indulgences: He bought a new Mustang convertible, and he joined the White Bear Yacht Club, a 1927 Donald Ross golf course on the edge of the lake. It was the club where Scott and Zelda Fitzgerald had lived in 1922, until being evicted for throwing too many drunken parties. His office was a five-minute commute to the golf course.

He performed two Friday nights a month with Night Beat at the Boom Boom Room, played golf three times a week at WBYC, and spent the rest of his time working on the stray cases that came his way—mostly divorce and missing-persons stuff. Nothing to get excited about, but enough to keep from using up the nest egg. He was not working all that hard at generating new business; he placed an ad in the Yellow Pages, let his former cop buddies know he was available for hire, then waited to see who rang the phone or walked in the door. At the rate it was going, he figured he could stay in business at least another year before he'd have to start hustling up clients or give up the White Bear membership. That would be incentive enough to work harder.

His knee—surgically repaired after a shooting while he was a cop—still hurt like hell on rainy days, but it was as good as it was ever going to get. He knew he should be working out more, but as long as he walked 18 holes three times a week, he was able to keep his weight around 180 and his legs in reasonably good condition. There wasn't a lot of running involved when you were staking out a cheating husband.

Now that he was no longer subject to the police department's rules, his sandy blond hair had grown out, as his cop pals continually reminded him. It wasn't rock-band long yet, but it was getting curly and harder to keep under his golf hat. He meant to go to the barber more often, but now that he didn't have to, it kept slipping farther down the priority list. He still kept himself clean-shaven, however. His golf tan accented his pale blue eyes and helped divert attention from the bridge of his nose, which was crooked from an old break.

He'd flown to Tucson in August to visit Caroline, the woman he'd met at the Masters. She'd gone back to using her maiden name after divorcing her golf-pro husband—a hopeful sign—but the rest of the picture was still cloudy. She had sold the ostentatious house at the private golf club that she used to share with her ex, and had stopped smoking—with a few backyard lapses—when she moved into her new house. She had a new job, too, working for the U.S. Citizenship and Immigration Services on border issues. Caroline was enjoying her life for the first time since long before her marriage broke up. She needed more time, she'd told Sam, to figure out what she wanted from life—and how a long-distance romance with an ex-cop fit into it. She said there was a chance—more than a chance, really—that he would be part of that life, but she wasn't ready to say when.

Sam wanted to be in Caroline's life. He was in his mid-thirties, and finding it lonely to be away from the police force. He had been used to not having anyone to greet him when he came home at night, but at least there'd been the crude jokes and camaraderie with his fellow cops during the day. Now he was thinking about getting a dog. When he was a kid, he'd had a German shepherd named Bart—a former police dog, brought home by his dad after it was injured in a chase. If he could find a dog as smart and loyal as Bart had been…but detective hours were unpredictable. Did he want to have to worry about running home in the middle of a stakeout to let the dog out? Or finding someone to take the dog when Sam had to leave town?

The band was his primary release, but not from job stress, like Hargrove and the others. Sam was battling boredom, and he didn't know what to do about it. He didn't want to be a cop again; he liked the freedom of being a private investigator. He could be relentless when a job had his full attention, and, working on his own, he didn't have to worry about being told to speed up or slow down on a case.

It was the cases themselves that were sucking the life out of him. When he was being honest with himself, he could admit that he didn't care whether Beth Cheslak was screwing Brian Johnson at their real estate agency, even if Beth's husband Bob was paying him $100 an hour to find out. It was tawdry work. But, it wasn't the prying and skulking that bothered him; it was the reason he was doing it. As a cop, he was Preserving civic order and Protecting the citizenry. He was helping a grieving wife, mother, or father find a small measure of relief by hunting down and locking up the murdering thug who'd ruined their lives. But catching Beth Cheslak coming out of the motel with Brian Johnson? That was a pay day, nothing more.

Marcus Hargrove brought "Ain't Too Proud to Beg" to its sudden ending, drawing cries for more from the dancers. He gave Sam and the band the signal for "Land of 1,000 Dances," and they all hit and held a B-minor.

"One, two THREE!" Marcus sang into the mic, and then Sam and the band let a solid D chord hang in the air while Marcus sang "ONE, two, three…" Then Bear played the descending bass riff, Stu began hammering the snare and hi-hat and the band kicked into the set-closer—you couldn't follow Wilson Pickett's "Land of 1,000 Dances" with anything except "Shout," and they always saved that one for the end of the night. When Marcus had finished screaming the final "ah, HELP me!"s, they put their instruments down, left the stage to the yells and applause of the exhausted dancers, and went to the bar for their beers—on the house.

"Phone call for you, Sam," Ted Tollefson said as he poured him a glass of Bass Ale from the tap.

"When did it come?" Sam said. He wiped his sweating forehead with the sleeve of his shirt.

"During 'Twist and Shout,' I think."

"Did they leave a number?"

"No. It was a woman. She's still on the line. Said she'd wait."

Sam took a deep gulp of his beer and then reached across the bar for the phone receiver that Ted held out to him.

"Hello?"

"Sam Skarda?"

"That's me. You'll have to speak up. It's real loud in here."

"Are you…Boston…tomorrow?"

"What's that?" Sam said. "I didn't catch that. Louder, please."

"…fly…tomorrow!"

"No, sorry, still not hearing you real well. Call me on my cell phone, and I'll take it outside."

Sam gave her his cell number. He was pretty sure she said she'd call him back, so he let Ted hang up the phone and took his beer across the room and out the front door. Sam sat down at one of the wrought-iron tables on the sidewalk in front of the bar, sipped his beer, watched the condensation drops trickle down the glass, and waited for his phone to ring. Something about going to Boston. He hadn't been there in ten years. Who did he even know there anymore?

The cell phone rang, and he said, "Sam Skarda."

"Hello, Mr. Skarda." It was a younger woman's voice. "My name is Heather Canby. I work for The Kenwood Companies in Boston. We have a job for you, if you're interested. Can you be here by tomorrow?"

"Depends on the job, I guess. Who did you say you work for?"

"Louis Kenwood."

Now the name registered. Lucky Louie Kenwood, owner of the Boston Red Sox. Why in hell would he want to hire Sam?

"The Red Sox owner?" Sam asked, to make sure.

"Yes, that's right."

"What you need is a young power hitter, not a detective."

"This is serious, Mr. Skarda."

The voice on the other end of the phone sounded all of about twenty-five. It sounded pretty, too. "Please, call me Sam. Now, what's the problem?"

"I can't talk about it on the phone," she said. "It's...extremely delicate."

"How'd you find me?"

"I talked to a Lt. Stensrud, at the police department."

"Doug, my former boss. How'd you get my name in the first place?"

"You were recommended by a very good friend of Mr. Kenwood."

That would almost have to be David Porter or Robert Brisbane, who had hired Sam at Augusta National. None of his contacts in Minnesota were pals with Lucky Louie.

"I guess I could catch a plane tomorrow," Sam said. He took another long sip of his beer.

"We'll cover all your expenses," Heather Canby said. "We'll put you up at the Taj Boston."

"Where's that?'

"Just a few blocks from our downtown offices. It's the former Ritz-Carlton."

"I know the place."

"We have a day game tomorrow. If you could be at our office by eight tomorrow night, we'll explain everything to you."

"You're in a hurry, aren't you?"

"Yes, we are."

"Why not get a local guy?"

"Mr. Kenwood doesn't trust anyone here for a job like this. That's why he consulted with...friends."

"David Porter?"

"That's correct," she said after a moment's hesitation. "He said we could trust you with our lives."

"Is it that serious?"

"No. It's more serious than that. Please call us the minute you arrive. We'll have Mr. Kenwood's chauffeur meet you at Logan and drive you into the city."

She left the Kenwood phone number.

"Don't you want to know my rates?" Sam asked.

"That's not important."

"It is to me."

"Whatever you charge, Mr. Kenwood will pay you substantially more."

"That works," Sam said.

"One other thing," she said. "You can't tell anyone you're meeting Mr. Kenwood. Don't even tell anyone you're going to Boston. I mean it. This has to be kept absolutely quiet."

"I'll have to tell my faithful Filipino houseboy where I'll be the next few days," Sam said. The beer was starting to have an effect.

"What?"

"Never mind." She was too young to get the Green Hornet reference, or too serious to have ever read a comic book. "I won't tell anyone anything. That's one thing we private eyes are good at."

"See you tomorrow, Mr. Skarda."

Sam was supposed to meet with Bob Cheslak Monday morning to tell him all about Beth and Brian. He wouldn't mind blowing that off.

Sam went back inside the bar and saw the rest of the band heading for the stage. Time for another set. They blasted through a string of dance-party oldies: "Good Lovin'," "Walking on Sunshine," "I'm So Excited," "Authority Song," "What I Like About You," "Satisfaction," and "Mony Mony."

When the set was over, Sam's shirt was clinging to him as sweat trickled down the small of his back. He grabbed another beer and headed back out to the tables on the sidewalk in front of the bar. Marcus Hargrove got a beer of his own and joined him. They sat at a table with an Amstel Light umbrella and watched the cars go by, some headed north toward the lights of the theater district, the others headed south past the technical college toward Loring Park, maybe to Uptown, with its funky shops and restaurants.

"Good set, good set," Marcus said, his head nodding in appreciation. "I still wish we could find a cop who played the sax."

Marcus stretched his long legs out onto the sidewalk. He had a shaved head and a gold earring, which might have made him stand out in the Minneapolis Police Department ten years earlier, but not anymore. The other cops considered him a prima donna because of his fondness for the media, and his tendency to break into Prince songs and moves as he strolled through the office. But when it came to dealing with street gangs, he was the best cop the department had. Some cops didn't like to work with him because he got himself dangerously deep into the neighborhood gang culture, straddling a fine line between being a liaison and a target. Sam knew him mostly through the band, but he would have been happy to work with a cop who put as much into his work as Marcus did.

"Yeah, a sax would sound great," Sam said. "We could do some of that old Junior Walker stuff."

"Add a trumpet, and we could do more Stax material."

"They wouldn't need to be cops. I'm not a cop anymore."

"You'll always be a cop," Marcus said, with his infectious cackle. "You just wear different threads."

"Hold it, Marcus," Sam said.

He took his hand off his beer and tapped Marcus' forearm.

"You see that car parked across the street? The green Civic, in front of the sandwich shop?"

Marcus flicked his eyes in the direction Sam had suggested, without moving his head. A young, bare-headed black male sat in the driver's seat, looking at Sam and Marcus, turning away briefly and then looking at them again. The traffic was light for a late Friday night.

"I see him," Marcus said. "I don't like him."

"Maybe he's waiting for somebody inside," Sam said. He took a sip of his beer without taking his eyes off the car.

"I don't think so. He's staring at us."

A Metro Transit bus went by, and as the bus passed the parked Civic, the young man at the wheel suddenly put the car into gear, did a squealing U-turn in the middle of the street and swung the car along the sidewalk in front of the Boom Boom Room. He raised his right hand and pointed a semi-automatic handgun out the open passenger side window.

"Get down!" Marcus yelled. He dived into Sam, knocking him off his chair and onto the sidewalk.

Sam heard the "pop pop pop pop" of four shots fired, clanging off the iron table and spraying chips from the brick front of Tollefson's bar, then the squeal of tires as the shooter stomped on the gas. Sam automatically looked for the license plate, and got a good read on it as the car roared away.

The cops inside the bar ran out to the street; one in uniform drew his service pistol and fired two shots at the Civic as it sped north on Hennepin and took a hard left at the first intersection, causing two oncoming cars to veer onto the sidewalk.

"Christ, are you guys all right?" the cop with the gun asked Sam and Marcus, who were lying in beer and broken glass on the sidewalk under their overturned table.

"I'm good," Marcus said. "Sam?"

"The punk was a lousy shot," Sam said.

"Lucky for us," Marcus said. He got to his feet and shook his arms to get some of the beer off his shirt. "Man, those fuckers are getting *bold*."

"You piss off some Crips today?"

"I piss somebody off every day," Marcus said, shaking his head. "But that's the first time this has happened."

Sam and Marcus agreed on the license plate number. The cop with the gun called in the drive-by shooting, describing the car, the driver, and passing on the license number. By now a dozen people had come out of the bar to see what the noise was about.

The other band members appeared to be more shaken up than Sam and Marcus were.

"You want to call it a night?" Bear asked them.

"Hell, no," Marcus said. "Nothin' more we can do about it now."

"Let's rock 'n' roll," Sam said.

# Chapter Three

*Caracas, Venezuela—*

Elena waited for her matching red travel bags to descend onto the American Airlines carousel at the Maiquetia Airport. She glanced outside through the terminal windows and wondered whether she would be able to find a taxi so late at night—and would the driver be a fast-talking bandit, like so many of them these days?

Her flight from Los Angeles had begun at 9:15 the morning before, and had been delayed in Miami for several hours by a mechanical problem. They had finally descended over the pitch-black Caribbean and into the airport fifteen miles north of Caracas at two a.m. Now Elena just wanted to get to her house, call her son to let him know she had arrived safely, and get off her tired, swollen feet.

When the bags eventually arrived, Elena shouldered the smaller one and wheeled the larger one to the Arrivals area of the nearly deserted terminal. No one was there to help her at the yellow Corporación Anfitriones desk, where travelers were advised to pay for their cab rides in advance. She wasn't going to wait for someone to show up; she had not slept a minute on the flight and wanted desperately to get home.

She walked out the front door and onto the sidewalk in front of the terminal. As soon as the automatic doors opened, the muggy September heat wrapped around her like a damp shawl, and the exhaust fumes assaulted her nasal passages, reminding her that she was back in urban Venezuela, land of pickpockets, muggers, and car-jackers.

A black cab with a yellow Taxi Astrala logo on the side was idling a few feet from the door. As soon as Elena signaled to the cab, the driver emerged from his vehicle and walked quickly to her.

"Allow me to assist with your bags, *Señora*," said the driver, a thin, younger man with a dark moustache, a white short-sleeved shirt, and a small-brimmed straw hat. He popped open his trunk, put Elena's bags inside, and opened the back door for her. Elena was surprised and impressed by such willing, attentive service. The Caracas cabbies were not famous for their courtesy.

"Where may I take you, *Señora?*" the cabbie asked.

She gave him her address in southeastern suburban Caracas and settled back for the half-hour ride home. Her husband, Victor, would have been asleep hours ago. She would have to de-activate the security system when she arrived.

The cab pulled away from the curb and merged into the sparse traffic exiting Maiquetia Airport. The driver, whose license identified him as Juan D'Aquisto, followed the Autopista/Caracas sign and stopped at a toll booth, then proceeded through the Boquerón I and Boquerón II tunnels. He took the left lane as they entered La Planicie tunnel, which would take them through downtown Caracas. For that reason, at least, Elena was glad that they were making this drive at night. She hated to look at the hillside shantytowns that ringed the downtown area—they reminded her that she had grown up in one of those tin-roofed hovels, with no water or electricity. Now, when she drove past, she could hardly believe that she or anyone else could possibly have lived like that. The shanties were piled on top of each other to the peaks of the surrounding hills, looking like a schoolgirl's slum diorama made of dented shoeboxes, with holes punched out for windows. Maybe someday she and her family could find a way to help those poor wretches…

Elena felt the tension of the long trip start to seep away, the pain in her feet begin to recede, her eyelids begin to droop. They opened again when she realized the cab was slowing down and pulling over, still inside the tunnel.

Flashing red lights reflected off the ceiling of the tunnel. Elena turned to look behind her. A Caracas Police van had pulled up behind them.

"*Policia*," the driver said.

"What is wrong?" she asked him.

"*No se*," he responded with a shrug. "I have done nothing."

Three police officers emerged from the van and walked up to the cab with guns drawn. One of them smacked the butt of his handgun on Elena's window several times, shouting at her to open the window. Terrified, Elena did as she was told.

"You will please get out of the taxi," the police officer ordered.

"*Por que?*" Elena stammered. "Is something wrong?"

"We will explain," the officer said. "But you must leave the taxi and come with us now."

Elena looked at the officer. He was a copper-skinned, well-muscled man who wore a short-sleeved, navy blue uniform shirt and, like the other two policemen with him, a hard-shelled riot helmet with the eyeshade pulled down to conceal his face.

Elena's first thought was that something must have happened to Victor, or to one of her children. But how did the police know where to find her? And why were their guns drawn? Crime was terrible in Caracas lately—maybe this was the way the police had to do things now. But it was all so upsetting. She just wanted to go home.

"*Por favor*," Elena said to the muscular officer as she got out of the cab. "Tell me what is happening. Is my family all right?"

"Into the van," the officer replied gruffly. Another officer in an ill-fitting uniform took Elena by the elbow and walked her to the police vehicle. "All will be explained shortly."

Elena allowed herself to be assisted into the back seat of the van with one of the officers, a thin young man with a moustache, while the other got behind the wheel of the vehicle and put it in gear, pulling around the cab and then stopping a few yards farther down the tunnel. Elena was looking out the window in front of her, wondering why they had stopped again, and where the third officer was. It must have been after three a.m. now—they were the only two vehicles in the tunnel, as far as Elena could tell. If only they would tell her what was going on.

She was so preoccupied with her concerns about her family that she didn't notice that the muscular officer had stayed next to the cab. Because of the silencer on the officer's handgun, she didn't hear the bullet he fired through Juan D'Aquisto's brain. She didn't see the blood that spattered the inside of the cab's windshield as though shaken from the end of a paintbrush.

A moment later the muscular officer got into the passenger seat, turned to the policeman at the wheel and said, "*Vamanos.*"

# Chapter Four

*Boston, Massachusetts—*

Sam's plane emerged from gray rainclouds and landed at Logan airport late the next afternoon. New England weather was holding form: When it was warm in Minnesota, it was usually crappy on the East Coast.

During the flight, Sam had tried to put together the few pieces of this puzzle. Why would a major league baseball team—the Red Sox in particular—need a private eye? Especially one from halfway across the country? The Red Sox had been expected to win their division again, but were trailing the Yankees, and were in danger of missing the Wild Card, too. Maybe if they could develop a couple of home-grown sluggers—another Yaz, another Rice—they'd really become the dynasty the fans and writers expected them to be. But those problems were beyond Sam's abilities to solve.

Sam had picked up the Red Sox addiction when he was a student at Dartmouth. A freshman from Minnesota who knew no one when he arrived in New Hampshire, he'd spent September mornings sitting on a rocking chair on the porch of the Hanover Inn reading the Boston Globe. The Red Sox were in a tight pennant race that fall with the Tigers and Jays, and the Globe baseball reporters and columnists revealed to him a depth and intensity about the sport that surpassed anything he'd seen in Minnesota. Hanover was a two-plus-hour drive from Boston, but all the locals—from the college's professors and administrators to the campus cops and janitors—hung on Ned Martin's radio play-by-play of each game. On Sundays, the Globe's Peter Gammons filled an entire page with inside dope from his notebook. Sam came to understand that the Boston Red Sox were more than a baseball team; they were the family narrative of New England.

Sam had to see this phenomenon for himself. He persuaded a guy from his dorm to drive them down to Fenway for a game in late September. Under the stands, Fenway was as dank as a bus station toilet, but out in the open air it was vibrantly alive, even as it retained the intimacy of a corner booth. It had everything he'd missed at the Metrodome, the sterile plastic auditorium where the Twins played. The stands buzzed with baseball chatter from fans who knew more about the players than they did about their own children. At Sam's first game, Ellis Burks won it for the Sox with a high, arching homer into the net above the left-field wall—known since Ted Williams' time as the Green Monster because, at 37 feet, 2 inches high and just 310 feet from home plate, it seemed to loom over the pitcher's shoulder.

From that night on, Sam was a shirt-tail relative of Red Sox Nation. Years later, he understood exactly what that curse-busting 2004 World Series meant to New England.

Now the team's owner had summoned him from Minneapolis to help him with a case that his assistant had described as more important than life or death. That was a nearly redundant way to describe Red Sox baseball. But he still couldn't guess what the problem might be, and why Heather Canby had insisted on secrecy.

After retrieving his bags at the carousel, Sam spotted a man in a dark suit, wearing a cap and holding a sign that said SKARDA. Sam hoisted his garment bag over his shoulder and approached the man.

"Are you Paul?"

"Yes, sir. Mr. Skarda?"

"Call me Sam. Ready to go?"

"This way, sir."

Paul O'Brien seemed a bit stiff. His thick, red hair was conservatively—and freshly—cut above his ears and his crisp white collar. Both the haircut and the suit must have cost a lot of money, but Kenwood apparently wanted a driver who could handle a car and look good doing it.

Sam tried to make conversation as they walked to the short-term parking ramp.

"Everything okay with Mr. Kenwood?"

"Yes, sir."

"Do you know why he wants me to meet him?"

"No, sir."

"Sox win today?"

"Yeah, 6-5. Luke Bowdoin hit a grand slam in the fourth, and Ken Adams struck out two guys in the ninth with a runner on third."

Paul's clipped responses and proper diction had evaporated, replaced by the universal language of New England—how the Red Sox did that day. Now his "r"s were starting to disappear; "fourth" sounded like "foth," and "third" sounded like "thad."

"Did Hurtado play?"

"Nah, they're sitting him down for a few days. The bum."

When they reached the Lincoln, Paul reverted to his chauffeur role, putting Sam's bags in the trunk and opening his door for him. Still, Sam felt as though he knew Paul now, or had known lots of guys like him. Red Sox Nation was a melting pot, bringing together M.I.T. professors and dock workers who couldn't communicate with each other about logarithms or bulkheads, but knew how many RBIs Jim Rice had in 1977.

Paul started the car and skillfully blended into traffic, heading for the Ted Williams tunnel.

"How'd you end up working for Mr. Kenwood?" Sam asked.

"I'd been driving truck for a few years," Paul said. "My cousin is the fleet dispatcher for the concession company that supplies Fenway. He heard Mr. Kenwood was looking for a driver, and he got me an interview."

"Let me guess—you're from South Boston."

"Southie born and raised," Paul said, his accent thickening with each word. "How'd you know?"

"I spent some time out here."

In fact, Sam could still be living in Boston if things had worked out differently. Instead of going to law school like so many of his fellow graduates, Sam moved to Boston, found a cheap apartment off Mass. Ave., and tried to put a band together. He'd found a compatible bass player and singer named Terry Donaghy, but the guitarists and keyboard players they met were either too egomaniacal or too introverted, while the drummers abused everything from cough syrup to their girlfriends. Sam took a crappy job cleaning an office building in Somerset, and played his acoustic guitar in the door wells around Harvard Square for spare change, hoping that a band would somehow congeal around him. It didn't happen. He was at a low ebb when his father, a Minneapolis cop, came out to visit him.

"Come home," his dad said. "This isn't the life for you."

Sam was twenty-two and not inclined to take career advice from his father, but he knew Dad was right. His own musical ability was limited, and his chances of success rested on the brilliance and unreliability of more talented musicians. Most were into drugs as much as they were into music, and even then Sam was beginning to resent the waste and sleaze of that lifestyle. It wasn't something he wanted to be around. His father had always hoped Sam would go to the police academy after college, and after the squalor of his musician's life in Boston, Sam decided it wasn't a bad idea. He went home with his father and signed up for the academy the following week.

Paul took the tunnel under the harbor into downtown Boston, arriving at the hotel as the streetlights were coming on. Paul opened the door for Sam and got his bags out of the trunk.

"You can check in and get settled," Paul said, once again the servant. "I'll wait here for you. We should leave in twenty minutes."

A cool wind was stirring the treetops in the Public Garden across the street as couples walked by on their way to dinner or a show. Sam was reminded of a similar autumn Saturday almost twenty years earlier when he'd gone to the same hotel, then known as the Ritz-Carlton, to have dinner with a friend's parents after the Harvard-Dartmouth football game. The old girl still looked like the prototype of an elegant big-city hotel. The exterior, at least, hadn't changed since the days when long-time Red Sox owner Tom Yawkey lived and drank there: the suspended marquee above the entrance, the sidewalk-to-ceiling lobby-level windows, and the granite gray façade that gave way to brick around the upper-floor windows.

Sam checked in and went up to his suite on the eighth floor. The living room had a wood-burning fireplace with marble inlays and an ornate wooden mantel, brass wall lamps on the built-in wooden columns on both sides of the hearth, and an oil portrait of some Revolutionary War figure hanging above the mantel. A glass-topped coffee table with a bowl of real fruit stood a few feet in front of the hearth, with two plush armchairs and a couch arranged around it. There was a walnut entertainment unit on the wall opposite the fireplace, and a matching desk and chair next to the draperied window that overlooked the Public Garden across Arlington Street. After admiring the view of the changing leaves and the swan boats in the Public Garden lagoon, Sam went into the bedroom, put his clothes in the closet and drawers, took off his sport jacket, and put on the shoulder holster and Glock 23 that he'd packed in his suitcase. He put his jacket back on and took the elevator down to the lobby.

The drive around the Common and down Boylston Street to One Financial Center took just a few minutes in light Saturday evening traffic. Paul had the car radio tuned to a classical music station.

"You like classical music?" Sam asked him.

"Not really," Paul replied. "It's what Mr. K. likes to listen to, so I don't change the station, except on game nights."

"I took piano lessons, and I still have trouble telling Mozart from Beethoven."

"Who are they?" Paul asked. The Boston inflection was creeping in again as he laughed at his own joke. "I'll take AC/DC."

A light rain began to fall, and Paul turned on his intermittent wipers. Other drivers began turning their headlights on, reflecting off the slickened streets. Boston could be a lot of fun, but it could be a gloomy town, too.

They parked in the underground garage and took the elevator up to the Kenwood Companies office suite. Paul directed Sam into Kenwood's office, where Sam immediately noticed the World Series trophy and the photo wall. You couldn't avoid the impression that Kenwood was a man who wanted to remind himself every day that he'd performed a miracle.

An older man and a young woman sat on a leather couch next to a low mahogany table with a tray of glasses and an ice bucket. An array of liquor bottles stood on a hutch next to the couch. The man stood up and walked over to Sam, holding out his hand.

"Hello, Mr. Skarda," he said. "Lou Kenwood. Thanks for coming on such short notice."

Kenwood shook hands the way you'd jostle a sleeping person to wake him up. He had a full head of white hair, a ruddy complexion, the requisite age spots on his forehead and cheeks, and a glint of determination in his eyes. He hadn't exactly jumped off the couch, but Sam sensed a raw energy from Kenwood that wasn't often present in men his age.

"I'd like you to meet Heather Canby, my executive assistant," Kenwood said. He turned to the young woman who remained seated on the couch. "You spoke with her on the phone."

Score one for the detective. As Sam had guessed, Heather Canby was somewhere south of thirty. She was also gorgeous—honey-blonde hair that was parted on the left and curved gently inward to the nape of her neck at an appropriate business length, light brown eyebrows—a sign that there wasn't that much dye in the hair—soft blue eyes set apart by a small, slightly upturned nose, and an upper lip that curved in a gentle semi-circle, as though in anticipation of something.

Heather wore a dark blue blazer and skirt, and sat with her legs crossed. Great legs—the kind a guy could spend too much time looking at when he was supposed to be focused elsewhere.

Sam reached across the table to shake Heather's hand. He looked in her eyes and sensed both skepticism of his abilities and defiance about her own, as though she were daring him to dismiss her. He was trying not to judge her by her looks, but so far the effort was failing. He could tell she knew it.

"Pour yourself a drink, Mr. Skarda," Heather said. She said it politely, while demonstrating that she wasn't there as a cocktail waitress.

"It's Sam," he reminded her. "And I'd be happy to. It's been a busy day."

He put ice cubes into a glass and found a bottle of Woodford Reserve on the liquor hutch. He poured himself a couple of fingers, took a sip, and sat down in a chair opposite the couch.

"I don't drink on the job," Sam said, in case his prospective employers were wondering.

"That's not iced tea in your glass," Heather said.

"I haven't taken the job yet," Sam said. "What's this about?"

Kenwood pulled a black envelope from inside his suit coat pocket and put it on the table in front of Sam. Sam reached over, picked it up, and read the extortion note in white ink that was signed by "Babe Ruth." He put it back on the table.

"Has that been dusted for fingerprints yet?"

"No," Kenwood said. "I don't dare show it to anybody. I don't think I can trust anyone to read the message and not tell someone about it."

"I can do it for you, if I can get my hands on a fingerprint kit," Sam said. "If there are any prints on it besides yours and mine, I could lift them and send a scan to a friend of mine with the Minneapolis cops. He wouldn't have to see the note."

"No," Kenwood said. "I'm afraid someone would talk. Whoever wrote that note is right: A gambling scandal would devastate baseball, and ruin what I've—what we have built here."

Sam took another glance around the office, which seemed to be a shrine to Lucky Louie Kenwood as much as it was to baseball or the Red Sox. No doubt a gambling scandal would seriously damage the game, but it was Kenwood who would be devastated.

"It would be like the Curse was never broken," Heather said.

"Well, you've won twice now," Sam said.

"The first one was the one that changed everything," Kenwood said. His voice nearly cracked with emotion. "If this—this lie—should become public, the press would tear that accomplishment to shreds. The newspapers, the twenty-four-hour cable channels—every day for weeks, for months, the story would be about investigations, gambling, and cheating. Here we've put together the best organization in the game. We're finally on top. Instead of celebrating our success, we'd spend all our time defending ourselves, while the media digs through our garbage."

"You know how the press is," Heather said. "They'd start questioning everything that's happened here since 2004."

"We beat the Rockies so easily, they'd probably start investigating that one, too," Kenwood said.

"The fans would stay with you."

"If anyone's more cynical than the Boston writers, it's the Boston fans," Kenwood said. "On top of everything else that's happened to this franchise, a thrown World Series would be ten times worse. I can't put our city and our fans through that."

"Any reason to think it's true?" Sam asked. He held Kenwood in his gaze while he took another sip of his bourbon.

"None," Kenwood said. "We won that trophy fair and square."

"Are you sure?" Sam asked. "Maybe the Babe knows something you don't."

"That's your professional advice—that we should pay this guy off?" Heather said.

"Can you afford it?"

"Theoretically, I can," Kenwood said. "But $50,000,000 is a lot of money, even for me, Mr. Skarda. And it would be difficult to transfer a sum like that to someone else without having to explain to the government what it was for."

"What if you told this guy to piss up a rope?"

"Then maybe he goes to the press, like he's threatening to do."

"We'd lose more in gate receipts, advertising and broadcast revenues than he's asking for," Heather said. "This season we're getting $300,000 per half-inning on those rotating ads behind home plate. If this becomes public, who's going to pay us those kinds of prices?"

"Then it sounds like it would be cheaper to pay him."

"We didn't bring you out here to advise us to pay off an extortionist," Heather said.

"I haven't advised you to do anything."

Sam was starting to feel irritated that Heather kept making premature assumptions, like the smartest kid in class trying to get one step ahead of the teacher.

"We're just talking through the scenarios here," Sam said. "Now, let's say, for the sake of argument, that you give this Babe his $50,000,000. If the Series really was fixed, a payoff won't change that. Somebody will still know what really happened—maybe a lot of somebodies."

Kenwood sighed and got up to pour himself a drink. He asked Heather if she wanted anything. She declined with a little sideways wave of her hand. There was a casual familiarity between them that transcended the standard boss-employee relationship.

"What I really want is for this to go away," Kenwood said. He returned to the couch. "Everything's good now. For the first time in four generations, this franchise doesn't feel as though some sort of hex is hanging over it. We brought optimism back to Boston."

"Some people say you've become a little arrogant."

"If so, we've earned it. But everything we've done will be ruined if this gets out."

No one said it, but the thought hung in the air among the three of them: That "we" was really an "I." If this scandal broke, no more Lucky Louie. His days as a hero would be over.

"What do you want me to do?" Sam said.

"Find out who sent this note. Find out if it's true. If it is, I guess we'll have to face up to that somehow. But if it isn't, I want proof, and I want this guy in jail. Quietly, if possible."

"It's tough to prove a negative. I can't prove to you that I didn't read a magazine on the flight out here."

"But millions of people watched that World Series," Heather said. "No one was paying attention to you on the plane."

"You'd be surprised. I caught several admiring glances from the flight attendants. Most of them were women."

Heather shook her head and looked away.

"Who else have you talked to?" Sam asked Kenwood.

"The only people who know about this letter are sitting here now. And my wife, Katherine. Paul, my driver, has heard some of my phone conversations, so he knows something is up, but he hasn't seen the extortion note."

"Your club president and general manager don't know about this?"

"No."

"So why did you tell Ms. Canby here?"

Heather squared her shoulders and assumed a convincingly offended expression.

"I tell her everything about my business," Kenwood said. "I couldn't run it without her. She's a graduate of Harvard Business School. Don't be put off by her legs, Sam."

"Never crossed my mind."

"I couldn't keep this completely to myself. I needed to be able to talk to someone I can trust."

"Besides Mrs. Kenwood?"

Kenwood nodded.

"Someone who knows this business as well as I do. Someone who works here every day and knows how much this could hurt us."

"Mr. Kenwood and I decided that our best approach was to investigate this note quietly, together," Heather said.

"It's going to be hard to find out anything if we can't tell anyone what we're trying to find out," Sam said.

"I know," Kenwood said. "That's why I called David Porter at Augusta National."

"You're a member?"

"Yes, for almost thirty years. I liked how you handled yourself at the Masters, but I wanted to be sure that you could be trusted to keep your mouth shut, so I called David. He recommended you without hesitation."

"There were lots of other cops working on that case. I just happened to be the one who was there at the right time."

"He's so modest, Lou," Heather said.

"Never mind. Sam, I believe you can help us now, or I wouldn't have sent for you."

For the next hour, Sam talked over the facts of the situation with Kenwood and Heather. Neither of them had ever heard Sox manager Gil Mahaffey or any of the players even suggest that the Cardinals—who went into the Series as a very slight underdog—had not tried their best in that Series sweep. Yet the writers and broadcasters who covered that Series were unanimous that the Cards did not play as well as they'd been expected to. They'd booted easy plays, missed signs, had runners picked off, hit poorly with runners on base, and their pitchers had been hammered.

In particular, the Cardinals' two best players, Ivan Hurtado and Alberto Miranda, had played badly. Hurtado, an All-Star right fielder, hit a home run in Game One, but was thrown out stealing three times, dropped a fly ball, misplayed several others, and hit only .211. After the Series, the Cardinals decided they didn't want to try to sign him to a long-term deal and traded him to the Red Sox for pitching prospects.

As disappointing as Hurtado's play was, he'd been stellar compared to National League Most Valuable Player Alberto Miranda. Miranda had been the first major league player since Babe Ruth to regularly play a position in the field when he wasn't pitching. He'd won 23 games as a starting pitcher, batted .328 with 27 home runs while playing 120 games in the field, and had gone to the mound from his third base position to post three saves late in the season. He'd made the cover of *Time* and *Newsweek*, heralded as the vanguard of a new kind of player, who would actually be a throwback to the multi-position players of baseball's early days. Writers kept predicting that Miranda would break down physically as the season progressed, but if anything, he seemed to get stronger as the Cardinals leaned on him more and more—that is, until the World Series. He batted just .188 with three singles and no RBIs, and he was shelled in his two starts. Worse, he'd thrown two balls away on potential double play grounders that could have got the Cards out of big innings.

The Cardinals, and the reporters who covered them, wrote off Miranda's poor performance to exhaustion from the supreme effort it had taken to get his team to the Series. In retrospect, it should have been expected, they said. The following season, Miranda went back to his normal workload, starting 30 games on the mound and playing third base when he didn't pitch. He was among the league leaders in both wins and home runs; all along, however, Miranda's name had been linked to steroid rumors. No one could believe a modern baseball player—even one as young and strong as Miranda—could excel at both hitting and pitching. A year after the Series, the Cardinals allowed Miranda to sign a four-year, $60,000,000 free-agent deal with the Dodgers, the team that had initially signed him and brought him to the big leagues as a skinny twenty-year-old.

The dismal World Series performances by Hurtado and Miranda had been forgotten in the lingering euphoria over Boston's long-awaited championship. But in light of the extortion note from Babe Ruth, they had to be considered prime suspects.

"But why would they have done that?" Heather said. "What did they have to gain?"

"Same reason the Black Sox threw the 1919 World Series to the Reds," Kenwood said. "Gamblers paid them to lose."

"Wasn't it obvious?" Heather said.

"I know you probably think I was there to see it, but I wasn't," Kenwood said, smiling slightly. "I do know that observers at the time were divided. Some didn't see anything suspicious. The White Sox manager, on the other hand, was sure something was wrong."

Sam had read about it, too. Eventually some of the players admitted to throwing games, and eight were thrown out of baseball for life. "No Gambling" has been baseball's Number One rule ever since.

Still, this case didn't add up. Those eight White Sox players were bribed with $10,000 apiece, which was more than their yearly salaries. But that was almost a century ago. Miranda and Hurtado were both making somewhere around $15,000,000 per year. They'd clear $50,000,000 in just over three seasons. On the free agent market, their next contracts could easily be worth over $100,000,000. Why would they get involved in something like this?

"Could be blackmail," Sam said. "If a player was using steroids, and somebody could prove it..."

"He might do something stupid to avoid being exposed," Kenwood said.

"What are the chances Hurtado's using?"

"I've never heard anything about it," Kenwood said. "Maybe he is, but he looks normal enough."

The first thing Sam had to do was get in touch with gamblers and bookies to find out if anything unusual had happened to the betting lines during the Red Sox-Cardinals World Series. He wouldn't have to tell them too much.

"I can start looking into this tonight," Sam said. "Maybe there's nothing to it."

"Be very careful what you say, and to whom," Kenwood said. "If this leaks out, I'll hold you responsible."

He stared steadily at Sam the way he must have stared down hundreds of business competitors over mahogany desktops. Sam had been pleased to discover that he was now considered a go-to guy in the high-finance sporting world. Earning that status had almost cost him his life, and could be lost quickly if he bungled this case.

"We understand each other," Sam said.

"Good," Kenwood replied. "Now, I want you to be my guest for tomorrow night's game. Sit in my suite with me and Katherine. I'd like you to get a feel for this franchise."

"I've been to Fenway many times, Lou."

"Oh?"

"I went to college up in Hanover."

"Dartmouth man," Kenwood nodded. "And you became a cop?"

"Like my dad."

"He must have set a powerful example."

"He did."

"Paul will pick you up at five sharp, in front of your hotel."

Sam put his drink on the table and stood to go, but Kenwood and Heather remained seated.

"There's one other thing," Kenwood said. "I want Heather to go everywhere you go, and be kept informed of everything you learn. If you have to leave town, she goes with you. She has my full confidence."

Sam looked at Heather, who clearly recognized that Sam wouldn't like the arrangement.

"Wait a minute, Lou," Sam said. "I don't work that way. When I was a cop, I knew my partners had the same training I had. I could count on them to have my back, and not make dumb mistakes that put us both in danger."

"Heather's an extremely competent young woman, Sam."

"I'm sure she is—no offense intended, Ms. Canby—but this work can be dangerous. Has she ever been in a fight, or been in a car chase, or had a gun pointed at her?"

"Are you expecting that kind of trouble?" Kenwood asked.

"That's just it—I have no idea what to expect. I have to be prepared for anything, and I can't worry about the safety of some desk jockey."

"Desk jockey?" Heather said, her eyes flashing. "Listen, I was on the ECAC women's crew champions, I've run the Boston Marathon three times, I'm a skeet shooter…"

"Yeah, and you ride English-style equestrian, and you studied fencing in Europe," Sam cut in. "Great, but none of that is going to help me find Babe Ruth, or keep somebody from putting a bullet through both of us."

Sam worked alone now, and liked it that way. It allowed him to be in complete control of his movements and his responses.

He doubted that Heather was equipped to do anything to help him, but she was definitely equipped to distract him.

"Sorry, Sam, but this is the way it's got to be," Kenwood said. "It's too much money and too much scandal to risk if I let you go out on your own. I'm too old to follow you around—much as I'd like to—but Heather can handle anything that comes up."

I'll bet, Sam nearly said out loud. He was tempted to walk away from the job. A case like this was the ultimate dark alley, and he couldn't begin to guess what he'd find at the other end. But he'd liked being the cop who brought down the bad guy at Augusta; it made him feel alive and valuable, in a way only aggressive investigative work could. He couldn't face the idea of returning to Minneapolis and tailing Beth Cheslak from motel to motel. Working for the Red Sox was almost like being called up to the majors again. Sam wanted this client.

"All right, we'll do it your way."

Heather picked up Sam's glass from the coffee table and stood up to return it to the hutch. Her sidelong glance at Sam contained a hint of triumph.

"I'm going over to my hotel to make some calls," Sam said. "If I turn up anything, I'll call you."

Heather took a business card out of the inside breast pocket of her blazer and handed it to Sam.

"Anytime, day or night," she said. This time, Sam thought he caught just the slightest upturn at the corner of Heather's mouth. Was she thawing out a bit?

Kenwood picked up the phone on the table and summoned Paul to give Sam a ride back to the hotel.

"You know what I dread more than anything?" Kenwood said as Sam headed for the door. "If this gets out, seeing some goddamn Yankee fan holding up one of those '1918' signs again, and underneath it '2004' with a line through it."

# Chapter Five

When he got back to his room, Sam placed a call to Marcus Hargrove.

"Hey, Sam," Marcus said. "What's up?"

"Just checking to see how you are. They catch that punk who shot at you?"

"Not yet. It was a stolen car."

"Figures."

"We'll get him."

"Say, Marcus, I need a phone number for Jimmy the Rabbit."

Marcus had joined Investigations a few years after Sam became a detective. He worked out of the organized crime unit, and though his specialty was gangs, he'd come to know most of the serious gamblers in the Twin Cities.

"What do you want with Jimmy?" Marcus asked. "You betting on Vikings games, now that you're a private citizen?"

"I haven't bet football since they made us drop the office pool."

"Yeah, same here," Marcus said. "I don't even watch much anymore. So why Jimmy?"

"Can't say right now, Marcus," Sam said. "I'm out of town, working on something kind of sensitive."

Marcus asked Sam to wait while he called up Jimmy's number on his computer. Jimmy the Rabbit's real name was Jimmy Waldrin. He'd been an outstanding high school athlete who'd later become a first-rate golf hustler. Sam had met him at one of those resort tournaments in northern Minnesota, where Jimmy finished second, sold all his shop winnings for 50 cents on the dollar, won a bunch of side bets and went home with more than three thousand bucks in his pocket. He lived in a nice four-bedroom Victorian near the old Guthrie Theater, drove a Mercedes convertible, and hadn't held a job since high school. He could be found most summer afternoons at one of the Twin Cities' private golf clubs, and most evenings at the ballpark or the racetrack. In the winter, he'd be at a downtown sports bar, keeping track of his pro and college bets in front of a bank of TVs.

Sam knew the sports books in Vegas adjusted the betting lines on a given game depending on how much money was being bet on either team, and if enough money suddenly came in on one team to change the odds, it was usually because of an injury or other significant piece of information. If somebody knew—or thought they knew—that a game was fixed, they'd put as much money as they could on the game, and that would definitely change the odds. If anyone in Minneapolis knew about the betting line being suddenly shifted during the Sox-Cardinals series, it would be Jimmy the Rabbit.

"Here you go, Sam," Marcus said. He read Jimmy's number off his contacts list. "Say, you gonna be around three weekends from now? One of the cops in the second precinct is getting married. He asked me if Night Beat could play the reception."

"Can't commit right now, Marcus. This case might wrap up in a couple of days, or I might be out of town for a while. I'll let you know as soon as I can."

"Damn unreliable musicians."

Sam dialed the number Marcus gave him for Jimmy the Rabbit. It rang several times, then Sam heard crowd noise in the background and a voice say, "Yeah." It sounded like a cell phone.

"Jimmy, it's Sam Skarda."

Sam heard a loud cheer in the background, and guessed that Jimmy was at the Metrodome.

"Sammy! Long time, babe. How ya hittin' em?"

"I still need strokes from you, Jim."

"I'll get a Good Citizen Award from the cops before you get a stroke from me. What can I do for ya?"

"How's the game going?"

"Twins up by three, but it's still in the sixth, and the Indians just got into the Twins' bullpen. This one ain't over."

"How much do you have on the Indians?"

"A honeybee. What's up?"

"I need to ask you about some recent World Series. Any sudden changes in the lines over the last six or seven years?"

"Nah, nothing I can think of. Why?"

"How about the Tigers and Cardinals in '06? Tigers were a heavy favorite, right?"

"Right."

"Any late money come in on the Cards?"

"Not really. Tigers just played bad."

"Marlins and Yankees in 2003?"

"Yanks were favored. Another upset, but the schmoes never saw it coming. I did okay."

"Sometimes the underdog wins," Sam said.

"That's right. That's why guys like me don't need real jobs."

"Red Sox-Cardinals?"

"Aw, Sammy, why you gotta bring up bad memories? I got killed on that one. Murdered. Lost the kids' college fund."

"I didn't know you had kids, Jimmy."

"I don't. But if I did…"

Sam heard the familiar foghorn voice of Wally the Beerman, the Dome's most recognizable vendor, bellowing "Who's ready?" as he passed Jimmy's seat.

"The Cards were underdogs, right?" Sam said. He was trying to steer Jimmy back to the subject at hand without sounding too focused on the Sox.

"Slight. After the miracle comeback against the Yanks, the Sox were the feel-good story. The rubes bet enough to make the Sox 8-5 favorites. Hell, I was hoping the line would go even higher. The Cards had the best record in baseball that year. They won

105 games—a great underdog buy. Besides, I thought the Red Sox would never win a Series."

"And the line never moved much?"

"Nah. I mean, maybe a little more St. Louis money came in after the initial line was set. But the dopes never stopped betting on the Sox. Pretty much 8-to-5 right up to the first pitch, if I remember right. What's this about, anyway?"

"Probably nothing. You know any bookies in Boston?"

"Sure."

"I'd like to talk to the guy who takes the most action."

Sam heard the pop of the catcher's mitt over the phone. Jimmy must have had good seats. Not surprising.

"There's a guy named Sal Bucca—I bet Big East basketball with him," Jimmy said. "I got his number on speed dial. Hey, you're not a cop anymore, right, Sam?"

"Come on, Jimmy, you know I left the force. You know everything."

"Yeah, but I gotta be sure. You're not working for them on this…whatever it is?"

"Nope. This is strictly private stuff. Nobody's going to get busted."

Jimmy gave Sam the phone number for Sal Bucca, but told him to hold off calling for an hour or so. Jimmy wanted to call Sal first, to let him know he could trust Sam.

"Tell him I'm staying at the Taj Boston," Sam said. "I'll call him from there."

Sam heard a sharp crack, heard the Metrodome crowd moan, and Jimmy shouted, "Double off the baggie! Gotta go, Sammy!"

Sam shut his cell phone and put it on the desk next to the television cabinet. He picked up the remote and turned on the TV—not exactly the most productive or entertaining way to spend his first night in Boston, but he had time to kill, time while waiting to call Bucca.

He was watching a rundown of the day's home runs on ESPN and listening to the raindrops on his window when he heard a knock on his door. He hadn't asked for anything from room service, and none of his old New England friends knew he was in town. He glanced at the shoulder holster he'd taken off and hung on the back of the desk chair.

Sam walked to the door and looked through the eyehole. Heather Canby was standing in the hallway with a leather bag over her shoulder, wearing the same blazer she'd had on in Kenwood's office. Sam opened the door.

"Hello, Sam," she said. She offered a cool smile, but still maintained the professional reserve she'd displayed in Kenwood's office. "I brought some homework for you."

Heather walked into the room and placed her shoulder bag on the coffee table. Her neck-length blond hair swayed softly from side to side as she walked. Sam could have stared into those soft, silky strands all night, if it had been polite to do so. Or even if it weren't...

She pulled a DVD case marked Red Sox-Cardinals World Series out of the bag and went to the entertainment unit, opened the TV cabinet, turned on the set, and inserted the disk into the DVD player. She quickly punched some buttons on the remote and the screen filled with a scene of riotous celebration in the Red Sox locker room following Game 4, accompanied by the Standells' recording of "Dirty Water."

"We must have sold 200,000 of these." Heather fast-forwarded through the introductory section. "But we never really looked at it before."

"We're going to now?"

"Is there somewhere you need to be?"

"No."

"Then have a seat."

Sam and Heather pulled the arm chairs close to the TV and went through the entire DVD, studying each key mistake by the Cardinals in slow-motion and freeze-frame. There was nothing on the highlight reel that would have ordinarily caught Sam's attention as being suspicious—but now, after reading the extortion note, several plays stood out. The first was the fly ball Ivan Hurtado dropped in the second inning of Game One. Alberto

Miranda, the starting pitcher, was already on the ropes, having given up three hits and a walk. Two runs had scored, and the Sox had runners on first and third when Luke Bowdoin lifted a lazy pop fly to shallow right. It was an easy play for Hurtado, who called off Cardinal second baseman Paul Weatherby and then seemed to take his eye off the ball at the last second, possibly watching to see if the runner on third was going to tag up. The ball hit off Hurtado's glove, and the runner on third scored. That made it 3-0 with runners on first and second, one out, and Miranda finished the Cards' chances when he fielded a grounder back to the mound on the next pitch and threw it into center field.

"I've seen stuff like that happen dozens of times," Sam said to Heather.

"I know," she said. "But if you were trying to throw a ball-game, isn't that how you'd do it?"

Hurtado later homered, but by then the score was 7-1. The final was 9-2, and the Cardinals were off to a demoralizing start. Neither Hurtado nor Miranda had a significant hit in the next two losses, and then Miranda overthrew third base on a one-out force play in the first inning of Game Four. The right play would have been to throw to second to start a double play. Instead, the first two runs scored in what became a five-run inning, almost assuring the championship for the Sox.

Heather replayed Miranda's overthrow to third a dozen times, and though it was hard to explain how one of the best players in baseball could make such a dumb mistake, it didn't look intentional. Then again, how could they tell for sure?

"There's no proof of anything here," Sam said. "You can see what you want to see."

"I see a couple of All-Stars playing like Little Leaguers," Heather said.

"Didn't Hurtado drop an easy one the other night? It happens."

"We're expecting you to give us more than that."

Sam started to speak, but managed to hold his tongue. He didn't need an office-bound twenty-something telling him how to do his job. If he had to report his every move to her—or worse, have her looking over his shoulder while he ran down every lead—he was tempted to catch the next plane back home.

Heather dug into her leather shoulder bag and took out a folded bundle of yellowing newspapers. They were October 2004 sports sections from the Globe, Herald, and New York Times, with game stories about the Sox-Cardinals Series.

"Lou and I have read through these, but we want you to look at them, too," Heather said. She handed Sam the stack of papers. "See if you can detect any sign that the writers thought something funny was going on."

Sam had to agree that rereading contemporary coverage of those games was a good idea.

"Why the Times?" he asked.

"For a neutral opinion."

Sam skimmed through the game stories, looking for accounts of Hurtado's muffed fly ball and the throwing errors by Miranda. All the writers ridiculed the horrible plays, but none suggested there was anything suspicious going on. As for Miranda's pitching, the beat guys from New York and Boston agreed: In those two big games, Miranda just didn't have it.

"Nothing here," Sam said, putting the papers down.

"That's what we thought," Heather said. "Now what?"

"A guy I know in Minneapolis gave me the number of a bookie here in town. I was about to call him when you dropped in."

"Don't let me stop you."

She gave no indication of leaving.

Sam used the hotel phone to call Sal Bucca, assuming the bookie would probably have caller ID The bookie would know the cops weren't likely to set up a sting operation at the Taj.

The call picked up on the first ring, and a heavy Boston accent said, "Yeah."

"Sal Bucca?"

"Who wants him?"

"Sam Skarda. Jimmy the Rabbit said to call this number."

"Hold on."

Sam waited about a minute, and then a different, raspy voice said, "Sal."

"Sal, my name is Sam Skarda. I'm a private investigator—I think Jimmy told you I'd be calling."

"Yeah."

They weren't a talkative bunch at Sal's place.

"Can I ask you a few questions over the phone, or do you want to meet someplace tomorrow?"

"Depends."

"On what?"

"What you wanna know, and why."

"I can't tell you why. It's confidential. But it has nothing to do with the cops. I need to know about some betting lines a few years back. No names. Just some numbers."

"What, you think we keep records on that stuff?" Sal uttered a harsh laugh.

Time to sweeten the pot.

"You think you could remember for ten grand?"

Sam looked across the room at Heather. She gave him a scowl and mouthed, "Ten grand?"

Sam nodded emphatically. She tilted her head to the side and put her palms up in resigned agreement.

"Still depends," Bucca said. His interest was now oozing through the phone. "I gotta see the money first."

"I can meet you tomorrow anytime before five p.m."

"You're at the Ritz, right?"

"Yeah. Well, it's the Taj Boston now."

"You must be workin' for Bill Gates."

"Not even close."

"Meet me at eleven tomorrow morning in the Common, corner of Tremont and Park." Bucca said it as "conna of Tremont and Pack."

"How will I know you?"

"Fat guy with a Sox cap smokin' a cigar."

"That sounds like lots of guys in Boston."

"I'm the ugliest one."

"Eleven o'clock," Sam said, and hung up.

"So who was that you were talking to?" Heather asked.

"A local bookie. Recommended by a friend of mine."

"If you go asking this guy a lot of questions about the World Series, isn't he going to get suspicious?"

"Bookies are born suspicious. But I'm not just going to ask him about the Sox and Cardinals. We'll go over the lines for a lot of games and different sports. He won't know what I'm looking for."

"He'd better not. Remember, the whole point of your investigation is to keep this story from going public."

"Look…" Sam said, but then thought better of telling her she was a beautiful but useless appendage, that he knew what he was doing, that he understood the assignment perfectly, and if she wanted the job done right she should head back down the stairs.

"What?" Heather said. She cocked her head innocently. "You don't like being told how to do your job?"

"No, I don't. That's why it's called private investigation."

"But the client pays your salary. You have to satisfy the client, don't you?"

Something about the way she said it caught Sam's ear, and by the expectant expression on her face, Heather knew it.

"Yes," he said.

"Want a drink?"

Heather reached into her leather bag and pulled out an unopened bottle of Woodford Reserve.

"Compliments of Mr. Kenwood. Do you have some ice?"

"No," Sam said, after some rapid contemplation about what he might be getting into. "I'll call down for some."

He picked up the phone and called room service for a bucket of ice.

"Hungry?" he asked Heather, covering the mouthpiece. "I haven't eaten yet."

"Neither have I. The pan-fried scrod is terrific. And you should ask for the Fireplace Butler."

"The what?"

"The Fireplace Butler. He brings whatever kind of wood you want, and lights the fire for you. I've always liked the cherry, but birch is quicker."

Sam put in the order for two servings of scrod and a bottle of Pouilly-Fuissé, and asked to be transferred to the Fireplace Butler. After hearing a rundown on the various woods—birch, cherry, oak, and maple—he went with Heather's cherry. He was in no hurry. The butler said he'd be right up.

"You do this a lot?" he asked her after hanging up.

Heather was seated in the armchair by the rain-spattered window, her feet up on the ottoman, her blazer unbuttoned, and her shoes on the floor. She couldn't have looked more comfortable if she'd been in a bubble bath in her own home.

"This is my favorite hotel in the world," she said.

A bellhop knocked on the door and left a bucket of ice. Sam poured a glass of bourbon on the rocks, handed it to Heather, and poured one for himself. She clinked her glass against Sam's and said, "Let's get to the bottom of this."

"The drink?"

Heather actually laughed. It was a rich, throaty chuckle, which suggested to Sam that perhaps she wasn't the ice queen he'd feared. But despite the drink and the laugh, she was still a business executive who had a $50,000,000 problem to solve. Maybe she was trying to find out whether Kenwood could really trust Sam to do the job. Whatever her purpose for visiting his room, Sam had done as much as he could do for the night, and it was time to unwind a little. If Heather didn't like a detective who was able to relax when he was off the clock, she could go back to the yellow pages.

There was another knock on the door, this time by the Fireplace Butler, a man in a plaid shirt and suspenders, carrying a basket of wood. He displayed a smile of practiced satisfaction, as though he'd just chopped down a cherry tree in the Public Garden, split the wood himself, and carried it up to Sam's room.

He opened the glass fireplace doors, arranged the logs in the fireplace and used kindling to begin a small blaze. Sam found a $5 bill in his wallet and handed it to the man, who nodded, put the bill in his pocket and picked up his basket.

"Just call if you need more wood," the Fireplace Butler said as he left.

Sam picked up the remote and checked the in-house video menu for music channels. They had the usual stale formats: blues, rock, contemporary, country, and smooth jazz. There was also a jack for an MP3 player. He plugged his iPod directly into the TV sound system.

"Want some jazz?" Sam asked her.

"Not that Kenny G crap…"

"No, I meant jazz."

He dialed up the jazz playlist from the menu and started with Cannonball Adderley's recording of "Autumn Leaves," with Miles Davis on trumpet.

"Now, that's not bad," Heather said when the music began filling the room.

Sam went to the window and pulled the drapes wide open so they could see the lights of the city through the streaks of raindrops.

"Do you work out?" Heather asked him.

"Not much," Sam said. He felt a flush of pride that this attractive younger woman seemed to be admiring his form.

"You should."

I walked into that one, Sam told himself.

When the waiter arrived with their scrod and their wine, they set their plates on the marble table in front of the fireplace and talked as they ate. She asked Sam how long he'd been a Minneapolis cop, and he told her about himself: about his father being a cop, about going to the police academy after college, about becoming a homicide detective, about being shot in the knee and taking almost two years off to rehab—mostly on golf courses.

"So why didn't you go back to the force?"

"It's in my blood, but not in my makeup. I need to call my own shots."

He changed the subject and asked Heather about herself. She was from Connecticut, and had grown up in a household with divided loyalties, including baseball. Her father was a Red Sox die-hard and a Yaz fan, while her mother loved Mickey Mantle and the Yankees. They'd divorced for other reasons, but Heather always thought the Yankees-Red Sox split played at least a small part. While the marriage was coming apart, Heather was attending a prep school in Massachusetts, and then Harvard. She came to side with her father after her first few games at Fenway.

"I learned to hate the Yankees," she said. "Paul O'Neill, Don Mattingly, Tino Martinez—and I really hated Wade Boggs when he went over to the dark side. And A-Rod—I bought one of those T-shirts from a street vendor, the one that said A-ROD DRINKS WINE COOLERS."

"How about Derek Jeter?"

"He's not so bad. I'm not blind."

She'd graduated with honors and then enrolled in Harvard Business School. The next summer she applied for an internship with the Red Sox, and got the position after a personal interview with Louis Kenwood himself. He asked her to apply for a fulltime job with his company when she graduated. She did, and within three years she'd become his executive assistant.

Sam's expression must have implied his suspicions.

"Lou's devoted to his wife," Heather said. "She has emphysema. Probably won't live to see spring training. I feel sorry for him. First his wife, and now this."

"Looks like he's dealing with his troubles pretty well."

"He's an amazing man—a very vital guy."

Sam still looked at Heather with skepticism. She wiped the corners of her mouth with her white cloth napkin and placed it on the table.

"I need more than a seventy-eight-year-old man—no matter how vital he is."

She stood up and began unbuttoning her silk blouse from the top. Sam had sensed a change in Heather's attitude toward him, sometime between the end of the DVD and the beginning of the

Woodford, but he wasn't expecting this. He quickly thought of Caroline as Heather got to the fourth button and drew open her blouse, revealing a not very business-like black bra that barely covered the bottom halves of her breasts. Caroline had not committed to him yet; he was technically a free agent. It still felt wrong, but that was part of what made it so irresistible.

Heather walked around to Sam's side of the table, and the room suddenly got a lot warmer. Sam glanced at the glowing logs in the fireplace; no, that wasn't it.

"If this is some kind of test to see if I can keep my mind on the job..." Sam said.

"It isn't."

She sat on his lap and moved her lips close to his. He reached up and put his left hand in her hair, running his fingers through the soft, smooth cascade and gently drawing her face the rest of the way to his. They kissed, Sam with a hunger for this beautiful woman he'd been looking at all evening, and Heather with the undisguised lust of someone who had not been sexually satisfied recently.

Sam helped Heather pull off her shirt as they continued to kiss, and he drew the cups of her bra downward, allowing her warm, round breasts to emerge. He ran the backs of his fingers gently upward against her nipples, and she shuddered. She began unbuttoning his shirt, and when she was finished he picked her up and carried her into the bedroom. They undressed quickly, and Sam pulled the duvet onto the floor. They could hear popping noises from the fire in the living room, and the rain began to drum harder on the window as Sam drew a sheet up to their waists.

"Are you using something?" Sam asked her. "I didn't pack anything. Didn't think I'd need..."

Heather rolled on top of Sam, sat up straddling his midsection, and ran her hands over his chest, her breasts slightly swaying.

"Don't worry," she said. "I'm on top of it."

# Chapter Six

Heather slid out of bed before eight the next morning and called Kenwood's office on her phone. She said she was having a meeting with Sam and would be in by noon. As she dressed, she seemed to slip back into the formality she'd displayed when Sam first met her. There was no morning-after playfulness, no touching, kissing, or implying that anything significant had happened between them. Sam was fine with that. He'd enjoyed her, but it was Caroline he thought of when he woke up and looked at Heather lying next to him. Was there something wrong with a night of delicious, meaningless sex between two consenting, unmarried, uncommitted adults? It bothered him that he was having a hard time answering his own question.

Heather left the room to go to a nearby bank and draw $10,000 from one of Kenwood's accounts, telling Sam she'd meet him in the lobby cafe for breakfast at nine. He was waiting for her at a table when she walked in, still wearing the blazer from the day before, and carrying her leather bag snugly under her arm.

"It's an odd sensation, walking down Boylston Street with $10,000 in cash." Heather took her seat opposite Sam. "It feels dangerous. I think I like it."

"Will Kenwood have a problem with you withdrawing that much money?"

"No. It's just business."

"Do you think he'd have a problem with you sleeping with me?"

"I don't know. And I don't really care. It's my business what I do when I'm out of the office."

"So that was a typical night for you?"

"No."

"You just couldn't resist me."

"I'm busy all the time. I don't meet a lot of guys, believe it or not. Once I found out we were going to be working together, I figured it would happen eventually. I just decided, why wait?"

"How did Lou meet his wife?"

The question caught Heather by surprise, and she momentarily dropped her eyes, as though she'd misplaced something.

"She was his secretary," Heather said. "Back in the '60s. He divorced his first wife and married Katherine. I've seen pictures of her back then. I've got to admit, she was hot."

"The pattern continues."

"What the hell do you mean by that?"

"You're hot, too."

"I'm not Lou's secretary."

Heather ripped open a packet of Sweet 'n' Low and poured a fourth of it into her coffee.

"I knew the minute you looked at me yesterday that you thought I was a bimbo," she said. "I get that all the time."

"So, if you think a guy doesn't respect you, you go to bed with him?"

"Don't you respect me?"

"I still don't know you all that well…"

"What else do you want to know?" she asked. She took a sip of her coffee.

"What do you like?"

"Fast cars. Riding western—you were wrong yesterday about English-style. Champagne. Escargots. New Zealand. The Wall Street Journal. What about you? What do you like?"

"Four-part harmony. A triple into the gap. A flush two-iron. Single-malt Scotch with a Bass Ale chaser."

"That sounded rehearsed."

"But true."

They ate in silence for a while. Sam could tell Heather was intelligent and well-educated, but she had a chip on her shoulder, too. Beauty was an asset she was willing to use, but unwilling to be defined by. Fair enough; it was time to find out whether she could be of any use to him.

"Does Kenwood have any other heirs besides Katherine?"

"He had a son from his first marriage, but he died a couple of years ago. A drowning accident somewhere on the West Coast."

"Was he in Lou's will?"

"I don't know. Lou never talked about him."

"Was he married?"

"If he was, Lou never heard from the wife."

"You will, when Katherine dies."

"That's Lou's problem, not mine."

"When Lou dies, who gets the team?"

"If he doesn't remarry, it will probably be put into some kind of trust, same as when Jean Yawkey died. Then it will be sold. That's how Lou got it."

They paid the bill at 10:30; Sam had to meet Sal Bucca at eleven. He told Heather he wanted to go alone.

"Lou says I go where you go," she said. "Besides, I'm not sure I trust you with all that cash."

"Hell of a thing to say to the man who took your virginity last night."

Heather smirked, then shouldered the leather bag, noticeably heavier with the cash inside.

"Won't Bucca know who you are?" Sam asked.

"I'm never in the papers. The reporters all want to talk to Lou, the club president, or the G.M."

They walked out the lobby doors onto Arlington Street. The previous night's rain had moved through, leaving the sidewalks cleaner and the air fresher. Tourists and office workers taking early lunches sat around the fountain in the Public Garden across the street, enjoying the crisp fall morning. Sam and

Heather crossed Arlington at Beacon Street and walked east toward Charles. Sam wasn't anticipating any trouble from Sal Bucca, but he was wearing his gun under his jacket, just to be the well-equipped private eye.

They crossed Charles Street and walked along the north boundary of the Boston Common, which was also bordered by Beacon, Park, Tremont, and Boylston, and abutted Boston's financial and government districts. They turned right at Park, where the 200-year-old steeple of the Park Street Church was being refurbished against the backdrop of modern skyscrapers. In the Granary burying ground next to the church, the headstones of Sam Adams, John Hancock, and Paul Revere poked up from the hallowed soil, a daily tourist attraction for visitors following the Freedom Trail.

There was a noticeable difference in appearance between the Public Garden and the Common; the lawn and flowers of the Public Garden were meticulously maintained by workers who speared stray paper and cigarette butts with spiked sticks and put the refuse into the trash bags slung over their shoulders. The Common was a different story. The grass was patchier, pigeons and squirrels fought over food refuse left behind by office workers around the two-level Brewer's fountain, and bums slept in the sunlight on the sloped hillside that led up to the Statehouse.

Sam stood by the fountain near the corner of Park and Tremont and looked around for the fat man in the Sox cap with the cigar, but saw no one fitting that description. He checked the time read-out on his phone: eleven on the dot.

He felt a tap on his arm.

"You Skarda?"

He turned to see a bareheaded, balding man with a crooked nose and a perfectly even set of false upper teeth standing next to him. The voice sounded like the first guy Sam had talked to when he called Bucca's number the night before. The face looked like that of a hockey player, or a boxer. Whatever he'd been, they'd had to stitch him back together a bunch of times.

"Yeah, I'm Skarda. Who are you?"

"I work for Sal. Follow me."

He began walking westward into the Common, and Sam and Heather followed. False Teeth turned and said, "She stays here."

"No, she doesn't," Sam said. "It's her ten thousand."

"Suit yourself."

They walked past the fountain and up the hill to a grassy spot shaded by two towering maple trees. A short, dumpy man with a two-day beard, wearing a Red Sox cap, was sitting on a bench under one of the trees.

"Where's the cigar?" Sam asked him.

"I'm tryin' to quit," said the man Sam assumed was Sal Bucca. "Who's the puss?"

"My banker."

Bucca turned to False Teeth. "Ya frisk 'em?"

"Not yet."

"I'm carrying a gun, Sal," Sam said. He opened his jacket to show the holstered Glock. "She's not."

"I don't give a shit about no gun," Bucca said. "I gotta check ya for wires."

False Teeth moved quickly to Sam, untucked his shirt, ran his hand up Sam's chest and back, then patted him down below the waist. Then he walked over to Heather, who took a half step backward as he approached.

"No, you don't," Sam said. He put a hand on False Teeth's shoulder. The goon slapped it away and reached for Heather's blouse.

Sam put his leg behind False Teeth's legs, reached across his chest to his opposite shoulder and pulled him backwards. False Teeth fell hard on his back, but reached into his jacket with his right hand as he went down. Sam was on him before he could pull his hand out, yanking his arm up behind his back. Sam reached into False Teeth's jacket, pulled out the gun, and threw it on the grass, then pushed False Teeth forward until his face was mashed sideways into the ground.

"If you don't want to spring for another set of uppers, keep your hands off her," Sam said. He tightened the painful angle of False Teeth's arm behind his back. "We're not cops. We're not working for the cops."

"Let him go, Sam," Heather said.

He looked up at her and saw that she had taken off her blazer and was unbuttoning her blouse. She pulled it open and showed Bucca her black bra, then turned around and lifted her blouse to show there was no wire on her back. Then she turned back to Bucca and hiked up her skirt to her panties, turned around once and dropped the skirt again.

"Satisfied?" she asked Bucca.

"You bet," he said.

Fifty feet away, a group of grade school kids was being led through the Common. Their teacher was busy explaining that the Common was the oldest municipal park in America, originally used for grazing animals and public hangings, while several of the boys in the group stared slack-jawed at Heather buttoning her shirt.

Sam and Heather sat down with Bucca on the bench, while False Teeth stood a few yards away, grimacing and flexing his shoulder.

"Sorry about my associate, there, but a guy like me can't be too careful," Sal said. "I got into this business right after that B.C. point-shaving shit back in '79. Then the Feds leaned on us bookies to try to bring down the Boston mob. I told 'em I don't know nothing about that. I ain't goin' to Walpole."

Heather took the cash out of her leather bag and handed the money to Bucca. He flipped through it with his thumb, and appeared satisfied.

"Now, whadya wanna know?" Bucca said.

Sam asked him about the betting lines on the Patriots Super Bowls, the most recent playoff series for the Celtics and Bruins, the recent NCAA basketball tournament games for Boston College and UConn, and all the Red Sox post-season series since 2002. Bucca provided detailed information on how the lines had shifted—or not—for each of those events. Nothing stood out, including the World Series. The Sox had been big favorites over the Rockies; no surprise there. They'd been slight favorites over the Cardinals, and as Jimmy had said, that line had barely moved.

"I ain't stupid," Bucca finally said. "I know what you're lookin' for."

Sam and Heather looked quickly at each other. Could he?

"Nobody can fix a game nowadays," Sal said. "Too many people know too much. You could still get a college kid to shave points, but who ya gonna bribe in the pros? The stars make too much money, and the scrubs don't have no impact on the game."

"What about that NBA ref?" Sam said. "He admitted getting involved with gamblers. He said some players might have shaved points."

"Look, that guy was a gambling addict, and everybody knows NBA players are knuckleheads. Amateurs coulda done that deal."

"So it could happen," Sam said. "If somebody had inside dope on a big game, and wanted to use the information, who would know about it?"

"The Vegas boys would know," Bucca said. "Manny DiMeola at the Stardust, or Jim Leone, the guy who sets the lines for LVSC."

"What's that?"

"Las Vegas Sports Consultants. They give the lines to most of the Vegas sports books."

Bucca explained to Sam that the Vegas bookmakers wouldn't dare try to do anything funny with the odds, or manipulate a game. They were already making plenty of money. Honest games kept them in business—a damn good business.

"You'd have to be looking at a gambler, maybe a guy who's connected. Like that bozo Rothstein, the guy who fixed the 1919 Series. I mean, there's guys like him in every city right now, high rollers and mob guys who know lots of jocks. Maybe one of them thinks they could get to somebody."

"Anybody like that here in Boston?"

"Aw, the only guy here who could have pulled off something like that was Donnie Sullivan. He had the operation in South Boston, but he ain't around anymore."

South Boston—Paul O'Brien was from South Boston. Probably a coincidence, Sam figured, but something to file away for later.

"What happened to him?" Sam asked.

"Disappeared. On the lam from the Feds. Or maybe he's in the witness protection program. Or dead. I dunno."

"How about Chicago?"

"Tony 'The Pony' Peloso would be the guy. He runs the Chicago Outfit. But he's tryin' to beat a federal murder rap. Besides, I never heard nothin' about him and a sports fix."

"St. Louis?"

"Lemme think…that group is pretty much busted up."

"L.A.?"

"Who knows? Not much goin' on out there. Sid Mink, maybe— but the L.A. boys ain't what you'd call a powerhouse outfit."

"Anybody else?"

"Like I say, they're all over. And it don't have to be a local guy. Rothstein was from New York, and he fixed a Series between Chicago and Cincy. But it just don't happen these days. Believe me. That it? Cuz I got business to attend to."

"That's it."

"Thanks for the dough," Bucca said. He stood up, and False Teeth fell in beside him as he began walking back toward Park Street. Then Bucca looked back at Heather and said, "And thanks for the show, sweetie."

He blew her a kiss.

Sam glanced at Heather to see if Bucca's last remark embarrassed her, but she appeared to give it no thought. Instead, she was smoothing out her skirt and blazer.

"I can't wear this back to the office," she said. "And it would take me too long to go back to my apartment. I'll change in your room."

"Into what?"

"There's a nice shop on Newbury Street, right around the corner from the hotel. I'll pick something up there."

They walked back toward the hotel through the Common, Heather's high heels making a clip-clip sound on the pavement. A few leaves had already fallen, though the trees were mostly still green. A bell from a nearby church steeple was tolling noon.

"Thanks for getting that ape off me," Heather said. "It looked like you knew what you were doing back there."

"Police training. I could have just shot him, but that would have attracted a crowd."

"We're no closer to finding Babe Ruth, are we?"

"You never know."

"So what's next?"

"We talk to guys who played in that Series. Can you get me into the Sox clubhouse before or after the game tonight?"

"That might not be the best way to do it. The locker room is kind of a zoo. There's always a dozen reporters and columnists wandering around in there. You don't want the beat guys from the Globe and Herald asking who you are. I'll see what I can do."

Sam wasn't sure what he expected to find out by talking to the players—and he had to be just as careful with a player as he'd been with Bucca. If one of them figured out what he was asking about, his discreet investigation would be blown open. There were no secrets in baseball—except, perhaps, for the biggest one in the game's history.

# Chapter Seven

*Caracas, Venezuela—*

Elena awoke to the now-familiar sights, sounds, and smells: a sliver of sunlight peeking through a crack in the cardboard-covered window above the torn, soiled mattress on the floor; the voices of screaming babies and hungry children in adjoining shanties; and the smell of rotting garbage and human waste permeating her filthy room.

She'd been imprisoned for several weeks—or was it a month now? She couldn't tell anymore. The days dragged by with a numbing, soul-sapping sameness. Any of three men would be there when she awoke—the skinny, droopy-eyed young man with the moustache, whom the others called Paquito; the mean, foul-smelling, stubbly-faced one named Hector, who sometimes kicked, pushed, and slapped her for his own amusement; and the copper-skinned, muscular leader that the other two always referred to as Jefe. He was the one who had stopped her cab in the tunnel, wearing a police officer's uniform. At first she thought he must have been impersonating a policeman in order to abduct her that night, but he often arrived and left wearing the uniform.

Elena knew approximately where she was, but for all the good that did her, she might as well have been a thousand miles into the rainforest. When she was allowed to stand, she could put her face to the crack between the cardboard and the edge of the window and see out over the endless tin roofs. There were no streets here, just a maze of narrow, muddy walkways and alleys, filled with the poor, the sick, and the young who lived in this hideous place by necessity, by inertia, or by birth.

It could have been Patare, or Libertador, Antimano, San Juan, Carapita…Elena did not know the names of all the shantytowns that hugged the hillsides overlooking Caracas. They all looked depressingly alike Some had electricity, water, and telephone service; the one she was in did not. She had not been able to clean herself in weeks. She was in the same clothes she'd worn on her flight into Venezuela. Her toilet was a bucket in the corner, emptied whenever one of her guards could no longer stand the smell.

At first they had left the room when she used it.

One afternoon she tried to yell through the crack in the cardboard to the people passing by on the narrow alley below her window, but if any of them heard her, they did not look up. There was no law in this part of Caracas, and it could cost people their lives to get mixed up in someone else's business. Within seconds of Elena's desperate cries, the brute named Hector rushed into the room, dragged her away from the window, and knocked her to the floor with a hard forearm to her temple.

"You think anyone will come to help you?" he said, laughing harshly. "*Nadie vendrán*! No one will help. No one cares here. If you want to eat—if you want to live—you keep quiet and do as we say."

Elena was not strong to begin with, not like her husband, not like her boy—and she grew much weaker eating the small, sporadic meals she was provided. The corn flour bread and cheese were usually moldy, and the occasional *platano* was always soft and bruised. Eventually she lost her appetite.

She sometimes asked why they were holding her, and when she could leave.

"It is not for you to know," the one called Jefe would say. "If all goes well, you will be returned to your family. If not…" .
Jefe shrugged.

He was the kindest, but the one she feared the most, because the other two feared him. One night he came to take his turn guarding Elena, and found Paquito asleep in his chair. Elena had not even noticed, because she had been asleep, too. But she awoke to the sound of Jefe beating Paquito mercilessly. He held Paquito up against the rough cinderblock wall with his powerful left arm and punched him repeatedly in the stomach with his right fist as Paquito screamed and begged for forgiveness.

"All I demand of you is that you remain awake!" Jefe said, delivering another sickening blow to Paquito's midsection. "Is that so much to ask for what I'm paying you? *Digame!*"

"No, Jefe, no…" Paquito moaned. Jefe loosened his grip and allowed the thin, young man to slide to the floor. "It will not happen again."

But it did.

Paquito's ribs were badly bruised from the beating he received from Jefe, and Elena saw him swallow a number of pills in the next few days. Whatever he was taking for the pain seemed to make him drowsier than usual. He would bring a thermos of coffee with him for his guard shift, but once the coffee was gone, it was all Paquito could do to keep himself awake. He would try to walk around the cramped shanty, humming to himself or singing along to a portable radio, but when the pain from his midsection became too great he would have to sit down again.

"Why do you stay here?" Elena asked him a few nights after the beating. "You are treated badly. You are a prisoner, too—no better than me. You should go to a clinic and see one of those Cuban doctors, and not come back."

"*Cierre su boca!*" Paquito said. "*Necesito el dinero.*"

"You could not need the money this much," Elena insisted. "What are they paying you? My family will pay you more if you help me leave."

Paquito shook his head slowly but emphatically.

"Jefe would find me, and kill me."

Elena had no answer for that, because she believed Paquito. From what she knew about Jefe, he would indeed kill Paquito, with no hesitation or remorse.

Jefe would sometimes talk to her about sports—he loved *futbol*, baseball not so much; religion—he believed the Catholic Church was a hypocritical sham, enriching itself while keeping the people poor and ignorant; and politics—Elena thought that Venezuela's president, Hugo Chavez, was a communist who would ultimately turn Venezuela into another failed dictatorship like Cuba, while Jefe thought he was the country's only hope to assume its rightful place as a South American power. But despite Jefe's willingness to talk to Elena, she found his eyes cold and unsympathetic, like a snake's. He was the kindest one only because he was the strongest and smartest; he knew she was under his total control and would not try to get away as long as he was around.

Hector was often drunk, always mean and simply looked for excuses to inflict pain on Elena. He must have been ordered not to molest her, because Elena could tell from the way Hector looked at her that he thought about violating her all the time. When he pushed her around, his hands were always on her chest. Several times he pulled the neck of her sweater open and looked down at her breasts. He even stared at her when she used the bucket, despite her pleas for him to avert his eyes. Elena was convinced Hector would have raped her every night if he weren't afraid of what Jefe would do to him.

Paquito was barely more than a boy. He did not have Hector's mean streak or Jefe's commanding presence. He was in this for the money, nothing more, and now that he was in so much pain, he was having trouble focusing on his responsibilities. The night Elena spoke to him about going to a doctor, she saw him swallow several more pills. He turned the radio up loud to a *llanera* station and walked haltingly around the small room, trying to sing along to the melodies. Elena knew he could not stay on his feet for very long, and once he sat down, she expected him to fall asleep. Hector was not due at the shanty until dawn.

Elena pretended to sleep, but listened to hear the sound of Paquito's breathing over the music on the radio. His breathing was labored when he first sat down, but then it became increasingly steady. For ten minutes she listened while he appeared to fall asleep. She forced herself to wait another ten minutes, then slowly raised herself from her mattress, feeling weak and frightened, but determined to slip past Paquito and out of the shanty.

She had no sooner risen to her feet than Paquito awoke with a start.

"What are you doing?" he demanded.

"I must use the bucket," she said. "*Excúseme, por favor*. I don't want to soil myself."

"Go ahead, then."

Elena said nothing. None of her captors had left her alone to use the bucket, since Hector had caught her calling down to the alley. At first it had been difficult, but she had become used to this further degradation.

She went to the corner, took down her underwear and urinated into the bucket. She returned to her mattress and curled up as if to sleep. Paquito once again stood up and tried to walk and sing, but his voice quickly became strained at the effort to force air out of his lungs. He sat down again, and within a half-hour he was asleep once again. This time his breathing was deeper and more rhythmic.

I must go now, Elena told herself. He will not hear me this time.

She rose again, quietly, and took slow, small steps past Paquito's chair to the tin door that led to the alleyway outside the shanty. The hinges were not expertly installed, but they were not rusty; Elena sometimes did not hear the door open when one of her captors came or went. The door was bolted from the inside with a metal L-latch that had to be lifted, turned and slid to the right. She could not see it in the dark, but found it with her hand and slowly slid the latch open. The door began to open to the inside by itself, making a louder creak than Elena had expected—loud enough, perhaps, to be heard over the music from the radio, but Paquito did not stir.

She held the door with both hands and gently eased it toward her until the opening was wide enough to slip through. She knew the door would not stay in the closed position if she tried to pull it shut behind her, so she left it open and began running down the dirt path beside the shanty to the alley below. It would take only a few moments to lose herself in the labyrinth of paths and alleys that crisscrossed Caracas' shantytowns. Eventually she would find her way down the hill and into the city, where surely someone could help her reach her husband...

Elena guessed it was sometime after midnight. She was disoriented, with no landmarks to guide her but the darkened outlines of endless, featureless, box-like hovels stacked atop one another. There were scattered lights in some of the windows, but the alley was deserted. She didn't dare knock on a door or ask anyone for help, for it was well known these neighborhoods were honeycombed with violent, desperate criminals—any one of whom might have been in league with her captors. She had to get down the hill, through the shanties, to the civilized part of the city.

She tried to run, but her legs would not work properly. She tripped over an unseen tire lying in the alley, fell to her knees and scraped her skin open, and tried to rise again in the dark.

Suddenly she felt herself being lifted from the ground by a pair of firm hands around her arms, and she heard a rough voice in her ear.

*"A donde vas?"*

She could not see the face, but the man was wearing a police uniform.

# Chapter Eight

Sam looked forward to being back at Fenway Park among the throngs wearing their B caps and Red Sox sweatshirts; to once again smell the Fenway Franks and gaze at the soothing green of the outfield grass and the famous left-field wall. They'd added seats atop the Green Monster since the last time Sam had been to Fenway. He hoped to go up there and see what the game looked like from the Monster Seats.

And yet, as he rode with Heather down Commonwealth Avenue in the back seat of Lou Kenwood's Lincoln, with the ever-deferential Paul in the driver's seat, he kept wondering, What if some of the games were a sham? What if a few ballplayers got so disillusioned with their contracts or their owners that they conspired with gamblers to throw a game now and then? It had happened before, and just because Sal Bucca said it couldn't happen again didn't make it so.

Paul had the car radio tuned to WEEI. The afternoon drive show was in its final hour before the Red Sox pre-game show, and the callers were venting their frustrations.

"Mike from Scituate—what's your take?"

"How long is Mahaffey gonna stay with Hurtado in right? The guy has obviously checked out for the year. I mean, I appreciate what Ivan has done for the Sox, but if he's gonna mail it in the rest of this year, let's sit him down and look at Burrows."

"I hear ya, Mike," the host said. "You might get your wish tonight."

"'Bout frickin' time."

"Eddie from Saugus, you're next."

"I agree with that last guy. Get Hurtado outta here, man. For fifteen mil, you'd think he could catch a stinkin' fly ball, for God's sake."

"So you wouldn't bring him back next year?"

"Hell, no. What's he want, four years at 22 per? We could get Naslund from Oakland plus a decent back-up catcher for less than that. Besides, I like the Burrows kid."

"I like him, too," the host said. "We'll be back in a minute, with Curt on a car phone, next up."

They approached Kenmore Square, the busy crossroads where Commonwealth, Beacon Street, and Brookline Avenue converged near Fenway. It was a few minutes after five, and already the fans, vendors, scalpers, and hang-out artists were pouring out of the T station entrances and choking the sidewalks. The fans on the streets were no doubt talking about the same things the callers to WEEI were talking about: whether they should re-sign Hurtado, the money it would take to get that reliever from Oakland, the Sox pitching rotation, that new right fielder from Pawtucket...

It all meant so much to the fans—and yet, if they found out the games weren't honest, it might suddenly mean nothing to them. If a World Series had been fixed, the damage would not only cripple baseball, but reverberate throughout pro sports.

Which raised the question that Sam kept coming back to: Did Kenwood really want to know that the Cardinals threw the Series to the Red Sox? If he found proof that there was a plot, what would Kenwood do then? Would he go to the commissioner, and then watch baseball attempt to endure its worst crisis in a century, while Red Sox Nation sank back into cynicism? Or would he pay off Babe Ruth and hope no one found out?

The Lincoln eased down Brookline and stopped in front of the Red Sox offices at Yawkey Way, which was closed off to vehicle traffic on game days. Eight red pennants with blue-and-white numerals hung from the brick exterior of Fenway Park, commemorating the years that the Red Sox had been World Champions: 1903, 1904, 1912, 1915, 1916, 1918, 2004, and 2007.

The conspicuous gap was the reason Kenwood didn't dare call Babe Ruth's bluff. The Sox were now out of that abyss, and never wanted to look back.

Paul dropped them off, and Sam followed Heather through the entrance to the team offices. She was wearing the black skirt and jacket she'd bought that afternoon, over a pink crew-neck top. The skirt showed off her legs without being too obvious about it, and her short hair bobbed gently back and forth like prairie grass in the breeze as she walked. The club employees they encountered all said hello to her, and Heather returned their greetings like the popular girl in high school being dutifully cheerful to the lesser beings.

They took an elevator up to the third level and found Lou Kenwood in the owner's glassed-in luxury suite, watching the Sox take batting practice. There was a bar and a poker table at the back of the suite, plush leather armchairs and sofas facing the field, and a wide-screen television monitor mounted in the wall. Classical music was being piped into the enclosed suite. Kenwood sat in one of the armchairs, a bottle of bourbon on the end table next to him and a glass of the brown liquid in his hand. He was the picture of a satisfied rich man enjoying his most expensive toy—except that the expression on his face was not one of satisfaction.

"Is Hurtado playing tonight?" Heather asked Kenwood when she and Sam walked in.

"No," Kenwood said. "Gil wants to look at Burrows for a couple of games."

Jason Burrows was the rookie right fielder just up from Pawtucket that everyone was buzzing about. Hurtado's injuries, occasionally indifferent play, and contract demands had eroded his standing with the Sox. It was widely assumed that he would not be re-signed in the off-season. But he was also the Sox player in the best position to know whether the Cardinals had thrown the series.

"I'd like to get a few minutes with Hurtado sometime tonight," Sam said.

"Sure," Kenwood said. "Why?"

"See what he remembers about the World Series."

"Don't push him too hard," Kenwood said. "He's not the brightest guy in the world, but he could figure out what this is about if you're not careful."

"I'll watch myself."

Kenwood was silent for a moment, then took a sip of his drink and turned to look at Heather and Sam.

"He called," Kenwood said.

"Who?" Heather said.

"Babe Ruth."

"When?"

"About twenty minutes ago. He called me here in the suite."

"How did he get this number?" Sam asked.

"How the hell should I know? That's something you ought to be figuring out."

"What did he say?" Heather asked.

"He said I had five days to come up with the money, or he'd call the Commissioner and the newspapers."

"What did you tell him?"

Kenwood got up from his chair and walked to the floor-to-ceiling Plexiglas window overlooking the field. None of the players fielding grounders and shagging flies noticed their owner wearily rest his forehead against the glass.

"I told him I didn't know how I could make a lump payment like that without causing suspicion." He turned back to face Sam and Heather. "He said I'd have to think of a way, or the story was going to blow wide open."

"Did you ask your staff if they could track where the call came from?"

"No," Kenwood said. He now sounded every minute of his 78 years. "I didn't want anyone to know…about this…"

Kenwood was petrified of losing his most beloved possession, and his fear was getting in Sam's way.

Sam questioned Kenwood as though he were a witness to a crime. What did the voice sound like? Smooth, calm, unhurried, Kenwood said. How old? Maybe 35...40. Any accent? Probably not from Boston, but hard to tell. Any background noise? Kenwood had to think for a minute. No, nothing. He hadn't really been paying attention to that. Any odd turns of phrase or unusual words used? No. How long did the call last? Not much more than a minute.

"How does he want to be paid?"

"I'm supposed to wire the money to an offshore bank account."

"Won't the government find out about it?"

"Probably not," Heather said. "Private financial transfers like that are still confidential."

"Don't drug cartels and terrorist groups use those kinds of transactions?"

"Sure," Heather said. "The Feds want offshore transactions made public, like they are in Europe, but U.S. businesses are fighting it."

"Why?"

"I don't want my competitors to know how much I'm spending, or why," Kenwood said.

"Kind of biting you in the ass now, isn't it?" Sam said.

Kenwood didn't respond.

"Did he say anything else?"

"He said, 'Get rid of the private eye. You're being watched.'"

That meant the plot wasn't necessarily a one-man operation. Babe Ruth could be anywhere, but he definitely had somebody in Boston.

"Are you going to get rid of me?" Sam said.

"I thought about it," Kenwood said. "But you're my only chance to get out from under this thing."

"All right, we've got five days," Sam said. "It looks like I'm going to have to talk to Alberto Miranda. Anybody know where the Dodgers are this week?"

"I'll check," Heather said. "Ellie can book our flight and our hotel."

"Are you sure Lou doesn't need you here?"

"No," Lou said. "Heather goes with you."

Kenwood poured himself another drink and sat back down in his chair, hardly seeming to notice that Sam and Heather were still there. The Red Sox players were leaving the field while a few of the Toronto Blue Jays were emerging from the third base dugout to limber up for their turns in the batting cage. Sam asked Heather for a quick tour of the ballpark—mostly to get away from Kenwood's despondency.

Heather took Sam past the upstairs offices of club president Michael Donovan, but they didn't stop in.

"He doesn't know we hired you," Heather said. "It would be better if he doesn't find out."

"Who am I, if anyone asks?"

"My boyfriend."

"And why am I getting the VIP treatment?"

"Because you're my boyfriend."

They took the elevator downstairs to the basement offices of general manager Joe Pagliaro and his staff. The walls were covered with dry-erase boards bearing the names of every player in every major league organization. An oversized bottle of champagne with the label WORLD CHAMPIONS 2004 sat on a filing cabinet. Pagliaro was on his phone, alternately waving his free hand in the air and tapping his index finger on his desk to emphasize a point he was making. Heather gave Pagliaro a wave, and he returned it with a harried half-smile—polite, but with some effort, Sam concluded. Pagliaro probably didn't like the authority Heather wielded in the organization, but it was at best a minor annoyance in a job filled with daily headaches.

"He's kind of a wreck these days," Heather said. "We were the beloved underdogs a few years ago. Now everybody expects us to do it every year. It's getting to him."

"Do he and Lou get along?"

"Well, they used to. But after 2004, there were…credit issues."

"What do you mean?"

"You know—who got most of the credit for bringing the championship back to Boston. Joe has his supporters in the media, and Lou has his. Lou hired Joe, so naturally it bothers him when a columnist writes that the Sox couldn't have climbed to the top without Joe Pagliaro calling the shots. There are egos involved. Both of them like to think they're the main reason we broke the Curse."

"And if somebody takes that 2004 Series win away…"

"It could get very ugly around here."

They went back up to the concourse level and walked outside to Yawkey Way. The second floor of the souvenir shop across from the ballpark had a row of six-foot windows displaying color posters of each player in that night's batting order. A five-piece jazz band played "Mercy, Mercy, Mercy" while fans sat at umbrella tables in the middle of the street, eating food from concessions stands that had been upgraded significantly since Sam had been there last. Instead of standing in a half-inch of water in the murky bowels of the ballpark, customers now lined up on clean pavement at food stands that sold pizza, barbecue sandwiches, Philly cheese steaks, and even Luis Tiant's own Cuban cuisine, in addition to hot dogs and beer. Success had turned a charming old dump of a ballpark into a merchandising gold mine.

They took the elevator back up to the suites level, walking past a gallery of Sports Illustrated covers featuring Red Sox ballplayers as far back as Jackie Jensen and as recent as Ivan Hurtado. At the far end of the concourse they emerged onto a metal walkway that led to the Monster seats atop the left-field wall. Sam had to get used to the idea that there was no longer a 23-foot net above the Green Monster to snag home runs that were headed for the windows across Lansdowne Street. Instead, there were now four rows of Monster Seats extending back from the edge of the wall. Heather picked out two unoccupied seats under the giant Coke bottles that were attached to the light standard near the left-field foul pole. Sam couldn't see the left-fielder beneath them, but it didn't seem to matter. The sun was setting over the seats along the right-field line, bathing the bleachers and center-field Jumbotron scoreboard in a soft, golden glow.

Everything about Fenway seemed perfect from these perches: the pale green of the interior walls, the emerald green of the outfield grass, the red-brown dirt of the infield and warning track, and the red seats that stretched from foul pole to foul pole. The glassed-in luxury suites and press box behind home plate gave the park a more modern feel, but the asymmetrical layout of the playing field and outfield seating areas was unmistakable evidence that you were in a ballpark that dated back to baggy flannels and pancake-flat fielder's gloves.

"Why didn't somebody think of this years ago?" Sam asked.

"When Lou bought the club, everybody thought they were already wringing as much money as they could out of the place," Heather said. "They were wrong."

Sam leaned over the wall to get a look at the most obvious nod to the past: the hand-operated scoreboard inside the Green Monster, directly below them.

"I've always wanted to see inside the scoreboard," Sam said.

"Not much to see, really. But we can go out there after the game, if you want."

They watched the first inning from the Monster Seats, but when a couple arrived with tickets to the seats Sam and Heather were sitting in, Sam said it was time to talk to Hurtado. Heather nodded. They went back to the suites concourse and took the elevator down to the clubhouse level. A guard stood outside the door to the Red Sox clubhouse.

"Andy, I'm going down the tunnel to talk to Gil for a second," she said to the guard. "Sam, wait here. I'll bring Ivan up from the dugout."

Heather disappeared down the ramp that led to the first-base dugout. In a minute she was back, trailed by a dark, wiry man wearing the blazing white home uniform of the Red Sox. He was obviously checking out Heather's legs as she walked ahead of him. Sam had seen Ivan Hurtado dozens of times on television. He seemed bigger in person, and younger.

"Let's go in here," Heather said, opening the door to the clubhouse.

Inside the deserted clubhouse were rows of floor-to-ceiling cubicles with the players' names and numbers on the facing edge of the shelves. There were chairs, tables, and couches in the center of the room, most facing a wall-mounted TV screen. Off to one side was the shower and the trainer's room. Gil Mahaffey's tiny office was just inside the clubhouse door, next to a table full of snacks: candy, gum, nuts, sport drinks, and pastries. The clubhouse smelled like a mixture of soap, sweat, styling gel, and deodorant. Sam had seen bigger dressing rooms at college gyms.

Ivan Hurtado took off his Sox cap and plopped himself down in one of the armchairs, looking around in a bored, distracted way.

"What's thees about, man?" he asked Heather. The way he looked at her, Sam suspected they knew each other in a capacity other than player and team executive.

"Ivan, I'd like you meet Sam Skarda. He's going to ask you some questions about the Series in '04."

"You a reporter, man?" Hurtado said. "Wait till after the game, like the rest."

"No. I'm doing some insurance work for the team," Sam said. That would be vague enough.

"Yeah, okay," Hurtado said, still petulant. "Shoot."

Sam asked Hurtado to think back to the first game of the World Series and describe what happened, from the first inning, when the Red Sox scored five runs off Cardinals starter Alberto Miranda. He watched Hurtado's expression intently as he raised the subject of the Series. There was no change; Sam could have been asking him about his electric bill.

"Alberto, man, he no have his good stuff," Hurtado said almost by rote, as though he'd answered the question a million times. "I know, cuz you no can heet his stuff when he's right."

"You dropped a fly ball that inning, right?"

"Oh, yeah, I take my eye off it when Weatherby cut in front of me."

"How'd Alberto look after that inning?"

"What you mean?"

"I mean, the look on his face. Did he look disappointed? Tired? Disgusted?"

"Oh, he disgusted, man. Like he no can figure out what the fuck is up with thees shit."

"Was he really bearing down?"

"Shit, yeah, man. He just no have it."

Hurtado was relaxed now, as though sitting in the clubhouse and talking about the World Series he lost was better than sitting in the dugout watching some kid from the minors audition for his job. Sam took him through the remaining three games of the Series, games in which the Red Sox won 3-1, 5-4 and 7-0. In the middle two games, several plays could have turned the games around. Hurtado said the Cardinal pitchers had pitched well in those games, but Boston's pitching had simply been better.

"We played bad, man," Hurtado said. "We coulda beat 'em. But they make a lotta great plays, and we fuck up too many."

"Infield play well?"

"Yeah, man, they all played good, except Alberto, he make a couple of bad throws. Everybody see that."

"Miranda didn't have a good Series, did he?"

"Not too good."

"He didn't hit well."

"No, man, but those Sox pitchers, man, they were fuckin' great."

"Is that pretty much how all the players saw it?" Sam asked. "Just a bad Series for Miranda?"

"Yeah, man, that's all."

"How about you? Did you give it everything you had?"

"What you mean, man?" Hurtado said. His eyes narrowed as Sam crossed into the taboo territory of questioning a professional athlete's effort.

"You and Alberto were the biggest stars on that team. Neither of you played well. I'm just wondering if there was a reason."

"No reason." Hurtado shrugged off the implication and regained his unconcerned expression. "I try my best. Alberto try his best. If we both play good, I don' think it make no fuckin' difference. The baseball gods, they was on Boston's side that year."

"I guess they were."

"Not thees year, though. Shit, we can't do nothin' right, man. I think we do better next year, but if they no want me here, I wanna go someplace else."

"I read that they offered you three years at $60,000,000, and you turned it down."

"It ain't about the money, man. Is about respect."

"I have a lot of respect for $60,000,000."

Hurtado blew a raspberry with his lips and began stretching, pulling one leg up to his chest with his hands clasped around the knee, then the other leg.

"If they want me, what the fuck am I doin' up here talkin' to you?" Hurtado said. "Maybe I go play with Alberto in L.A. He my brother, you know?"

"You guys pretty close?"

"Hell, yes, man."

"You see him in the offseason?"

"Not so much anymore. We no play winter ball together since the Series."

"But you talk to him?"

"Yeah, we call each other."

"How's he doing?"

"Not so good, man. They write fuckin' shit about him, too. Reporters, man. It's 'steroids this,' 'steroids that' all the time now. Alberto, man, he clean, but no one believe it."

"How do you know for sure?"

"I just know, man. He don' do that shit. He don' need to."

"How about you, Ivan? Have you ever tried steroids?"

"Oh, man." A pained look crossed Hurtado's face. "How many times I gotta say it? Never. No fuckin' way. That stuff will kill you."

"It can make you great, too."

"Not if you ain't great already."

Sam thanked Hurtado for his time, and the ballplayer stood up and looked around, as if trying to decide whether to return to the dugout or simply leave the ballpark. He gave Heather one more lingering glance, then turned and walked down the tunnel to rejoin his teammates.

"You two ever go out for a milk shake?" Sam asked Heather after Hurtado left.

"Once or twice," Heather said. She smiled slightly. "I wanted to make him feel at home after the trade."

"So, you know him. Do you believe him?"

"Honestly? He's too proud to intentionally play bad, and he's too emotional to keep quiet about it if he did."

"I didn't think he was lying, either. But I've been wrong before."

"Do you want to talk to any of the other players?"

"No, I got what I needed here," Sam said. He stood up and began walking toward the exit. "We need to talk to Alberto Miranda."

"How do you know he's the guy?"

"If a fix was on, they couldn't have done it without him."

# Chapter Nine

Lou Kenwood was no longer alone when Sam and Heather returned to the owner's suite. Paul sat at the bar on the upper level, and a woman in a wheelchair sat next to Kenwood, watching the game. An oxygen tank with two round gauges was attached to a holder behind the wheelchair, and a tube extended from the tank under the woman's arm.

"Oh, there you are," Kenwood said. The woman next to him did not turn around. "Paul, would you leave us for a while?"

"Sure thing," the chauffeur said. He got up from his stool, walked out of the suite, and closed the door behind him.

"Did you talk to Hurtado?" Kenwood asked Sam.

"Yes."

Sam approached the woman in the wheelchair and extended his hand. Heather remained at the back of the suite.

"I'm Sam Skarda."

"Excuse my manners," Kenwood said. "Sam, this is my wife, Katherine."

Kenwood's voice was a bit slurred. He might have been on his third or fourth bourbon.

"Pleased to meet you," Sam said.

"Hello, Sam," Katherine said. "I'm so glad to meet you. I hope you can help us."

Katherine Kenwood's grip was not forceful, but she did not simply lay her hand in Sam's palm, either. She put what strength she had into it.

She had definitely been a beauty in her day, and—except for the inevitable wrinkles, an age spot here and there, and the oxygen tube that ran under her nose—that day had not yet officially passed. Her hair was an elegant gray with silver streaks. Her eyes were a bit watery, but the hue remained a vibrant blue. She had the small, pert nose of a debutante, and her mouth, though widening with age, looked like the inviting kind that many men would once have wanted to kiss, and probably had. Her jaw line was sharp, almost regal, with no obvious signs of facial work so common to wealthy women of her age. What she had was what nature had given her, and nature had been generous.

"What did Ivan say?" Kenwood said.

"He said the Cardinals played hard, and he and Miranda tried their best. They just didn't have it."

"Would you expect him to say anything different?" Katherine said.

"I would have expected him to show some reaction if he knew the Series had been fixed," Sam said. "He didn't. I believe him, for now."

"So do I," Kenwood said. "Are you going to talk to any of the others?"

"No. After watching the DVD and reading the game stories, it would have to be Hurtado and Miranda. Definitely Miranda."

"When are you going to talk to him?"

"As soon as I can."

Sam pulled up a chair and sat next to Katherine. Heather asked from the bar if anyone wanted a drink. Sam declined.

"Make mine a martini, sweetheart," Katherine said.

"Do you think you should?" Kenwood asked.

"Why the hell not?" Katherine said. She laughed in a low, rumbling tone that didn't sound as much bitter as resigned. "I'm dying, Sam. I smoked two packs a day for thirty years, and it caught up with me."

"I'm sorry," Sam said. He noted the slight rasp in her throat as she spoke.

"So am I. Christ, I don't want to die. I wanted to be around to see us win another championship. But it had to be this year…"

Sam didn't know what to say, but he appreciated Katherine Kenwood's bluntness. She was making the best of the cards she'd been dealt, facing death with the kind of grace everybody hopes they'll have.

They sat in silence for a while, watching the game. It was in the sixth inning; the Blue Jays were leading 6-4, and the Sox had runners on second and third with one out.

"Gil should put on the squeeze here," Kenwood said.

"It's a bad play when you're down two runs," Katherine said. "What is it with you and bunting, anyway?"

"Look where Johnson's playing," Kenwood insisted. "He's two steps behind the third base bag, and Davis can bunt."

"He won't."

"Gil's got to get the crowd back into the game. You want to put ten on it?"

"Sure, I'll take that bet," Katherine said.

There was a hint of what must have been the old playfulness between them, the residual familiarity of sharing thirty years and hundreds of ballgames together.

Davis swung away at the first pitch and fouled it back.

"I guess Gil doesn't like the squeeze here, either," Katherine said.

"There's only one strike. He's got one to play with."

Davis took a pitch outside for ball one, and didn't start to slide his hand up the bat as if to bunt. He stepped out of the box and checked the third base coach's signals.

"That's a different sign than he got on the last pitch," Kenwood said.

"You missed the indicator," Katherine said. "There's no play on."

"Look at Mitchell's lead. He's farther down the line. Watch…"

The Blue Jays pitcher delivered, Mitchell stayed where he was and Davis whistled a line drive past the third baseman, who had started to cheat in. It was now 6-5, runners on first and third, still one out, and the crowd was suddenly on its feet, roaring.

Silently, Kenwood pulled his wallet out of his pants pocket and extracted a ten dollar bill, handing it to his wife.

"Why do I bet with you?" Kenwood sighed. "You must be into me for a couple of thousand bucks by now."

Katherine took the bill, put it in the pocket of her sweater, and gave Sam a satisfied grin. Sam returned the smile, then glanced quickly at Heather. She was not smiling.

"Sam, I understand you're going to be leaving town, with Heather," Katherine said.

"That's right."

"I wonder if you could come out to the house tomorrow morning before you leave."

"I could. Why?"

"I'd like you give me a shooting lesson."

Sam glanced at Lou Kenwood, who simply shrugged and turned back to the game.

"Why?"

"Lou leaves me alone at the house too often. It's on an isolated point, sticking out in the ocean. With all that's going on now, I don't feel safe there."

Sam must have looked perplexed by the request, because Katherine felt compelled to explain.

"Just because I'm dying doesn't mean I don't care about protecting myself," she said. "I bought a pistol, but I need someone to show me how to use it. You were a police officer, weren't you?"

"Yes. I'm still licensed to carry."

"Then you could take an hour or so to show me how to shoot, couldn't you."

It was a statement, not a question. And since the man paying his salary didn't voice any objection, Sam agreed.

"Wonderful. I'll have Paul pick you up at your hotel right after he drops Lou at his office. Say, about 8:15?"

"I'll be ready."

◇◇◇

Neil Diamond's "Sweet Caroline" blared out of the stadium loudspeakers after the Red Sox took the lead in the bottom of the eighth inning. The capacity crowd roared along with the "bom-bom-BOM" chorus, kept singing after the song faded out, and continued to sing until the Sox closer threw his second pitch in the ninth. Sam couldn't help but think about a woman named Caroline who lived in Tucson, and wonder if their good times would ever seem so good...

Heather took Sam down to the clubhouse level, waiting for the game to end so they could walk out to the left-field scoreboard. After the final out of the 7-6 Boston win, the players exited the dugout and headed up to the clubhouse while the crowd sang along with "Dirty Water" as it blared from the p.a. system.

"You were getting awfully chummy with the Missus," Heather said as the players filed past.

Sam wondered if he was hearing a tinge of jealousy in Heather's voice.

"I like her," Sam said simply. "She's a smart, interesting woman."

"She's a drag on Lou's time and energy," Heather said. "I know that sounds harsh, but it's true."

"God forbid you should get old someday," Sam said.

"If I end up in a chair, I hope someone puts me out of my misery."

Sam couldn't tell whether Heather's lack of compassion was restricted to Kenwood's wife, or to mankind in general.

They took the tunnel down to the dugout, now deserted except for the equipment man picking up bats, helmets, and towels. The floor of the dugout was covered in seed shells, gum wrappers, Gatorade cups, and drying saliva. Sam stepped over the worst of it and went up the steps to the field level, where the grounds crew was removing the bases and smoothing the infield with a small tractor. Sam turned to look back up into the stands. While the aisles were clogged with exiting fans, a few stragglers remained seated, not wanting to let go of their visit to this jewel of a ballpark. A dozen security cops stood on the dirt of the infield warning track, looking into the stands for anyone who thought they could get away with jumping over the low retaining wall onto the field. At least on this night, no one was drunk or foolish enough to try it.

Sam and Heather walked behind home plate and along the warning track that paralleled the third base line to the left-field corner. When they reached the Green Monster, Heather took him to a small doorway cut into the hand-operated scoreboard, just below the AT BAT indicator. Heather pulled the door outward, and they stepped over the foot-high threshold and into the dim, dusty room behind the scoreboard.

Inside, there was a long corridor about six feet deep, with head room limited by the slanted concrete abutments on the wall opposite the scoreboard. Three men in shorts and t-shirts were extracting green metal plates with white numerals from the scoreboard slots above their heads, and hanging them on the corresponding pegs against the wall behind them. Their night was over, except for the cleanup. It was hot inside the scoreboard, the men were sweaty, and they looked glad to be finished.

"Hiya, Heather," said one, a wiry, dark-haired guy with sideburns and curly dark hair on his legs. "Givin' a tour?"

"Hi, Danny," Heather replied. "Yeah, Sam here wanted to see Fenway's real glamour location."

"Well, it's all yours," Danny said. "We're outta here."

"That's the last one," said one of the other scoreboard workers, hanging up a final number.

"You gonna be a while?" Danny asked Heather.

"I thought I'd show Sam some of the autographs in here."

"Joe Mauer came in last week and signed, right over there—above Pudge's name," Danny said. He pointed to a spot on the back wall where a signature stood out in fresh, bold Sharpie strokes.

"We'll shut off the lights," Heather said.

The three scoreboard operators picked up their jackets and their plastic Coke cups and walked out onto the field. Heather showed Sam one of the eyeholes through which the operators watched the game, and he could see the three men heading toward the infield. The lights were still on in the park, but the stands were now empty except for the custodians picking up garbage from row to row.

He turned back to Heather, and saw her taking off her jacket.

"It's hot in here," she said. "Aren't you a little warm?"

The question didn't seem to require an answer. She smoothed her hair back with both hands, her breasts making round shadows on her tight, pink crew-neck shirt; she gave her head a little shake, not taking her eyes off Sam. Then she walked up to him and kissed him. While they kissed, she untucked his shirt from his pants. Sam looked quickly around. Here? Inside the Green Monster? Well, why not?

He pulled a folding chair over to him and sat down, with Heather facing him. He unzipped his pants and she pulled her skirt up and took off her underwear, hanging it on one of the pegs that held the scoreboard numbers. She straddled him on the chair while Sam caressed her breasts, first outside her shirt, then pulling it up gradually and loosening her breasts from her bra.

"Anyone else coming in here tonight?"

"I can't remember if that Girl Scout troop is tonight or tomorrow night," Heather said.

He picked Heather up and leaned her against the inside of the scoreboard for support. While he was entering her, he could see the field through one of the peepholes. He wondered if his thrusts were causing any visible movement in the wall—but there was no one on the field to notice anyway.

Heather's eyes were open, looking off into the distance behind him. He closed his own eyes and kissed her while his left hand caressed the smooth curve of her small, taut ass, and his right hand played among the smooth strands of her hair. When he opened his eyes again, Heather's eyes were fixed on a spot somewhere near the far corner of the floor.

"What are you looking at?" he said into her ear.

"Nothing."

She curled her thigh around the back of Sam's leg and arched herself backward as Sam kissed her breasts. She moaned, but Sam glanced at her face and saw that her eyes were still fixed on the same spot.

He adjusted his stance so he could turn his head to follow her gaze. Two rats were emerging cautiously from the shadows fifteen feet from where they stood.

"Jesus!" Sam said. He started to pull away, but Heather clung to him and thrust her hips closer to Sam's.

"Finish," she said.

Sam kicked the folding chair toward the corner and the rats scurried back into the darkness.

When they were done, both glistening with sweat, Sam eased himself back onto the folding chair while Heather got dressed.

"Is that the standard tour, or did I get the special?"

"That's a first for me, too," Heather said, pulling on her bra. "And I wasn't expecting an audience."

"It didn't seem to bother you too much."

"Well, this isn't the Ritz...or the Taj."

The overhead lights were being turned off a few minutes later as Sam and Heather emerged from the scoreboard and walked back to the infield. They used the gate next to the third base dugout that led into the grandstand and went up the aisle, stepping on black, flattened pieces of chewing gum that must have dated back to the days when Mel Parnell was pitching.

When Sam and Heather emerged from the stadium onto Yawkey Way, there were still fans milling around, mostly drunk and loudly celebrating the victory as they drifted toward Brookline Avenue and the T station in Kenmore Square. Take this away from them, Sam thought, and they'd find something else to get drunk and yell about—but it would never be the same as their unquestioning love for the Sox. They decided to get a bite and a drink at the Cask 'n' Flagon on Lansdowne before catching a cab.

"So you're really going out to the Kenwood house tomorrow," Heather said.

"Yeah. What should I expect?"

"I don't know. I've never been invited."

# Chapter Ten

Kenwood's Lincoln was waiting for Sam in front of the hotel at a quarter after eight. Heather had called to tell him that the Dodgers were in the middle of a homestand. She'd booked them on an L.A. flight leaving Logan the next morning. Sam had been in Boston for two nights now, and already he was getting restless to leave. He hadn't accomplished much; he'd found no convincing evidence that the Series had been fixed, and he'd established a borderline-kinky sexual relationship with his client's assistant.

On second thought, not bad for less than 48 hours work, most of which was on the clock. But there seemed little left to do here, unless Heather wanted to do it on Old Ironsides.

"Good morning, Mr. Skarda," said Paul O'Brien, who was waiting to open the back door of the limo. "Sleep well?"

Sam scanned Paul's face to see if he might have meant anything extra by that, but there appeared to be no hidden intent. Sam settled deeply into the black leather seat. There was a pot of hot coffee and a carafe of orange juice on the fold-down buffet shelf in front of him, and a Boston Globe in the magazine rack. Paul pulled smoothly out into traffic while Sam poured himself a cup of coffee and opened the paper.

"Paul, how long have you worked for Mr. Kenwood?" Sam asked.

"Ten years, sir."

"What happened to his chauffeur before that?"

"I don't know. I think Mr. and Mrs. Kenwood drove themselves. But they were getting older, and then Mrs. Kenwood got sick."

"Do you know anything about Kenwood's son?"

"No, sir. We—they—didn't hear from him. I never met him."

"What was his first name?"

"Bruce, I think."

"How'd he die?"

"Drowned in the Pacific—somewhere in California."

"Did Lou go to the funeral?"

"No."

Odd, Sam thought. Unless Bruce Kenwood had been in a monastery or a mental ward somewhere, you'd think he'd have wanted to stay in touch, just to try to get his piece of the pie. But the children of rich people were an unpredictable subset. Some grew up with a sense of entitlement, while others had a desperate need to prove that they could make it on their own. Sam knew both kinds, and didn't particularly envy either.

"Why do you think Bruce stayed away?"

"I really don't know. But I don't think he and Mrs. Kenwood—Katherine—ever got along."

That would make sense. He'd resent his father's new wife.

"I think he got into some trouble—taxes or something," Paul continued. "Then he died. The Kenwoods never talk about him."

"What about your family, Paul?"

"Mine, sir?"

"Big Sox fans, I'd guess."

"Oh, you know it," he said, again dropping the formal veneer. "Me and my brothers—my brothers and I, we grew up goin' to Sox games. My dad was at Fenway for Game Seven in '67. He said losin' that game broke his heart. Then 1975 did it all over again, and the playoff in '78...hell, I remember that one. I was just a kid, but I can remember my dad cryin' when Yaz popped out to Nettles to end the game. But the '86 Series, when the ball went through Buckner's legs, that was the worst. It took him most of spring trainin' the next year to decide whether he was gonna watch the Sox anymore. Course, he did. Still never misses a game on TV, even after he got sick…"

"What's he got?" Sam asked.

"Alzheimer's. Pretty far along now. He didn't really know what was going on when the Sox beat the Rockies."

"He must have loved it when the Sox beat the Cardinals."

"Greatest moment of his life," Paul said, his voice quavering. "Back then, he knew what was gonna happen to him. When we got the last out, he turned to my ma and said, 'I can die happy.'"

Sam let a few moments of silence pass, then said, "Does he still watch the games?"

"Yeah. Every once in a while he asks if we've traded that goddamn Buckner yet."

They took the same route out to Marblehead Neck that Kenwood used, hugging the shoreline on Route 1 through Revere, Lynn, and Swampscott, passing industrial areas, beaches, apartment buildings, and a few trendy restaurants and shops, with sailboats bobbing offshore and gulls swooping down for snacks. Traveling against morning commuter traffic, it took just 30 minutes to cover the 15-mile drive to Ocean Avenue, which ran across a narrow, sandy isthmus and connected Marblehead Neck to the mainland.

The Kenwood house was at the north end of the Neck on a leafy, two-lane road with homes isolated from the passing traffic by thick hedges and stone walls. The entrance to Kenwood's place was marked by two towering maples on either side of a gated brick driveway that concluded in a circle with a flagpole in the center, from which flew the American flag and 2004 and 2007 World Series Champions banners. To the left of the circle was a two-story, four-car garage in the same weathered, gray cedar-shake style as the main house, which had four chimneys and seemed to sprawl across the high point of the property like a series of smaller houses pressed together. A stone stairway led up to the main doorway, and Sam could see through the windows that the view from the back of the house was going to be spectacular—nothing between the Kenwoods and the rocky shore but a long, sloping green lawn, and nothing beyond that but France.

Paul went in ahead of Sam and announced loudly that they had arrived. Katherine Kenwood was in the living room bump-out, her wheelchair facing the wide bay windows that looked out over the jagged point that jutted into the ocean. The morning sun was sparkling on the calm water, and Katherine seemed reluctant to turn herself around and surrender the view.

The spacious living room, with hardwood floors, wood-beamed ceilings, and a stone fireplace, was furnished with sturdy-looking but obviously antique wooden furniture mixed with more comfortable and contemporary couches and armchairs. The living room was open to an adjoining study, with floor-to-ceiling bookshelves, a grand piano, a globe in a wooden stand, and a compass, a sextant, a maritime map, and other nautical knickknacks on the walls, all of it suggesting New England whaling days. The Kenwoods were relatively new to their wealth, but their house was a study in old-money taste.

"Let's go out to the porch," Katherine said.

Paul gripped the handles of her wheelchair and pushed her through the open door that led from the living room to a covered porch with wooden floorboards. Three-fourths of the porch was sheltered by the overhang from the second floor, supported by shingled wooden pillars; the far end was open, and bathed in sunlight. Katherine was sitting in the covered side. Sam selected a white wicker rocker to sit in, facing the ocean.

"Bring us some coffee, would you, Paul?" Katherine said. "And bring my pistol out here. It's on the dining room table."

Katherine looked even more striking in the daylight than she had in the owner's suite the previous night. Despite the lines around her eyes and the corners of her mouth, the natural light brought out the smooth delicacy of her complexion; the ocean seemed to reflect back to Sam in her deep blue eyes, and her fine, silver-blond hair rustled in the gentle breeze off the water.

It wasn't difficult to see past the oxygen tube that ran across her upper lip and imagine why Lou Kenwood had left his first wife for this woman.

"This is a fantastic house," Sam said, looking to get the conversation started.

"Everyone loves it." Katherine's words and breaths were measured. "We looked for two years...before finding this place. I wish I never had to leave."

Sam didn't know what to say to that. Katherine's condition seemed worse than it had the previous night. She wore a shawl over her shoulders and a blanket across her lap, despite the moderate morning temperature. While Sam was wondering how to sound consoling without conveying pity, Katherine reached under the blanket and pulled out a pack of cigarettes.

Paul returned with coffee and the pistol. He placed the silver coffee tray and the gun—a Beretta Bobcat—on the end table between Sam and Katherine, and pulled a light out of his pocket and lit Katherine's cigarette. Then he walked back into the house.

"Want one?" she asked as she inhaled.

"No, thanks. Does Lou know you're still smoking?"

"Of course. He has Paul buy them for me."

"You didn't smoke last night."

"Fenway is smoke-free, my dear."

"Even for the owner's wife?"

"We must set a good example."

"Does your doctor know?"

"Don't judge...until you're sitting where I'm sitting," Katherine said. She took another draw and then slowly exhaled. "I haven't got much left...besides these. What about you? What are your bad habits?"

"I like a stiff drink, but I don't like being drunk. I haven't touched drugs since college. It's a control thing, I guess."

"Not much, as far as failings go."

"I've got a temper. I got rough with some of the worst assholes when I was a cop—just because it made me feel better. I let the job get to me sometimes."

"Ever marry?"

"No," Sam said. "Close once. Probably would have been a bad idea."

"That's been a while."

"Yeah. It has."

"Are you the workaholic type, Mr. Skarda?"

"Not exactly. I could let it go when I wasn't on duty. I played a lot of golf."

He smiled at that, and so did Katherine.

"So I've heard," she said. "You played varsity at Dartmouth."

"How'd you know?"

"Lou had you checked out."

"By Heather?"

"Isn't she a dear?"

Sam was on dangerous ground now. It would only be natural for Katherine to harbor some resentment toward her husband's pretty young assistant—after all, that's where Katherine came in. But she might not be pleased to suspect that Sam was having sex with her, either. Lou, Katherine, Heather, and Sam were supposedly the only four who knew what was going on, and the loyalties seemed to be divided on all sides.

"She has her good qualities," Sam said.

Katherine laughed and changed the subject.

"So, how on earth did a Dartmouth man become a police officer?"

"My dad was a Minneapolis cop."

"And your mother?"

"She was a junior high music teacher."

"Interesting combination. I assume you're musical."

"Guitar, a little piano."

"Could you play something on our piano? It never gets used anymore."

"If there's time. What about you? What's your background?"

Katherine told him that she was born and raised in Boston, an Irish-Catholic girl—Katy Kelly, in those days—whose father was a lawyer and whose mother stayed at home and raised seven kids. All of them lived and died with the Red Sox. She'd gone to Wellesley, did some modeling after college, and eventually got into retail. She took a job as a buyer with Kenwood Companies, and moved into the corporate office when Lou was still acquiring his fortune. Her family disapproved when Lou divorced his wife to marry Katherine, and they didn't really come around until Lou bought the Red Sox. Then all was forgiven.

"What's your take on the extortion plot?" Sam asked.

He studied Katherine's face while she thought of a way to answer. Lou was almost too emotional about his team to analyze the situation clearly. He doubted that Katherine's mind was similarly clouded.

"I take it at face value…until I find out otherwise," Katherine said. Her breathing was becoming shorter. "We weren't supposed to even get to the Series. Nobody ever thought we'd sweep. It was exciting, but I remember thinking…that it was almost too good to be true. I guess this doesn't really surprise me."

"Why not? Nobody's tried to fix a World Series for ninety years."

"As far as you know, Sam. And if it's really been that long… another one was overdue, don't you think?"

"But the Black Sox fix was about a cheap owner and under-paid players. That's not what's happening here."

She took a drag on her cigarette, snuffed it out in the ashtray that Paul had brought out with the coffee, and wheeled her chair toward the open side of the porch.

"Let's go out here in the sunlight," she said. "I've spent 70 years protecting my skin. I don't think I need…to worry about that anymore."

Sam followed her to the sunlit deck overlooking the sloping emerald lawn and the ocean. Katherine lit another cigarette and turned to look at Sam.

"My father told me the whole story…about the 1919 World Series," she said. "Comiskey was a short-sighted miser. He low-balled his players every year at contract time…even though they were the best team in the league. There was no free agency. He didn't pay them because he didn't have to. It wasn't hard for the gamblers to find eight fools…willing to risk their careers for some extra cash. Ballplayers always grab for the easy money. I haven't met one yet who thinks more about his legacy…than the size of his house."

"Money keeps a lot of people from seeing the big picture."

"They were all suspended for life. Don't you think every one of them would have given the money back…if they could have stayed in baseball?"

"Sure, but they knew Comiskey was screwing them."

"They also knew throwing games was wrong, but they got greedy," Katherine said. She paused to inhale from her cigarette, then coughed. "Just because we're paying the Ivan Hurtados of the world $15,000,000 a year to play baseball…doesn't mean we've wiped out greed."

"No, it doesn't."

"It's in man's nature to want more. And it's especially in a pro athlete's nature. That's how they judge themselves…by how much more money they're making than the other players. It will never change."

"I haven't noticed many owners worrying about their legacy, either," Sam said. "Most of them just want to squeeze every dime out of the franchise."

"I know," Katherine said. "I don't want that to be our legacy. When we're gone, I want people to remember the Kenwoods as the best owners Boston ever had."

"You're on your way. Two World Championships…"

"That's not what I mean. What good does all our money do…if we simply become the new Yankees…buying the next Japanese star…or the next Cuban defector? I've been talking to Lou…about establishing a foundation…or charitable trust."

"Like the Yawkeys?"

"Something like that. Something that will help people…after we're gone. That's how I want to be remembered."

Katherine's watery blue eyes did not waver from Sam's.

"The opposite of Charles Comiskey," he said.

"Comiskey was hated by his players, and he hated them. Lou loves his players…and he's sure they love him. This would kill him if it turns out to be true."

Sam believed her. Kenwood struck him as the kind of guy who could technically own other human beings and still convince himself that the bond between them was about love, loyalty, and mutual respect, rather than money.

"What about you?" Sam asked. "Do you love the players?"

"I love the Red Sox."

Sam gazed beyond the sun-splashed deck to the glittering ocean. If it weren't for Katherine's oxygen hose, the Kenwoods would have seemed the most fortunate people on the face of the earth.

"Why do you want me to show you how to shoot a gun?" Sam asked. "You seem pretty safe here."

"I didn't want to say this in front of Lou…when we were in the suite," Katherine said. She leaned closer to Sam. "Odd things have been happening. I'm afraid someone wants to kill me."

"Why do you think that?"

"I've had strange phone calls. Hang-ups, when Lou isn't home."

"Probably telemarketers."

"No, it's more than that. Paul can tell you. Someone ran a red light, almost hit us on our way into town last weekend. If Paul hadn't seen him coming…and slammed on the brakes…"

"What happened to the other car?"

"It sped away."

"Anything else?"

"There was a gas leak…in the basement a few days ago."

"Who noticed it?"

"One of the boys from the lawn service."

"Maybe he caused it."

"I don't know. Maybe. But with this extortion note…I just don't feel safe. Somebody is coming after us. I want to be able to protect myself. Now, how about that shooting lesson?"

"We can't do it here."

"Of course not. We'll do it out there."

She pointed to the ocean.

"Paul, would you bring the car around?" Katherine called. "We're ready to go to the yacht club."

# Chapter Eleven

It took Paul five minutes to get Katherine out of the house and into the car, and three minutes to drive to the yacht club, on the bay side of The Neck. They parked among the Jaguars, Cadillacs, and Chrysler 300s, passed through the weathered old clubhouse, built in 1895, and boarded *The Katy K,* a 55-foot mahogany and teak Chris Craft Constellation built in 1961 and renamed by Kenwood when he bought it in 1980. A special hydraulic ramp lifted Katherine in her wheelchair from the dock to the deck of the yacht.

"We used to have…lots of parties on this boat," Katherine said. "The last one was right after last year's World Series."

She looked off to the horizon as Paul skippered the boat out of the bay, past dozens of anchored sailboats and cruisers, and into open water. In less than a half hour, the coastline was barely visible, several miles in the distance.

"I'm sure this is far enough, Paul," Sam said.

He stood up and turned Katherine's wheelchair around to face over the stern. There were no other boats in sight—just a few seagulls. He picked up the Beretta that she had brought with her. It was a small semi-automatic with an eight-round magazine for .25 caliber cartridges, a favorite among women for personal protection. It fit Katherine's hand well, and it was probably the biggest gun she was capable of handling.

"It's a nice gun," Sam said. "I don't think it's got much of a kick. You might be able to get a few shots off with it."

"Well, let's see," she said.

Sam pointed to a darkened spot on the water about 30 feet from the stern of the gently rocking boat and told her to aim for that. He had her place the fingers of her left hand in front of her right hand for a two-fisted grip, and told her to extend her arms and squeeze the trigger slowly. When the gun discharged, Katherine's hands recoiled upward and her chair rolled backward several inches. He looked at her to see if she was hurt or frightened, but the look on her face was one of determination mixed with satisfaction.

"I did it," she said. "I put that bullet right where you told me to."

"Not bad," Sam said.

"I want to do it again."

"We'd better set the brake on your chair. I don't want to have to fish you out of the ocean."

Katherine fired ten more shots, each of them fairly close to the target Sam had picked out for her, before her hands and arms began to tire. The big cruiser was riding smoothly on the gently rolling waves, but Sam was nevertheless impressed with her marksmanship. He showed her how to remove and insert the magazine, and made sure she knew where the safety was.

"Did you bring your gun?" Katherine asked him.

"Yes."

Sam took out his Glock 23 from the holster under his jacket and handed it to Katherine.

"It's heavier than mine," she said.

"More stopping power."

She handed the gun back to him, and he fired three quick rounds into the ocean, the splashes kicking up in a tight pattern. He hadn't fired the gun since that spring, in Georgia. As he lowered the Glock and continued to gaze at the spot in the water where his bullets had disappeared, Katherine noticed the look in his eyes.

"You've killed someone with that gun...haven't you?"

"Yes."

Katherine was quiet for a moment, then said, "Is my gun powerful enough?"

"For what?"

"To kill a person…with one shot?"

"If you put the bullet in the right place, it is. Besides, I don't think you could handle anything bigger. Better to hit someone two or three times with a small gun than miss with a big one."

Paul had begun to turn the big Chris Craft around when Sam noticed a boat coming at them from behind, kicking up a wake. It looked like one of the high-performance ski boats he often saw on White Bear Lake, maybe a 25-footer, with a V-hull and a big MerCruiser engine, possibly 350-horse. There was one person visible in the boat—and he appeared to be heading directly for the *Katy K*.

"Do you recognize that boat?" Sam asked Katherine. She turned to look where Sam was pointing.

"No, I don't think so," she said.

Sam continued to watch as the boat closed the gap, then changed course slightly to pass the *Katy K* on the starboard side. If the guy at the wheel was just out for a jaunt in the open water, he was coming way too close to their space. Sam put his hand on the butt of his Glock and pushed Katherine's wheel-chair away from the stern rail and toward the steering column, which was protected by the boat's gunwales. As he turned back to look at the speeding inboard, the man in the boat picked up a submachine gun from the seat next to him and pointed it at the *Katy K*. Bullets riddled the side of the big cabin cruiser, chipping away at the wood and fiberglass.

Sam dived for Katherine's wheelchair and pulled it over on its side as she screamed and fell onto the deck. He pushed her over to the stairs that led below, and Paul lowered her down to the lower level by her arms. When the gunfire ceased, Sam crawled to the stern and peered over the railing. The inboard was doing a fast, tight circle around the *Katy K* and coming around again from the port side. Once again the machine gun spat fire and bullets thudded into the boat's gunwales. Sam could see the man at the controls of the inboard—a dark-haired white guy wearing a black nylon jacket and blue jeans. He was a good 40 feet from the *Katy K*, but Sam was sure he'd never seen the man before.

"Sam…what's happening?" Katherine gasped from below deck.

"Somebody's trying to kill us," Sam said. "Stay down there!"

Paul scrambled to the steering wheel and crouched behind it.

"What should I do?" he asked Sam. "Make a run for it?"

"We'd be sitting ducks. Hold it steady. If he gets close enough, I might be able to take him out."

The inboard was circling behind the yacht, and the man at the controls fired off more rounds over and into the yacht as he tried to steer his boat. He put the gun down to turn his boat to the left and come closer to the *Katy K*. The gunman pushed the throttle open again, and as the outboard gained speed he raised the submachine gun. Sam braced his gun on the railing and fired at the man. The shot missed, and the gunman veered the boat sharply to the right when he heard the sound of Sam's shot. He opened the throttle and sped out to sea, but when he was well out of range, he turned the boat and began to circle back toward the *Katy K*.

"He's coming back," Sam said. "Paul, go below and check on Katherine. Then get her gun and take the port side. I'll go to starboard."

"This is starboard."

"So I'm not nautical. Get the goddamn gun."

Sam crawled on his stomach to the other side of the boat and waited. Then he heard Paul's voice calling to him from below deck.

"Sam! Katherine's been hit!"

"I'm all right," Katherine called, in a weak voice. "Never mind…about me."

Sam had no choice. The inboard was approaching the *Katy K* again from the starboard side, and Paul wasn't there to hold off the gunman. Sam heard several more rounds rip into the starboard side of the boat as the inboard engine seemed to go into idle.

Then he heard the engine engage again, and it sounded like the gunman was coming around the bow to get a look at the port side. Sam was ready for him. He braced his gun on the yacht's railing, and when the inboard appeared around the bow, Sam fired a shot that shattered the smaller boat's Plexiglas windshield. The gunman realized he was too close and turned the bow of the inboard toward open water, letting the throttle full out, but as he turned away, Sam fired three more shots. The second and third shots hit the man in the head and back. The inboard shot forward into open water, while the gunman toppled backward into the ocean. He flopped his arms weakly, opened his mouth, and took in crimson saltwater. He eventually stopped moving, and his body disappeared beneath the surface.

Sam ran to the steps that led to the lower compartment.

"Katherine, are you all right?"

He heard her heaving breaths. Paul was already helping her up the stairs, readjusting her oxygen tube.

"I'm...all...right," she said between gasping breaths. "The... bastard...just...nicked me."

Blood dripped from what looked to be a flesh wound on her right forearm. Sam pulled her bloody hand away from the wound and saw that the bullet had indeed just grazed her arm. Paul opened a cabinet under the steering column and pulled out a first aid kit. He applied an antiseptic wipe to Katherine's wound, then covered it with a gauze pad and wrapped it with surgical tape. Sam was more concerned about Katherine going into shock than he was about the wound itself. He had her lie down on a reclining deck chair. Her face had been ashen, but in a few minutes she began to get control of her breathing, and some color returned to her cheeks.

"Paul, are you okay to take us back?" Sam asked.

"Bastard missed me," Paul said, the Boston accent reappearing. "What happened to him?"

"I shot him. He didn't float."

Sam looked out beyond the *Katy K*'s bow and saw that the driverless inboard had almost vanished in the distance, headed full throttle to the middle of the Atlantic.

"We need to get you to a hospital," Sam said to Katherine, who was now sitting up. "And we need to talk to the cops."

"I'm...all right," Katherine wheezed. She motioned for Paul to help her back into her wheelchair. "You...can't...report this. The police will...ask questions."

"They tend to do that," Sam agreed.

"She means, they'll find out about the extortion note," Paul said.

"How much do you know about it?" Sam asked. He studied Paul's face.

"Enough. And I know cops. They don't keep secrets."

"Did either of you tell anyone we were going to be on the yacht today?"

"Only the harbormaster at the yacht club," Paul said.

"Look, somebody knew we were going to be out here," Sam said. "Somebody tried to kill us. I don't know who, and I don't know why, but this is getting pretty damned hard to keep a lid on."

"There's...no body," Katherine said. "No boat. Nobody has...to know."

"I killed a man."

"He had it comin' to him," Paul said, in the pugnacious tone of a Red Sox fan who'd just punched a Yankee fan in the face.

Sam knew he hadn't committed a crime. More than that, he knew the Kenwoods were paying him to help them save their baseball team, and if he reported this murder attempt, there would be no way to keep the whole story from ending up in the papers and the evening news.

If a driverless inboard was reported by a fishing trawler, he'd just have to withhold what he knew about it for a while. If somebody at the yacht club noticed the bullet holes in the *Katy K* and asked questions, Katherine would just have to play the proper Bostonian and tell them to mind their own business. But one thing was certain: Sam had been shot at twice within the past seventy-two hours, and he was getting tired of it.

◇◇◇

When they returned to the Kenwoods' house, Sam helped Paul get Katherine up the steps and into her bedroom, where she said she wanted to take a nap. Paul checked the dressing on her wound, called the Kenwoods' home health nurse to come over for a few hours, and then drove Sam back to his hotel in the Lincoln.

"Katherine thinks someone's trying to kill her," Sam said to Paul from the back seat. "What do you think?"

"I don't know," Paul said. He didn't turn his head. "Maybe someone's trying to kill you."

Sam thought about the events of the last few days, and called Marcus on his cell phone.

"Sammy, what's happenin'," Marcus said. "You back in town?"

"No, I'm headed to L.A. for a few days. You find that drive-by punk yet?"

"Yeah, we found him."

"Why'd he do it?"

"He can't say."

"Can't, or won't?"

"Can't. He's in a coma."

"What happened?"

"We found him in a crack house in North Minneapolis. He'd been shot five times."

"Is he going to make it?"

"Too early to say."

Shit. Sam needed some answers, and no one had them. All he knew was that he couldn't find Babe Ruth—but Babe Ruth might have found him.

# Chapter Twelve

Sam sat in one of the armchairs in his hotel suite, staring into the ashes of the cherrywood fire from two nights earlier. He went over the facts of the case so far, and found as many holes as there were in the side of the *Katy K.*

Someone was shaking down the Red Sox for $50,000,000. Someone was supposedly willing to admit he threw the World Series. Lou Kenwood didn't want to pay the extortionist, but he didn't want the story to become public, either. Lou was worried that a gambling scandal would shatter his reputation as a savior and gravely wound both the Red Sox and Major League Baseball. On top of all that, someone had twice shot at Sam, once when he was with Marcus, the other time when he was with Katherine Kenwood and Paul O'Brien.

Who had not been around when the bullets began to fly? Lou Kenwood. Heather Canby.

But Sam came back to Paul O'Brien. Paul was from South Boston, home of the Boston mob. He'd been a truck driver— probably involved with the Teamsters. His father was dying of Alzheimer's disease. Beyond the financial motivation, a son with peripheral ties to the major leagues might just be willing to participate in a fix if it meant his father could celebrate a World Championship before he died. If it were to turn out that the Series really had been fixed, the senior O'Brien wouldn't even know; according to Paul, his disease was so far advanced that he didn't know what year it was.

Paul had been on the boat when the gunman opened fire, and unlike Katherine, he had emerged unscathed. He'd seemed unusually calm for a man who'd almost been murdered by a hitman—a hitman who'd been tipped off that they'd be on the boat.

Sam called Heather.

"It's your private eye," he said. "What do you know about Paul O'Brien?"

"Why?" Heather said, sounding surprised by the question.

"We were shot at today on the Kenwoods' yacht. Katherine thinks somebody's trying to kill her. I think somebody's trying to kill me. It all makes me want to know more about O'Brien."

"Let me close my door," Heather said.

She put the phone down. When she returned, she spoke in a quieter voice:

"First, Lou trusts Paul with his life."

"What about you?"

"What I think doesn't matter."

"Sure it does. I'm asking."

"I've wondered about him. He's from a rough background."

"Did you run a criminal background check on him when you hired him?"

"I don't know. That was before I got here."

"Look it up," Sam said. "See if you can get me his full name, age, address, and Social Security number."

"All right. Why?"

"I want to run him through the national crime computer."

He heard her fingers clicking on a keyboard. After a minute or so, she read Sam the information.

"I don't like this," Heather said. "Lou would really be angry if he knew you were looking into Paul for any reason."

"Yeah, well, he'll be angrier if he loses his team. Somebody knows I'm working for Lou, and they don't like it. That guy on the boat today sprayed us pretty good, but Paul wasn't hit."

"Were you?"

"No. But Katherine took one in the arm."

"Is she all right?"

"I don't think she's any worse off than she already was. Look, I know a guy in town who grew up in South Boston about the same time Paul did. I'd like to go see him. Have you got a car?"

"I'll be at your hotel in forty-five minutes," Heather said.

Sam had received a nice note from Terry Donaghy after the Masters back in April, but they'd last talked more than three years ago. After Sam left Boston, they'd kept in sporadic touch as Sam got deeper into his police career and Terry played in a series of bands while holding down bartending jobs. According to his note in April, he was still working at Sweeney's Tavern in South Boston, not far from where he'd grown up. Sam looked up the number in the phone book and was told by a woman who answered the phone that Terry was expected in around four p.m. Sam hoped to talk to Terry before the place got crowded.

He was waiting outside the Taj on Arlington Street when he heard the roar of a motorcycle coming down the one-way street from Beacon. The loud pipes echoed off the façade of the hotel, and Sam was irritated that the owner of the bike was disturbing the quiet calm of the early-autumn afternoon. Then the Harley-Davidson pulled up in front of the hotel, and when the rider's red-and-blue Red Sox-themed helmet came off, Sam realized it was Heather. She was dressed in a black leather jacket with tight blue jeans and black mid-heel boots.

"Is that yours?" Sam asked her, pointing to the Harley.

"Yes. It's easier to get around the city with one of these."

She shook out her honey-blond hair, tilting her head back and raking her fingers from her forehead to the back of her neck.

"I hate helmet hair."

"Then why wear one?"

"Mandatory helmet law in Massachusetts."

"What's the fine?"

"Thirty-five bucks."

"Big deal."

"Lou makes me wear it." She looked embarrassed. "It's in my contract. If I want to ride the bike, I have to wear the helmet."

"Where's mine?"

Sam looked at the back of the bike, where most riders kept spare helmets, if they had one. Nothing there.

"We're only going to Southie, you wuss," Heather said. "Get on."

Sam shrugged and put his leg over the seat, grabbing Heather around the waist. She was about as big around as a rolled-up throw rug. Sam was afraid that he'd pull her off the bike if she accelerated too quickly, but as she gunned the accelerator, put the bike into gear, checked over her shoulder, and then pulled out into traffic, she had no trouble resisting his backward pull.

"Watch your hands," she yelled over her shoulder. "I can only do one thing at a time here. What's the address?"

Sam yelled into her ear that Sweeney's was located near the corner of West Broadway and Dorchester. Heather nodded and kept the bike on Arlington until it turned into Herald, and then took a right at Albany, which ran parallel to I-93. Sam kept glancing sideways, and noticed that they were getting a lot of interested stares from people in cars and on the sidewalks. They turned left at West Broadway and went about a half-mile up the street until they reached Sweeney's. When Heather pulled the bike over to the curb in front of the bar and took her helmet off, Sam again noticed that they were getting looks from the people nearby.

"Another first for Boston," Sam said. "I should be in the history books with Sam Adams and Paul Revere."

"What do you mean?" Heather said as she smoothed out her hair with her hand.

"Think about it. Have you ever seen a guy on the back of a motorcycle driven by a woman? I never have."

"No, I guess I haven't either."

"Neither have these people," Sam said. He gestured toward a few curious onlookers. "Until now."

The block was undergoing a facelift. The sidewalks were being replaced, and the businesses around the tavern had obviously diversified in recent years: a Chinese restaurant, a Payless

Shoes, a coffee shop with free wi-fi, and a small international grocery that sold fresh tortillas and falafel. They walked into the saloon, a narrow storefront with raised pub-style lettering spelling Sweeney's over the door. There was a small window on either side of the open door, and a neon Budweiser sign hung in one of the windows, with the words "Boston Red Sox World Champions 2004" underneath the beer logo. Maybe the newer one hadn't arrived yet.

It was much darker inside; while Sam's eyes were trying to adjust to the light, he heard his name called out.

"Sam Skarda! You old piece of shit! What are you doin' here?"

Sam recognized Terry's voice, though it was harder to recognize Terry himself as he came walking around the end of the bar and grabbed Sam's hand. Terry had shorter hair and more bulk than he'd had a decade ago. He'd been the bassist and lead singer in their short-lived band, a gifted entertainer with a strong rock voice—his dad had been an Irish tenor who sang every year in Southie's St. Patrick's Day parade—and the kind of soulful eyes that made women want to come back and see the band night after night. His eyes still looked full of life, even in the dim light of the tavern.

"Who's your knock-out friend?" Terry asked. His instincts for applying the charm to attractive women had not diminished.

"Heather Canby, this is Terry Donaghy."

"At your service," he said. He kissed Heather's hand. She looked him over and smiled, but did not seem impressed. She'd been schmoozed by men who were just as charming, and much farther up the food chain.

There were two older men sitting at the bar, both smoking and wearing jackets that seemed a little heavy for the fall weather. One of the half-dozen booths on the opposite side of the room was occupied by a balding guy who was engaged in a hushed conversation with a chubby woman who had dyed-black hair and hoop earrings. The bar smelled like the tap hoses needed a good cleaning.

"This guy," Terry said, putting an arm around Sam's shoulder, "was a fuckin' hero at the Masters this year."

"So I've heard," Heather said. She forced a polite smile. "Sam, you wanted to ask some questions."

"Let's get a booth," Sam said.

Terry checked with the guys at the bar to see if they needed a refill, then followed Sam and Heather to the farthest booth from the door, next to a small corner bandstand where Sam recognized Terry's old sunburst-finish Fender Precision leaning up against a covered amp. Terry asked Sam and Heather if they wanted anything, but they declined.

"I see you're still playing, Terry," Sam said. He gestured toward the tiny bandstand.

"The owner lets us play once a week, for tips," Terry said. "I'm trying to put a CD together—you know, original stuff. But studio time is expensive, and I gotta work most nights."

"I hear you," Sam said.

He thought about what it might have been like if he'd stayed in Boston after college. Would this be his life, too? He saw Heather looking around the bar as though she were observing a zoo exhibit.

"So, you said you wanted to know about a guy," Terry said.

"Yeah. Paul O'Brien. He would have been in school around the same time you were."

"Lotta O'Briens in Southie."

"He was a truck driver. Now he's a chauffeur. Kind of big, red curly hair."

"Oh, yeah, I knew that guy. Paulie. His younger brother Johnny was in my class. What'd he do?"

"Nothing, as far as I know. Where's Johnny now?"

"Walpole," Terry said, lowering his voice. "He, uh, kind of got mixed up with Donnie Sullivan and that bunch."

"Gambling?"

"Yeah, I guess. Maybe some drugs, too."

"Ever hear that Paul was into any of that stuff?"

Terry shot a glance over his shoulder at the two guys sitting at the bar.

"It's not such a good idea to talk about, you know… Sullivan…around here."

"I thought Sullivan had disappeared."

"He did." Terry was now talking almost in a whisper. "But he's still got guys around…"

He moved his eyeballs sideways toward the bar, without moving his head. Sam glanced up at the two guys at the bar, and saw that one of them was staring back at their booth. Maybe he was checking out Heather. Maybe not.

"So you don't know anything about Paul O'Brien?" Sam asked.

"You're like, what? A private investigator now?"

"Yeah. Not a cop."

"Look, Sam, I'd help you if I could. I just don't know anything. I remember the guy—kind of tall, red hair, right?"

Sam nodded.

"But that's all. His brother got in trouble, but as far as I know, Paulie is clean. Or, he was."

"Well, it was a long shot," Sam said.

"Maybe not," Terry said quietly. His eyes darted toward the bar again. "I'm just saying, it's not a good idea coming down here and asking about guys like him."

"I don't want to get you in any trouble, Terry. You know that."

"I know. Geez, it was good to see you again. You still playing?"

"I'm in an oldies band with some of the cops I used to work with. We play maybe twice a month."

"You gotta keep your hand in, right?"

"That's right."

"How long you gonna be in town? We should go out and see some bands, or jam."

"I'd love to, but we're leaving for L.A. tomorrow."

"The two of you?" Terry said. He looked back and forth between Sam and Heather. "That should be fun."

"It's business," Heather said. She stood up. "Nice to meet you Terry."

She extended her hand to him, and Sam got up, too. He handed Terry his card.

"If you can think of anything else," Sam said quietly.

"Yeah, definitely. You comin' back to town?"

"Don't know yet. I'll call you."

Terry gave Sam a hug and watched him walk out to the street with Heather. Then he went back behind the bar and got the two men refills, without being asked.

# Chapter Thirteen

*Caracas, Venezuela—*

Elena felt herself being lifted roughly from the ground by a man with strong arms. It was too dark to see anything but the dim outline of the shanties on either side of the narrow walkway where she'd stumbled. A baby was crying somewhere up the hillside, and a dog began barking when the man who held her by her wrists asked her where she was going.

"Nowhere," Elena stammered. She was afraid to look at the face of the man in the police uniform who held her. She was sure it was Jefe, and that he would now drag her back to that filthy room and beat her. She would never escape her prison.

"It is very late, and very dangerous for a woman like you to be in this place," the man said.

He did not sound like Jefe. Elena cautiously looked up at the face in the darkness, and was able to make out a round-headed man wearing a cloth paramilitary cap and a blue-and gray camo uniform. He was a police officer, but not the one who had held her captive for weeks.

"Can I trust you?" Elena asked him.

"Of course. *Policia.*"

"I do not trust the police anymore," she said. "What is your name?"

"Sgt. Arturo Cordoba. You may trust me, *Señora.*"

"Please, take me from here. Anywhere."

"But why…"

"There is no time to talk. I've been kidnapped. Take me to your headquarters—*por favor!*"

The officer nodded. These kidnappings were becoming commonplace. Elena obviously was not from here. You could tell by how she spoke. She might have money. If he could get her back to the central part of town, to his precinct headquarters, he could reunite her with her family. There might be a reward. But the kidnappers were likely nearby. They must move quickly and quietly.

Arturo put his hand around Elena's shoulders to steady her as they walked. She appeared malnourished and weak; she wobbled like a drunk as they descended the narrow walkway between the ramshackle structures of tin and cinderblock. Rats scurried across their path, but Elena was beyond concern about them. She was going to be free, if she could just stay on her feet until they got out of the maze of shanties.

"*Hola!*" she heard Arturo greet a man walking up the path toward them.

"No, no!" she hissed into his ear. "*Silencio!*"

"Do not worry, *Señora,*" Arturo replied. "I know this man. He is *policia,* too."

A cold wave of dread washed over Elena. She buried her face into Arturo's uniform and clung to him with both arms. Arturo stopped when the other man reached them.

"*Hola,* Arturo," Elena heard the man say. "Who have you there?"

Elena nearly collapsed, sick with fear. She knew the voice. It was Jefe.

"*No se, amigo.* She says she's been kidnapped. I'm taking her to headquarters. We'll straighten this out."

Elena felt a strong hand reach for her chin and twist it forward, so she was now facing the copper-skinned, muscular man in the tight blue police uniform. He smiled in recognition—a deadly smile containing no humor.

"*Buenos noches*, Elena," Jefe said. "Out for a walk?"

"No, no," she said, trying to turn her face away from him—but his powerful grip held her jaw where he wanted it.

"You know her, *Jefe?*" Arturo said.

"Yes, he knows me!" Elena began to shout. "He is the one who has kidnapped me!"

Jefe clamped his hand across Elena's mouth. Arturo looked at Jefe with surprise, then began to reach for his service pistol. He was not fast enough; Jefe roughly threw Elena to the ground and slammed his riot stick across Arturo's hand, causing it to recoil from his holster in pain. Jefe then spun Arturo around and pulled the riot stick against his throat with both hands, lifting the policeman off the ground. Arturo kicked furiously, but Jefe's riot stick was crushing his windpipe. He soon lost consciousness and went limp, yet Jefe continued to choke him until, even in the dimness of the alley, the horrified Elena could see the man's face begin to darken. When Jefe was sure the officer was dead, he let him crumple to the ground.

Elena began to scream as Arturo's limp arm landed in her lap. Jefe bent down to her, sweat glistening off his face, and put the riot stick under her chin.

"*Silencio!* Or you will be lying dead here, next to your friend!"

Elena stopped screaming, but could not stop crying. Could a police officer really be murdered here in the middle of Caracas, with no one to come or care? She felt herself being lifted around the waist by Jefe, who began walking back up the path between the shanties. No lights had come on, despite Elena's wails; the baby she'd heard earlier continued to cry, and now several dogs barked, but there were no faces peering out of windows, no voices calling to see what the trouble was, no figures appearing outside the shanties to offer assistance. Even the rats seemed to be cowering in the shadows.

Farther up the hill, one person dared peer out of a doorway as Jefe led the sobbing Elena through the narrow alley. It was an old man, holding a threadbare blanket around his shoulders. He walked out into the alley and stared quizzically at the muscular man in the police uniform and the distraught woman whom he seemed to be dragging along with him.

"*Boracha*," Jefe said. "She's had too much to drink tonight." The man nodded and returned to his shanty.

Within minutes, Jefe had dragged Elena back to the doorway of the shanty she'd escaped from. The radio was still on, playing the county music Paquito liked. Holding Elena around the waist with his left arm, Jefe opened the door to the shanty with his right hand, still holding his gun. He walked in, pushed Elena onto her mattress and kicked the chair legs out from under Paquito, who woke with a start when he landed on the floor.

Paquito rubbed his eyes and looked up at the figure of Jefe standing over him, riot stick poised above Paquito's head.

"Jefe, no, *por favor...*" Paquito begged, when he realized what had happened.

Those were the last words Paquito ever said. Jefe's club smashed into Paquito's face, shattering his nose and sending a spurt of blood onto Elena's skirt. Jefe followed with what seemed like an endless series of blows to Paquito's skull, beating the young man to death while Elena sobbed on the mattress.

# Chapter Fourteen

*Los Angeles, California—*

Waves of hot air shimmered above the tarmac as Sam and Heather walked through the air-conditioned LAX concourse to the baggage area. Sam didn't mind the idea of walking out into that heat; Boston had left him with a chill, and he was looking forward to warming up under the Southern California sun.

They picked up their bags and caught the shuttle to the Hertz lot. Heather had reserved an Audi Quattro, but decided to switch to a BMW convertible when they got to the rental counter.

"Detectives aren't supposed to call attention to themselves," Sam said quietly as Heather filled out the paperwork.

"I'm not a detective," Heather said. "If we get into a chase, this baby might come in handy. It hit a top speed of 180 on a test track."

"God help us."

They walked out to the lot, found the car, and put their bags in the back seat. Heather started to get into the driver's seat, but Sam said, "Hold it. I'm driving."

"No, you're not. This car was my choice."

"We're not playing bumper cars at the amusement park. You hired me to do a job—and driving is part of the job."

Heather shook her head and got behind the wheel, closing the door. She fastened her seat belt, then looked up at Sam, who was still standing next to the driver's side door.

"You're partly right—we hired you," she said. "So you'll do as we ask. If you don't like it, you can go back to Minneapolis."

Sam hated to ride shotgun, especially when he didn't know anything about the driver. But Heather was paying the bills. He got in the passenger side and connected his iPod to the car stereo and dialed up a '70s L.A. rock playlist: Eagles, Jackson Browne, Linda Ronstadt, Poco, the Flying Burrito Brothers, and CSN&Y. "Already Gone" was playing as Heather squealed out of the Hertz lot and onto Sepulveda, heading north for Santa Monica.

She was wearing a pair of tortoiseshell sunglasses, a white sleeveless shirt, a pink skirt, and designer sandals with toenails painted to match her skirt. She looked like she was born and raised on a movie lot in Beverly Hills.

They were booked into the Loews Santa Monica Beach Hotel, a luxury resort just south of the Santa Monica Pier on Ocean Avenue. Sam asked her why they were staying in such a posh spot.

"Lou's on the Loews board of directors," she said. She adjusted her sunglasses. "He insisted."

The hot streets of L.A. were a jarring change from chilly, edge-of-autumn Boston: The palm trees rustled in the heavy breezes that surged northward from Mexico, and the concrete roadways seemed on the verge of melting. Heather got on the 405 heading north, and though the traffic was sluggish, they made decent time as Heather kept changing lanes, sliding into small openings, and constantly accelerating and braking with a deft touch. When she spotted the exit for the Santa Monica Freeway, she quickly maneuvered through four lanes of traffic to get into the right lane. She was so aggressive that Sam started glancing around for L.A. freeway nut-jobs who might pull a gun on them, but it was clear to him that she knew what she was doing.

"Where'd you learn to drive like that?" Sam asked.

"Driving between Hartford and Boston. They say L.A. traffic is bad, but the Mass Turnpike is no picnic, either."

"You didn't get those skills on the freeway."

"I went to one of those performance driving schools in South Carolina a few years ago."

"Why?"

"Just for the rush. Know what I mean?"

Sam had to admit that he did. Most cops feed off that kind of adrenaline—yet it was always heightened by the fear that some civilian would accidentally get hit.

The more he learned about Heather, the less certain he was about her. She was one of only five people who knew he was working on this case, and it was becoming harder to ignore the possibility that at least one of them was responsible for the two recent drive-bys. When he told her about the attack on the *Katy K,* Heather had seemed genuinely surprised and concerned, but agreed with Katherine that they couldn't call the police.

"You'll have to be more careful," she'd said.

But she didn't seem to be afraid of being around a man who'd possibly been the target of two failed hits. She didn't seem to be afraid of anything. Sam didn't want to discuss it on the crowded flight to L.A., but he thought about it from the time the plane lifted into the air over Boston Harbor, while he was thumbing through the latest Golf Digest, while he was eating the dry ham-and-cheese sandwich and drinking two overpriced Scotches, and he was still thinking about it when it was time to put the tray tables up on their descent into LAX.

What if Heather was in on the extortion plot?

It could be a way for her to end up with a much bigger chunk of Kenwood's money than she'd ever earn working for him. Being assigned to work with Sam was a perfect way for her to monitor his every move, and to orchestrate his murder. Maybe she'd had sex with him just to gain his trust, and to create a little complacency. If Sam were killed while trying to find Babe Ruth, it might just convince Kenwood that he should stop messing around and make the payment. *Hey, Lou, we've done all we could do to try to fend this guy off,* she could say. *He's obviously dangerous and determined—let's just pay him what he wants, and this all goes away.* A few weeks later, Heather quits her job, moves to the Caymans with a share of $50,000,000, and no one ever finds out.

Sam couldn't spend any more time distrusting her. As Heather maneuvered through the sluggish traffic on the Santa Monica Freeway, Sam reached into the back seat of the BMW for his suitcase, unzipped it and pulled out his Glock. In the lane next to him, a woman driving a Prius—adorned with "Kerry-Edwards" and "Visualize World Peace" bumper stickers—saw the gun and veered onto the shoulder of the highway, frantically punching her cell phone keypad as her car came to a halt.

Sam rested the gun in his lap and watched the breeze play with Heather's hair, which had assumed an extra shade of gold under the California sun. Eventually Heather turned to look at him, and noticed the gun.

"What's that for?" Heather asked—puzzled, but not alarmed.

"I want an honest answer from you," Sam said. "Are you part of the plot?"

"What?"

"Did you set up the hit on me?"

"What the hell are you talking about?"

"Somebody knows I'm on the case." Sam fingered the trigger of the Glock and turned it so the barrel pointed at her waist. "I want to know how they found out."

"You're out of your fucking mind," she said, with a short laugh.

"Am I? I don't think Lou is trying to have me killed—why would he bother to hire me? Katherine? Paul? They could have both been killed yesterday, along with me. But you weren't there."

Heather hung her head forward so that her hair brushed the steering wheel, laughing to herself. Then she threw back her head and laughed even louder, a genuine peal of mirth.

"I'm glad you find this amusing," Sam said. "I started losing my sense of humor after the first bullet missed my head yesterday."

Heather turned to look at Sam, brushed the blowing hair out of her face and held her index finger up to silence him.

"Listen, dumbass," she said. "I wasn't going to tell you this if I didn't have to, but it looks like I have to. Lou and I are lovers. We have been for three years."

"So?"

"So I want to find whoever is behind this plot as much as Lou does. Maybe more."

"Why?"

"Because as soon as Katherine dies, Lou's going to marry me."

Was she lying? The only way to know for sure would be to ask Kenwood. But Sam believed her. It fit with what he sensed the first time he saw Heather and Lou together in his office. Heather might have been smarter than Steven Hawking and have a better business mind than Warren Buffett, but when you see an old tycoon hire a beautiful young woman, you tend to think her résumé wasn't everything.

Sam didn't care whether she married Kenwood or not. Ethically, it put him, at best, in a gray area. It wasn't as though he was sleeping with his boss' wife—not yet, anyway. Sleeping with Kenwood's mistress wasn't much different from a drug dealer getting ripped off by another drug dealer—the guy getting ripped off wasn't going to go to the cops. And there wasn't much chance of their being caught. Kenwood wasn't going to hire another detective to trail the detective he'd just hired.

What did concern Sam was finding out that the members of Lou Kenwood's innermost circle—his executive assistant/lover and his wife—did not necessarily share the same motivations.

"So you marry Kenwood, and then he dies—someday—and you get it all," Sam said. He took his hand off the gun. "The business, the team, the money—everything."

He expected her to show some indignation at the implication she was a gold-digger, but if she resented it, it didn't show in her eyes.

"That's right."

"You'd be the Anna Nicole Smith of the American League."

"I can live with that."

Kenwood was estimated to be worth more than a billion dollars. A woman could ignore a lot of insults for that kind of money.

"It's happened before," Sam said. "The owner of the L.A. Rams married a showgirl. When he died, she got the team."

"I'm no fucking showgirl. I've trained for this job. I'd be a damn good owner."

"I'm sure you would."

"Oh, don't give me that bullshit. It's all over your face. You think because I'm young, and a woman, that I have no business owning and running the Red Sox."

"I don't think that at all. I just think you're not prepared for the shit-storm you're going to face when it all comes down. Fortune-hunting bimbo is probably the kindest thing you're going to be called. The late-night talk show hosts will cut you to pieces."

"I can take it."

"What about the team going into a trust after Lou dies?"

"Lou decided he doesn't want to do that. He'd rather keep the team in his family."

"If he doesn't remarry after Katherine, there is no family."

"Then it's lucky he found me."

"Don't be surprised if somebody sues you."

"My lawyers will kick their lawyers' asses. This is all legal, all above-board. Lou loves me, and I really do love him, too. We make each other happy."

"Well, not completely."

Heather shot Sam a quick squint and returned her gaze to the road. At least Sam could relax a little now. He was reasonably certain that Heather wasn't trying to kill him.

He watched the Hollywood sun work its magic on Heather's hair, and realized that she was born for this kind of life. She was going to love the attention that came with being the owner of a major league baseball team, even if Sam couldn't picture her dedicating the next thirty years to the nuts and bolts of running the Red Sox, when she'd have the money to be hobnobbing with stars and celebrities on the West Coast. Katherine Kenwood once had movie star looks, too, but baseball was her passion, and so was New England. She'd belonged in Boston, overlooking the icy Atlantic; Heather, on the other hand, was L.A. to her core.

"Were you going to shoot me?" Heather said. Her tiny smile suggested she hadn't been worried.

"Sure. On an L.A. freeway, who'd notice?"

◇◇◇

They were greeted by a bellman under the orange awning in front of the hotel. He took their bags out of the trunk and gave the keys to the valet parking attendant.

"Will you be needing the car again this evening?"

"Maybe," Sam said. "I don't know yet."

They had adjoining ocean view suites on the eighth floor. Sam's room had a queen-sized bed and a sliding glass door that opened out to a deck, from which he could see the sun setting over the ocean, and the lights twinkling beneath the mountains up the coast. It was a gorgeous view, but it wasn't getting him any closer to the identity of Babe Ruth.

He called directory assistance and got the number for the Los Angeles Times. He was connected to the newsroom.

"Russ Daly, please," he said.

"Would you like his voicemail?"

"No, I'd like Russ Daly. Is he in?"

"He's rarely in the office, sir, but he checks his messages."

"Fine."

Daly was the acerbic, nationally syndicated sports columnist for the L.A. Times whom Sam had met at the Masters that spring. Despite the image he cultivated on TV panels as an overweight wise-ass, he was a razor-sharp observer of the sports scene, and he was somebody Sam was convinced he could trust. If he promised Daly that he'd be the first journalist to get the story after everything was resolved, Sam could share some of the details of the extortion plot without seeing it in the paper the next morning. And at this point, there was nothing else Sam could do to get information without giving out some of his own.

Sam heard the beep on Daly's answering machine.

"Daly, this is Sam Skarda. I'm in L.A., working on a case. It could be a very big story. I can let you in on some of it in exchange for some information. Call me."

He was about to hang up when he heard a rasping voice say, "Daly."

"I thought you weren't in," Sam said.

"That's what I tell 'em to say at the switchboard. I'd never get any work done if I answered my phone. So what's the story, Skarda? You still a cop?"

"No, I've gone private."

"Who you workin' for these days?"

"I don't want to get into it over the phone. Have you eaten?"

"Let's see...I had a hot dog, one of those big pretzels, and a couple of tacos at the Dodger game this afternoon. So, no, not really."

While Daly was talking, Sam heard a knock on the door. He walked over to open it and found Heather standing barefoot in the hallway, wearing one of the white terrycloth robes that hung in each guest bathroom. He motioned for her to come in.

Daly said there was a pizza place on South Broadway, two blocks from the Times building in downtown L.A. He could be there by seven. Sam told him he had no idea how long it would take to get downtown from Santa Monica.

"Take the 10," Daly said. "This time of day, you can do that in a half-hour, tops."

Heather had let the robe fall open. Underneath, she was wearing an orange and yellow string bikini that she could have carried on the plane in her coin purse.

"My driver can do it in twenty minutes," Sam said.

"Oh yeah? Who's your driver?"

"I'll introduce you when we get there."

"Get where?" Heather said when Sam hung up. "I thought we'd go down to the pool. Have a drink or two. Recover from our jet lag."

"Sorry. I'm meeting Russ Daly of the Times downtown at seven. You're welcome to come."

"Why are you talking to a newspaper guy?"

Sam could not help staring at Heather, thinking that she must spend a lot of time at the health club to keep up a set of abs that looked that good in a string bikini. And, from what he could see—and he could see almost everything—Heather did not have a tattoo. A big point in her favor; it must have been her Harvard background.

"Because right now I'm spinning my wheels," Sam said. "I need to talk to somebody who knows the Dodgers, and knows L.A. I trust Daly."

"You'd better be able to trust him." Heather pulled the robe closed and headed toward the door. "If any of this ends up in the paper, Lou will fire you."

◇◇◇

It was twilight when they got back on the freeway, the time of day when Southern California is at its best. Everything seemed to have an extra glow, like one of those painted postcards of Hollywood in the '30s. Even the tail lights on the freeway had a soft neon charm to them. The oppressive heat had faded into the evening, replaced by a comfortable warmth that made Sam want to stay outside all night.

Heather didn't seem to pay much attention to the weather or the scenery. She made it her personal obligation to get to the restaurant faster than Daly's prescribed travel time. They pulled up in front of Bonfetti's Pizza in just over fifteen minutes.

Downtown L.A. is low on glamour by Southern California standards. It could be any business district in America, so when Heather opened up the driver's side door of the red BMW and slid her model-slim legs out of the car, it was as though she was delivering a little bit of Tinseltown to the button-downs. Sam was glad they weren't going undercover; then again, he could arrive with Heather almost anywhere, and no one would notice he was there.

There were sidewalk tables outside the restaurant, but Sam didn't see Daly. They went inside, where the artificial coolness gave Sam goosebumps. He glanced at Heather, who had exchanged the bikini for a miniskirt and tight white top. She had bumps, too.

Daly's bulky frame occupied half of a booth near the back of the restaurant. He had a pint of beer in front of him and a menu spread open. His thinning hair was uncombed, and his frayed navy blue golf shirt was only partially tucked into his blue jeans, and covered by a light blue, pit-stained seersucker jacket. Sam figured he had to be pulling down at least $200,000 per year for his syndicated column and his frequent TV work, but judging from his wardrobe, he was closer to homeless than famous.

Daly did a double take when he saw Sam and Heather approach.

"That's your driver?" he said, his voice nearly cracking in surprise. "I gotta tell you, Skarda, you do seem to gravitate toward nice-lookin' babes."

"Thanks," Sam said. He introduced Heather. "It's a beautiful night. Why don't we get a table outside?"

"I'm a big fan of air conditioning—cuts down some on the sweat," Daly said. He waved his hand dismissively toward the door. "Heather Canby...why do I know that name?"

Daly gave Heather a slow up-and-down inspection, only partly intended to jog his memory. "I got it—Red Sox, right? You work for Lucky Louie."

"That's right," Heather said. She displayed the same noncommittal expression that she'd first given Sam when they'd met. Sam doubted that it meant she intended to sleep with Daly, too.

"So what's this about?" Daly said. "Or do you want me to guess?"

Sam started to explain the situation, but a waitress with streaked green hair and two thin metal rings pierced through her lower lip came up to the table. Sam ordered a beer; Heather, a Chardonnay. Daly ordered an extra-large five-topping pizza.

"Great crust here," Daly said. "The help is kind of a freak show, but that's L.A."

"From this point on, we're off the record," Sam said.

"I can't even put it in my notes column that the guy who saved the Masters is in town this week with a blonde from the planet Va-Va-Voom?"

"No. You never saw us."

"Fine. What's up?"

"Think about this: What's the best thing that's happened to Boston in decades?"

"When the Sox broke the Curse of the Bambino."

"Right. What's the worst thing that could happen to Boston now?"

"Being nuked by terrorists."

"What if that 2004 Series turned out to be fixed?"

Daly took a long swallow from his beer while Sam and Heather waited.

"The Cardinals played like pukes in that Series," Daly said. "You think they threw the Series?"

"An extortionist is claiming they did."

"How much does he want?"

"Fifty million."

Daly whistled, finished his beer and caught the waitress' attention, pointing to the empty glass.

"You got problems," Daly said to Heather.

"I know. And I didn't want Sam to tell you about it, either. You know what would happen if a rumor got out that the World Series was fixed?"

"Yeah, yeah—the American public would lose faith in all their institutions, the stock market would crash, anarchy would run wild in the streets, Major League Baseball would go out of business, and the Boston Red Sox would be worth zero."

"It may be funny to you, Mr. Daly—"

"It's Russ, honey."

"But not to me. Not to Lou Kenwood. And not to all those Red Sox fans who said winning that Series made their lives complete."

"Why is it that the pretty ones always take themselves so seriously?" Daly asked Sam. "I know what's really bothering your boss. If this gets out, he stops being Lucky Louie, the Man Who Saved Red Sox Nation. He'll be just another rich sucker whose expensive plaything blew up in his face. Am I close?"

"I think you made a big mistake trusting this guy, Sam," Heather said. Color rose into her cheeks as she turned back to Daly. "You've got to promise to keep quiet about this."

"Look, sweetie, I already agreed that this conversation would be off the record. You know how long I'd have lasted in this business if I double-crossed a source?"

Heather looked back at Sam, and he nodded.

"I dealt with reporters for years in homicide," Sam said. "They'd cut each other to pieces for a story, but they won't burn their sources. Not if they want to keep reporting."

"I wouldn't trust a Boston writer with this story," Heather said, now on the defensive.

"Neither would I," Daly said.

Sam laid out what they knew: the handwritten extortion note on black paper, the deadline and procedure for the payoff, the gambling insiders who didn't raise red flags when Sam talked about the Red Sox-Cardinals Series, and the conversation with Hurtado.

"You want my opinion on that Series?" Daly said. "I actually had my doubts when Miranda threw that ball away in Game One. But the more I thought about it, the more I figured he just cracked. It was a long season; he might just have been worn out from pitching and playing third base. Nobody's been able to do that since the deadball era. And maybe all the steroid talk got to him."

"You think he's using steroids?" Sam asked.

"Human growth hormone. As far as I'm concerned, they're all guilty now, until they prove to me they're innocent. I mean, just look at these guys. Mickey Mantle would be a shrimp today. I don't think they get that way naturally, but hey, I could be wrong. Unless they get caught receiving a supply, there's no proof, 'cause HGH doesn't show up in urine, and the union won't let the players take blood tests. But I know what I see."

"The HGH must have quit working for Miranda in the Series."

"It could have been a lot of things. He wasn't the first big name to choke in the World Series. Ted Williams was a lifetime .344 hitter. You know what he hit in the 1946 Series?"

".200," Heather said.

"Very good," Daly said. "Nothing I like better than a pretty girl who knows her baseball."

Heather didn't seem to be charmed by Daly's style, but Daly was used to that.

"I need to talk to Miranda," Sam said. "If it did happen, he's part of it. If it didn't…"

"Then what?" Daly said.

"Then I've got to figure out who's trying to shake down Lou Kenwood."

The pizza arrived, and Daly got busy making it disappear. Sam and Heather helped out.

"This guy, Babe Ruth," Daly said between bites. "He says a player will come forward and admit to throwing the Series if Kenwood doesn't cough up?"

"That's right," Heather said.

"Think he's really got someone?"

"I don't know."

"And would he go through with it if Kenwood doesn't pay?"

"I think Kenwood will pay, if I can't find who's behind this," Sam said.

He looked at Heather. She shrugged her shoulders, looking discouraged.

"Why would a player do that?" Daly said. "First, why would he throw the World Series? There can't be enough money in it, compared to what these guys are already making."

"That's what the bookies tell me," Sam said.

"And why would he come forward? Somebody would have to be leaning on a player pretty fuckin' hard to get him to ruin his career like that."

"That's what I was thinking," Sam said. "Maybe the player's being blackmailed."

"And who'd do that?"

"Have you heard of a guy named Sid Mink?"

The columnist snorted.

"Who hasn't? He's the biggest crook in town."

"Could you see him being involved in something like this? Miranda started his career in L.A."

Daly rubbed his hands across his face and leaned back in the booth.

"He's into drugs and prostitution, for sure," Daly said. "Beyond that, I don't know. The L.A. mob has always been considered a bunch of underachievers. They're called the Mickey Mouse Mafia. The East Coast families push them around. They can't keep their territory under control."

Daly went into a brief history of the L.A. mob since Bugsy Siegel, who came out from New York in the '30s to cut himself in on the West Coast rackets and establish gambling in Las Vegas. When Siegel was murdered in 1947, Jack Dragna took over and developed some influence with the labor unions in Hollywood. But he couldn't keep Siegel's underboss, Mickey Cohen, from holding on to a big piece of the L.A. vice action. The mob tried to kill Cohen a half-dozen times, but they never hit him. He eventually went to jail for tax evasion—the Feds had to get him, since the local cops and the movie industry seemed to tolerate, if not take orders from, Cohen. Now Sid Mink was the guy who ran the rackets in L.A., but he was no better than any of the previous bosses at keeping the other local hoods in line.

"Is Mink into sports?" Sam asked.

"He's always at the Lakers games, and I see him at the track. He's got a box seat at Dodger Stadium, too."

"You don't need to go to a game to fix one," Sam said. "You don't even need to be in the same town."

"Lemme put it this way," Daly said. "If Miranda was involved in this, Sid Mink might know about it. But would he be behind it, or be able to do anything about it? I don't know."

"I need to talk to Mink."

"That shouldn't be hard to arrange."

"But first, Miranda. Got a number?"

Daly pulled out his cell phone and began scrolling through his directory. When he got to Miranda's entry, he pushed the button and waited. He got Miranda's voice mail and left a message for the player to give him a call.

"Weeknight off, I'm guessing he'll be at a club somewhere. He'll get back to me."

"What kind of a guy is Miranda?"

"I thought he was a good kid when he came up as a rookie—before the Dodgers traded him to the Cardinals. He was just a scared, skinny kid from South America who didn't know much English and had warning-track power. But he started bulking up while he was here, and then he blossomed in St. Louis. I was glad the Dodgers got him back, steroid rumors and all. But he's changed. A hell of a ballplayer, but he's kind of a playboy now. You don't always know what to expect with him after a game. Some nights he'll make sure to give you something you can use, and other nights—more and more, lately—he'll blow you off."

Daly went back to eating, and his phone rang five minutes later. It was Miranda. Daly told him he had a guy who wanted to talk to him about an opportunity to make some money.

"No, I don't want to call your fuckin' agent, Alberto. I'm just doing you a favor. This guy's a friend of mine. He'll be leaving town in a couple of days."

Miranda agreed to meet them at a nightclub called Quasar, in Hermosa Beach. He'd be in a first-floor cabana with a few of his friends.

"We'd better get moving," Daly said. "I hear that place fills up by eleven."

"Dance there often?" Heather asked.

"Do I look like I dance?"

He pried himself out of the booth and waddled toward the front door, brushing pizza crumbs off his sport coat and onto the floor.

# Chapter Fifteen

Sam and Heather followed Daly to a ramp a block away and waited until he emerged in his black Buick Lucerne. He led them onto the Harbor Freeway, then exited on Artesia Boulevard. Sam plugged in the iPod, which spit out Bob Seger's "Hollywood Nights" as they followed Daly toward the ocean.

"You're really into music," Heather said.

"It blocks out stuff I'd rather not think about."

"No, I mean, it's important to you."

"Yes—I guess I got that from my mother," Sam said. He took in the lights of the city as the Silver Bullet Band pounded through the instrumental break. "She was a music teacher."

"Was?"

"Retired. She's living in Duluth now. She grew up there."

"How about your dad?"

"He died fifteen years ago. He was a cop."

"Was he killed?"

"No—unless you want to blame cigarettes."

"That's one thing I'll never understand—smoking. You get one pair of lungs. Why not take care of them?"

"I suppose the current Mrs. Kenwood wishes she had."

"Too late now."

"I guess that's why she still smokes."

"She does?" Heather said, looking at Sam with surprise.

"Lou sends Paul out to buy them for her."

The corners of Heather's mouth turned up slightly.

They found Quasar a few blocks from the beach. A line stretched halfway down the block from the ropes at the entrance to the two-story building, illuminated by electric-blue spotlights on the metallic façade. Sam could hear the hip-hop music from inside the club, pulsating like a giant car stereo. Not his style of music—but then again, this wasn't a social night out. The young people waiting to get in were dressed in expensive jeans and shoes, the women wearing low-cut, bare-midriff tops and constantly touching up their makeup and lipstick with hand-held compacts, while the spiky-haired young men gave off the distinct aroma of cologne and styling gel.

Daly met them at the entrance, and walked up to the host at the head of the line, a black guy with diamond and gold grills in his teeth and biceps that looked as if they could bend steel girders. He took a look at Daly's ratty clothes and flabby physique and started to laugh.

"Man, ain't you lookin' for the wrasslin' matches?" the bouncer said.

"No, we're looking for Alberto Miranda."

"He ain't in there."

"He's in there," Daly said.

"No, he ain't, and you ain't, either. But she can go in."

The bouncer pointed at Heather, flashed his gem-studded smile and lifted the rope, but she stayed where she was. Daly rolled his eyes and took out his cell phone. He punched Miranda's number and then handed the phone to the bouncer. When Miranda answered, the bouncer stammered and said, "Yo, uh…Alberto?"

When Miranda confirmed his identity, the bouncer told him there were three people outside who wanted to see him. He listened, said. "Sure, man," snapped the phone shut and handed it back to Daly as though it had just turned to gold.

"He says to go on in. He's at a cabana on your left as you walk in, first floor, about halfway back in the room."

The mystified tone never left his voice as they walked past him and up the steps into the club.

Inside, the sound was so oppressive that Sam thought the walls were going to collapse. Every time he'd been in L.A., he'd made it a point to go out to a club and catch at least one band or solo artist. But this was barely music. Daly was actually wincing at the decibel level; he mouthed the words "Please, somebody, kill me." Heather was oblivious to everything. She cruised past the blue leather couches and the elevated dance floor and headed for the gold beaded curtains that separated the private cabanas from the public areas. Heads turned to gaze at her as they walked through the club, and Sam hoped he wouldn't have to deal with some coked-out playboy trying to make a pass at her. If it were up to him, he'd let her handle it, but he worked for her. If she needed a bodyguard, that's what he'd have to be.

Heather pulled one of the cabana curtains aside, and they found Miranda seated on a couch with a woman sprawled on either side of him. One was nibbling on his ear, while the other had her hand in his lap, rubbing back and forth. Two large, dark Hispanic men materialized from either side of the cabana as they began to walk in, stepping in Daly's way. Miranda shook his head at the two men and held his hand up, indicating it was all right for Daly to come in. Sam and Heather followed. Sam saw Daly lean over and say something to Miranda, but he couldn't hear what it was. Then Miranda got up, shook Sam's hand, kissed Heather on the cheek and motioned for them to follow him.

They walked around the dance floor to a stairway that led up to the second floor, and they emerged in a hallway that led to a closed door. Miranda knocked, and after a few seconds the door opened. They went inside and found themselves in a private, glassed-in suite overlooking the dance floor, not unlike Lou Kenwood's suite at Fenway Park.

A white man with swept-back silver hair and a black open-collared shirt was sitting in a leather armchair watching the dancers, while a large black man wearing a sideways NY ballcap, baggy mid-shin cargo pants and an oversized Detroit Red Wings jersey stood by the door.

"Alberto, my man," the white guy said. He got up to give Miranda a soul shake and a hug. "Great game today. You're amazing, dude."

"Thanks, bro," Miranda said. "Kenny, I need a favor, man. You know Russ Daly of the *Times*?"

Daly nodded but didn't make a move toward Kenny.

"Sure, I read your stuff, Daly. Honored to have you here."

"Likewise," Daly said, with absolutely no sincerity.

"Daly, he writes good stuff about me," Miranda said. "Some of those other bitches, man, they write lies all the time. Not Daly. If he rips me, I deserve it. If I play good, he says so."

"That's me—fair to a fault," Daly said.

"I need a quiet place to talk to these people," Miranda said to Kenny. "Okay if we use your suite?"

"That's what it's here for, Alberto. I was about to make the rounds anyway. Take as long as you want. Tito, let's go."

Kenny's ingratiating manner changed abruptly when he spoke to his assistant, or bodyguard, or whatever he was. They walked out and Miranda took the club owner's seat. Daly, Heather, and Sam sat down on a couch facing him.

"Now, what's this all about, Daly?" Miranda said. "Something about me making money?"

He spoke with much less of an accent than his pal Ivan Hurtado. He'd been playing baseball in America for about eight years, and he'd worked hard on his English skills to bring in endorsement money. He was the entire package—tall, muscular, neatly groomed with short hair and no goatee or moustache. In his tailored Italian suit, it was hard to tell whether Miranda had the steroid-enhanced physique that was obvious on some players. What was not hard to tell was that Heather couldn't take her eyes off him.

"Alberto, Ms. Canby and I work for the Boston Red Sox, and this isn't really about money," Sam said. He leaned forward from the couch to try to engage the Dodger player, who looked as relaxed as though he were expecting a commercial pitch from a soft drink company. "It's about your World Series with the Red Sox."

"What about it?" Miranda said, suddenly wary.

"Did you try your hardest?"

"Hey, fuck you, man! Hell yes, I try my hardest!"

Miranda's eyes flashed, and his accent became more pronounced.

"It didn't look that way," Sam said. He figured he had nothing to lose—Miranda wasn't going to talk about this with anyone else. "It looked like you were trying to let the Red Sox win."

"Why you say that?" Miranda said. He was shouting now. "That's fucking bullshit, man!"

"I'll tell you why I say that. Somebody is demanding $50,000,000 dollars from the Boston Red Sox owner. He says unless he gets the money, a player will come forward and claim the World Series was fixed."

"Who the hell is this guy, Daly?" Miranda said.

"Detective."

"A fucking detective?" He was on his feet now, waving both hands at Sam as if to say, 'Get that shit out of my face.' He walked to the window, looked out over the dance floor and then turned to face Sam.

"I play as good as I can, man. My arm hurt. I couldn't pitch like I can. That's it. That's all I got to say."

"We're not trying to get you in trouble, Alberto," Heather said. She got up and walked to the glass wall next to the ballplayer. "We're trying to help you. Really."

She put her hand gently on his shoulder, and he looked down at her hand, then at her. It appeared that Miranda could not quite understand Heather's role in the proceedings. Women who looked like her normally came to clubs like this for one thing—to meet men like Alberto Miranda and go home with them. This one, however, was with a man who was accusing him of betraying his team and his sport. Miranda took her hand off his shoulder. He looked intently at Heather, then crossed his arms and leaned against the glass.

"You want to do something for me?" Alberto said, still staring at Heather. "Suck my dick."

"Hey," Sam said. He started to get up.

"Never mind, Sam," Heather said. She went back to the couch and sat down next to him. It probably wasn't the first time she'd heard that proposal in a business meeting.

Sam had known Miranda would not admit to the plot. But he wanted to see Miranda's reaction—and the reaction was angrier and more defensive than Sam would have expected if Miranda were totally in the dark.

"So you're not the guy who's going to go to the press and the Commissioner and tell them the Series was fixed?"

"It wasn't fixed, man, that's what I'm telling you!"

But Miranda had averted his eyes from Sam's when he was first asked the question. Something was going on. Sam decided to take it in a different direction.

"Do you know a guy named Sid Mink?"

This time Miranda held his gaze.

"Yeah, I heard his name. I don't know him."

"You know what he does?"

"Sure, I guess so. Organized crime. Mob stuff."

"That's right. But you don't know him."

"No. Never met him. Never talked to him. We got to stay away from dudes like that, man. Baseball rules."

This time, Sam was inclined to believe Miranda, though he wasn't sure why. He knew Miranda wasn't telling the whole truth, but Sid Mink's name had barely registered with him. Something was going on, and Miranda knew something about it, but it looked like Mink wasn't the guy running it.

"Are you on steroids, Alberto?"

"Hey, man, I don't got to talk to you anymore," Miranda said. He walked up next to the couch and glared down at Sam. "You come here, insult me, insult my family—"

He broke off, took a last, long glance at Heather, then walked out the door, slamming it behind him.

"That went well," Daly said. He looked up at the ceiling and shook his head. "I think I've had my last interview with Alberto Miranda."

"Sorry," Sam said. "But I had to ask him straight out, to see how he took it."

The door opened again, but it wasn't Miranda returning. It was Kenny and Tito, and they didn't look happy.

"Hey, asshole," Kenny said. He walked up to Sam, stopping when their faces were inches apart. "I don't appreciate you coming in here and hassling my guests."

Tito had walked around beside Sam and suddenly put his hand around Sam's arm, squeezing it hard and digging his fingers into the muscle.

"He's got a gun, boss," Tito said.

"Get him out of here. All of 'em."

Sam shook his arm to try to free himself, but Tito's grip was too tight. He looked out the door and saw two more bouncer types waiting for them.

"We'll leave quietly," Sam said. "Keep your hands off the young woman."

"Sure, sure, anything you say, dickwipe," Kenny said.

He pushed Sam and Daly out the door, then grabbed Heather by the arm and roughly pulled her along with him. Tito and his fellow goons escorted the three of them down the hallway to the stairs.

"Just so you know, Skarda, you're on your own here," Daly said. "I'm a peacenik."

"Daly, I don't ever want to see your fat face in here again," Kenny said. "I never read that puke you write, anyway."

"That hurts," Daly said.

Then Kenny looked at Sam.

"And as for you, whatever your name is, if I see you anywhere, anytime, I'll break your legs."

"You'll need more than the Jackson Three here," Sam said.

Kenny stopped walking, turned to face Sam and punched him in the stomach. Sam tried to spin sideways out of Tito's grasp, but one of the goons grabbed his other arm and held him so Kenny could hit him two more times.

"Stop that!" Heather screamed.

"Shut up, bitch," one of the goons said. He grabbed her by her hair and pulled her head back.

The door to the stairway opened and Alberto Miranda came running through it, accompanied by a burst of pounding dance music from the main floor. He went straight for the goon who had Heather by the hair, grabed him and shoved him against the wall. Two rapid blows from Miranda's elbow to the side of the goon's head dropped him to the floor. Sam shook himself loose from Tito and pulled his gun just as the other thug was drawing a knife from under his shirt.

"Don't," Sam said. He aimed the gun at the thug's heart. "Put it down."

The knife clattered to the floor. Miranda went to stand in front of Heather, who was clutching the back of her head in pain.

"You all right?" he asked her.

"Yes, I think so," she said, her voice coming in little gasps. "Thanks."

"Now, we're walking out of here, and we don't need any help," Sam said. He moved the gun from Kenny to Tito and the goons, and back again.

Kenny nodded to his bouncers. Sam held the gun on them while Daly, Heather, and Miranda walked down the stairs. Then Sam started to follow, but he turned back to address Kenny.

"The name's Sam Skarda, Kenny. Like you said, anytime, anywhere."

Kenny was disinclined to make a smart comeback with the muzzle of a Glock pointed at his balls.

Sam found Heather, Miranda, and Daly on the sidewalk outside the club. Miranda was patting Heather and stroking the back of her head.

"Thanks, Alberto," Sam said. "I'm glad you came back."

"No problem, man," Miranda said. He had his arm around Heather's waist. "That fuckin' Kenny's a weasel."

"Here's my card." Sam took one out of his billfold and handed it to Miranda. "If you want to talk…"

"Nothing to talk about, man. Like I told you, I played my best in the Series. I got nothing more to say."

But Miranda took the card and put it in his coat pocket. He asked Heather one more time if she was all right, and she smiled at him and said she'd be fine. He gave her a long squeeze, and their eyes lingered on each other for another moment. Then Miranda walked over to the valet stand and asked to have his car brought around. He pulled out his phone and made a call while he was waiting. By the time the valet brought his car—a Jaguar—Miranda had been joined by the two women who'd been sitting with him in the cabana. They both slid into the Jag with him, and he drove off—checking to make sure that Heather was looking at them as they passed by.

"What's he got that I haven't got, except looks, money, and a great body?" Daly said as Miranda's tail lights receded.

"I don't know what to make of him," Heather said. "First he comes off as a spoiled, piggish jock, and then he turns around and..."

"Becomes your knight in shining armor," Sam finished.

"Yeah. Strange guy..."

"I'd go with your first impression," Daly said.

"So you think he's involved in this?" Sam asked Daly.

"I still don't know if anything happened. But he's got something up his ass."

Sam agreed, but he was at a loss to know how to prove it. Another night had slipped by, and he was no closer to figuring out what, if anything, was going on, or who was behind the extortion note. Now there were just three days left before the money had to be wired to Babe Ruth's offshore bank account. Three days to find the Babe; after that, Kenwood was out $50,000,000, or baseball had its worst scandal in a century.

There was only one other man in town who might have some answers.

Sid Mink.

# Chapter Sixteen

If Sam had been working the case as a cop, he could go to the L.A. police and talk to their organized crime unit about Mink. They could fill him in on chapter and verse of Mink's illegal activities, his known associates, his usual hangouts, and his most dangerous habits. But as a private investigator, he might not get much cooperation from cops he didn't know. And he'd probably have to give more answers than he'd get. Kenwood hadn't been willing to get the Boston cops mixed up in this, so the same caution had to apply in L.A. The story couldn't get out. Cops were pretty good at keeping their mouths shut when it came to cases they were working on, or protecting the safety of one of their own. But they could also spread a juicy rumor faster than a Hollywood gossip columnist.

There had to be another way to get in touch with Sid Mink—and fast. All he could think of was talking to another bookie—an L.A. bookie. If Mink was running the kind of enterprise everybody said he was running, the bookies would know how to reach him.

It was almost midnight when Sam and Heather got back to their hotel. He told her he was going to call Jimmy the Rabbit before turning in. She said she was going back to her room to call Lou and tell him they'd talked to Miranda. Sam was not surprised that Heather didn't suggest spending the night together. She'd had a tough night, and if there was anybody she wanted to curl up with, it would be Miranda. Since he wasn't around, she went to bed alone. That was all right with Sam—now that he knew about Heather and Kenwood, his ethics were telling him to keep his hands to himself.

Sam got an answer on Jimmy the Rabbit's cell phone.

"Jimmy?"

"Bad timing, whoever this is. I gotta get back to the table."

"Sam Skarda. You at the card room?"

"That's right. I'm down three hundred, Sammy. I gotta get healthy."

It was just after two a.m. Minneapolis time. Jimmy would be playing poker all night in the card room at the Canterbury Park racetrack. He could afford to take a few minutes off.

"Jimmy, I need to talk to an L.A. bookie. A guy like Bucca in Boston."

"You in L.A. now?"

"Yeah. Santa Monica."

"Right on the beach, huh?"

"Yeah."

"Must be nice."

"Got a name and a number?"

"Sammy, what do I get outta this?"

"Nothing. But if I'm ever in a position to do you a favor with the Minneapolis cops…"

"Which you won't be."

"Don't be so sure."

"Phil Minervino."

"How's that?"

"L.A. bookie—Phil Minervino."

Jimmy gave Sam the number, and told him it was the same deal—wait an hour until Jimmy could call him up and vouch for Sam. Then he hung up.

Sam waited until almost one a.m. and called Minervino. He explained who he was, and said he needed to get in touch with Sid Mink. It was urgent.

"It's always urgent," Minervino said, in a bored tone.

"You know how I can talk to him?"

"You like the ballgames?"

"Sure."

"You can usually find Sid at Dodger Stadium. He's got a field box down the third base line. There's a game tomorrow night."

"Got a seat number?"

"Section 25, Row 15, seats one through four."

Sam wrote the seat numbers down, thanked Minervino and hung up. He hadn't thought it would be that easy. Apparently the mob scene was a little more laid back in L.A. than it was back east.

◇◇◇

Sam was awakened by a knock on his hotel room door at ten a.m. He glanced out the window—the sun was already starting to burn through the coastline haze, and the shadow of the ten-story hotel stretched across the sand to the edge of the ocean. He had no reason to get up, and the fact was, after finishing off a couple of Scotches from the mini-bar and listening to Sade on his iPod before going to bed the night before, he didn't much feel like getting up. But he got up.

Heather was standing in the hall, wearing the white terrycloth robe, when he opened the door.

"Too early for a swim," Sam said, turning back toward the king-sized bed, intending to crawl back in till the cobwebs cleared.

"I don't want to swim."

He turned around to look at her again. She walked into his room, closed the door, untied the cloth belt that held the robe together, and pulled it open. This time, no string bikini.

"I feel so pale," she said. "See? My tan lines are gone."

She was right. Her splendid body had only the slightest trace of an old swimsuit line—one that must have been daring even for her, as the suggestion of darker skin ended just a millimeter or so above her pinkish-brown nipples. Suddenly, Sam wasn't feeling so groggy.

"Did you talk to Lou last night?" he asked.

"He'd gone to bed."

"Did the Sox win?" He was staring at her breasts, and didn't care whether the Sox won, but he wanted to slow things down.

"They beat the Jays 3-0. Let's celebrate."

She walked over to him, lifted the shoulders of her robe and pulled them aside, letting it drop to the floor. Then she tried to back Sam toward the bed, but he held his ground. Now that he knew Heather was going to marry Kenwood, he had made up his mind to end the sex between them.

Heather noticed the bullet wounds left by the gunshot he'd taken almost three years ago. In the sunlight coming through the balcony door, the scar tissue over the entry and exit wounds had a light purple hue. It wasn't nearly so ugly as it used to be. His knee swelled up sometimes when he'd been walking for several hours, losing most of its definition; by morning it usually resumed its normal size. Heather bent down, put her hand on one of the scars, and ran her index finger along its length. Sam sat on the edge of the bed.

"Does that hurt?" she asked.

"No. When it hurts, it's inside. It wakes me up sometimes."

"Is it ever going to be—you know, normal?"

"Not until I get a replacement. I lost too much cartilage."

"Who shot you?"

"Bad guy. He's dead now."

"Did you kill him?"

"No. Somebody else did."

Heather's phone rang in the pocket of her robe, which was still lying on the floor. She reached down to get it, looked at the incoming number, and said, "It's Lou."

Sam lay back against the headboard while Heather sat with her naked back to him and went over recent developments: They'd made contact with Alberto Miranda through Russ Daly, the Times columnist; she thought Daly could be trusted, though she didn't much like him. As for Miranda, he denied everything, but both she and Sam thought he was hiding something. There'd been a little incident at the night club where they met him last night, and he'd turned out to be a pretty good guy. She might be able to get him to talk.

"You want to talk to Sam? He's right here," Heather said. She handed Sam the phone.

"Time's running out, Sam," Lou said. "I'm supposed to wire the money in three days."

Heather had crawled between Sam's legs and begun to slide up and down against him.

"I know, Lou. We're going as fast as we can here."

Heather smiled and increased her tempo.

"You think Miranda's the key to this thing?" Kenwood asked.

"Yeah, I'm pretty sure." Heather was slowly advancing northward, her breasts grazing his chest.

"I don't like you talking to Daly," Kenwood said. "He's nationally syndicated. He's on ESPN all the time. This could be all over the country by tomorrow."

Heather was now breathing in his ear, and she'd taken his free hand and placed it on her right breast.

"I trust Daly completely, Lou," Sam said. He was fighting for control. "He could have screwed me over in Augusta, but he kept his word. He was the only way we could get to Miranda."

Heather had her full weight on Sam now, and put her mouth on his while Kenwood said: "Everything going okay between you and Heather?"

"Fine," Sam managed to say after pulling his lips from hers.

"I know having her around might make it more difficult for you to do your job, but I feel a lot more connected and informed if she's right there with you."

"Connected—right," Sam said. He clenched his teeth. "Heather's right here. She wants to talk to you again."

He handed the phone to Heather, who pushed her hair out of her face and covered her mouth with her hand while she laughed quietly. Then she lay back on the bed and said, "We're working very well together, Lou. I don't think Sam has any complaints."

She told Kenwood she'd call him later that day, and closed the phone.

"That was a very disrespectful way to treat your fiancé," Sam said.

"Oh, come on." Heather still sounded playful. "He gets what he needs from me."

"But you don't get what you need from him?"

"No, he's great—really. But I don't think he expects me to be totally satisfied by a man who's fifty years older than I am."

"I'll bet he does."

"Well, then he's…unrealistic."

Sam got up off the bed and put his pants on.

"What are you doing?" she asked.

"Sorry, but I've got work to do. Besides, I'm sure I'm no Alberto Miranda."

Heather ignored the remark.

"You know, there's a piano in the lobby bar," she said. "Why don't you play me a song the next time we're down there?"

"If there's time," Sam said.

In fact, he had no intention of playing a song for Heather. He knew what happened whenever he played piano or guitar for a woman. There was something almost unfair about it, as though he somehow magically became Billy Joel, or Bruce Springsteen, or Harry Connick, Jr., or whoever their favorite singer was. Sam had no qualms about using that effect to his advantage, but only when he wanted the relationship to go somewhere. He realized he had been betraying his client, and that led to thoughts about how Caroline would react if she knew. Heather saw no moral dilemma, but that didn't absolve Sam—or make it any easier to break it off with her, either. If he gave up the sex, he wasn't all that sure he would like what was left between them.

"I've got some calls to make," Sam said. "Then we're going to Dodger Stadium tonight to meet Sid Mink."

"Oh? Is he expecting us?"

"My guess is yes."

Heather went down to the pool while Sam called Doug Stensrud at the Minneapolis Police Department. His old chief of detectives was at his desk when Sam's call went through.

"Hey, I haven't heard from you since your retirement bash," Stensrud said. "What's new?"

Stensrud had been Sam's first partner when he joined the force, but after Doug got promoted, he and Sam had developed a more formal relationship. Stensrud had taken it personally when Sam decided not to return to his job in the detective bureau.

"Not much," Sam said. "How's my replacement working out?"

"Fantastic," Stensrud said. "He's cleared four unsolved cases in two months. A real go-getter."

"You're lying," Sam said. "If I couldn't solve them, they stay unsolved."

"What do you want me to do, beg you to come back?" Stensrud said. "We're doing fine without you. Hope you're not getting any bedroom windows slammed on your fingers."

"Not yet," Sam said. "I could use a favor, though."

"I was waiting for this," Stensrud said.

"Could you just run a couple of names through the NCIC computer for me?"

"All you ex-cops think you can use our resources any time you want. Remember, Sam, the national computer system is supported by public dollars. You have your clients, and I have mine—the taxpayers."

"By the book these days, huh, Doug?" Sam asked.

"Yep—ever since you took all that training we gave you and walked out the door with it," Stensrud said. "And don't try to get around me by going to one of your buddies. We don't have time to do fishing expeditions for you."

"Well, gee, thanks for your time, Doug."

"Hey, stop by and see me some time. We'll go have a beer. Relive old times."

"Like this one?"

Sam hung up. Then he called Marcus Hargrove.

Hargrove's answering machine said he was away from his desk, which was usually the case. Marcus didn't spend much time in the office. Sam left a message asking Marcus to call him. He'd tried the front door, but Doug Stensrud was being a prick. Sam knew he could count on his fellow band member to help get background information on Paul O'Brien, whether Stensrud approved of it or not.

With several hours to kill, Sam decided to find out more about the black sheep of the Kenwood family. Sam called the concierge and asked where he could find the nearest public library. Told that the main branch of the Santa Monica library was just five blocks from the hotel, he walked there and spent several hours going through the L.A. Times index, looking for references to Bruce Kenwood. He found two stories: a four-year-old brief about a fire at a warehouse, owned by a Bruce Kenwood, and a story a year later about a Bruce Kenwood who was lost and presumed drowned in a sailing accident off Catalina Island. It wasn't clear if it was the same Bruce Kenwood in both stories, and neither story tied him to the Kenwood family in Boston. Sam ran a computer search for "Bruce Kenwood and Los Angeles," but found no matches. He returned to the hotel, told Heather about his fruitless efforts, and they had an early dinner before leaving for the Dodger game.

They took the Santa Monica Freeway downtown, then joined up with the Pasadena Freeway, which took them northward toward the mountains. Within minutes they were part of the crawling backup of traffic trying to get to Dodger Stadium.

The stadium was built on the former site of a Chicano hill-side neighborhood called Chavez Ravine, a few miles north of downtown. The ballpark opened for business in 1962, four seasons after the Dodgers moved from Brooklyn to Los Angeles. It took that long for the city to work out the political difficulties of commandeering the land and converting it from a condemned neighborhood to a baseball showplace. With its 56,000 seats over six spectator levels, muted pastel décor, a 300-acre footprint with 21 terraced parking lots and 3,400 trees, the San Gabriel Mountains to the north and the skyscrapers of Los Angeles to the south, Dodger Stadium was almost the anti-Fenway—even though it was now one of the oldest ballparks in baseball. Generations of baseball fans could immediately identify the chevron-shaped roofing that shaded the top seats of the outfield bleachers, with solitary palm trees waving beyond the fence.

Sam had been there before, and while he much preferred the gritty quirkiness of Fenway Park, he could understand why the Dodgers drew more than three million people per season, even when the team was having an off-year. Dodger Stadium was a pleasure pavilion in Lotus Land.

Fenway Park had a few celebrity fans, but nothing to compare to the Dodgers. Over the years, actors, singers, and comedians—Doris Day, Milton Berle, Cary Grant, Frank Sinatra, Linda Ronstadt, Keanu Reeves, David Hasselhoff—had made it their business to be seen and perform at Dodger games.

Sid Mink wasn't your standard celebrity; the TV cameras weren't going to linger on Mink while Vin Scully told some amusing tales about how he'd muscled his way into L.A.'s drugs, gambling, and prostitution trades. Mink didn't go to Dodger games for the attention it might bring. He just happened to like baseball. And he liked people who bet on baseball.

But he didn't particularly care for people he didn't know. When Phil Minervino called underboss Bernie Tosta, and Tosta called Mink to tell him to expect a visit in his field box by a guy named Sam Skarda, Mink was irritated. Why couldn't he simply watch the ballgame in peace? The season would be over soon, the track would be open again—he'd rather talk there. The ballpark was where he went to forget about business. Now he'd have to bring an extra man with him to the game—some dumb chump who didn't know an infield fly from a fielder's choice, and couldn't care less.

The stadium lights were on, the sky was a flaming orange to the west, and the temperature was still in the mid-80s when Sam located Mink's box seats—great seats, just a few rows up from the Dodger dugout on the third base side. Sam had insisted that Heather not be with him when he sat and talked to the mobster; somebody might recognize her, maybe even take a picture of her with Mink. It would be disastrous if a Red Sox official were seen conversing with a known racketeer at a major league ballpark. He promised he'd tell her everything that was said, and Heather reluctantly agreed to stay in her seat, a section above and to the left of Mink's box.

"Sid Mink?" Sam said to the three men seated in the four-seat box.

"Could be," said the biggest one. He turned his head slightly, but didn't look at Sam.

"Sam Skarda." Sam offered his hand.

Mink briefly took Sam's hand, as though it were a summons. Sam slid into the vacant seat next to him.

There wasn't much room. Mink was as round as an over-stuffed leaf bag, spilling over into the vacant seat where Sam squeezed in, and onto the bodyguard sitting on his opposite side. He wore a blue Dodger cap pulled down low over his eyes, an open-collared short-sleeved silk shirt, polyester slacks, and had a blue satin Dodger jacket the size of a small tent draped over the back of what appeared to be a larger than standard seat. He had curly gray sideburns and bushy eyebrows, and his smooth, Southern California tanned skin seemed stretched too tightly across his chubby face, like a balloon about to burst.

As with Miranda, Sam decided to confront Mink directly. They were out in the open; even the two broad-shouldered, short-haired men sitting to Mink's left would have to think twice about trying to get rough with him—which would definitely be to Sam's advantage, since he'd left his gun in the car.

"I'm not wired," Sam said. "Pat me down if you want. I'm a private detective. The last thing my client needs is to get the cops involved."

Mink nodded to the bodyguard seated next to him.

"You heard the man, Joey Icebox."

Joey Icebox was a round-faced, dull-eyed man who was so thick through the chest and torso that his jacket seemed to be stuffed with insulation. He stood up, squirmed into the narrow space in front of Sam, and ran his hands up and down Sam's legs and torso so unobtrusively that the fans sitting around them might have thought he was just trying to get past Sam and go up the aisle for a beer. The bodyguard finished and sat down between Mink and the other bodyguard, a gawky, slender man with a prominent nose and the kind of Caesar-style haircut George Clooney used to wear, though he looked nothing like George Clooney.

"Are you Babe Ruth?" Sam asked Mink.

Mink now turned to look at Sam directly. At first his expression was one of irritation, but then it turned to mirth.

"Christ, I wish," he said, laughing loudly and turning to look at the bodyguard on his left. "You hear that, Joey? Leon? This asshole wants to know if I'm Babe Ruth."

Mink's two companions laughed with him, then Mink returned his gaze to Sam.

"Wrong guy, pal. I'm Willie Mays. Don't I look like Willie Mays?"

"Yeah, Willie Mays," Joey Icebox said, laughing at his boss' joke. "'Cept, he turned white."

"Why do you waste my time with stupid shit like that?" Mink said to Sam. "I came here to watch the fuckin' ballgame. Get lost."

The two bodyguards started to get up to enforce Mink's invitation, but Sam remained seated.

"I think you'll want to hear this," Sam said. "It's about fixing ballgames."

Mink put his hand out to stop his boys.

"Make it quick. If I'm not interested by the time the next guy comes to the plate, Joey and Leon will walk you to your car."

Sam took a look around, partly to make sure no one in the adjoining seats was paying attention to them, but also to assess the reality of Mink's threat. It wouldn't be smart for one of Mink's boys to rough him up in front of 45,000 witnesses.

The Dodgers were batting in the bottom of the third, and the lead-off hitter had just singled to left. The crowd was making noise, while the p.a. system played the "Charge!" bugle call. It was safe to talk, but Sam kept his voice low to make sure he wouldn't be heard by anyone else over the steady buzz of the crowd around them.

"I work for the Red Sox. Somebody calling himself Babe Ruth wants $50,000,000 from Lou Kenwood, or a player will go public that he fixed the Cardinals-Red Sox World Series."

Mink snorted with disgust.

"That's bullshit."

"Total fuckin' bullshit," echoed Joey, who had leaned over to get an earful.

"Why tell me?" Mink said. "I got nothin' to do with crap like that."

"I think Alberto Miranda is the guy Babe Ruth is talking about. And they say anything that goes on in this town, you know about it."

"That's right," Mink said. "I do."

Mink turned and raised one of his bushy eyebrows at Joey, who seemed to be his second-in-command. Sam couldn't read the gangster well enough to know whether he was telling the truth about not being involved, but Sam knew he definitely had Mink's interest. The second Dodger hitter had popped out, and a new batter was digging in at the plate. Mink made no effort to have Sam removed from his seat.

"Kenwood's thinking of paying," Sam said.

"Why the fuck would he do that?" Mink said. "Lemme tell ya, I watched those games, and there was no fix. The Cards played like shit, everybody knows that, but it was straight up."

"How do you know?"

"I see fifty-sixty games a year from this seat. The Dodgers even widened this one for me. I know baseball. If there was something funny goin' on, I'd know."

"True or not, somebody's shaking down the Red Sox. You know what would happen if a rumor got out about that Series being fixed."

"If Lucky Louie wants to throw his money away, it's no skin off my ass."

But Mink's eyelids were twitching as he stared off into center field. Like any baseball fan, it wasn't lost on him that the public needed to believe in the integrity of the sport. And like anyone who made money from gambling, he knew it would be just as bad for his income as it would be for Lou Kenwood's if fans lost that belief. Besides, if it was somebody in L.A. making $50,000,000 on this scam, they'd be strong enough to come after him next.

On the field, the Dodgers had a runner on second with two out, and Alberto Miranda stepping to the plate. The buzz in the ballpark rose as the big right-handed hitter dug in. He looked god-like from this vantage point, a supremely well-proportioned warrior tightly packed into his dazzling home white uniform. The pitcher for the Padres appeared nervous, taking a long time between pitches as he repeatedly glanced over his shoulder to keep the runner close to the bag at second. The pink tint in the western sky was muted now, painting the blues, oranges, and yellows of the three main seating decks in even deeper shades. It was an idyllic place to be discussing the ugliness of cheating and blackmail.

"Baseball's a beautiful game—Skarda, is it?" Mink said. He jabbed his index finger into Sam's upper arm, then pointed to the field. "It takes most of these guys four or five years in the minors just to learn enough to stay up here. If a pitcher figures out how to throw a ninety-four-mile-per-hour split-finger pitch just off the black, he'll make millions. And the hitter who learns to lay off that pitch, get ahead in the count and drive the ball into the gap makes millions, too. The stands are filled with people who believe that what they're watching is something so good, so perfect, and so fuckin' hard to do, that it's worth spending fifty bucks for a good seat to watch these guys do it.

"Only some fuckin' punk would tamper with that," Mink said. "Nobody with any class would try to pull this shit."

Mink looked genuinely angry now. Did he suspect someone? A rival gangster? Sam wasn't sure how hard to push for names, but as long as he had Mink's attention, he might as well play off the man's aggravation—and the alleged inferiority complex of the L.A. mob—to see what he could get.

"I heard you were the guy who could help us out," Sam said.

"Yeah? Who told you that?"

"Cops, reporters, bookies. Lots of people."

"What do they say about me?"

Mink was too eager. Why should he care what people were saying about him? All that "Mickey Mouse Mafia" stuff must make Mink and his outfit insecure about their own status. It was time for Sam to pour on the bullshit.

"You run a tight ship," Sam said. "You don't take shit from anybody. Everybody fears you—the cops, the unions, the Hollywood studios…"

"They got that right," Mink said. "Nobody fucks with me."

He pulled out a cigar and started chewing on the end, but didn't light it. There were NO SMOKING signs scattered around the ballpark, just like at Fenway. Sam assumed Dodger Stadium had put their signs up first. And Mink, despite being a professional lawbreaker, showed no inclination to flout the stadium's smoking rules.

"I've got three days left to find out who's behind this," Sam said. "The payment's due on Friday."

"How's Kenwood supposed to pay off fifty million bucks—offshore bank account?"

"That's right."

"There are ways to find out who owns those accounts."

"I know, but Lou still has to keep this quiet, even if he figures out who Babe Ruth is."

"This kind of thing is no fuckin' good for anyone," Mink said. "I make plenty of money on suckers who want to bet on ballgames. I don't need this shit."

He turned to Joey and said something to him in a low voice that Sam couldn't make out. He leaned a little closer, but just then Miranda smashed a curve ball into right-center field, and the runner on second scored standing up when the first baseman cut off the throw to the plate. The crowd roared its appreciation. Dodgers 1, Padres 0.

"Gimme your phone number," Mink said to Sam over the crowd noise.

Sam recited his number while Joey punched it into his cell phone.

"I'm on this," Mink said. "When I got something, I'll call you."

"Clock's ticking," Sam said.

"Hey," Mink said, grabbing Sam's jacket. "I told you, I'm on it. Now get outta here."

Sam returned to the seat where Heather was waiting for him, and told her that Mink was going to help them find Babe Ruth. Heather was not impressed.

"He's probably just blowing you off," she said. "We're running out of time."

"Don't worry—Mink's humiliated. His authority has been challenged. He's highly motivated."

Sam pulled out his cell phone and dialed Russ Daly. He got the answering machine and told the columnist he had one more question to ask. A few minutes later, Sam's phone rang.

"Daly," the raspy-voiced columnist said. "You're lucky I'm such a lovable, caring guy. After last night, I should get a restraining order against you."

"That's hilarious," Sam said. "Hey, I just talked to Sid Mink."

"You get his autograph?"

"He says he's not involved, but he thinks he might know who is."

"Is he going to let you in on it?"

"He said he'd call."

"They always say that. Then you wait around, pass up calls from other mobsters, and end up missing the big dance."

Daly was right. Sam couldn't wait around hoping that an L.A. drug lord would decide to help him find Babe Ruth. He had to get moving. At least he was sure of one thing: Whoever was trying to kill him, it wasn't Mink. Sam wasn't even sure Mink could pull off a hit if he tried.

He looked over at Heather, who was nibbling from a box of popcorn and brushing stray kernels off her denim mini-skirt. He still wasn't sure he could trust her. She could be playing all sides of this game, with the intent of being the last one standing when the Kenwood fortune changed hands. All the more reason to find Babe Ruth—now.

"Where does Miranda work out?" Sam asked Daly.

"At the stadium, like everybody else."

"No, I mean off-season—weight-training. He must go to a gym."

"Oh, that—there's a gym in Glendale that a lot of the local jocks go to, called Roy Laswell's."

"Any rumors of steroids being distributed there?"

Daly snorted.

"You know a gym that doesn't have steroid rumors?"

"You know what I mean. There are steroid rumors about Miranda. The cops must be looking at the place."

"Our federal courts guy says the government has been trying to nail Laswell for a couple of years now. Nothing yet."

"What's the place like?"

"Big, cushy, pimped out with all the newest machines, crawling with muscle-bound creeps."

"Is there a Roy Laswell?"

"Yeah—unless it's some guy playing Laswell in their ads."

"Thanks."

Sam snapped the phone shut and told Heather they were leaving. She nodded, stood up and put the popcorn box on the concrete in front of her seat. They squeezed past a couple of schoolgirls waving signs at the TV cameras, and Sam glanced up at the JumboTron screen on the scoreboard to see if the girls had been selected. To his surprise, the camera was focused on

Heather as she stood in the aisle, hand-combing her short blond hair, her elbows up in the air and her breasts bouncing slightly against her white cotton tank-top. The teenage girls next to them started yelling at Heather to move, and stuck their signs up in front of her. When Heather glanced up at the screen and realized what was going on, she laughed.

"You're blowing our cover," Sam said.

They walked up the aisle toward the exit.

# Chapter Seventeen

It was not quite nine when they got back to the BMW, illuminated to a shiny gleam under the arc lights in the Dodger parking lot. Sam slid in behind the wheel before Heather could and held out his hand for the keys. Heather shrugged and handed them over.

Sam called directory assistance on his phone and got the number for Laswell's Gym. The gum-chewing girl who answered the phone at the gym said they were open till two a.m., and once Sam deciphered her Valley Girl accent, the directions weren't hard to follow: Pick up the Golden State Freeway just north of the stadium, go north on the Glendale Freeway, and exit on Colorado Boulevard.

He found the game on the radio. The Dodgers were now up by three in the bottom of the sixth. According to Vin Scully, Alberto Miranda had just hit a two-run homer to pad the lead—and a steady stream of cars was already leaving the lot. Dodger fans were famous for leading all of major league baseball when it came to beating the traffic home. Scully went through the American League scores. The Sox had beaten the Blue Jays for the third straight game, while the Yankees lost to the Orioles again. It looked like the Sox were crawling back into the A.L. East race.

The drive to Laswell's took about fifteen minutes. On the way, Sam told Heather about Daly's description of the gym. He assumed Laswell would be a character similar to Kenny, the owner of Club Earache—tightly wound and protective of his famous clientele. Sam told her they would tour the gym as prospective customers, and see if they could strike up conversations with some of the regulars.

The gym was on a wide commercial street where hot cars cruised back and forth, the drivers looking for excitement in the sultry coastal darkness. Sam parked in the gym's adjoining lot, and they walked in to find a brightly lit, spacious main exercise room decorated primarily in blue with orange and yellow accents, with unseen fans forcing fresh air currents through the dense aroma of sweat and body oil. There were both free weights and resistance machines near the main entrance, with stair-climbers, treadmills, and elliptical machines farther back. Apparently Roy Laswell thought it was good advertising to put the oil-slicked hardbodies out front, and let the blubbery treadmill types slave away in the farther reaches of the big room.

Sam went to the reception desk and spoke to a young woman who wore a plastic nametag that said "Kaylee." She was thumbing through a Muscle & Fitness magazine. She had teased-up hair and wore a blue sleeveless workout suit—calculated to show off the definition in her biceps—that matched her eye shadow. When Sam said hello to her, she glanced up at him and revealed her yellow chewing gum when she smiled. She removed one of the ear buds attached to her MP3 player.

"My wife and I are thinking of joining. Is there someone who can give us a tour?"

"Not tonight." Kaylee glanced at the clock by the door. "I've got to stay by the phone. The other staffers on duty are conducting classes. We do tours between nine and six o'clock. But you're welcome to look around."

"I hear you have some pro athletes who work out here."

"Oh, yeah. Some of the Dodgers do. A couple of Lakers and Kings. Roy's good friends with lots of them."

"Is Roy here tonight?"

"No. You could try back tomorrow."

"We'll just take a walk through, if that's okay."

"Sure, whatever."

She turned back to her magazine, and Sam scanned the room, looking for guys who appeared over-supplemented. There were several possibilities; the sounds of guttural grunts and clanking metal drew Sam's attention to the free-weight side of the room.

"Are we interested in the one-month trial membership or the half-year introductory offer, honey?" Sam asked Heather.

She gazed at a trio of rippling, sculpted specimens wearing snug singlets and broad leather belts spotting for each other at a weight bench, then reached over and squeezed Sam's right bicep.

"I think you'd better sign up for the full year," she said.

"Hey, easy," Sam said. "Or I might not step in the next time you get manhandled."

"Handle this," she said. She grabbed his crotch.

One of the weightlifters happened to catch Heather's quick strike and broke into a leering grin.

"We interrupting something?" the guy asked.

"She's just doing some weightlifting," Sam said.

The three lifters didn't even smile. Sam walked over and sat next to the weight bench where two of the men were spotting for the third. One appeared to be Hispanic, while the other two were white guys with short, buzz haircuts that revealed scars on their scalps, the kind most often acquired from a broken bottle in a bar fight. None of them was particularly big, but their muscles were. Heather might have been impressed, but to Sam, they looked like normal guys wearing fake plastic muscle suits—except that the veins and the bulges were real.

There was a terraced rack of round free weights next to the bench, and another low rack of dumbbells against the mirrored wall. The guy on his back looked to be benching 300 pounds.

"We're thinking of joining the gym," Sam said. "You guys like it here?"

"Yeah, it's okay," one of the spotters said. "Membership fee's not bad. They keep the equipment up to date."

"Some of the pros work out here, I hear," Sam said.

"Yeah, a few."

"Some Dodgers?"

"Yeah, they come in."

"How about Alberto Miranda?"

"Yeah, he's in here a lot in the off-season."

"You guys know him?"

One of the spotters turned to the other and gave him a look. His companion looked back at Sam and said, "Yeah, we know him."

They didn't seem to want to continue the conversation. "You guys get like that just lifting weights?" Sam asked.

"What do you mean?" one of the spotters said. The guy on his back set the barbell down in its holder and swung himself to a sitting position. He didn't look friendly.

"Oh, you know," Sam said. "What about those supplements? Creatine, HGH, steroids—"

"Hey, FUCK you!" the weightlifter said. He pushed Sam backward hard enough to make him nearly fall off the weight bench he was sitting on. Sam got to his feet, looking for something to defend himself with as the three bodybuilders advanced toward him, but Heather stepped in front of him.

"Cool it, guys, okay?" she said. "He didn't mean anything."

"Nobody comes into our gym and tells us we're on juice," said the Hispanic-looking weightlifter. "Get the fuck outta here."

"Nice friendly place you got here," Sam said. He wasn't ready to back away.

A door banged open at the back of the gym. An older man with a shaved head and a gray Fu Manchu moustache, wearing a black tank-top and black running pants, walked as quickly as he could past the exercise machines to the weight area where Sam and Heather were being confronted by the Bash Brothers. The man's hands were balled into fists, and his angry gaze bounced back and forth between Sam and the lifters. Sam tried not to laugh; the man had muscles, but his skin hung loosely on his neck, and his shoulders and biceps had the surface consistency of oatmeal. He must have been on the cover of magazines when he was forty years younger, but now he looked like one of those tabloid photos of an aging, sagging movie star caught sunbathing.

"I told you guys I don't want no more fights in here," the man said to the trio of lifters. "I'm sick of this shit. What's goin' on here, Jesus?"

"Sorry, Roy," the Hispanic bodybuilder said. "But this dickhead here started asking us about steroids. I ain't gotta listen to that bullshit."

Roy turned to Sam and said, "What's your problem?"

"No problem," Sam said. "I take it you're Roy Laswell?"

"Yeah—so what?"

"The receptionist told us you weren't here tonight."

"Maybe I came in when she wasn't lookin'. Now, what the fuck do you want?"

What did Sam want? His cop instinct was to suggest they go back and talk in Roy's office—but then what? Sam would ask him if Alberto Miranda had gotten steroids from anyone connected with Laswell's gym, and he knew damn well what the answer would be. The Three Stooges would be asked to escort Sam to the curb. He'd already lost some face with Heather, and he couldn't see the wisdom in pushing things to a point where he'd have to bounce his fist off one of these rock-hard goons to maintain his dignity. That was the problem with being in private practice: Everybody else had people. Kenny had three guys, Mink had two guys, and now Laswell had three guys. Sam had Heather. Heather had her own talents, but they weren't of much use here.

"Look, I'm sorry, Mr. Laswell," Sam said. "We were just checking the place out to see if we wanted to join. Maybe I was out of line. You read so much about bodybuilding supplements, so I just asked a question."

"My husband's an idiot," Heather said. She shook her head with a slight eye-roll. "He says the first thing that pops into his mouth."

Laswell was looking steadily at Sam, using whatever remaining brainpower he had, mixed with whatever muscle-growth cocktails he was downing, to try to get a fix on him.

"I don't think this guy's no idiot," Laswell said. "I think he's an asshole. I want you both outta here—now. And don't come back."

"Fine with me," Sam said. He took Heather by the elbow. "Let's try Bally's."

They walked back toward the door, the entire gym having gone silent to watch the owner quell the disturbance.

"Bye now," Kaylee said with a wave—looking up from her magazine with her ear buds back in place—as Sam and Heather passed her desk.

Back at the BMW, Sam leaned against the driver's side door with his hands on the car's finish and his chin nearly touching the buttons of his golf shirt. This was not going well. All he had going for him right now was the word of a crime boss that he'd help find Babe Ruth. Miranda had given them nothing, and the trip to the gym had nearly turned into a disaster, except to establish that there were some hair-trigger steroid cases pumping iron in the same health club where Alberto Miranda worked out—and that he'd needed Heather to jump in to save him from a beating.

He hated himself for his next thought. Hated himself, but at this point, with the hours slipping by and Babe Ruth no closer to surfacing, Sam had no choice. Miranda was still the key to the whole thing—the only one who knew for sure what had happened, or not happened, during the World Series. They had to get to him again—and this time, he had to talk.

"Heather..." Sam said, not knowing exactly how he was going to phrase his request.

"Quiet," she said. "I'm calling him."

She was sitting in the passenger seat of the convertible, her cell phone to her ear and a hand up to keep Sam from saying anything more.

"Calling who?"

"Alberto. Shhh, it's ringing."

"Where'd you get his number?"

She looked at him with an expression that said, "Are you from outer space?"

Sam should have known. Miranda had done what any other millionaire pro athlete would have done after meeting a hot blonde like Heather. He got her phone number and called her later. Maybe that's why she hadn't talked to Kenwood the night before. At any rate, Heather now had Alberto Miranda's number in her call list.

"Alberto—Heather Canby," she said with a musical lilt. "Great game tonight…Of course we were. We were sitting behind your dugout, about thirty rows up…Listen, I thought maybe we could get together tonight…No, no, Sam's just…well, you know, we work together, but…"

Sam smiled. He'd been on the verge of pimping Heather out to Miranda, and now she was doing it herself—though she certainly didn't seem offended. This was the up side of casual, recreational sex: Whatever jealousy Sam might have felt was more than compensated for by the prospect of getting some useful information out of Miranda.

"I don't know where the players' entrance is…" Heather was saying. "Oh…sure, I can find that…Will you be ready in twenty minutes? Great. See you then."

Heather clicked off the phone and turned to Sam.

"Back to the stadium. I've got a date."

# Chapter Eighteen

Vin Scully was wrapping up the post-game show after the 7-2 Dodger victory when Sam and Heather got back to the stadium. The lights of downtown Los Angeles burned brightly to the south as they drove around the ballpark, until they found a section of the lot where several dozen luxury cars were clustered together under the watchful eye of a couple of security cops. Sam recognized Miranda's Jaguar, with the California vanity plate "AM 19"—his initials and uniform number.

Several dozen autograph seekers and baseball groupies clustered along a metal barrier near the clubhouse door, waiting for the players to emerge. Sam stopped the BMW and turned to Heather.

"We've got to get him to talk—tonight," Sam said.

"I know. It might take a while, though. I've got to earn his trust."

She looked at Sam with the same knowing expression he'd seen the first time they'd met in Kenwood's office. She wasn't going to tell him what she was prepared to do. She didn't have to.

"I'm going to follow you," Sam said. "I'll keep out of sight, but I'll be nearby, wherever you go."

"Why? I'll be all right."

"I know, but I haven't got anything better to do. If you learn anything, we can move on it right away."

"I might not be done until morning."

"Fine. Just don't turn it into brunch and a matinee."

Heather got out of the car and walked over to the group of fans waiting along the barrier by the players' entrance. The kids waiting for autographs didn't pay much attention, but the waiting women looked at Heather as though she'd just walked into their kitchen and taken the roast they'd set out for dinner.

Ten minutes later, Alberto Miranda came out, wearing brown tailored slacks and a cream-colored Tommy Bahama sport shirt. The fans clamored for him to come over to the barrier, waving programs, baseball cards and notebooks for him to sign. He worked his way down the barrier, signing, unsmiling but dutiful. When he spotted Heather, he broke into a grin. He gestured for her to walk around to a gate where a guard let her through. He put an arm around Heather's waist and walked her to his Jag, disappointing dozens of young women who'd waited around after the game, hoping for the same invitation. While the autograph hunters turned their attention to other players who'd come out of the locker room, Miranda's sleek sports car sped off toward the limitless possibilities of L.A.

Sam put the BMW in gear and followed at a distance. A red BMW convertible wasn't the ideal car for a tail, but it wouldn't stand out all that much in L.A. And Miranda had no reason to think he was being followed.

Sam followed Miranda south on the Pasadena Freeway and stayed with him when he exited west onto the Santa Monica Freeway, headed toward the ocean. Traffic was not as constipated as in the daytime, so Sam could stay several hundred feet behind Miranda without worrying about losing him.

He dialed up Don Henley's "Boys of Summer" on the iPod. He'd always wanted to drive in L.A. with the top down, listening to that insistent synth riff, Mike Campbell's ominous guitar fills swooping like a pack of malevolent seagulls, and those desperate lyrics about a dying summer love—with a title borrowed from a book about the Brooklyn Dodgers, which in turn was borrowed from some famous poem...who wrote that? Yeats? Keats? Dylan Thomas? Tennyson? He should have paid more attention to his

English poets in school, and less time studying batting averages and chord progressions.

Sam figured he was one of many men cruising the L.A. freeways listening to the same song that night, and thinking the same vaguely paranoid thoughts about a woman—it was a Southern California cliché, for sure. But he didn't care.

Some guys could sustain a sexual relationship with a woman without getting the least bit involved, but Sam wasn't that kind of man. His thoughts bounced back and forth between Caroline and Heather. Don't look back, the song advised. He'd agreed that a cooling-off period was the right thing to do when Caroline went back to Tucson. But what did that mean? There were no rules. No advice, either. Don't look back...he could see both of them, feel them, smell them...never look back...Heather's shiny blond hair and hard-eyed focus on what she wanted...Caroline's dark, silky hair and her optimistic, I-can-get-through-anything smile...summer was coming to an end, even here in Los Angeles...

Heather...Caroline...Kenwood...Miranda...don't look back...

Miranda's car was nearing La Brea when Sam's cell phone rang. The guitar riff continued to peck in the background as Sam opened his phone. It had to be either Daly or Mink.

"This Skarda?" he heard an unfamiliar voice ask.

"Yeah. Who's this?"

"Sid wants to meet with you. Tonight."

"Where?" Sam asked. He kept his eyes on Miranda's tail lights. He wasn't sure he wanted to leave Heather on her own—she might get something out of Miranda sooner than later, considering how effective she could be with men who enjoyed sensational blondes. And what man doesn't? Yet Mink was just as likely to give him some vital information—and you don't refuse offers from the Sid Minks of the world.

The voice on the phone—it sounded like Mink's tough-guy companion Joey Icebox—gave Sam directions to a Mexican restaurant called Dos Mujeres in Inglewood. Then he hung up.

Sam exited on La Brea and headed south. Heather wouldn't know that he had stopped following her, or why, but she could take care of herself. Obviously.

Dos Mujeres was located a couple of blocks past the Hollywood Park racetrack and casino on West Century Boulevard. Driving by, Sam glanced at the casino, a newer building with a soft pink four-story façade and a metallic art-deco rotunda that extended over the circular driveway to a lighted waterfall facing the street. Airplane noise from LAX completed the area's ambiance of hustle and edgy commotion.

Sam pulled into the parking lot at Dos Mujeres and found a spot near the front door. He locked his gun in the trunk of the car, knowing Joey would just pat him down again anyway. He thought about putting the top up on the convertible, but there was nothing in it worth stealing, after he unplugged his iPod from the car stereo and put it in his jacket pocket.

A black Cadillac pulled into the lot and stopped in front of the entrance. Joey Icebox jumped out of the car, followed by Leon with his Clooney haircut. They scanned the parking lot with the self-importance of a couple of Secret Service agents. Joey noticed Sam and nodded to him. Then Mink struggled out of the back seat, having exchanged his Dodgers jacket for a huge, ill-fitting brown sport coat. He had a lit cigar in his hand, but when he reached the steps of the restaurant, he tapped the ashes of the cigar and ground it into a wooden pillar just below the NO SMOKING sign. Then he put it back in his mouth and walked through the door that Leon held open for him. Joey gestured at Sam to follow them. In the vestibule, Joey did another quick frisk on Sam, then motioned for him to go in ahead of him.

The sound system was playing contemporary Latin pop, with drum machines and synthesizers instead of accordions and trumpets. The decor was the typical potted ferns with colored Mexican blankets hanging from stucco interior walls. Substitute red checkered tablecloths for the chips and salsa, Chianti for the Dos Equis, and Dean Martin music for Selena, and Dos Mujeres would be the classic mob hangout. Sam didn't have any urgent desire to be wearing his gun, but he didn't know much about organized crime in L.A., either. Maybe gangsters here were as relaxed as the city they controlled; maybe not. Sam couldn't shake the feeling that Mink was as much Hollywood as he was Mob; that he and his boys had never missed an episode of "The Sopranos," and had "The Godfather" memorized line by line.

"Good evening, Mr. Mink," the ruffled-shirted host in the lobby said. He sounded nervous. "We weren't expecting you."

"I got a whim," Mink said with a shrug. "The usual table, Jorge."

He pronounced it hor-GAY, letting the emphasis linger purposely on the second syllable. The host did not correct him.

Jorge led them through the restaurant to a booth in the corner that was occupied by a man and woman with three young children. Their food had just been served, and the woman was trying to calm one of the kids, who didn't like the looks of his plate of rice and beans.

"We'll need to find you folks another table," Jorge said to the couple.

"What the hell," the man said. He looked behind Jorge to see Mink and his men waiting impatiently. "I didn't see a 'Reserved' sign on this table."

"Oh, sorry," Joey said. He reached into his sport jacket. "Here it is."

He pulled out a Smith & Wesson semi-automatic and laid it in the middle of the table. Without another word, the man grabbed two of the kids by the arms and pulled them out of the booth. The woman picked up the youngest one and followed her husband without making eye contact with Mink or his goons. The youngest child stared wide-eyed back at Joey Icebox over his mother's shoulder, and Joey stuck out his tongue. The little boy covered his eyes and screamed.

"I'll have this cleaned up right away, Mr. Mink," Jorge said. He waved furiously at one of his busboys.

The table was wiped down and re-set in less than a minute. Sam sat next to Leon on one end of the booth, with Sid Mink in the middle and Joey on his other side, where he could keep an eye on the front door. In another minute, three plates of food appeared, and another waiter placed a drink in front of Mink. Each plate had a different entree; Mink's was three large enchiladas, a stuffed burrito, and sides of refried beans, rice, and pico de gallo; Joey Icebox had a chimichanga; and Leon had three tacos. One of the waiters asked Sam if he was going to order, but Sam waved him off. His stomach wasn't in the receiving mood for Mexican food.

Mink put a few hasty, ungraceful forkfuls of food in his mouth, had several sips from his drink, then returned to his dinner plate and finished it off before speaking to Sam. He pushed his empty plate away and chewed on his unlit cigar.

"You sure you don't want anything, Skarda?" Mink asked.

"No thanks."

"Get him a drink, Leon."

Sam wasn't going to argue: "Dos Equis."

Mink leaned toward Sam and spoke softly. His breath smelled of cigars, whiskey, and cilantro. Not all that unpleasant, really.

"The guy you're looking for is a Spic hustler named Frankie Navarro."

"How do you know?"

Mink looked at Joey, then at Leon.

"How do I know, he asks. I got people everywhere. Take it to the bank, pal—Navarro's behind this. He's been nipping around the edges of my business for a while now. A bookie here, a drug dealer there. Nothing to make me mad enough to do something about it. It's a big town. He likes to pump iron, thinks he's a tough guy. I hear he was in a couple of movies. But he's a dumb punk who's way over his head on this one."

Mink put the cigar in his mouth and worked it around like a lozenge, waiting for Sam to ask more questions. Sam had a dozen of them, but he wasn't sure which one to ask first. The most obvious one was why Mink was bothering to tell him. Sid

Mink's say-so might be reliable, but it didn't get Sam any closer to proving anything, or stopping it. It had to be in Mink's interest, as well as Louis Kenwood's, to terminate the extortion plot—and he'd have to help—but Sam wanted to hear Mink say it.

"What are we going to do about it?" Sam asked. He stared coolly at Mink, though he didn't feel cool. He was about as far out of his comfort zone as he could get, talking to mobsters in a strange town about a rival mobster.

"We?" Mink said. "When did you become one of my guys?"

"I can't wait for you to clean this up," Sam said. "My job is to tell Kenwood he doesn't have to worry about Babe Ruth anymore. And I have to know that it's true."

Joey Icebox put one of his large hands over the closed fist on his other hand and rubbed his knuckles, then said, "Only one way to be sure you don't have to worry about Navarro."

That's as far as Sam wanted to take that discussion. He couldn't be party to planning a hit, assuming these guys could pull it off. If they did, and the cops defied the odds and did something about it, Sam would go down with Mink and his boys. Mob guys loved to make everybody think they were running smooth, trouble-free organizations, but Sam knew there were always wiseguys trying to position themselves to move up, others falling out of favor, and a cop strike force trying to exploit the rivalries. For all Sam knew, Joey or Leon could be wired by the Feds, working to bring Mink down. Sam didn't have police affiliation anymore; good intentions wouldn't help him in court if he was caught on tape discussing how to eliminate a rival mobster.

"How do you know you can trust me to talk about this?" Sam asked Mink.

"We had you checked out," Mink said with a wave of the cigar. "Didn't take long. You used to be a cop in Minneapolis. You got shot a couple years ago, went into private practice, and you've been peeping in bedroom windows for the last few months until Kenwood hired you. And somebody tried to gun you down right after that."

"You know about the boat?"

"What boat?" Mink said. "I'm talkin' about that fucked-up drive-by in Minneapolis."

So the kid lying in a coma back in the Twin Cities had been gunning for him, not Marcus. And that meant somebody knew Kenwood was going to hire him almost from the minute Heather called him—or even before. Navarro might not be a big-timer like Mink yet, but his reach was long; he'd found a guy in Minneapolis to try to take him out, and a guy in Boston, too. When the Minneapolis gang-banger failed, Navarro sent somebody else to shut the kid up. He didn't need to worry about the guy in the speedboat. His talking days were over.

So who was giving Navarro information? It had to be either Heather or Paul O'Brien—and Heather had had other chances to get rid of him since they left Boston. He needed that background check on Kenwood's driver.

"If Navarro is such a punk, how did he put all this together?" Sam asked. "Sounds to me like he's getting ready to come after you."

"Bring it on," Mink said. "I let him hang around, run his cheap operations because I didn't think he had the brains or the balls to do anything that could hurt me. But suddenly he's ambitious. The only way he becomes anything in this town is if he takes me out, and that ain't gonna happen."

Mink looked at Joey and Leon, both of whom nodded silently.

"We're gonna go see Frankie tonight. Your problem's gonna go away. You want to come, be our guest."

Sam had to think this through. He couldn't take Sid Mink's word that killing Frankie Navarro was the end of the Babe Ruth problem. At the very least, he needed to hear Navarro admit he was behind the plot. He also needed to know who had tipped him off that Kenwood had hired a detective. And a dead Frankie Navarro could do neither of those things.

"Can't you just lean on him a little?" Sam said. "Scare him into talking, then run him out of town?"

"Evidently, he don't scare," Mink said. "He thinks he's safe. He's got his own soldiers."

"Musclebound shitheads," Leon said, speaking for the first time.

"You don't scare an ambitious punk," Mink said. "You get rid of him. I don't like it when it comes to this, but here we are."

Sam's cell phone rang, and he looked at the incoming number. It was Heather.

"Sorry, I have to take this," Sam said. He got up from the table.

"You comin' with us, or you just want to read about it in the papers?"

"Hold on a minute," Sam said.

He walked to the bar by the host stand on the other side of the room, took a stool, and asked Heather where she was.

"I'm at Alberto's house in Pacific Palisades," she said. "He wants to talk."

"That was fast."

"He likes me."

"He's a man."

Heather sighed.

"It's not like that. And I tried."

"What do you mean?"

"I mean I was ready to go to bed with him, but…" Her voice trailed off, and then Sam heard her footsteps and the rustle of her clothes. It sounded like she was walking through a hallway, with the phone held to her side.

"Sorry," she said, in a quieter voice. "I don't want him to hear this. He's…not capable."

"That's hard to believe."

"No, we…he couldn't do it. So we started talking. He brought up the World Series. I mean, it started pouring out of him. He kept saying the same thing—he tried his best, he didn't throw the Series. But he was getting really upset. He won't tell me what's going on, but he wants to. He's in trouble."

"What now?"

"Can you come over?"

Sam glanced back at the booth where Mink sat with his boys. They looked like they were ready to leave.

"Things are popping here, too."

"Where are you?"

"At a Mexican restaurant in Inglewood with Sid Mink and his two buddies. He told me who's running the scam."

"Who?" Heather said. Sam listened closely to her voice to see if there was any hint that she was worried about Sam learning who Babe Ruth was, but he couldn't detect it. She sounded excited.

"A local mob wannabe named Frankie Navarro."

He let the name hang in the air. After a pause, Heather said she'd never heard of him.

"Ask Alberto if he's heard of him."

"Okay."

He could hear Heather asking Miranda the question, and he heard the ballplayer say something in an agitated tone of voice.

"That's it," Heather said. "He knows him."

Her phone was silent again for a moment as Miranda said something to her. Then Heather spoke again.

"He wants you to come over, now. He says he'll tell us what's going on."

Sam thought he had the pieces put together now, or most of them. Navarro had somehow gotten to Miranda. Steroids, probably. Maybe it was true—maybe Miranda had thrown a game in the Series to keep Navarro from exposing his steroid use. But it still didn't explain why Navarro thought Miranda would be willing to admit he'd thrown a World Series game if he wasn't willing to admit he'd used steroids. Steroids got you suspended; throwing a ballgame got you kicked out of baseball for life. Even a jock ought to be able to figure that one out.

Sam looked at Mink again. If Mink killed Navarro tonight, Miranda's problems might be over, and so would Lou Kenwood's—if, in fact, Navarro was Babe Ruth. Maybe that was the easiest way to let this play out. But whatever Mink did tonight, Sam couldn't be there. He had to talk to Miranda.

He got directions to Miranda's house from Heather, and told her he could be there in less than an hour. Then he put his cell phone in his pocket and returned to the table.

"I'll have to decline your invitation, Sid," Sam said. "Something's come up."

"Suit yourself," Mink said, shrugging. "You're the guy who said you had to talk to Navarro. Could be your last chance."

"I can't be two places at once. Can I call you later tonight?"

"You got Joey Icebox's number in your phone."

Mink threw down some bills and got up from the table.

"If you got something you wanna say to Frankie," Mink said, "you better call early."

# Chapter Nineteen

The L.A. freeway system is known for apocalyptic gridlock, road rage shootings, and high-speed chases taped by TV choppers, but late on a Wednesday night, a private eye with a fast car could get from Inglewood to Pacific Palisades in under thirty minutes. Sam took Century Boulevard toward the airport and got on the San Diego Freeway going north. Keeping an eye out for CHP speed traps, he held the BMW at a steady seventy-five, with the iPod pumping out the Eagles' "Desperado." He was in the mood for L.A. outlaw music. He didn't much care for "Hotel California" and all the bloated radio hits the Eagles put out after that, but early Eagles was a different story. Cops—and ex-cops—resonated to songs about Wild West gunslingers.

He took the Santa Monica Freeway west and headed toward the ocean, picking up the Pacific Coast Highway within a block of the Loews hotel. He flashed back to that morning, when Heather had come into his room for another tumble. He'd assumed that she'd had sex with him back in Boston to eliminate any suspicions that he might have had about her relationship with Kenwood—and it had worked, for a while. So yesterday she'd admitted she was going to marry Kenwood—but was that true, or a necessary cover story because he was getting too close to the truth about the extortion? It was a lot easier to sleep your way into money than steal it, at least if you had Heather's skills. But he only had Heather's word that she would someday be Mrs. Lou Kenwood. If she was lying, she took a chance that he wouldn't dare ask Kenwood himself. Did he dare? It might get him kicked off the case, but he'd been shot at and pushed around—he had a right to know for sure where all the loyalties lay in this mess.

But that was for tomorrow. Tonight, he was headed north on the Coast Highway toward one of L.A.'s swankiest neighborhoods to have a come-to-Jesus with one of the world's richest athletes. That was enough to worry about for the time being.

The lights of the coastal homes reflected off the ocean as the highway bent to the west near the seaside town of Castellammare. The vegetation-shielded bungalows along the beach seemed to be just waiting to be buried under the sandy cliffs on the opposite side of the road, which looked as if they could collapse across the highway in a light drizzle. He took a right at West Sunset Boulevard and headed up into the hills, following Heather's directions until he came to Palisades Drive. From there it was three miles of thick hedges and palm trees to Miranda's ornate, Spanish-style mansion in the shadows of Topanga State Park. He pulled into the circular driveway in front of the house, and a motion-detector light came on. Then the service door next to the four-stall garage opened, and one of the men who had been with Miranda at Quasar the night before—a tall, dark-skinned guy with a black nylon skull cap who looked like an ex-Laker—emerged to look him over.

Everybody had guys.

"Alberto's waitin' for you," the man said, motioning for Sam to follow him. They went through the service door, avoiding the main entrance with its pillared steps and tile-roofed overhang.

They walked through the kitchen—large enough to be the galley for a cruise ship—down an open hallway past a spiral staircase to the second floor, and out onto the patio that overlooked the lights of Pacific Palisades and the ocean beyond. Heather was sitting on a lounge chair next to Miranda when Sam walked out. She stood up and came over to him.

"Alberto, you remember Sam," she said. She touched Sam's arm the way one would communicate to a child that the person who'd just walked in was not someone to be frightened of. Miranda nodded, but did not stand up. He turned his head toward the ocean and ran his hands across the top of his head from front to back, apparently trying to clear his mind of something.

"What's up?" Sam said. He was feeling impatient. Frankie Navarro could be dead already; he needed to know what Miranda knew, now.

Heather walked back to Miranda and sat next to him, putting her left arm over his shoulders and talking soothingly to him.

"You've got to confide in someone, Alberto," she said. "We can help you. Just tell us what's going on."

Alberto looked up at Sam.

"That son of a bitch kidnapped my mother."

"Which son of a bitch?"

"Frankie Navarro."

The story began pretty much the way Sam had it figured. Then it dropped off the table like a knuckleball.

Miranda admitted that he'd begun experimenting with steroids a year before the Dodgers called him up, but he didn't find the right mixture until he started working out at Laswell's gym. A couple of the older Dodgers introduced him to a Dr. Seth Whitlinger, a friend of Laswell's who ran his own lab and came up with an undetectable human growth hormone. Whitlinger began shopping it around to pro athletes, insisting the stuff was the best in the big leagues; in addition to 30 or 40 major league players, Miranda said, Whitlinger's HGH was being used by more than 100 NFL players, several Olympic track champions, and dozens of Tour de France bicyclists.

The stuff was expensive, but Miranda was willing to try almost anything to make it in the Major Leagues. Life in Venezuela was abysmal. He wasn't going back there.

After a half-dozen injections, Miranda could tell the HGH was improving his power and stamina. His arm bounced back much more quickly after pitching, and he had more than enough energy to play third base and bat on the days when he didn't pitch. The Dodgers didn't know how to use him, however, and shipped him to the Cardinals for established pitching. Miranda kept up with the injections in the off-season, and quickly became a star in St. Louis.

But then the urine screening done by the Commissioner's office became more sophisticated, investigations were stepped up, and players started getting caught for steroids and suspended. Miranda didn't know what to do; he didn't want to bring shame and disgrace to his family, but he knew he couldn't continue to play at his current level without the HGH. He had become a celebrity jock, and he loved the money, the cars, the house, the women, and the lifestyle too much to risk becoming a mediocre player. His mother and father were so proud of him. He could finally buy them things, like the ranch outside of Caracas. He was a hero in his homeland.

Even though Dr. Whitlinger assured him that he'd never get caught—it took a blood test to find HGH, and the players' union would never agree to blood testing—Miranda always feared that one day he'd wake up from this dream. Someone would rat him out, or they'd develop a new test, or the players' union would cave in. Then, just a few weeks before the playoffs, when the Cardinals were in L.A. on their final West Coast road trip of the season, his fears were realized.

Roy Laswell called him at his hotel and asked him to come by the gym. Something about a promotional appearance that would pay him a lot of money. Miranda didn't particularly want to do it, but Laswell had befriended him when he was nobody, and had introduced him to Dr. Whitlinger. He owed him—and the tone in Laswell's voice suggested that this was one of those times when the debt was being called in.

In Laswell's office, Miranda was introduced to a muscular dude named Frankie Navarro. Navarro was not a fan, and not a nice man. He told Miranda he knew all about Whitlinger's HGH formula. He had a copy of Miranda's injection schedule, in Whitlinger's handwriting. The Commissioner's office wouldn't need a blood test to suspend him. If the Cardinals made the World Series—and at this point they were almost a cinch to win their division—Navarro wanted Miranda to see to it that the Cards lost. Otherwise, Navarro said, he'd blow the whistle on Miranda's HGH use. He'd be suspended from baseball. He'd be disgraced.

Miranda walked out of the meeting in a daze, terrified that he was going to lose his career. Yet he was not willing to let down his teammates.

"I say to myself, 'Alberto, just see what happens,'" he told Sam and Heather. "Maybe this guy, he's bluffing."

On the day before the World Series began, Navarro called Miranda at his house.

"He say, 'Last chance, Alberto. Throw the Series, or I tell the world you're a drug cheat.' I tell him, 'Stick it up your ass, man.'"

Then Miranda played terribly in the World Series anyway. He was embarrassed, but he swore that he played as well as he could. He just couldn't get Navarro's threats out of his mind. The harder he tried to concentrate and block out his possible suspension from baseball, the more nervous and tentative he became.

"You can't play this game when you think about something else all the time," Miranda said.

He got up from his lounge chair and walked to the balcony overlooking the lights along the coast. A cool ocean breeze had dropped the temperature, and Heather began to shiver.

"So you tried as hard as you could, but you played like crap and lost anyway," Sam said. "That should have made Navarro happy, right?"

"No, man," Miranda said. "He call me again, after the Series, and say he lose millions of dollars."

"Betting on the Cardinals?"

"No, because he don't bet on the Red Sox. When I told him I was not gonna throw no games, he decide not to bet. He say,

'If I know you gonna play like that, I coulda made millions.' He say I screwed him."

He'd heard nothing from Navarro after that—not until last month, when Navarro called him again, right after Miranda's mother had come to L.A. for a visit, and then left to fly back to Caracas. This time, Navarro told Miranda that he had better be prepared to go to the Commissioner's office and admit he'd thrown the World Series. When Miranda laughed at him and asked why he should do that, Navarro asked about his mother.

"He say, 'How's Elena doin'. I say, 'How do you know my mother's name?' Then he tell me he had her kidnapped.

"I say, 'She just flew home yesterday after she visit me.' He say, 'Try to call her.' I call my mother and father's house. She never came home. My father is upset, but he don't know where to look, what to do. Then somebody call him and say, 'Don't call the police. Your wife is safe. She will come home when we get our money. But if you call the police, we kill her.'"

"I don't know what he want me to do, man," Miranda said. He was facing Sam now, anguish etched on his face. If it hadn't been so dark on the deck, Sam thought he'd have been able to see tears in Miranda's eyes. "I did not cheat, but I will tell the Commissioner anything if they let my mom go free."

Now it made sense, in a bizarre, mob-think kind of way. Navarro was pissed off that he'd missed his big payday, so he came up with an idea that could land him an even bigger pile of cash. Big enough to give him the leverage he'd need to take down Sid Mink. Of course Miranda would cooperate with Navarro if his mother's life was on the line. But why was Miranda spilling his guts now? Sam glanced at Heather, who'd gone over to stand next to Miranda. He saw that she was shivering, and took off his own jacket and put it over her shoulders. There was something between them, and apparently it wasn't just sex—or sex at all, if he could believe Heather's story.

"You won't have to go to the Commissioner," Sam said. "Navarro is bluffing. He wants the Red Sox to pay him to keep you quiet."

"If they pay, will he let my mother go?"

Sam didn't say anything. He wanted to be reassuring, but who knows what they were planning to do to *Señora* Miranda? If she disappeared, she could never testify. Her best chance to come out of this alive was getting to the kidnappers' location before they knew the plot had fallen apart.

Sam checked the time on his cell phone—almost two. He'd been there over an hour.

"Heather, we've got to call Sid Mink," Sam said.

"Why?"

"When I left him, he was on his way to kill Frankie Navarro. If that happens…"

Alberto Miranda finished Sam's thought.

"If that happens, my mother's dead, too."

# Chapter Twenty

Frankie Navarro sat in a lounge chair beside the small, six-foot-deep pool in his fenced-in back yard, sipping an energy shake and watching his girlfriend Fawna, who was perched on the edge of the pool in a yellow-and-red bikini, swishing her legs back and forth in the tepid water. Dead bugs, orange leaves, and a few of Fawna's cigarette butts floated on the pool's surface, backlit by the underwater lights. The water seemed to ripple to the rhythm of the Def Leppard music that throbbed out of the speaker he had placed in his living room window.

As usual, Frankie felt hemmed in by the redwood fence that separated his back yard from his neighbors'. Fawna's scrawny, matted Pekingese had left a little pile of crap in just about every square foot of dirt and dead grass around the pool deck. He'd yell at her to clean it up, and she'd do it for a day or two, and then forget again. The neighbors—Russian émigrés on one side, a gay couple on the other side—didn't like the noise when he yelled at Fawna, or the loud metal music he liked to play at night, but he didn't give a shit. They were afraid of him; after coming over to complain once, and seeing the muscles on Frankie and the guys who hung out with him, the neighbors didn't come over again.

He'd wanted to be close to the movie action, but West Hollywood was becoming a zoo, and this was no way for a crime lord or a successful actor to live. But it wouldn't be long now…

Frankie's cell phone rang, and he thought about not answering. Let it ring. It's almost midnight—he didn't feel like talking to anybody, and it would just cost him minutes on his cell plan. Besides, in two days he'd be so fucking rich, he'd have to hire guys who'd hire other guys to answer his phone for him.

Ah, fuck it—he picked up and said, "What?"

"Hey, Frankie, it's Larry."

Frankie's agent, Larry Eldin, hadn't called in months. Hell, Frankie wasn't even sure he was a client anymore. The last gig Larry'd got for him was a two-scene, one-line role in a grade D sorcery flick called "Wizard Killer." He played a warrior whose big moment was getting his own head cut off in a sword fight. The *papier mâché* model of his bloody head, jammed onto a pike on the wall of the castle, got more screen time than Frankie did. Straight to video. Even his mother never saw it.

Still, Frankie couldn't help but feel that old excitement. He'd been in L.A. for fifteen years now, getting by on the crumbs Sid Mink let fall to the floor. Acting sure as hell didn't pay the bills. Five movies, total—unless you counted that recruiting thing he did for the Navy down in San Diego. Shit, more people saw that on TV than all his movies combined.

But Frankie's ship was about to come in. Once he got rid of Sid Mink, he'd be Bugsy Siegel all over again. Those Hollywood snobs would trip over themselves inviting him to their parties. They'd see what they'd been missing—a good-looking guy with a build like Stallone or Arnold could only dream about now. He could be the next Rambo, the next Rocky, the next Terminator. The Latin Stallion—no, that didn't sound quite right, but why the fuck couldn't it happen? If they wouldn't cut him in, he'd cut himself in. In two days, he could do it.

And now his agent finally calls. It pissed him off—just when everything is starting to look up, suddenly the lazy asshole finds something.

"Yeah, what is it, Larry?"

"Damnedest thing, Frankie. I just got a call from a producer who's making a big-budget action flick, and he saw you in that thing, what was it called—'Death Bus.' I guess it was just on TV or something. Anyway, he loved you, and he had an actor walk off the set this afternoon, right as they're starting to shoot. He's up the creek for a big, strong guy to play a…what was it…oh, yeah, the leader of a biker gang. You can ride a bike, can't you, Frankie?"

McQueen. Brando. Fonda. Hopper. Navarro.

"Hell, yes, I can ride a bike. What, are you shittin' me? I rode out here on a hog fifteen years ago from New Mexico."

He'd also sold the bike fourteen years ago, and hadn't ridden one since, but Larry didn't have to know that.

"That's great," Larry said. "He'd like his casting guy to meet you tonight. You'd be on the set tomorrow, if it works out. Somewhere out by San Bernardino."

"It's gotta be tonight?" Frankie said. "You mean, like, right now?"

"If you want it. Lotta lines, pays good. I think you're on screen for, like, a quarter of the flick."

"Really? That much."

What am I doing, Frankie wondered. I don't need this now. I need to keep my eye on the ball here. Payday in two days, unless something comes out of nowhere to fuck it up. I should just lie low, stay close to the phone, then start counting my money. But this flick, I'd have lots of lines, Larry said. On screen for, what, twenty, twenty-five minutes? How great would that be? Shit, I've been sticking with this guy for years and he's got me nothing but crowd scenes and auditions for 'Muscle-bound man in tank-top' roles. I can't pass this up. I can't—not when I'm finally getting something from the little cocksucker.

"What's the producer's name?" Frankie asked.

"Williams. Robert Williams."

"Never heard of him."

"I think he's one of those wine-and-microchip guys from Napa who's made a ton of money and has always wanted to get into the movies."

I know the feeling, Frankie thought. Except for the ton-of-money part.

"And what's the name of the movie?"

"Uh…lemme think…'Day of Doom,' 'Day Before Doom,' something with 'Doom' in it. I haven't seen the script, but the guy says it's one of those save-the-world-from-the-Apocalypse things."

"Anybody else in the cast that I've heard of?"

"I can't remember right now…"

"Do I get a sex scene?"

"Look, Frankie, do you want this or don't you? I gotta tell you, it's been tough finding films you're right for, and you're not gettin' any younger. This could be a breakthrough for you. You do this, I could start getting you more mature action parts. But it's only on the table tonight. The guy's got two other actors he's ready to call if you don't want it."

"Yeah, okay. I want it. Where do I meet him?"

Larry gave him the address of an office park in Inglewood, not far from Frankie's house in West Hollywood. Frankie was surprised that a movie producer would set up a meeting there, but he had to admit that he didn't know what the fuck these producers thought or how they operated. If he did, he'd have been in more pictures. Besides, this Williams guy was new to the business, he needed somebody right now, and the casting director was taking the meeting. Maybe the casting director lived in Inglewood. Who knew? All Frankie cared about was that he was going to be in a movie, with lots of lines. Big budget, with a theatrical release this time. For that, he'd drive to fuckin' Tijuana.

"Fawna, I'm goin' out," Frankie said. Fawna hadn't paid attention to the phone conversation. Of course, Fawna didn't pay much attention to anything when she was on blow or ecstasy, which was most of the time. Lost in her world. Great lay, if she wasn't too high. But Frankie knew he could do better. Next week, with the money and the movie role, he was putting this puke-hole of a house up for sale, and shopping for something in Palos Verdes. Fawna wasn't coming with him.

He went inside the house and called Jesus. He wouldn't need an entourage—that would look bad for a supporting actor. But it made sense to bring one guy with him. You never knew.

Ten minutes later, a dinged-up Chevy Tahoe pulled up in front of Frankie's one-story stucco house, shrouded by two short, fat palm trees. Jesus got out and walked to the door. It was still warm out, and Jesus wore a black tank-top that showed off his bulging triceps and delts. Jesus was smart, though; he never worked his body to the point where he had a better set than Frankie. If Frankie was busy and couldn't get to the gym for a few days, Jesus didn't pump, either. Sometimes he spotted for Gino and Mikey, but he always stayed a few reps behind the boss.

"Kinda late," Jesus said when Frankie met him at the door. "What's up?"

"My agent called," Frankie said. "Can you believe it? I was gonna see about getting his face on a milk carton. Says he's got a job for me, starting tomorrow, but I gotta meet the casting director tonight."

Jesus shrugged. He knew the boss was obsessed with getting into the movies. He didn't know why, and he didn't care. Jesus drove the car, muscled the pushers and bookies, and didn't ask Frankie a lot of questions. It wasn't a bad job—you had to look over your shoulder to make sure one of Sid Mink's guys wasn't around, but Jesus could take care of himself. Besides, something told him Frankie was going to be moving up in the world someday, maybe soon. He had that thing, what did they call it? Charisma. He wasn't some porky, dried-up old fart like Mink. Frankie had balls, good looks, and the energy it took to be somebody. Lately Frankie'd been making lots of plans, something about a kidnapping that was going to pay off big. He wouldn't give Jesus all the details, but it involved one of the Dodger players who worked out at Laswell's. Frankie just told Jesus to be patient, because the money was going to be rolling in pretty soon. Jesus had heard that kind of talk before, but this time it sounded like the real thing, and he liked that.

Jesus had the Tahoe's radio tuned to Que Buena, the Hispanic music station. Frankie didn't like that down-home, old country shit; it was for small-timers, homeys, guys from the barrio who weren't ever going to make it. He hit the scan button, looking for classic rock. He was pumped up about this acting gig, and he needed some high-energy headbanging to match his mood. He wanted to walk into that audition like a rock star. He settled back when he found a station playing "Beautiful Girls" by Van Halen.

He couldn't help thinking about the Alberto Miranda deal as Jesus piloted the big SUV down La Cienega. He'd received an update earlier that morning. Elena Miranda was still under Jefe's control, getting weaker, definitely, but she'd live long enough for the money transfer on Friday. Then Jefe would turn her loose, let her wander around until she found her way home or someone found her. It didn't matter. The shanty would be torched by then, all traces of Jefe and his team destroyed. Jefe would get his cut, to divide up among his partners any way he saw fit. Frankie expected Jefe to kill them; that's what Frankie would do. Dead kidnappers don't talk. As for Jefe, a million bucks should buy his silence. If not…well, anybody could be killed, anytime, anywhere.

Except, apparently, that private dick from Minnesota. He'd missed Skarda twice, and that really pissed him off. Now Skarda was somewhere in L.A., but he didn't seem to be getting any closer to finding Frankie or figuring out what was going on. And Skarda didn't have enough time left. There was nothing he could do to stop Kenwood from paying off now. Maybe a week ago Frankie would have passed up this audition; there was too much up in the air then, too many ways that things could go wrong. Jefe might have let Elena get away, Miranda might have gone to the cops, Kenwood might have refused to pay…but none of that happened. He was almost home free, and it was time to expand his horizons. The money, the acting job, the new house, the new girlfriends…life was about to get very, very good.

Jesus got on the 405 at Florence and exited five minutes later at West Century. They found the address they were looking for in a complex of boxy, two-story office buildings between the freeway and the eastern edge of LAX. With the constant hum of the freeway and the din from the arriving and departing jets, it wasn't the kind of location where you'd try to get a lot of thinking done. He hoped they had a halfway quiet room for the audition.

Jesus pulled into the parking lot outside the building they'd been directed to. The main entrance was a glass door near the north corner of the building, with the address stenciled in black numbers on the stucco wall next to the building. The front of the building was not lit, but from the streetlights along the curb, Frankie could tell that a company name had been spelled out in three-foot-tall letters above the door at some point, but the letters had been taken down a while ago, leaving a faint outline behind that he couldn't read. There was a light on inside, illuminating two of the windows that faced the street, but the blinds were drawn.

There were two other cars in the lot, a new Cadillac and an old Nissan. So nobody was driving a Mercedes or a Hummer—big deal. Probably just the casting director and an assistant, maybe a makeup artist or something. These Hollywood producers didn't get rich by going to auditions at one in the morning.

Jesus parked in front of the entrance and got out of the SUV first. Frankie was checking his hair in the mirror behind the sunshield, so he didn't see Leon come from out of the shadows beside the building, walk up to Jesus, and put a bullet through his temple. But Frankie did hear the sharp pop, followed by someone pulling his door open and grabbing him by the arm. He tried to yank free and reach for the gun in the glove compartment, but he heard the mechanical sound of a semi-automatic being racked next to his ear, and a familiar voice:

"You wanna die, Frankie?"

# Chapter Twenty-one

Frankie eased his hand away from the glove compartment and slowly turned to see Joey Mattaliano—Joey Icebox, they called him, because he was built like a Frigidaire—with a gun pointed at the base of his skull. Through the open driver's-side door, Frankie saw the other guy who was always with Sid Mink. Leon somebody. He had a gun, too, pointed directly at Frankie's face. Frankie might be able to make a quick move and out-muscle Joey Icebox, but Leon would blow him away. Frankie looked down at Leon's feet. He could see Jesus' arm on the asphalt driveway, blood-streaked and immobile. He must be dead. Jesus.

It was a set-up. They'd got to his fucking agent, that no-good piece of shit.

The sweat was pouring down Frankie's body, seeming to pool in his shorts and freeze around his genitals. Mink must know about the kidnapping. But how? He hadn't told Jesus any of the details. Maybe Jesus had said something to Mikey or Gino; you couldn't trust those two to go get a sandwich without shooting their mouths off to somebody, trying to prove how tough and important they were. Could Miranda have talked? But that would be crazy—he had to know his mother would be killed the moment anyone even suspected what was going on. Maybe it was Jefe; Frankie'd never met the guy, so who's to say he didn't try to cut a better deal for himself with Mink?

Frankie knew he had just a few minutes, or even seconds, to bargain for his life.

"Look, Joey, let me talk to Sid," Frankie said. "Please. We can straighten this whole thing out."

"What thing would that be, Frankie?" Joey asked.

"Come on, Joey. I know Sid knows. I was always gonna cut him in. Right from the start—honest. I just couldn't let anybody else know about it until it all went down. But Sid's gonna get his cut. Friday. Just lemme talk to him. Joey. Joey. Please."

The door to the office building opened, and Sid Mink walked slowly down the steps, swinging his big gut from side to side. He'd shut off the lights inside. He walked over to the SUV and looked down for a moment, staring at the spot where Jesus lay.

"Guy's name was Jesus?" Mink said, looking at Leo, then at Frankie. "This one ain't gonna rise again."

Frankie had thought Mink was soft and old; he thought he could take him down. But it looked like he'd been wrong. Mink wasn't washed up yet. That weary-old-fatman-at-the-Dodger-game act was a phony. But if he let Mink in on the plan, he'd have to give up maybe half of his take. Besides, Joey Icebox and Leon and maybe some of the other guys in Mink's organization would know, too. Fuckin' mobsters couldn't keep their mouths shut. He should have just set up Mink for a hit—get it over with, bang, boom. Joey and Leon would be taking orders from him now.

Instead, he was going for a ride—one way.

Joey and Leon hauled Frankie out of the SUV and shoved him into the Cadillac. Then Leon went back to the SUV and got the gun out of the glove compartment. Mink got into the passenger seat, Leon got behind the wheel, and Joey sat in the back, holding a gun to Frankie's ribs.

"What should we do about the Nissan, boss?" Leon asked Mink.

"Leave it. It's clean."

The other car had been a dummy, just to convince Frankie that there really was a meeting at the office building. He should have smelled it; the car was a piece of shit, something Joey Icebox or Leon drove over from a chop shop. Not even a studio flunky would drive a crate like that.

Joey backed up and turned the car toward the exit to the street. Mink didn't say anything, so Frankie knew they already had his future figured out. He was going to be taken somewhere, shot and dumped. But first, they'd want to find out what he knew.

They were on the 405 heading north toward the hills when Mink finally spoke.

"So Frankie Navarro thought he was big enough and smart enough to pull a $50,000,000 scam to fix the World Series— that's what we got here, Frankie?"

Sid didn't know Frankie very well. They'd crossed paths a few times at neighborhood festivals, political fundraisers, and the occasional social gathering at the home of mutual acquaintances. Frankie had decided right after arriving in L.A. that he and Mink were different breeds of cat, and he'd never get anywhere working for him. Mink was old-school, a relic from the days when the L.A. mob had some juice. Frankie wanted no part of it; he had to be free to do his own thing, to pursue acting at the same time he was building up his own little network of dealers and book-ies. Besides, L.A. was changing. Mink was more comfortable dealing with white gamblers and black dope pushers; Frankie knew the barrios. Frankie wasn't from East L.A. or Mexico, so he knew he'd never be able to move up in the Latino gangs. He worked the fringes—Mink assumed the La Raza boys looked out for him, and the Latinos figured Frankie was in good with Sid Mink.

Frankie had just pushed it way too far.

"It's not like that, Sid," Frankie said. "Like I told Joey Icebox—I was gonna cut you in. You know that. I just didn't want to tell the world, you know? It was a tricky deal. If some-body talked…"

Mink lit his cigar and pushed the button on the door to roll his window down halfway. He took a long drag and, instead of blowing it out the window, blew it at Frankie.

"See, that's what I don't get," Mink said. "You're tellin' me you didn't trust me? YOU didn't trust ME?"

"No, I don't mean it that way, Sid," Frankie said. Shit, everything he said came out wrong. There had to be something he could say, something he could offer Sid, that would keep him alive. Think, Frankie.

"How did you mean it?"

"I...I..."

"C'mon, you fuckin' little spic punk piece of shit!" Mink yelled. Now the veins were standing up in his neck, and he leaned over the back seat to get his face closer to Frankie's. "I gotta listen to people tellin' me we're the Mickey Mouse Mafia. They say the cops are laughin' behind our backs, that the unions don't respect us no more, and the newspapers write editorials about our 'declining influence.' I'll show you 'declining influence.'"

Mink reached over into Leon's jacket and took out his Walther PPK with the silencer still attached. He pointed it at Frankie's right bicep and pulled the trigger. The bullet tore through Frankie's arm.

"Christ!" Frankie screamed. He clutched at the blood that poured out of his arm.

"You think you're so fuckin' tough, you and those muscle boys you hang around with," Mink said, his cigar hanging wet from the corner of his mouth. "What good are your muscles doin' you now, huh Frankie? You look like a fuckin' clown, like one of those dumb stiffs from a fuckin' beach movie."

Frankie's arm hurt like hell, but he wasn't going to whimper for Sid Mink. Joey handed him a handkerchief and said, "Here. Don't bleed all over the upholstery."

Frankie pressed the handkerchief to the gaping wound, but it quickly became soaked with blood, and looking at it made him woozy. He had to come up with something soon, think of something before he couldn't think anymore, before Mink shot him in the head. They wanted something from him, or he'd be dead already. What was it?

"Now, you're going to tell me how your little scam worked," Mink said. "How you thought it up. How you got to Miranda. Did he throw ball games? Was he on the juice? I wanna know, Frankie—that ain't information you're gonna wanna take to your grave."

"He was on the juice, Sid—Christ, anybody could see that," Frankie said, between gasps of breath. His arm felt like it had been ripped off his body. "We train at the same gym. I got his injection schedule from the doctor who was givin' him the stuff."

"You usin' too, Frankie?"

Even at a time like this, when his life was dangling by a sinew, Frankie was reluctant to admit that he'd been on the same powerful mixture of steroids, HGH, and muscle-building supplements that many of the ballplayers used. All the work at the gym wouldn't have got him ripped without it. He wanted the punks on the street, Mink's mob, and the Hollywood crowd to think it was all about the lifting, but the barrel of a gun was powerful truth serum.

"Yeah, yeah, I use, Sid."

"But bullets don't bounce off you."

"No, guess not."

Joey and Leon laughed. Frankie, for all his pain, tried to laugh too. It came out more like a choking sob.

"So, what, you figured you'd blackmail Miranda? Poor guy comes over here from Colombia, or wherever the fuck he's from, and he gets mixed up in steroids so he can get better at his job. He wants to be an American baseball hero. Then a drug-shooting piece of garbage like you—doing the same shit, just to try to look tough—you threaten to rat him out if he don't throw World Series games?"

"Yeah, that's about how it was," Frankie groaned. Not entirely, but he had to hold onto something to bargain with.

"You know what really pisses me off, Frankie?" Mink said.

Frankie flinched, hearing the anger return to Mink's voice and expecting another shot to be fired.

"It's baseball you're fuckin' with. There's enough shit in this world. Why you gotta fuck up one of the only good things we got left?"

Frankie didn't answer, and Mink made a disgusted grunt at the back of his throat and turned to watch the freeway. Leon had gone east on the 105, and then merged onto the 110 heading north toward downtown. Frankie couldn't figure out where they were headed. It looked like they weren't going to toss him off a cliff into the ocean. Maybe up into the hills to dump his body in a canyon.

"Sid, what do I gotta do to stay alive?" Frankie said. His heartbeat raced and his breath came in short, panting gulps.

Mink faced forward, watching the road and saying nothing.

"Half, Sid. I'll give you half."

Mink remained silent, while Joey chuckled to himself, his gun still poking into Frankie's ribs like a letter from the future.

"Where we goin'?" Frankie asked.

"Since you love baseball so much, I thought we'd let you out at Dodger Stadium," Mink said. "Nobody there now—you'll have the parking lot all to yourself."

Frankie immediately visualized his own body, lying crumpled on the asphalt in a lined parking space outside the ballpark, waiting to be discovered by the first employees to arrive in the morning. He couldn't let it end that way.

The light traffic allowed Leon to reach Chavez Ravine in twenty minutes. Mink was still holding Leon's Walther—it looked like he was going to do it himself, instead of having Leon or Joey Icebox do it. It didn't normally work that way, but Mink probably wanted word to get out that he was the trigger man. It would boost his sagging ratings.

Leon had reached the outer gates of the stadium parking lot and was pulling in when Joey's phone rang.

"Shut that fucking thing off," Mink said. "We got work to do here."

Joey pulled the phone out of his pocket and looked at the number on the display.

"It's Skarda."

◇◇◇

In Pacific Palisades, Sam heard Joey's voice and the background sound of a car's engine. They were driving somewhere, probably with a gun in Frankie's mouth.

"Joey, put Mink on the phone," Sam said.

It was past two now. Sam had gone inside Miranda's house to make the call. He'd started to shiver, and he didn't know whether it was because of the falling canyon temperatures, or the certainty that if he didn't stop Mink from killing Frankie Navarro, Miranda would never see his mother again.

Technically, Sam had no stake in Elena Miranda's fate. But he had a big stake in whether they could prove Frankie was behind the extortion plot. Miranda's say-so wasn't good enough.

"Make it quick, Skarda," he heard Mink say. "Frankie's about to become unavailable for comment."

"Where are you?" Sam said.

"Let's just call it an undisclosed location. A smart private eye like you should be able to figure it out by tomorrow night's news."

"Don't kill him, Sid."

"Funny, he's been saying the same thing. But I haven't heard a good reason not to."

"Because he's not the guy who dreamed this whole thing up. He's just the front man."

"What do you mean?" Mink said. He'd been projecting a cold confidence, the kind he would have needed as he was rising up through the ranks in the '60s and '70s, and had undoubtedly lost in recent years. But now Mink sounded less sure of himself again.

"Think about it. Miranda says his mother has been held captive for at least three weeks now. Even in Venezuela, that costs money. You need at least two guys, probably three, to keep up a round-the-clock watch in a kidnapping. Has Frankie Navarro got the kind of money or contacts it would take to recruit a foreign kidnapping team, keep them in supplies for a month, and pay them enough to keep them on the job?"

Mink didn't say anything. Sam could almost hear the rough, scaly skin on Mink's fingers, nervously rubbing the smooth metal of the gun he was about to use to kill Frankie.

"Is he smart enough to put something like this together?" Sam continued. "Is he a deep thinker, a patient guy, or more of an impulsive type?"

"How the fuck should I know?" Mink bellowed into the phone. "All I know about him is he tried to blackmail Miranda. He admitted it. That's good enough for me."

Sam could sense Mink's finger tightening on the trigger. He had to get through to him.

"Of course, he admitted it," Sam said. "He's trying to save his life. But he knows more than he's telling you. If you kill him, you'll never find out who put him up to it. Kenwood will never know. Hell, Kenwood might get another note from Babe Ruth tomorrow afternoon. He'll pay up. Miranda's mother will be dead and somebody else will have gotten away with 50 million, right under your nose."

Again there was a pause. Mink had to realize that he was about to make a big mistake killing Frankie.

"Yeah, well, we took a vote here," Mink finally said. "Three of us want to kill the cocksucker. Even with your vote, it's still three to two. The polls are closed. So long, Skarda."

# Chapter Twenty-two

*Caracas, Venezuela—*

"How much longer?" Elena asked Jefe, in a dreamy, defeated voice.

She lay on the filthy mattress, disgusted by her own smell, beyond hunger and now simply wishing to sleep until someone came to set her free, or until she died. She didn't care which anymore.

Jefe knelt at her side, a plate of *pabellon con baranda*—plantains, rice and beans—on the floor and a forkful of the food in his hand. He held it up to her mouth, but Elena would not open for him. He shrugged and ate the forkful himself.

"*No se,*" Jefe said. "Maybe two days, maybe three. Not much longer."

He scooped up another forkful of the food and held it up to her mouth. Elena rolled her face away from him. A fly landed on the fork, and Jefe blew it away, scattering a few kernels of rice into Elena's hair. He reached out and picked the rice out of her hair, kernel by kernel, and threw it on the floor.

"You must eat," he said to her.

"I don't want to."

He reached over to her and gently turned her chin toward him. She'd been a beautiful woman; Jefe could see that. She still had admirable features, with just enough peasant stock to differentiate herself from the usual society whores of the Venezuelan aristocracy that Jefe hated so much. Elena had new money—her rich ballplayer son had allowed the Mirandas to leap from the working class to the status of landowners. She bore her new station well, but the fierce pride that had been in her eyes the night they'd kidnapped her had all but burned out. Her expensive clothes were now soiled rags, her hair was a tangled, matted mop, and sores were forming on her arms and legs. It couldn't be helped, Jefe told himself; he was not going to wash and dress her each day. But he did have to feed her. A dead hostage does no one any good.

Besides, he liked her. She had shown enough courage, when she still had the strength, to try to escape. She had never lost her dignity or her defiance, and in their conversations she had passionately and convincingly defended the capitalism that had allowed her son to sell his athletic abilities for American riches. But she was now rapidly losing her strength. If she didn't eat, she'd be dead in a couple of days.

Holding her chin, he pulled her lower lip down with his thumb and put the forkful of food to her mouth. She would not move her jaw, but even the effort to keep it from being opened was too much for her. Jefe put the food in her mouth, and to keep from choking on it, she attempted to chew and swallow. It was difficult at first, and she gagged, half sitting up to clear the food from her throat. She managed to take a few more forkfuls, then lay back on the mattress and covered her face with her arms.

"*No mas,*" she said.

"I will put this aside for later. You need more."

"My son is going to pay," Elena said. She had slipped back into her near-trancelike state. "Then I will go home."

"It's not that simple. I have told you before. It is not your son who must pay. We are waiting to hear from Kenwood, who has far more money than your son will ever have."

"Kenwood," Elena said. She repeated the name slowly as though she'd never heard it before, though Jefe had told her who Kenwood was several times.

"A rich Yankee, very rich," Jefe said. "When he pays, you are free to go."

Jefe laughed to himself. He knew enough about American *beisbol* to know that Lou Kenwood, of all people, would not want to be referred to as a Yankee. But Elena would not get the joke.

Jefe wanted this to be over, too. A million dollars—his share—would set him up for life, allow him to leave the police department and become a landowner like the Mirandas—though certainly in another country. But there was so much more to do, and the waiting, the constant watching over Elena, and worrying that someone would discover them, perhaps try to rescue her—it had been a long, aggravating month. He didn't know how much longer he could stand it. Truthfully, if he had not had Elena to talk to, an intelligent, prideful woman instead of those two ignorant fools he'd hired—now down to one—he might have gone crazy. He was earning his million, no doubt. He would not have the slightest pang of guilt when he killed that drunken lecher, Hector. He deserved Hector's share, too.

He was not so certain about killing Elena Miranda. She had been through so much, and he really did admire her son for all he had accomplished. It would have been easy for an Alberto Miranda to accept the crushing poverty and lack of opportunity in Venezuela, slip into a gang, deal drugs, and end up dead or in prison before he turned twenty. That was the fate of so many in Caracas; as a cop, Jefe saw it every day. But, like Jefe, Alberto Miranda wanted more from life, and had the focus and determination to achieve his dreams. Those dreams were about to end, but there were far sadder stories in Venezuela. Soon, it would be Jefe's turn to have what he wanted.

The only light in the shanty came from a table lamp in the corner of the room, on the opposite side from the waste bucket. Elena now dozed on the mattress. Jefe hated it when Elena slept. There was nothing to do here, ever, except talk to her. Hector was not due to arrive for three more hours, and Jefe had no faith in Hector's abilities or character. Now that Paquito was dead—his body carried to the nearest landfill in the middle of the night and dumped like a sack of garbage—Jefe had assumed his shift. He took time off from the police department, stayed later at the shanty and returned earlier, so Hector would not have to put in more hours. He thought Elena's dirty, weakened condition might have lessened Hector's obvious lust for her, but he still hated to take that chance. As Elena got weaker, Jefe wondered if he should just kill Hector now, and assume full-time guard duties. She wasn't going anywhere.

Jefe was sleepily opening and shutting the cover of his cell phone when it rang. He checked the number on the incoming call. Jefe was surprised; he wasn't supposed to get a call for two more days.

"*Hola*," Jefe said.

"How is she?"

"Getting weaker," Jefe said. "I'm trying to make her eat."

"She can't die. Not yet."

"She can't last much longer, and there's nothing I can do about that. She's been here too long."

"Do you have some place you can move her to?"

"Why?"

"There's a detective asking questions. I think he's getting close."

"How can he find us? The only ones who know…"

"I don't trust Frankie. I never have. If that detective finds him, he might talk."

"So kill him."

"Who, Frankie?"

"Him, the detective…kill whoever you have to kill."

"Jefe, I don't know if you've ever been to the U.S., but it's not like Caracas. You don't just kill people here and dump them in the street."

"I have seen that on American TV many times."

"Anyway, get ready to move Elena. Where could you take her?"

Jefe thought for a minute. His house was out; he lived in a nice enough place that the neighbors would notice if Elena managed to wander out of the house, or if they saw Hector coming and going every five or six hours. But Hector—he lived in a place not much better than this shanty. He used to have a wife and three daughters, but they moved out a few months ago after the oldest one accused Hector of touching her. He lived alone now, with nothing, which was why Jefe had known he'd be a good hire for this job. Moving to Hector's house would work for a couple of days. Then, when the money came through, Jefe could blow Hector's brains out in his own house, put the gun in his hand and leave a stupid, illegible suicide note, just the kind a man like Hector would write.

Though she deserved to die in a better place, he would probably have to kill Elena there, too.

# Chapter Twenty-three

"Mink hung up," Sam said.

"He's going to kill Frankie," Miranda said. "My mother will die. Call him back. Please."

"Let me call him," Heather said.

She took the phone from Sam and pushed the redial. Sam wasn't even sure Joey would pick up. Mink might have told him to turn his phone off while they dragged Frankie out of the car, made him kneel down in a ditch, and put a couple of hollow-points in the back of his skull. Nobody liked being interrupted in the middle of a job.

Heather stood in the living room with her right arm across her midriff and her hand under her left elbow, listening to the phone ring. She looked as though she were waiting impatiently for a vendor or a sponsor to answer her call. She showed no signs of panic, despite the reality that this was the most important business call she'd ever made: If she got no answer, or—absurd as it might have seemed, the mobster's voice mail—Frankie Navarro was history, and so was Elena Miranda.

But Heather got through.

"Is this Sid? Oh, Joey. Hi. My name is Heather Canby. I work with Sam Skarda, for the Boston Red Sox. Listen to me: Don't kill Frankie Navarro. My boss will pay you to let him live." There was a momentary pause, then Heather said, "Sure. I'll talk to him."

Heather glanced up at Sam. The cool expression on her face perplexed him. Was she doing this for Miranda, out of concern for his mother? Was she doing it so she could find out who was really behind the extortion plot? Or was she doing it because she was part of Frankie's scam, and was trying to save her co-conspirator's life? Sam wished they printed scorecards for shake-down operations. He had no idea who was playing for which team anymore.

He sat down on a leather armchair and waited to see what happened when she talked to Mink. That's all he could do now. Two lives were in Heather's hands from this point on.

"Is this Sid?" Heather said, turning on the charm in her voice like a charity fundraiser buttering up a wealthy donor. "Hi, Sid. Heather Canby, executive assistant of the Boston Red Sox. Look, I'll make this simple. Frankie Navarro has information we need. We'll pay you $1,000,000 to not kill him."

She waited for a moment, then said, "Any way you like. Wired to a bank account, cash in untraceable bills, securities...you name it."

Another pause.

"Yes, we'd like to talk to him tonight. Where can we meet you?"

She looked around for something to write with. Sam tossed her a small notepad he always kept in his pocket, and a golf pencil with an eraser. He had hundreds of those pencils lying around his house, and he was in the habit of carrying them for taking notes. When one got dull, he threw it away and put a sharp one in his pocket.

Heather wrote something down, then showed it to Miranda.

"How long will it take us to get there?"

Miranda looked at the address and said, "This time of night, twenty minutes, half hour."

"We're in Pacific Palisades," Heather said to Mink. "We can meet you there at...about three. Good. See you then."

She closed Sam's phone and handed it to him. Where he'd failed, a beautiful woman with a million bucks to throw around had succeeded. So much for a dozen years of police training.

"Where we going?" Sam asked.

"Laswell's gym."

Sam did a quick calculation. Laswell's was obviously a comfortable hangout for Navarro. Those human dumbbells he'd bumped into at the gym must have been members of Frankie's gang. Sid apparently wanted to take Navarro back to his own turf to lure the rest of his oiled-up freaks out of hiding. It didn't much matter to Sam who came out of that meeting alive, as long as Frankie was one of them. As for the rest, it couldn't happen to nicer guys. Sam had a passing thought that they ought to invite Kenny and his thugs at Quasar to the party, too.

"All right, this is going to be bad," Sam said. "Heather, you're staying here with Alberto. Write out a check to Mink for a million bucks, or an I.O.U.—whatever mobsters take. I'll bring it with me to Laswell's."

"What are you talking about?" Heather said. "You know I go where you go. That's the deal."

"Not to a mob hit, for Christ's sake."

"Everywhere."

Maybe Mink and his crew would get there first. With any luck, the shooting would be finished by the time he and Heather arrived.

Miranda wanted to come, too, but Sam told him they'd call him as soon as they knew anything.

"Be smart about this, Alberto," Sam said. "You won't do your mother any good if you get shot in a mob crossfire. And if things go down the way I think they will, the cops will show up. When they find you there, you'll make the papers all over the country—'Dodgers All-Star at gangland slaying.' Your family doesn't need to read that."

Miranda nodded helplessly. He looked exhausted. Sam wasn't even sure how he'd found the energy to play ball the last few weeks, and still go out to clubs at night. Well, on second thought, there was the HGH …

Heather walked over to Miranda, whispered something in his ear, and kissed him.

"It will be all right," she said aloud. She held Miranda's hand for a lingering moment. "We'll call you as soon as we know something."

As she and Sam headed to the front door, the ballplayer slumped onto a couch in the living room and picked up a remote control. He pointed it at the floor-to-ceiling audio unit built into the wall, surrounding the wide-screen video monitor. Hip-hop music filled the house. His knees were bouncing up and down, though not in time to the music, and he rubbed the side of his head with the remote. Sam could only imagine what it had been like for this man, with both his career and his mother's life hanging on the edge of extinction for weeks on end. No wonder he'd finally opened up to Heather. He was a 'roided-up bundle of nerve endings, ready to blow.

They were a couple of miles from Miranda's house, Sam driving the BMW down West Sunset toward the ocean, the stars blinking through the light haze overhead and Heather sitting beside him, when he asked the question he couldn't hold back any longer.

"What did you mean, he couldn't do it?"

"I mean, I think the steroids have made him impotent," Heather said.

"How far did you get?"

"Far enough. I suppose you want to know how big he is?"

"Sure. I can't get enough of celebrity penis stories."

Sam heard Heather sigh, and even in the dark, he could sense the disgusted look on her face. He'd seen photos of bodybuilders on stage with their enormous muscles and their minuscule swim suits. That wasn't the only thing that was minuscule; Sam had always assumed that the supplements those guys took to increase muscle mass had an inverse affect on their equipment.

"He's no bigger than you, if that's what you want to know," Heather said.

"I didn't..."

"But he can't do it. He wanted to, and to be honest, so did I."

"I'm having trouble dealing with all this flattery."

"Hey, don't get all possessive on me. It's not about you. Anyway, I just feel bad for the guy."

"Yeah, I know what you mean. Mansion in Pacific Palisades, $20,000,000 per year contract, world-class athletic ability, adored everywhere he goes…"

"You know what I mean. His mother."

"Okay. I'll try to be more sensitive."

"How are we going to get her free?"

"That's not what you hired me for."

"We're paying you to end this, and it doesn't end until Miranda can tell Babe Ruth to fuck off. So what's your plan?"

"I'm really hoping something comes to me by the time we get to Laswell's."

First things first: They had to find out who had bankrolled Frankie—assuming Sam's theory was correct—and then find the bankroller, preferably before the night was over. When the sun came up, it would be Thursday. Then they'd be down to twenty-four hours.

They reached Laswell's gym a little after three. They'd put in a very long day, and Sam should have been feeling the fatigue by now, but the adrenaline pumping through him had kept his eyes wide open on the drive across town. Nothing like the prospect of walking into gangland warfare to hold your attention.

The lights in Laswell's main exercise room were still glowing, though the hours painted on the glass doorway said 6 AM - 1 AM. Sam didn't expect to see Mink's Cadillac on the street in front of the building, and he was correct. If Mink had already brought Frankie here, they must have used an employee entrance behind the building. There was another car on the street by the front door—a dark blue Chevy Impala. Sam parked behind it and got out to look in the Impala's windows. He saw several CD jewel cases by Latino and hip-hop artists in the front seat. Two gym bags and a creased copy of Monster Muscle Magazine were visible in the back seat. It looked like Frankie's pals had already arrived.

Heather had gotten out of the car and was walking to the front door.

"Hold it," Sam said. "Let me go in first."

"Fine with me."

Sam drew his Glock and held it down at his side. He put his left hand on the door handle and gave it a turn. It was open. He pushed the door ajar and took a step into the vestibule. There was an inner door that led to the reception area, where they'd met Kaylee hours earlier. Sam could see through the inner door that she was not around anymore. He couldn't see anyone else, either, though the lights were blazing throughout the building. He opened the inner door and motioned to Heather to follow him. There was no sound anywhere in the gym, but Sam knew people had to be inside, somewhere, or the front door wouldn't be unlocked. The question was, how many of them were alive?

Sam walked cautiously over to the reception area and picked up the receiver on the telephone. He heard a dial tone and gently replaced the receiver. His gaze turned past the idle exercise machines and weight benches to the doorway at the back of the room, the door Roy Laswell had emerged from. That must be where the action was—or had been.

"Hey! Anybody here?"

Sam instinctively dropped to his knees when he heard Heather's piercing shout from a few feet behind him. Maybe Sam hadn't adequately explained the likelihood of encountering trigger-happy wiseguys.

"Shut up," he hissed at her. "Trying to get us killed?"

Heather ignored him and walked down the center row of machines toward Laswell's office. Sam got up from his crouch and followed her, holding the gun out away from his side so he could either drop it or use it, as the situation dictated. Heather reached the door to the back offices, opened it and went down a short hallway. Sam had nearly caught up to her when she turned to her left in an open doorway, looked inside, and put her hand to her mouth.

"Oh. God," she said. She backed into the hallway.

Sam could smell them before he rounded the corner.

The room had a desk, filing cabinets, track shelving with weightlifting and bodybuilding trophies, and the bodies of two men lying on the floor. Both had been shot in the face, one lying atop the other, their blood pooling together in a dark circle beneath them. Sam recognized the guy on top as one of the weightlifters who had tried to push him around earlier. He didn't recognize what was left of the face of the guy underneath. Was it Frankie?

"See, I always thought muscles were overrated."

Sam heard Sid Mink's voice coming from a room on the other side of the hallway. The sign on that door said "Roy Laswell, Owner" but when Sam crossed the hall and looked in the office—plastered with photos and posters of pro athletes and barely human strongmen—he didn't see Laswell. Instead, he saw Mink, Joey Icebox, and Leon, with a brawny, dark-haired man tied to a chair and a gag stuffed in his mouth.

"Skarda, meet Frankie Navarro."

Sam looked Frankie up and down. He was clean-shaven with a dark complexion, at least part Hispanic, and his black hair was moussed up in trendy little spikes. He wore a silver cross on a chain around his neck, and a black sleeveless shirt that showed off his bulging biceps, one of which had a fresh, ugly bullet wound through it, leaving partly dried streaks of blood down his forearm. He had on a pair of navy blue jogging pants with a red stripe on the side, and white running shoes that were spotted with blood. The expression in his eyes was wild and desperate.

Mink sat behind Laswell's desk under a poster of Alberto Miranda dropping his bat and striding out of the batter's box. Mink's curly silver-and-gray hair gleamed like a crown under the fluorescent light overhead, and his eyes sparkled with a renewed vigor that Sam hadn't seen at Dodger Stadium or at the restaurant. The act of snuffing Navarro's posse had seemingly dropped ten years from Mink's round face.

Joey Icebox sat on the edge of Laswell's desk, one foot on the floor next to Frankie. Leon was on the other side of the room, holding a Walther PPK as though he wasn't through using it yet.

"Put your gun on the desk, Skarda," Mink said. Sam did as he was told.

"Who's the babe?" Joey Icebox asked.

Heather was standing behind Sam in the doorway to Laswell's office. Sam was trying to think of a way to get her out of there without having to reveal her identity when she said, "Heather Canby. I work for the Red Sox."

Sam could have groaned out loud.

"I gotta pat you down," Joey said.

It was obvious that Heather had no place to conceal a weapon, but Joey Icebox crossed the room toward Heather as though headed to a buffet line. She sighed and pulled up her top to show her bra, turned around, then hiked up her skirt. She turned back to Joey and said, "Satisfied?"

"Not yet," he said with a grin, but Mink growled, "Joey, calm down."

Mink now had the identities of two witnesses to a gang slaying—just the kind of thing someone in his position would normally find inconvenient. Then again, the more people he killed tonight, the more ways the cops would have to come after him.

"You like Leon's work, over there across the hall?" Mink said. "Face shots are an old custom in this business. Now their mothers can't have open caskets."

Sam knew the best way to get out of this alive was to convince Sid they were on his side.

"Before you kill Frankie, let me ask him a couple of questions," Sam said.

"Be my guest," Mink said. "We're not going anywhere—for a while."

Sam kicked the underside of Frankie's chair, causing the front legs to elevate several inches off the floor and slam back down. The kick had the dramatic effect Sam had hoped for, but it also

made his big toe hurt like hell. Sam ignored the pain and got his face right into Frankie's.

"Are you Babe Ruth?"

Frankie shook his head violently. Sam reached out and pulled the gag out of his mouth. A torrent of words gushed out.

"It wasn't me, God, I swear it wasn't me, I was just doing this for another guy, and I was gonna cut Sid in, even though he would never have known about it, but I had to go behind Sid's back at first because this guy made me swear not to tell."

"What guy?" Sam asked. "I need a name."

"Babe Ruth."

Sam picked up his other foot and slammed it into the seat of the chair between Frankie's legs, shoving him back against the wall so hard that a bodybuilding trophy fell from a shelf overhead. The trophy landed on Frankie's shoulder, near the bullet wound. Frankie cried out in pain.

"That's what he called himself," Frankie whined. "I don't know his name. I swear to God!"

"Then why did you agree to blackmail Miranda?"

"For the money, man. Why else?"

"We've been through all this, Skarda," Mink said. He pulled a fresh cigar out of his pocket and lit it up, throwing the match on what had been an immaculately clean floor. Laswell might have allowed some dirty characters to hang around his gym, but he didn't like a dirty office.

Between puffs on the cigar, Mink explained that he had brought Frankie to the gym after Sam's phone call. Using a key Frankie had for the back door, they'd let themselves in and made Frankie call Mikey and Gino, his two remaining associates—the other one, Jesus, having experienced his own sudden demise earlier that evening. Frankie told them to meet him in Laswell's office, but when they arrived, they met Leon instead, who herded them into the room across the hall and put an end to their greedy, insubordinate lives—using the gun they found in Jesus' SUV, of course.

That got Frankie's tongue moving. Blackmailing Miranda before the World Series was his own idea, but when it didn't work, he decided to let it go. Miranda figured he didn't have to worry about Dr. Whitlinger's injection records, as long as the league wasn't requiring him to take a blood test. He could just deny he'd ever taken HGH, and it would be the word of an international baseball superstar against the word of some nutty chemist that no one had ever heard of.

That's when "Babe Ruth" had contacted Frankie with an offer to split $50,000,000 if he went back to Miranda with a different offer: Go public that you threw the Series, or your mother dies.

"How did Babe Ruth find you?" Sam asked Frankie. "Who knew about the World Series blackmail plot?"

"Just those guys," Frankie said. He gestured out the door with his head. "And Jesus, my bodyguard."

"Could one of them have talked to somebody?"

"Ask him," Frankie said. He glared at Mink, who shrugged.

"How did you know for sure that Miranda's mother was kidnapped?"

"Babe Ruth put me on the phone with the guy who has her. I heard her crying."

"Could be an act."

"They sent a photo. I showed it to Miranda. It's her."

"Where's the photo now?"

"I burned it."

Sam looked at the plain, white-faced clock on the wall opposite Laswell's desk—four a.m. It looked like the night cleaning crew had already been through the building, but Laswell or someone else was likely to arrive soon to re-open the gym. They had to get Frankie out of there and figure out how to find Babe Ruth. And Sam had to get Heather away from what was sure to become a highly publicized crime scene.

"Do you have any idea where Babe Ruth lives?" Sam asked.

"Somewhere in L.A., that's all I know," Frankie said.

"Did you have a phone number for him?"

"No. He always called from pay phones. I checked the num-bers—different every time."

"How were you going to get paid?"

"There was gonna be a drop-off somewhere. He was gonna call me when the Red Sox paid up."

"And Babe Ruth was sure they were going to pay?"

"Yeah. He said, 'I know these people. They're afraid of bad publicity. They'll pay up.'"

Anybody could have guessed that, but something about the way Frankie relayed that conversation resonated with Sam. He'd felt all along that there was something too inside about the case—the way someone seemed to know everything that he did, and everywhere he went. He kept thinking about Paul O'Brien. The guy had seemed totally loyal to the Kenwoods, but Sam still didn't know enough about him to rule him out as the insider.

"Say, sweetie, you mentioned something on the phone about a million bucks," Mink said to Heather. "I kept this scumbag alive for you. Time to pay up."

Sam had wondered how Heather was going to handle this moment—ask Sid if he accepted American Express? But Heather had already figured out her play.

"Not yet, Sid," Heather said. "Not until we find out who Babe Ruth is. If you want to kill Frankie now, go ahead. But he's the only link we have to Babe Ruth, and to Miranda's mother. If you kill him now, Miranda's mom dies, the whole thing becomes public, and the offer's off the table."

"You weren't going to pay, anyway," Sid said angrily.

"That's not true. Lou Kenwood keeps his word, and I speak for Lou Kenwood. You'll get your money when we get Babe Ruth."

"That's a different deal. Make it two million."

"One-five."

"Two."

Heather held Mink's gaze, waiting for a sign that he was bluffing. Finally she said, "Done."

"Cash."

"How am I supposed to get my hands on two million in cash?"

"Lucky Louie sits on the boards of half the banks in this country," Mink said. "You'll find a way."

"I don't suppose you'd let us take Frankie back to the hotel with us," Sam said to Mink.

"Look, Skarda, you should be glad I let the punk live this long. Don't push me."

"Why are you so determined to kill him?" Sam said. "You killed his boys. I think he gets the message."

Mink sighed and leaned his forehead on his hand, tapping his head with his fingers. He flicked an ash on Laswell's desk, took a deep breath and pointed the end of his cigar at Frankie.

"If I let that piece of shit live, every two-bit punk in L.A. is gonna think he can walk all over me. Despite what you might have heard, I run this town—the whole town, see, not just the white neighborhoods, or the black neighborhoods—every neighborhood. Frankie knew the risk he was takin' when he decided to pull this job without my say-so. Now, he pays the price. He dies. End of story. I can't have nobody laughing at me because I didn't clean up the garbage around here."

"Nobody will be laughing when they find those two guys in the other room," Sam said. "And we need Frankie alive."

"Don't worry about Frankie. Anytime you want to talk to him, give us a call. We'll put him on, if he feels up to it."

# Chapter Twenty-four

"Frankie's still lying."

Sam had been silent as they drove back to the hotel, while he played all the scenarios over again in his mind. Something still didn't add up. "Babe Ruth" didn't pick Frankie at random to run the kidnapping scam. He knew about the earlier blackmail attempt. One of Frankie's boys might have talked, but there were other possibilities.

When Sam told Heather that Frankie was lying, she didn't seem impressed with his deductive skills.

"Of course he's lying," she said. "He figures he's going to die by the time this is over, anyway. The sooner he tells all he knows, the sooner Mink kills him."

Sam glanced away from the road to look at Heather. She had brought a red three-quarter-sleeve jacket with her, and had slipped it on when they got back in the convertible for the ride back to Santa Monica. The pre-dawn air was making Sam shiver, but Heather seemed unfazed—either by the temperature or the thought of negotiating a $2,000,000 deal with mobsters. Sam wouldn't have imagined how hard-edged she could be. Even looking at her now, there was a disconnect between the cover-girl looks and the hard-boiled—not to say cynical—analysis that was coming out of those nicely rounded lips. Sam had worked with cops who were more trusting of human nature than Heather was. The violent world they were navigating didn't seem to daunt her, either, though she obviously hadn't enjoyed finding two dead mobsters in a heap at Laswell's gym.

Somewhere along the way, Heather had learned that there wasn't much difference between a CEO with financial leverage and a crook with a gun. Both would use whatever means they had at their disposal to get what they wanted, if they wanted it badly enough. You just had to know when they were bluffing, and when they were ready to pull the trigger.

And then there was Frankie Navarro. What would it take to get him to give up Babe Ruth? A gun to his head hadn't worked. Killing his three soldiers hadn't worked. What did he want—besides his life? Obviously he'd blackmailed Miranda in the first place for money. Heather was already paying Mink to keep Frankie alive. Could she pay Frankie to talk? Probably not. Frankie would see it for the empty gesture it was. What good was money going to do him if Mink killed him?

No, all Frankie wanted now was to live. If Sam could figure out a way to make that happen, he might get Frankie to talk.

"How much do you think Lou would pay to cut this thing short?" Sam asked Heather. "You've already promised Mink two million. It might cost a lot more than that to keep Frankie alive until we find Babe Ruth. How high would Lou go before he just says 'Screw it' and wires the $50,000,000 to the Babe?"

Heather had her arms folded in front of her. She didn't immediately reply. Sam knew she was doing the cost-benefit analysis in her head. They were exiting off the freeway near their hotel when she finally spoke.

"Lou can afford the $50,000,000, and that's probably the most likely way to keep all of this quiet, but he'd sure as hell rather pay nothing. But if he pays off Mink for anything over $10,000,000, with Frankie Navarro still alive, what guarantee does he have that no one talks? One loose end shoots his mouth off, he's wasted enough money to buy a starting pitcher."

"So you figure we've got, maybe, eight million more to work with?"

"Max."

Sam pulled the car up to the valet stand at the hotel, and waited until a young man in a burgundy vest emerged from the lobby to take the keys. It was not quite five in the morning; the sun would not be coming up for another hour and a half. He bought a copy of the L.A. Times from a stack near the front desk and leafed through it as he and Heather rode up to their rooms.

"Good news," Sam said to Heather.

"What?"

"Sox beat the Yankees. They're just four back. And the murders at Laswell's gym won't be in the paper till tomorrow."

◇◇◇

Sam was desperate to get some sleep, but he checked the clock next to the bed and picked up the phone. It was past seven a.m. back in Minneapolis—not too early to call Marcus Hargrove at home.

He heard the sleepy cop's voice answer, "Hargrove."

"Marcus, it's Sam Skarda. You didn't return my call."

"Hey, man, you know what time it is?"

"I need a favor."

"Here's a favor: I won't slap you upside the head the next time I see you."

"Late night?"

"What do you think?"

"How's the kid in the coma."

"He came out. Not doing too good, but looks like he'll live."

"I need you to ask him about a guy named Frankie Navarro."

"What about him?"

"Small-time L.A. mobster trying to make the bigs. Can you run an NCIC search on him, Marcus? I need anything you can get. I wouldn't ask you, but there are lives at stake. And don't let Stensrud know. He already turned me down."

"Hey, you know I got your back, but you gotta tell me what's goin' on here."

Sam couldn't ask Marcus to go fishing without doing him the courtesy of telling him why, but he still had to keep the core issue a secret. He told Marcus he was working for the Red Sox, who were being shaken down by an L.A. mobster named Frankie Navarro. He suspected that it was Navarro who'd sent the Minneapolis gang-banger to whack him, but he had to find out how Navarro knew he'd been hired.

"I know this is a lot to ask, but I've got two more names for you to run," Sam said.

"Hell, all I was gonna do today was arrest a couple of Bloods on a murder charge. That can always wait."

Sam ignored the sarcasm and asked Marcus to run a background check on Paul Eugene O'Brien, thirty-seven-year-old white male, born in South Boston, now a professional chauffeur in Boston. He gave Marcus O'Brien's birth date, address, and Social Security number, and said he once worked as a truck driver and would have had a commercial driver's license, and maybe a Teamster membership, in addition to a chauffeur's license.

"And get me whatever you can on a Bruce Kenwood. He was the son of Lou Kenwood, the Red Sox owner. He drowned somewhere on the West Coast a couple of years ago. See if he left a wife or a kid."

"I'll see what I can do," Marcus said with a sigh. "How soon you need it?"

"Noon."

"You mean noon, my time?"

Sam thought about it. Noon there would be ten in L.A. Hell, he could use more sleep, but....

"Yeah. Call me at this number, or on my cell."

Sam gave him the hotel number, hung up, kicked his shoes off, and crawled under the covers of his bed without undressing.

If Heather came knocking, looking for something to take her mind of Miranda, she could keep knocking.

The call came at 11:30, and pulled Sam out of a sleep so deep and dreamless that he was unsure where he was. He stared at the ceiling, then looked over his shoulder at the palm trees and sandy beach outside his balcony window. Santa Monica. The Loews hotel. The phone. Marcus.

"Yeah, Skarda," he mumbled.

"Got what you wanted," Marcus said. "Ready?"

"Hold on."

Sam sat up in bed and grabbed the hotel note pad and a pen from the nightstand.

"Okay, go."

Frankie Navarro came first. He was 36, born in Albuquerque, moved to L.A. fifteen years earlier after a string of arrests for small-time stuff like burglary and drug possession, now lived in West Hollywood, did a four-year stretch at the Federal Prison Camp in Lompoc, California, for drug distribution, and had been mentioned in several organized crime investigations in L.A. He was also a bit-part player in several action films, the most prominent being "Death Bus." Marcus had an address for him in West Hollywood. Sam took it down.

"I didn't have his acting credits, but the rest of it checks out," Sam said. "What about the punk who shot at us? Does he know Navarro?"

"Nathan DeWayne Shelton denies knowing Navarro, but the way the kid reacted to the name, there's no doubt he's heard of him. He was surprised we knew about Frankie."

"Okay, what about Paul O'Brien?"

Marcus didn't have much of a paper trail on O'Brien, other than that he was thirty-seven, graduated from South Boston High School, now lived in Salem, Mass., had worked for the Kenwood Companies for the last ten years as a driver, was a member of the Teamsters, and had been in trouble with the law only once—arrested for gambling at an after-hours club in South Boston when he was twenty-two.

"What did he do between high school and getting hired by Kenwood?" Sam asked.

"Commercial driving jobs. Delivery truck, courier service, school bus—"

"That gambling bust would keep him from driving a school bus now, wouldn't it?"

"Depends on the school district, I suppose. It wasn't like he was making book. It was just misdemeanor sports betting."

Even so, Sam didn't like the sound of it. He was investigating a sports betting case, and guess what pops up in Paul O'Brien's background check? The primary cash crop of the Boston Mob was gambling. On the other hand, O'Brien had a good job and hadn't been in trouble for a long time. Most wiseguys weren't employed, and didn't have clean rap sheets for fifteen months, much less fifteen years.

"Anything on Bruce Kenwood?"

"I think you're going to find this interesting," Marcus said. "He was the only child of Louis Kenwood and his first wife Mary. Born in Springfield, Mass., went to Phillips Exeter Academy—what's that, some snooty prep school?"

"Yeah. New Hampshire."

"And then a couple of years at Amherst before dropping out. He might have been expelled—can't tell. He enrolled at U.C. Santa Barbara a couple of years later, but never got a degree. He started a couple of businesses in Santa Barbara that went belly-up…"

"What kind of businesses?"

"First real estate, then financial planning. He got nailed for back taxes and did some time in federal prison."

"Don't tell me…"

"That's right. Lompoc."

"Same time as our boy Frankie?"

"The sentences overlapped."

"Then what?"

"Bruce Kenwood got out five years ago. He got into the sports memorabilia business, but that tanked. Investigated for arson after a warehouse fire in Anaheim burned up about thirty million baseball cards from the '80s and '90s that he couldn't sell. Nothing was proven."

"So his insurance company settled?"

"Looks that way."

"Then what?"

"Drowned in the Pacific while sailing. Body was never found."

"Any family?"

"No."

Babe Ruth's face was finally coming into focus. Lucky Louie's son was a serial scam artist and, very likely, an acquaintance of Frankie Navarro. As the son of the owner of the Boston Red Sox, Bruce would have been intimately familiar with Ruth's role in the so-called curse that had hung over the franchise for nearly a century; and as a New Englander, he'd have known how much a betting scandal would tarnish the long-awaited World Championship. If Bruce were still alive, it would explain everything: Bruce, bitter over being excluded from the family business, would be extracting his revenge no matter what happened with Miranda. If his father decided to pay the hush money, Bruce took a huge gouge out of the Kenwood fortune, putting it back in his own bank account. And if Lucky Louie refused to pay, and Miranda went public with the fix story to save his mother's life, the Red Sox owner lost something he valued far more than money.

But Bruce Kenwood was supposed to be dead. If he wasn't, Frankie would know.

Whoever Babe Ruth was, Sam had to convince Frankie that giving him up would be in his best interests. Kicking his chair again wasn't the answer; Sam's big toe still hurt from that stunt.

He rang Heather's room. No answer. He punched her speed-dial entry on his cell phone. She picked up on the third ring.

"Where are you?" he asked.

"At the pool. Come on down."

"No, you come up. I think I know who Babe Ruth is."

"Then get your ass down here and tell me."

# Chapter Twenty-five

Sam put on a pair of shorts and a T-shirt and took the elevator down to the pool, in a courtyard facing the beach and surrounded on three sides by the hotel. The pool was protected from the wind and shaded by perfectly spaced, identical palm trees, each trimmed at the same height. Plush chaises circled the pool, and a patio with umbrella tables separated the pool area from the sand. Dozens of people were sunning on the beach or splashing in the breakers, but Heather had set up shop on one of the lounge chairs at poolside. She wore a wide-brimmed straw hat and sunglasses, a tiny blue string bikini, and was sipping iced tea through a straw while reading a copy of Forbes, strategically propped on her bikini bottom at an angle that did not block the sun from hitting her stomach or thighs.

Heather felt Sam's shadow when he arrived, and put down the magazine.

"So who's Babe Ruth?" she asked.

"Bruce Kenwood."

"He's dead, remember?"

"Maybe. But I don't think so."

Sam pulled up a chair and sat down.

"Did you know?"

"Of course not," Heather said. She lowered her sunglasses and looked into Sam's eyes. "I had no idea."

"Do you know him? Have you ever talked to him?"

"No. All I know about Bruce is that Lou was embarrassed by him and didn't want anything to do with him. As far as I know, Lou hadn't talked to him for years before he died."

"Did you know he was in prison here in California?"

"No, but it doesn't surprise me. Lou said he was no good. That tells you something."

"He was in the federal prison camp at Lompoc the same time Frankie Navarro was there."

"So they knew each other."

"Seems like too much of a coincidence. And they never found a body when Bruce supposedly drowned."

"Where are you getting all this?"

"Cop friend of mine. Don't worry, he doesn't know the whole story."

"Now what?"

"If you're done browning, we have to take a field trip."

◇◇◇

Sam showed Frankie's address to the concierge in the hotel and got directions to Ogden Drive in West Hollywood. As they drove there, Sam explained to Heather that he hoped to find some connection between Frankie and Bruce Kenwood at Frankie's house—perhaps a way to contact Bruce without going through Sid Mink. If they could find Bruce without Frankie's help, it would save Lou Kenwood $2,000,000. And if the $50,000,000 extortion plot failed, Sid Mink just might let Frankie live.

Sam stayed on Santa Monica Boulevard until he got to La Cienaga, then went south to Ogden Drive. He had the radio on, listening for newscasts. Several stations had the story about the two bodies found shot to death in Roy Laswell's gym in Glendale. Apparently the cops hadn't released their identities yet, but at least one station was already going with "execution-style murders" to describe the crime. That news wouldn't help Laswell's business, and Sam wasn't sympathetic.

On the streets of West Hollywood, gawking tourists and gay couples drifted in and out of antique shops, jewelry stores, and trendy restaurants. The basic motif was sweaters tied around the neck and T-shirts with filthy slogans. There wasn't much in the way of glamour on display, but that depended on your definition; Sam's imaginary point of reference was Hollywood in the '30s and '40s, before the hippie music culture took root in West Hollywood. Sam would have loved to be on the Sunset Strip in the short-lived heyday of the Byrds, the Doors, and Buffalo Springfield, but sex and drugs had soon replaced film and music at the core of that scene. He could understand why a star-struck kid like Frankie Navarro would think West Hollywood was the place to be when he arrived from New Mexico, but he could also see why a struggling actor would soon find drug trafficking an easy way to make a living off the desperate and disillusioned kids who ended up here.

Frankie's house was a vaguely Spanish-style bungalow with peeling paint, shrouded in shrubbery and short, fat palm trees and squeezed onto a narrow lot with a one-lane driveway that ran past the house from the street to a garage behind the house. Right out of a Joan Crawford movie. Sam and Heather walked up the front sidewalk, looking around for neighbors or any other signs of life, but it appeared to be a quiet afternoon in Mr. Navarro's neighborhood. Marcus had said that Frankie had no family, so Sam didn't expect anyone to answer the front door when he knocked. He was surprised when the wooden door opened just as he was about to turn the knob.

They were greeted by a sleepy-eyed woman who looked older than she probably was, thanks to day-old makeup and large, fake breasts that looked ready for their 50,000-mile tuneup. She stood in the foyer wearing a long T-shirt and nothing else that was apparent. Her reddish-blond hair was mussed in a way that suggested she'd just gotten out of bed. Sam knew the feeling.

"Yes?" she said, in a voice that was more innocent than the face suggested.

"Hi," Sam said. "My name is Skarda. I'm a private detective. This is my associate, Ms. Canby."

The woman at Frankie's door stared at Heather for an extra beat. Then she glanced back at Sam with the renewed interest of a woman who felt compelled to pull herself together in the presence of a guy who could attract such a good-looking companion.

"Can I help you?" she asked.

"I hope so," Sam said. "This is Frankie Navarro's house, right?"

"Yes. What's he done now?"

"That's what we're here to talk about…Miss…"

"Springs. Fawna Springs."

"Pretty name," Heather said. Sam suspected she was trying not to laugh.

"It's my stage name, but I'm having it changed legally, when I get enough money."

"Mind if we come in, Miss Springs?" Sam asked.

"Call me Fawna. Sure, come on in."

She opened the door, and Sam and Heather followed her past the entryway to a messy kitchen and into a messy living room with throw pillows and magazines on the floor, empty beer cans on the coffee table, and a pair of panties on the back of the couch. The walls were decorated with cheaply framed, crookedly hung movie posters—"Rocky III," "Terminator," and "Under Siege." The carpet was stained with what looked, and smelled, like dog urine. Sam realized the yapping he'd been hearing was coming from somewhere in the back yard.

Fawna sat down on a corner of the couch, pulled up her legs, and crossed them. She was wearing underwear. She lit a cigarette from a pack on the coffee table.

"Where's Frankie?" she said. "He didn't come home last night. He's not dead, is he?"

"No," Sam said. "He's with Sid Mink."

"Oooohhh," Fawna said slowly, as though she knew that should mean something to her, but she couldn't figure out what. The ashtray in front of her was overflowing with butts, so she tapped the ash from her cigarette into a beer can. Sam saw what he thought was cocaine residue on the coffee table. Frankie and Fawna were certainly living the good life in L.A.

"Here's the thing, Fawna," Sam said. "Frankie's in real trouble, and we need to get in touch with a guy named Bruce Kenwood, who might be able to help him out. Recognize the name?"

Fawna tilted her head back and blew a cloud of smoke into the air above her, holding the pose in a way that suggested she was trying to place Kenwood's name. Sam wasn't so sure she wasn't just trying to piece together the verbs and nouns in his sentence to see if she could understand it.

"What was that name again?" she said.

"Bruce Kenwood."

"Uh-uh. Never heard of him."

"Does Frankie keep an address book, or a list of phone numbers, something like that?" Heather asked.

"No. It's all in his head. Frankie's really smart."

Sam saw no point in getting into that debate. Instead, he explained to Fawna that Frankie was being held by Sid Mink—a rather lethal mobster who had a long-standing grudge against Frankie and was keeping him alive only because Heather was paying him to. This arrangement was subject to termination at any time. Frankie's termination. Sam figured Fawna got the parts about money and Frankie not being dead yet.

"What can I do?" Fawna said.

"Let me look around the house and see if I can find any connection to Bruce Kenwood," Sam said.

"Frankie wouldn't like that."

"No, I suppose not. But if I don't talk to Kenwood soon, Frankie will be dead, and none of this will matter. So I don't think he'd mind right now."

Fawna looked troubled. All the expressions on her face—troubled, perplexed, worried, bored, curious—seemed to be poses learned from an acting coach.

"Go ahead," she said. "Our bedroom is next to the kitchen."

Sam started with the kitchen, looking for phone numbers written on scraps of paper, the cover of the phone book, or even on the wall, which wouldn't surprise him in this house. He found one on a matchbook cover, dialed it, and got an auto-repair shop. There was nothing on the refrigerator; normal people put messages to and from themselves on the fridge with magnets, but that was the one place in the house that was free of clutter. Maybe they hadn't heard of refrigerator magnets.

Fawna was right—there was no address book or phone list. Sam wished he could get his hands on Frankie's cell phone, but that was probably in a flood basin somewhere next to a freeway.

"Where do you keep your bills?" Sam called to Fawna, who was still sitting in the living room with Heather. A conversation between the two had yet to materialize.

"Umm…in the bedroom, I think."

Sam braced himself for more disarray, and was not disappointed. The bed looked like it had not been made since the sheets were new—if they ever were new. There was maybe two or three square feet of open floor space between the piles of clothes, though dozens of unused hangers dangled in the open closet. Half the dresser drawers were pulled open, with clothes falling out of them as though trying to hurl themselves onto the floor to join the party. If he hadn't seen the rest of the house, Sam would have assumed someone had already been there ahead of him, turning the place upside down.

There was an end table under a window next to the bed, piled with unwashed glasses, empty Miller Golden Draft cans and bottles, a clock radio running either two hours late or ten hours early, a People magazine, an ashtray, and a bra. No bills there. Sam looked on top of what appeared to be Frankie's dresser and found a stack of envelopes—water company, power company, phone company…

The phone bill was a month old, and the list of numbers called did not immediately reveal anything. Sam walked back into the living room and asked Fawna if she recognized any of the numbers. She looked at it with a squint, handed it back to Sam and shook her head.

"He only calls three people, really," she said. "Jesus, Mikey, and Gino."

Sam took out his cell phone and called the number that appeared most frequently on the list. He got an answering machine that said, "This is Jesus. Leave a message."

No point in that.

He called the other two most-called numbers. One belonged to Mikey, whose answering machine also picked up. When Sam called the last number, he got a tremulous female voice.

"Hello?"

"Is Gino there?" Sam asked. He braced himself for the answer.

"No," the woman said, her voice breaking. "He...he died last night..."

"I'm sorry. Please accept my condolences."

"Who...who is this?"

"Los Angeles County Court. His name came up for jury duty. We'll find someone else."

He hung up.

No other number on the monthly bill had been called more than once. Sam didn't want to go through the list asking for Bruce Kenwood, or Babe Ruth. That wouldn't get him anywhere, and they didn't have time for it. It would be Friday in nine hours.

He spent another half-hour poking through the clutter in Frankie's house—in the garbage pail under the sink, in the urine-splashed magazine rack in the bathroom, amid the piles of especially dirty clothes that had somehow found their way to the laundry room. He even did a search around the pool in the back, where he found piles of dog shit and a couple of used condoms, but no notes, letters, or phone numbers that could lead him to Bruce Kenwood.

He went back in the living room and sat down on an arm chair that smelled like marijuana and taco sauce. Heather was perched on the edge of a folding chair, trying to keep as little of her designer skirt in contact with the household furnishings as possible.

"Okay, that was a waste of time," Sam said. "Now we have to do this the hard way. Fawna, does Frankie have a car?"

"Sure," she said. "He's got a Mercedes in the garage in back. But Jesus usually drives when Frankie goes somewhere."

"Can you drive it?"

"Sure. I mean, not very well. It's a stick. Frankie doesn't let me use it much."

"Good enough. You're going to use it tonight."

# Chapter Twenty-six

Heather turned right off Beverly Boulevard and pulled into the parking lot at Pan Pacific Park, a sprawling complex on the edge of West Hollywood with ballfields, basketball courts, picnic tables, barbecue pits, and an auditorium with a faux-'30s Art Deco-style marquee. It was accessible from several surrounding streets, always busy, and the nearest public place Sam could think of for their meeting with Sid Mink.

He had called Mink and told him he knew who Babe Ruth was—he just needed to have Frankie tell him where to find the guy. He insisted on doing it in a public place where he, Heather, and Frankie could all feel safe. Mink agreed to bring Frankie to Pan Pacific Park at seven p.m., and Sam agreed to bring Heather and $2,000,000 in cash.

Paper bags, cups, and bottles were strewn around the half-full parking lot, and plastic shopping bags were stuck to the low chain-link fence that bordered the lighted soccer field, where two teams of teenagers were playing a game in front of about 50 spectators. Mink's Cadillac was parked next to the fence, near a picnic table, under a eucalyptus tree. There was another black car, a Chrysler 300, next to the Cadillac, with three men sitting inside. Mink had brought even more guys. Great.

Sam told Heather to back into a spot in the row opposite Mink's cars. He got a gym bag from the back seat—a bag he'd found in Frankie's closet—and handed it to Heather. As they walked across the lot, Joey Icebox emerged from Mink's Cadillac and approached them. Sam put his arms out, opened his jacket, and allowed Joey to frisk him.

"I'm not wearing my gun," he said, though he knew Joey would check anyway.

Heather was wearing a sleeveless pink tank top and a turquoise mini-skirt that couldn't have concealed a butter knife. Joey Icebox looked as though he wanted to go in for the full-cavity strip search.

"Take it easy, Joey," Mink said. He pointed to the bag. "The money's in there?"

"Yeah. Where's Frankie?"

This was the part Sam had worried about. Sid Mink didn't have to produce Frankie Navarro. All he had to do was reach over and take the gym bag. Upon opening it, instead of $2,000,000 in cash, he'd find old copies of Us and Entertainment Weekly. At that point, the shooting would start.

But Sam had counted on Mink's desire to find out who Babe Ruth was—who was this guy who had the chutzpah to try to pull a $50,000,000 job right under Mink's nose? He wouldn't find out if he simply grabbed the cash and killed Frankie.

"Leon!" Mink yelled over his shoulder. "Get Frankie out here."

The back door of the Caddy opened, and Frankie Navarro got out of the car, with Leon right behind him, his right hand concealed under a jacket over his arm, prodding Frankie from behind. Frankie's puffy face was various shades of blue and purple, with some dried red for accent. Sam could only imagine what the rest of him looked like under his jacket and running pants. Mink's boys must have worked him over for hours. He looked worse than Stallone ever did at the end of a "Rocky" movie.

They stood facing each other in the middle of the parking lot—Sam and Heather on one side, the battered Frankie flanked by Mink, Joey Icebox, and Leon on the other. Sam glanced over at the other car; the windows were now rolled down and three unfriendly faces stared through them at Sam and Heather.

"Frankie, I know who Babe Ruth is," Sam said.

"Bullshit," Frankie said.

"His name is Bruce Kenwood. Lou Kenwood's son."

"He's dead."

"No. He isn't. You know he isn't. You met him in prison at Lompoc. When he got out he looked you up, found out you'd tried to blackmail Alberto Miranda, and figured out a scheme with an even bigger payday. He's the guy who set up the kidnapping in Venezuela, and sent the extortion note to the Red Sox."

Sam could see why Frankie had never made it as an actor. He was trying to play defiant, but his eyes were saying the game was up.

Mink pulled out a cigar, lit it, and blew a cloud of smoke into the air between them, a smile spreading across his face.

"Son of a bitch," Mink said. "Kenwood's own kid. Makes me glad I never had any."

"Where do we find Bruce Kenwood?" Sam asked Frankie.

"I ain't telling you nothing," Frankie mumbled through his cracked, bruised lips. He looked up at Sam with a question in his eyes: Are you going to get me out of this, or what?

Sam had counted on that. Frankie was still holding out for the one thing he needed: his life.

"We could beat it out of him," Joey said.

"Looks like you already tried," Sam said.

"We'll find that cocksucker sooner or later," Mink said. He looked up at Sam and said, "I think our business is concluded, Mr. Skarda. You got the name. I want my money."

"What about Frankie?"

"His time's up. Hand over the money, and get the fuck outta here."

Joey Icebox took a step forward to take the bag from Heather.

"It's all here," she said. She unzipped it as if to show Joey the bundles of cash. Then she reached in, pulled out Sam's Glock and pointed it at Joey's forehead. Sam took that opportunity to grab Frankie.

"Do what I say and you'll live," Sam hissed into Frankie's ear.

He and Heather backed away from Mink's men toward their convertible. Heather dropped the gym bag in the parking lot and handed the gun to Sam just as the doors to the Chrysler 300 opened and the three men started to get out with their guns drawn. Sam squeezed off two shots, one that shattered the back windshield of the Chrysler 300, the other embedding in the driver's-side door, which was quickly pulled closed again as the three thugs dived out of sight inside the car.

"Keep your hands out of your jackets," Sam said to Joey Icebox and Leon, who were glancing nervously at each other, waiting for an order from Mink, who looked indecisive. An ambush in a deserted fitness club or parking lot was one thing, but gunning people down in the daytime, with dozens of witnesses nearby, wasn't Sid Mink's thing. His mouth hung open as Sam swung the Glock toward him; he probably hadn't had a gun pointed at him in 20 years.

Sam pushed Frankie into the back seat of the BMW, jumped into the passenger seat and kept the gun trained on Mink and his boys while Heather started the car.

"Go! Go!" Sam yelled.

He had time to fire two more accurate shots, taking out the rear tires of the Chrysler 300, and then got off a third that whistled past Mink's head and cracked the rear window of his Cadillac. Heather burned rubber toward the exit. Everyone at the soccer game—kids, parents, referees—had heard the shots and the squeal of tires. They didn't need to be told to dive to the ground, cover their heads, and wait for the shooting to stop.

As the BMW roared away, Mink reached down to look in the gym bag. He pulled out a fistful of magazines and furiously threw them across the lot, then pointed at the receding BMW and yelled something to his men. Joey, Leon, and the three guys in the Chrysler 300 all had their guns out and began firing, but Heather had already put too much distance between them. Sam could see Mink and his men run to their cars. The Chrysler 300 wasn't going to be much use with bullet holes in the rear tires, but the Cadillac was soon following them.

And now the timing had to be perfect. Sam knew that even with Heather's driving skills, the West Hollywood traffic wouldn't let them shake free of Mink. She just had to stay ahead of him for four blocks…

Traffic was sluggish on Beverly Boulevard as Heather got to the end of the driveway and looked for an opening to make a left turn. Then, instead of turning left as they'd agreed, Heather hung a hard right and started heading east.

"No!" Sam yelled. "What the hell are you doing? Follow the plan, goddammit!"

"I just want to try something," Heather said.

Mink's Cadillac screeched out of the parking lot, gained speed and closed on the BMW. The Cadillac had nearly caught them when Heather stomped on the brakes and executed a perfect 180 degree skid-turn. Leon attempted to do the same but nearly lost control of the car, fishtailing onto the boulevard and trapped sideways in front of honking oncoming traffic.

"They never let us do that on the street at performance school," Heather said, grinning.

Once they turned west, Heather veered over to the far right lane, cutting off a Porsche, whose driver slammed on the brakes and the horn simultaneously. Heather then swung back to her left to get around a beer truck, while Mink's Cadillac finally managed to merge into westbound traffic about a block behind them. Leon and Joey could not get a clear shot off, but they were closing the gap as Heather was boxed in by the beer truck on her right, a limo on her left, a minivan with South Dakota plates in front of her, and a double-decker Hollywood tour bus in front of the beer truck. The tour guide stood on top of the bus, speaking into a megaphone while pointing out locations from recent movies.

Frankie was lying face up across the back seat of the BMW, not daring to lift his head high enough to see what was going on. Sam turned around in the front seat and peered past the headrest to keep track of Mink. He could see the Cadillac weaving from lane to lane, trying to make up the distance between them. Sam still had his gun in his hand, but he wasn't going to risk firing a shot in traffic. He knew Sid wouldn't feel so constrained.

They were doing about thirty miles per hour as they crossed Spaulding, then Stanley, and approached the intersection at Genessee. Ogden would be next, but Mink's car was now only one length behind them.

"Remember, you're taking a right at this corner," Sam told Heather.

"I can't," she said. "I can't get over to the right lane. That damn bus is blocking me."

Sam rose from his seat. He was almost parallel to the bus driver, whose window was open. Sam heard the tour guide atop the bus telling the tourists through his megaphone, "We're nearing the location where the lava poured down the street in the movie 'Volcano.' Remember how the cars just melted in that glowing red wave? Talk about global warming!"

The bus driver, a paunchy man wearing checkered suspenders, turned to look out his side window and saw Sam aiming his Glock at him.

"Stop the bus! Now!" Sam shouted.

The driver stared incredulously at the barrel of Sam's gun, then heard a gunshot and saw his side-mount rearview mirror shatter. Sam hunched back down in his seat as the bus driver stomped on his brake. The bus halted immediately, sending the tour guide tumbling forward to his knees and his megaphone clattering onto the street. Heather quickly took the opening, jerking the wheel to the right and cutting in front of the bus in the middle of the intersection to go north on Genessee. Mink's car was stuck behind the bus.

"Not too fast," Sam said to Heather. "Wait until they make the turn. We don't want to lose them."

"What the fuck are you talking about?" Frankie wailed. "Of course we want to lose them!"

Sam heard a shot fired from Mink's car, which was still trying to maneuver around the tour bus.

"Where does Bruce Kenwood live, Frankie?"

"I don't know!"

"Stop the car," Sam said to Heather. He pointed his gun at Frankie's head. "Get out, Frankie."

"What? No—they'll kill me!"

They heard two more shots; one of them hit a palm tree on the boulevard a few feet from them, and the other pinged off the BMW's windshield.

"Where's Bruce Kenwood?"

"Palos Verdes!" Frankie yelled.

"I need an address."

"I'm tryin' to think, dammit! It's 20—no, 2120 Yarmouth Road. Now let's get the fuck out of here!"

Sam looked back at the intersection, where Mink's Cadillac had cleared the tour bus and was now speeding up Genessee toward them.

"Okay, hit it," Sam said to Heather.

Heather slammed the car into gear and sped a block down Genessee, then did a skidding left onto Oakwood Avenue. Sam took out his cell phone and speed-dialed a phone number he'd entered into his directory while he and Heather were at Frankie's house with Fawna.

"L.A. Sheriff's Department, West Hollywood station," he heard the dispatcher answer.

"You know that double homicide at Laswell's Gym in Glendale last night?" Sam said. "The guys who did it have been in a car accident at the intersection of Oakwood and Ogden," Sam said. "Get here fast."

He closed the phone as Heather was reaching Ogden, going close to 60. She hit the brakes and skidded into a right turn, then stomped on the gas again. Mink's car was less than a half-block behind them.

"Hey!" Frankie said, cautiously raising his head above seat level to look around. "That's my house!"

And that was Frankie's Mercedes in the driveway, visible as the BMW gathered speed past Frankie's yard, but not visible to the car chasing them, thanks to a thick hedge separating Frankie's driveway from his Russian neighbor's yard. And that was Fawna sitting in the Mercedes, putting the car into neutral when she heard Heather sound the horn as the BMW sped by. Fawna stepped out of the car and watched it roll down the driveway and into street just as Mink's Cadillac rounded the corner and started to accelerate. At the wheel of the Cadillac, Leon had no chance to stop.

The Cadillac slammed into the side of the Mercedes, spinning both cars around until they were facing in the opposite direction from the vanishing BMW.

The rear half of Frankie's car was caved in, and the hood of the Cadillac had buckled in two and was shoved up against its windshield. Even if Leon had been able to get the smoking engine started again, he couldn't have seen where he was going.

Leon, Joey Icebox, and Mink all got out of the car to look at the damage. Joey noticed Fawna standing in the driveway where the Mercedes had been.

"Hey, you stupid bitch!" he yelled at her. "What the fuck were you thinking?"

Joey strode over to Fawna as though he intended to beat the hell out of her, but as he reached for the cowering woman, they all heard police sirens begin to wail, coming south on Fairfax and getting louder.

Heather had seen the wreck in her rearview mirror; Sam saw it while he looked backward between the front bucket seats. Frankie heard it, but couldn't bring himself to look.

Heather slowed down when she got to Oakwood and took a left. She went two more blocks west, this time under the speed limit on the residential street, until she got to Fairfax. She waited there at a red light as four squad cars roared through the intersection, sirens wailing and lights flashing.

"Nice timing," Heather said to Sam.

"Nice driving," he said.

They exchanged the kind of glances that had led them to bed in the past few days—but things had changed between them. Maybe for the better.

"Have you ever been to Bruce Kenwood's house?" Sam asked Frankie.

"Yeah, once or twice."

"We need to go there now. Can you find it?"

"Yeah, I guess."

"After that, we're going to the airport. You'd better leave town for a while."

"Fine with me."

# Chapter Twenty-seven

Sam was convinced that neither Mink's gang nor the cops were following them, but he had Heather avoid the freeway and take city streets—La Cienega to Washington, Duquesne to Jefferson—until they picked up the 405 near Marina Del Rey. They exited again on Hawthorne Avenue and headed south toward the oceanfront promontory that was Palos Verdes. On the way, Sam gave Frankie the quick version of how he and Heather had tracked him down.

"After I found out you two had been locked up together, suddenly the 'lost at sea' story didn't ring true," Sam said. "The rest was easy to figure out."

Especially when he realized Frankie didn't have the money or the brains to pull off the job himself—but Sam kept that thought to himself.

"So where does Bruce get his money?" Sam asked. "Palos Verdes is a pricey neighborhood, right?"

"Yeah," Frankie said. "Even the pool boys drive Hummers out there."

"And Brucie never got any money from Dad, right?"

"That's what he told me," Frankie said. "Ever since the step-mom came into the picture. But he got almost a million from that insurance settlement when his warehouse burned down."

Frankie told Sam that Bruce Kenwood had been a marked man from the day he walked into Lompoc. Few of the inmates knew who his father was, but the stink of privilege, prep school, and wealth was all over him. He was immediately dubbed Preppie, and then Richie Rich, and then Richie Bitch. By then he was literally the bitch of one of the nastiest prisoners in Lompoc, an arson and forgery specialist named Dingo. Bruce never ratted out Dingo for repeatedly raping him, possibly for fear of being murdered, but more likely, Frankie speculated, because the arrangement came to suit him. No one messed with Bruce as long as he was Dingo's bitch.

"Did you ever have a go at him?" Sam asked Frankie.

"Hell, no," Frankie said. "I wasn't in there long enough to turn queer. Can't say the same for Brucie, though."

"What do you mean?"

"I mean, maybe he liked it. How do you put up with that shit night after night unless part of you kind of gets off on it? Bruce is a strange dude, man."

"But you got to know him."

"We were on the same cell block. I'd, like, talk to him at chow, or, you know, in the exercise yard. Hell, I felt sorry for him—at first. But as long as Dingo was around, he was safe."

"What happened to Dingo?"

"Somebody strangled him in the shower. He was a real prick."

"How did Bruce manage after that?"

"Not too well, I'd guess. But that's about the time I got out."

"How much longer before he contacted you?"

"A few years, maybe."

Frankie said he'd gotten a call from Bruce after the Red Sox won the World Series. He wanted to meet Frankie for a drink, and Frankie figured it couldn't hurt. He'd already decided to take the Bugsy Siegel route to the top in L.A. He was going to be a smooth, good-looking crime boss who knew all the Hollywood heavy hitters—and he wanted to know anybody in town who had money, or could pull strings for him. Bruce Kenwood's dad was a big shot. So what if he'd taken it up the chute in prison? A guy did what he had to do.

When they met at a bar, Frankie had the creepy feeling that Bruce was hitting on him. Hard to blame the guy, Frankie told Sam, when he saw the kind of shape Frankie was in. He'd been in a couple of movies and was hoping for more work, so he kept his weight down, his reps up, and his hair looking good. The side benefit was that the two-bit mobsters who used to blow him off before he went to prison were starting to treat him with more respect. Frankie felt like a guy on his way up. Maybe Bruce Kenwood could help him.

They talked about the movies. Frankie was looking at trademarking some kind of nickname—maybe the Satin Latin, or the Hispanic Panic.

"You know, like Stallone was the Italian Stallion," Frankie said. Sam glanced over at Heather, who was doing her best to keep from laughing.

Then Bruce had switched subjects. He wanted to talk about sports. He'd been in the memorabilia business, which hadn't worked out too well, but he was still looking for a way to make some money off the pros. Frankie asked him why he didn't just go to work for his dad, but Bruce said that would never happen. Then Bruce said he'd heard that Frankie pumped iron with some of the Dodgers. He asked right away about steroids.

"Did that piss you off?" Sam asked.

"Nah," Frankie said. "Some guys get pretty touchy about that, but I figure, all of them action heroes did it, and they made it big in the movies. I don't tell the world, but why should I be ashamed? When I show up to collect a debt, nobody asks me if my biceps are real. Which reminds me, I got a bullet hole in my right arm that I should get looked at."

"Maybe we can help you out with that," Sam said. "Tell me more about meeting with Bruce."

Frankie and Bruce had gotten to talking about which major leaguers were using illegal substances, and Frankie finally mentioned trying to blackmail Miranda. Bruce got real interested, but Frankie said Miranda couldn't be blackmailed. He wasn't afraid of the Commissioner finding out he'd used HGH—they couldn't test for it, so he thought he was safe. That's when Bruce said he knew a way they could make a lot more money off Miranda than by blackmailing him. Bruce said it would take him a while to put everything together, but he'd call Frankie when the plan was set—if Frankie was interested in making about $25,000,000.

"Interested? Shit, yeah, I was interested," Frankie said.

Then Frankie read about the sailing accident, and how they couldn't find Bruce's body. So much for that, Frankie figured. But he got a call from Bruce a while later, inviting him over to his house. Frankie asked him what the fuck was going on—he was supposed to be dead. That's what I want people to think, Bruce said.

Bruce was alive, all right, living in a house in Palos Verdes. When Frankie got there, Bruce poured him some top-shelf booze, rolled some very potent joints, and went through the extortion plan. He'd found some guys to kidnap Miranda's mom in Venezuela; all Frankie had to do was make the contact with Miranda, and send the letter to Lou Kenwood. Bruce would take care of everything else.

"How did you know Kenwood had hired me?" Sam asked.

"Bruce told me."

"How did he know?"

"You got me."

Sam again looked at Heather.

"It wasn't me," Heather said. She brushed a strand of blowing hair out of her eyes. "I told you that."

"Bruce just said Kenwood hired a dick, and I should take care of it," Frankie said. "I put out two contracts on you, but I didn't hire the best people. I figured that would change when I got Kenwood's money."

"Do you think it was O'Brien?" Sam asked Heather. "I found out he got popped once in Southie on a gambling charge."

"I don't know. He always seemed loyal."

"Most guys are loyal to whoever pays best," Frankie said.

They stayed on Hawthorne as it became a winding residential street in the hills of Palos Verdes. They occasionally caught glimpses of the ocean to the west, but Bruce Kenwood's house was on a sloping, tree-shaded lot that faced east.

"Bruce is supposed to be dead," Sam said. "Who owns the house?"

"It's in his girlfriend's name," Frankie said.

"Girlfriend? Who's that?"

"Kimberly something. I never met her, but Bruce says they've been living together here."

That complicated things. Sam had been hoping to surprise Bruce, show a little force, maybe wave his gun around for effect, and scare him into admitting the whole plot and telling them how to find Elena Miranda. There was no telling how much the girlfriend knew, or what she was willing to do to protect Bruce.

They might both give it up immediately.

Or they might be armed, desperate, and willing to pull the trigger.

There was a light shining through the only window that faced the street. Sam told Heather to drive the car up the hill past the house and park it a block away. He didn't want Bruce to spot them coming; he also didn't want Heather getting in the way if Bruce got desperate and began shooting, but he knew he couldn't talk her into staying in the car. He decided to send Frankie to the door. Bruce would have no way of knowing what had happened in the last twenty-four hours. He probably wouldn't be happy to see Frankie show up without an invitation, but he wasn't likely to shoot him, either.

In Minneapolis, Bruce Kenwood's one-story ranch-style house with the three-car garage in front might have sold for $400,000; here, Sam knew it would easily list for over $1,000,000, even without an ocean view. There were nice landscaping touches around the yard—the driveway was lined with purple and white flowers, and there was a two-tiered fountain with a small statue of a nymph inside a brick-lined pool, surrounded by stone pavers and three dwarf orange trees. Yet even in the dark, the property looked run-down; the driveway flowers were wilted or dying, there was no water in the fountain, the lawn hadn't been mown recently, the oranges on the trees looked diseased, and the stucco on the front of the house was cracked.

Frankie walked up the sloping driveway while Sam and Heather stood in the shadows against the side of the garage. There was a porch light above the front door, but the nearest streetlight was half a block away, and Bruce didn't have a yard light. Sam heard Frankie ring the doorbell, wait 20 seconds and ring it again. Then he heard the door open. He cautiously peered around the side of the garage and saw a woman of perhaps 40 standing in the doorway, talking to Frankie. She wore a pair of khaki walking shorts that showed off smooth, tanned legs. Her floral print shirt was untucked, and the tails were tied across her midriff. She had thick, curly brunette hair that hung below her shoulders, and she twirled a few strands of hair in her right hand as she talked to Frankie. She looked safe enough. Sam decided to introduce himself.

"Come on," he said to Heather. They walked around the corner of the garage to the front door. He kept his gun in the shoulder holster, but his jacket was open. He could get to it in a second, if necessary.

"Evening," Sam said to the woman in the doorway. "Kimberly, is it?"

"Yes," she said, in a low, wary voice. "Who are you?"

"A friend of Frankie's here. This is Heather Canby. We're looking for Bruce."

"As I told—Frankie, is it?—Bruce is out of town."

"When will he be back?"

"Saturday—or was it Sunday? This weekend, sometime."

She smiled at Sam, but something was going on. She knew. She was lying for Bruce. She should have been less polite and more freaked out about three strangers showing up at her door at night. She didn't ask what they were doing there, or demand to see I.D.'s. Unless Bruce got visits like this all the time, Kimberly was covering something up.

"I'd offer you something, but it's really very late," she said. Her eyes suggested that she was about to go back inside. "Can I tell Bruce why you were here?"

"It's about sports collectibles," Sam said.

"I'm sure he'll be interested. He could call you. Do you have a card?"

Sam did, but he wasn't going to give her his private investigator's business card. Heather opened her purse and handed Kimberly her card. Kimberly scanned it quickly.

"Oh, the Boston Red Sox," Kimberly said. "Bruce will be sorry he missed you. If that's all…"

Now Sam knew she wasn't being straight with them. Bruce Kenwood wouldn't live with a woman for any length of time and not tell her—if she didn't figure it out for herself—that he was the son of the owner of the Red Sox. But Sam wasn't going to force himself into her home at gunpoint and make her tell him where Bruce was. There had to be some other way.

He looked at Heather and shrugged.

"Guess we're done here," he said.

"I guess so," she said. "Nice to meet you, Kimberly."

Heather reached out to shake hands. She seemed to be examining the bone structure of Kimberly's hand, turning it sideways and rolling the fingers in her palm. Then she pulled Kimberly forward suddenly, reached up with her left hand and grabbed Kimberly's hair. With a downward yank, the wig came off.

"Bitch!" said the man, who was wearing a tight nylon skullcap under the wig. His voice dropped to a lower register.

"Jesus Christ!" Frankie said. "Bruce?"

Bruce Kenwood pulled his hand free of Heather's and tried to get inside the house, but Sam kicked the door shut as Bruce tried to slip through it. His hand was caught in the door frame, and he screamed in pain. Sam grabbed Bruce by the chin and pushed it upward so the top of his head was pressed against the house. The Adam's apple and razor stubble were now apparent. Sam slammed his fist into Bruce's stomach; he doubled over, moaning and gasping for air. Frankie got in a punch with his good arm, too, but Sam pushed him back, opened the front door and shoved Bruce inside. They followed him in.

Sam gave Bruce another hard push backward toward the couch, and he fell into it, not putting up a struggle. He looked up at Sam, Heather, and Frankie, who stood around him in a semicircle, glancing quickly back and forth from one to the other. His hand slowly went up to the top of his head, pulled the hairnet off and threw it on the floor. A lazy grin spread across his face, and he started to laugh.

"Took you guys long enough," Bruce said, like a teenager who'd been caught making prank phone calls.

The interior of the main floor was designed as a great room, with a large fireplace between the living and dining areas. The walls were decorated with framed posters of Fenway Park and the Green Monster, and portraits of famous Red Sox players: Ted Williams, Carl Yastrzemski, Carlton Fisk, Roger Clemens. The biggest portrait of all hung on the wall above the couch in the great room: a young, trim Babe Ruth, standing in front of a row of empty bleachers, his hands on his hips, RED SOX arched across the front of his pure white jersey. The Babe's soft, small-brimmed ballcap was tilted over his left eye; his face had not totally filled out yet, but the wide nose and broad upper lip were unmistakable. The Babe was staring hard at something slightly to the right of the camera, as though he saw his future coming—the brief ascendancy in Fenway, followed by glory with the Yankees as the Red Sox crumbled—and didn't know exactly what to make of it. His pensive gaze dominated the room, making Sam want to turn and look over his own shoulder to see what the Babe was staring at.

So this was it—the house that Ruth built, so to speak.

"One more day, and Dad would have sent the money," Bruce said. "It's Heather, right? He was going to pay up, wasn't he?"

"Probably," Heather said. She looked at the slim, fey man on the couch with a mixture of amazement and repulsion.

"Where's Elena Miranda?" Sam said. He took a half step closer to Bruce, in case he doubted Sam's willingness to get rough with him again. But Bruce kept grinning, almost as though he was hoping for more.

"Oh, she's in good hands, but I don't know how much longer," Bruce said.

"If she dies, you will, too," Sam said. "Kidnapping is a capital offense."

"I know," Bruce said. Then, as if answering a test question: "The death penalty for kidnapping was reinstated in 1994. Big whoop. I guess this means you're willing to have this whole story become public. Dad will love that."

His smirk vanished, and he glared at Heather. She did not back down from him, but instead shook her head slowly in utter contempt.

"Just tell us where Mrs. Miranda is," Heather said. "If she dies, Alberto won't have any reason to keep quiet. But if we can get her back alive, nobody has to know about this."

Bruce put his hand over his mouth and made a show of yawning.

"C'mon, Brucie, the game's over," Sam said. "Your only way out of this is to tell us where Elena is."

"She's in a shanty in Caracas, right under the cops' noses. At least she was. But I told my man down there to move her yesterday. I'm not sure where she is now."

"Who's your man?"

"A deputy police chief named Guillermo Llenas. They call him Jefe."

"So, if we find Jefe, we find Elena."

"Yes, but you've got a little problem."

"What's that?"

"If anything goes wrong, he's supposed to kill her."

"So call him and tell him your dad paid up," Heather said.

"It won't matter," Bruce said. He looked at Sam with satisfaction in his smile. "He's supposed to kill her if Dad pays, too."

Heather let out an exasperated groan. There didn't seem to be any way out; the story was going to hit the papers as soon as Elena Miranda's body was found. Sam understood the public-relations nightmare she was looking at. He could see the words in enormous type on the front pages of the Globe and the Herald: "Kidnap," "Red Sox," "Murder," "Extortion," "Steroids," "Blackmail," "Organized Crime," "World Series," and worst of all, "Fix." The reporters would be digging through the details for months, every new revelation leading the local newscasts. Eventually, after the criminal charges, lawsuits, and trials ended, and after all the books were written, the truth might eventually sink in with the public. Until then, the Red Sox, Cardinals, all of Major League Baseball—and Lucky Louie—would have the stench of scandal clinging to them.

"Call Jefe," Sam said to Bruce. He took his gun out of his holster and held it with the barrel pointing to the ceiling. "Call him and tell him the whole deal is off. Let her go. Get out while there's still a chance to save yourselves from prison, or the electric chair."

"He'll know it's a bust, you bonehead," Bruce said. "The second he gets a call from me telling him to let her go, he'll kill her. Kidnapping is a death-penalty offense in Venezuela, too—doesn't matter what happens to the victim. He might as well kill her—if she's alive, she can identify him."

Sam and Heather locked eyes, hitting on the same thought simultaneously. They didn't dare call the Caracas police, because at least one of the cops was in on the kidnapping. There could be more cops involved, and they would have no idea which ones they could trust. Elena's only chance was for them to go to Venezuela and find her.

It was nearly ten p.m.—there might still be time to get on a plane.

"I'll call the airport and see if they can get us two seats to Caracas tonight," Heather said.

Heather already had her phone out of her purse and was punching 411 on to her keypad.

"Make it three," Sam said.

Heather stopped and looked quizzically at Sam.

"Three seats?"

"We don't know squat about Venezuela, and we have no way of finding this guy, Guillermo Llenas," Sam said. "But we know somebody who does."

Heather smiled and sat down at the dining table to make the calls.

# Chapter Twenty-eight

Sam paced the living room, trying to focus on what they could do when they got to Caracas. But he kept glancing at the smirking face of Bruce Kenwood, sitting comfortably on the couch in his designer shorts and print blouse. There was a hint of foundation on his face, a touch of blush, a tasteful stroke or two of mascara and eye-shadow, and a light application of rose-colored lipstick. Frankie, meanwhile, was seated across from Heather at the dining table, his jacket draped over a chair, clenching and unclenching his right fist and rubbing his left hand over the ugly dried bullet hole in his arm. He kept glancing out the window.

A more unlikely pair of conspirators, Sam had never seen—the foppish preppie cross-dresser and the vain, ambitious hustler with B-movie looks whose only talent was violence. It was surprising enough that they'd ever met—but to almost pull off a $50,000,000 extortion plot, right under the noses of both the mob and Major League Baseball...

"Why the women's clothes, Bruce?" Sam said.

"After I faked that sailing accident, I needed a new name. I figured, why not be a woman? I have to say, I've enjoyed it."

"So you're a transvestite?"

"To tell you the truth, Skarda, I don't know what the fuck I am. I used to think I might be bi. Then I was somebody's bitch in prison. And now—well, let me put it this way: You and Heather both look pretty good to me. She *is* good, isn't she?"

"Shut your mouth."

"Touchy, aren't we? Think Dad knows you're screwing his girlfriend? Aren't there any ethics in your business?"

"I didn't know she was his girlfriend," Sam said. "How did you know?"

"Lucky guess. I know Dad. He dumped Mom for an office bimbo who looked like Heather."

Sam glanced at Heather, who had her phone to her ear and didn't react to Bruce's comment. Maybe she was tough enough to withstand the leers and wisecracks she'd face when she married Kenwood. She was certainly calm enough now, taking the insults of her would-be stepson without flinching. If Sam had been in her place, he'd have kicked Bruce in the balls. But Heather was made of some tough stuff; along with her training in risk management, marketing, mergers, acquisitions, and balance sheets, she'd prepared herself for being hated.

"So who was your inside source? Paul O'Brien?"

"Yeah."

"He told you they hired me?"

"That's right."

"What's his cut?"

"A million."

"What were you trying to accomplish?" Sam asked. He'd figured out the who and the how, but the why still didn't make any sense. "Wasn't there any other way to get some of your old man's cash?"

"Not this much," Bruce said. He crossed his legs and looked at a pack of cigarettes on an end table next to the couch. "Mind if I smoke?"

"No—in fact, I'd like to be there to watch you fry," Sam said.

"I meant a cigarette, asshole," Bruce said. He reached over for his pack of Marlboros. Every East Coast college man Sam ever knew smoked Marlboros.

"So why the elaborate plot?" Sam persisted.

"Look, it wasn't about money," Bruce said. He lit his smoke and inhaled. "Not to me."

"It was to me," Frankie said.

Bruce waved his hand with the cigarette at Frankie and rolled his eyes.

"I wanted to embarrass my father," Bruce said to Sam. "Even a low-grade intellect like you ought to be able to figure that out. He divorced my mother, married that gold-digging bitch, and suddenly nothing I did was good enough for them.

"You know, my dad basically forced me to become a Red Sox fan when I was a kid. He made me play Little League. He took me to dozens of games at Fenway every summer. He quizzed me on the box scores at breakfast every morning.

"At first I hated all of it—I couldn't hit and I couldn't throw. Even the fat kids in school ran faster than me. Dad called me a sissy. He was disgusted that I didn't like to play baseball. But after I read a book about Babe Ruth, it all took hold. His father abandoned him at that orphanage. I identified with him."

"Sorry, Bruce, but I don't see it," Sam said. "Babe Ruth was a throwaway kid from the Baltimore slums, and you're the son of one of the richest men in America."

"You don't get it, because you're like everybody else—an ignorant moron. After my father divorced Mom and married Katherine, he exiled me to prep school. I was 12 years old. He never visited. He was—oh, let me think, what was the excuse? Wait, I've got it—'too busy.'

"The Babe was never too busy to do something for a kid. He was just a big kid himself. He never judged anybody, even though they always judged him. Once I got the Babe, I started to get the game. I read everything I could about the Red Sox, and all the stupid mistakes they've made—starting with selling the Babe to New York.

"Look around at this place. It's my fucking shrine to the most inept team in baseball history. Ted Williams—greatest hitter since the Babe, never won a World Series. Carl Yastrzemski—played twenty-three years, all with the Sox, won a triple crown, but never won a Series. Carlton Fisk—hit one of the most famous homers in World Series history, but the Sox didn't win, and then they lost him when they forgot to mail his fucking contract. Roger

Clemens—maybe the best pitcher of the past century, six Cy Youngs, but never won a Series in Boston.

"There should even be a picture of Willie Mays. Did you know they gave him a tryout, but didn't sign him because he was black?"

Sam nodded. It was a familiar story.

"I was like every fan in New England," Bruce said. "I grow up thinking that I could have done better running the team—and then my Dad buys them. I'm in heaven, right? By then, I knew so much about baseball I could have run any department in the organization. But I got in some trouble in college, and that gave my dad and my stepmom all the excuse they needed. They didn't want me anywhere near the team. So I said, fuck them, I'll make it on my own."

"And how'd that work out for you?" Sam said.

"You apparently know all about me—you tell me."

"You get popped for tax evasion, you go to prison, the Sox finally win the World Series, your dad is the hero of New England, and you're no part of it."

Bruce nodded, but didn't look up.

"So you decided to take a big bite out of your dad's bank account, and spoil his greatest achievement. If it all becomes public, so much the better. Am I close?"

"If you say so."

Heather got up from the table, holding her cell phone at her side and said, "Sam, I can get three on the 2:15 a.m. flight to Caracas. It gets there at 2:45 tomorrow afternoon. Alberto will meet us at the airport. But there's a problem. Do you have your passport?"

"Yes. I bring it with me whenever I leave town. Habit."

"Well, I didn't bring mine."

"Then it looks like you stay here. Alberto and I can handle this."

"No fucking way. Alberto won't go without me."

"Then we do have a problem."

Sam stared at the ceiling, trying to think of someone he knew who could expedite a passport clearance for Heather. Passports were administered by the U.S. State Department. Maybe someone with the Minneapolis bureau of the FBI? No—Sam didn't have a pal in that office, and even if someone there could eventually get through to a State Department official at this time of night, it would take too long. Someone from Augusta National? He knew of at least one former secretary of state who was a member there. But Sam would have to go through David Porter to contact him; he didn't have Porter's number, and had no way to know where he might be tonight.

Augusta reminded him of Caroline. Caroline worked for Citizenship and Immigration Services, which used to be the INS. Last Sam knew, the INS was part of the State Department. Maybe...

He punched Caroline's number on his speed dial, and heard her sleepy voice. It was getting late in Tucson, too.

"Sam? I was about to go to bed."

"Alone, I hope."

"No, with David Letterman. You don't usually call this time of night. What's up?"

"Caroline, I need a huge favor, and I'm in a hurry. I'm working a case in L.A., and we need to get on a plane tonight for Caracas."

"We?"

"My...uh...client. Trouble is, she doesn't have her passport with her. We flew out here from Boston."

"That's tough," Caroline said. She didn't sound the least bit sympathetic.

"Do you have any contacts in the State Department? She's got a passport. She just doesn't have it with her. There's got to be a way to get her on the plane."

"Why does it have to be tonight?" Caroline said. "You could have somebody overnight her passport, and fly out Saturday."

"Too late," Sam said. "A woman will be dead by then."

"Then maybe the police ought to be handling this one," Caroline said. There was an edge in her voice that reminded Sam why he and Caroline were giving each other space. The daughter of a career military man, Caroline understood cops and soldiers all too well. She'd been determined to not get involved with a man like her father, who felt it was his duty to risk his life. Sam knew this was exactly the kind of phone call Caroline didn't want to get from him.

"Caroline, please," Sam said. "I have to keep the cops out of this. It can't become public. I can explain why later, but for now, if there's a phone call you can make, I'm asking you to make it."

"I don't know, Sam," Caroline said. "It's late. And we're not part of the State Department anymore. We're Homeland Security now."

"Call your boss. He must know somebody at State. Whatever it takes. We've got to get on that plane."

"Can't you go alone?"

"I'd love to, but…it's complicated. I can't prevent a murder if we don't both get to Venezuela."

Caroline was silent for a moment. Sam didn't blame her a bit for hesitating. He was asking her to put her own credibility on the line for him, when he couldn't even tell her what the case was about. He also might be asking her to do the impossible.

"What's her name?" Caroline finally asked.

"Heather Canby. She lives in Boston."

"I need her full name, address, birth date, and Social Security number. And I need the airline and flight number."

"I'll get it. Thanks, Caroline."

Sam got the information from Heather and relayed it to Caroline, who repeated it back to Sam—making a special point to emphasize the year Heather was born. Sam let it go. Caroline said she was pretty sure her boss could get through to an under-secretary at the State Department.

"Don't take any stupid risks—please, Sam."

"I won't," he said. He glanced at Heather, and then felt an overwhelming urge to tell Caroline he loved her. But it wasn't the right time.

After hanging up, he told Heather they were leaving for the airport.

"What about me?" Frankie said.

"We'll take you with us. After we get to the airport, you're on your own."

"And me?" Bruce said.

"Frankly, my dear..."

Sam heard a car pulling up to the curb outside the house. He looked out the window and saw that the car's headlights were off. He quickly crossed the room and flipped a light switch. The overhead light fixture went out, but a floor lamp near the window remained lit. Heather went to the side of the window, reached over and turned it out while Sam crouched next to the couch. The house was now in darkness, and Sam could make out the car in front of the house.

"It's the Chrysler 300 from the park," he said to Heather. "The rear window has plastic taped over it. They must have changed the tires."

"How did they find us?" Heather said quietly.

"I don't know. I guess Mink has his ways."

"Who's Mink?" Bruce asked. Suddenly he didn't sound so smug.

"Sid Mink. He's the cocksucker that killed my friends," Frankie said. "Thanks to you."

"Do you have any guns in the house, Bruce?" Sam asked.

"Yes. One."

"Get it."

Bruce got off the couch and ran down a hallway. Sam heard the sound of a drawer being opened and closed. He came back with something gleaming and metallic in his hand, though it was too dark to see what kind of gun it was.

"Don't get any stupid ideas, Bruce," Sam said. "If you shoot us, there'll be no one between you and Mink's guys."

"Who…the FUCK…is Mink?" Bruce almost screamed.

"L.A. mob. He's very upset with you and Frankie."

Bruce groaned.

Then a bullet shattered his front window and hit the portrait of Babe Ruth. A volley of gunshots ripped through the window and embedded into the back wall of the great room. Bruce dived for the floor, where Sam, Heather, and Frankie already were pressing themselves as flat as they could get.

"Give Frankie the gun," Sam said.

Bruce slid the handgun across the wood floor to the spot where Frankie was curled up. Frankie looked it over as well as he could in the dark.

"Smith & Wesson?" Frankie called to Bruce.

"How the fuck should I know? I just thought I should have a gun in the house. I traded a '56 Mantle for it."

"Is it loaded?"

"I have no idea."

Frankie pulled back the slide, got into a crouch and fired four shots at the car parked in front of the house, then dived back to the floor.

"Do you have another clip?"

"What's a clip?"

Sam knew this standoff wouldn't last long. The mobsters weren't going to stand at the end of the driveway and have a firefight in the middle of a residential neighborhood. The cops were already on their way. All he cared about was getting out of the house before the thugs could finish the hit. Whatever happened to Bruce and Frankie—well, they'd earned it.

"Where's your back door?" Sam said to Bruce.

"Through the dining room, take a left. It's off the kitchen."

"What's in your back yard?"

"A deck. A garden."

"Is it fenced?"

"Yes. Six-foot redwood."

"Is there a gate?"

"Yes. Off the garage, left side of the house."

"Locked from the inside?"

"I can't remember."

"Heather, let's go," Sam said. "I really hate getting shot at."

Sam crawled toward the dining room as another barrage of bullets screamed through the broken window. The portrait of the Bambino was hit again; it dropped off the wall, bounced off the couch and clattered to the wood floor. Heather stopped crawling until the shooting ceased, then crab-walked on all fours to the dining room. Frankie stood up and pumped several more shots toward the street.

"You can't leave!" Bruce yelled at Sam. "They'll kill me!"

"I hope so," Sam said. "But I think Frankie can handle this."

"Thanks, amigo," Frankie said, sounding like the action hero he'd always wanted to be. "But what about that ride to the airport?"

"Some other time," Sam said.

He grabbed Heather's hand and dragged her up to her feet. They sprinted out of the dining room and through the kitchen, which had utensils, pots and pans hanging from a chef's rack above a center cooktop island. A sliding glass door led out to the deck. Sam glanced through the door and saw a dark figure coming around the left corner of the house toward the deck. He pulled Heather to the floor.

"It's Joey Icebox," Sam said.

Joey was holding a gun in his right hand and taking cautious steps up to the deck, trying to see into the house.

"You go out first," Sam told Heather.

"Me? Why me?"

"Because he won't kill you."

"How do you know?"

"You're a woman. Mobsters mostly whack guys."

"Mostly?"

"Look," Sam whispered. "To a mobster, there's just two kinds of women: Madonnas or whores. Madonnas are off-limits when it comes to hits. Their mothers and sisters are Madonnas."

"What about whores?"

"Look, we're running out of time. You distract him, and I'll take care of the rest."

Heather got up from the kitchen floor and grabbed the handle of the sliding door. Joey saw her in the window and pointed his gun at her. Heather smiled at him and opened the door, walking out onto the deck.

"Where the fuck do you think you're going?" Joey said. Then that look came over him again, the one where he began visually stripping her, in anticipation of doing it for real.

"I'm getting out of there," Heather said. She walked past him toward the steps that led down off the deck. "I don't want to get killed."

Joey turned to grab her arm as she walked by. He put his hand on the strap of her tank top and began yanking it downward. Heather tried pushing him away, and as they struggled, Sam stepped quietly through the open door, out onto the deck, and swung the metal skillet he'd taken from the chef's rack. The sound of cast iron hitting skull was a mixture of a clang and a crunch as Joey collapsed in a heap on the deck.

"Why didn't you just shoot that slobbering pig?" Heather said as she pulled her tank top back into place.

"Strict office policy at the Skarda Agency: Never shoot a mobster. It's grounds for instant dismissal."

They heard more gunshots coming from the front of the house. Sam grabbed a folding chair from the deck and carried it over to the fence. The best way back to the car was through the adjoining yards. He wasn't going to give Mink's boys another chance to take a shot at him.

Sam braced the deck chair against the redwood, stood on it, and boosted Heather to the top of the fence. Before dropping over into the neighbor's yard, she turned to look at Sam.

"How did you know that stuff about mobsters never shooting women?" she asked.

"I think I read it somewhere."

They heard several more gunshots, and then the sound of sirens wailing in the heavy coastal air, getting closer.

Sam followed Heather over the fence. They ran through the adjoining back yards, got into the BMW, and drove away just as several police squad cars rounded the corner and converged on Bruce Kenwood's house.

# Chapter Twenty-nine

The flight to Caracas was three-quarters full. The seats were mostly occupied by families, many with children and babies, but it was so late that most of them were asleep. Sam was rarely able to sleep on a plane, but this flight would be an exception. He expected to be out cold by the time the plane leveled off. The adrenaline rush he'd felt when the bullets started flying at Bruce's house had subsided, and the desperate weariness of the long week began settling over him again.

They'd had enough time to get back to the hotel, pack their bags, and meet Miranda at the United terminal. On the way to the airport, Heather called Lou Kenwood and filled him in on what had happened that night: His supposedly deceased son was Babe Ruth; the mob had tried to kill Bruce, though he might have survived; and the plot had been broken up, but they still had to keep Alberto Miranda's mom from being killed or it would all hit the papers anyway.

"One other thing," Heather had said. "Bruce told us Paul O'Brien is in on the plot. Fire him."

Kenwood had been almost too stunned to reply. He said he'd fire Paul immediately.

"Be careful, please," Kenwood told her. "I don't want to lose you."

"Don't worry, Lou," she said, though there was plenty of reason to worry.

Caroline had managed to reach someone at Homeland Security, who had reached someone else at the State Department, who had in turn reached someone else at Homeland Security who had secured clearance for Heather to fly. As they boarded the plane, Miranda told them he had called some friends in Caracas who promised to help him track down Guillermo Llenas—Jefe—and rescue his mother from the byzantine shantytowns surrounding the city.

Sam sat next to the window, with Heather in the center seat and Miranda on the aisle. Sam was still awake when the drink cart came by. He ordered a Scotch to help himself settle down.

"This is the first time I fly coach since they call me up to the big leagues," Miranda said.

"Sorry, but this is what's left when you book at the last minute," Heather said. "We couldn't wait."

"No, no, it's okay," he said to Heather. "The seats are small, but no big deal. We have to get there."

"What did you tell the skipper?" Sam asked. He was concerned that Miranda going AWOL from his team would be a big story in the L.A. media, leading to more questions.

"No problem. I call him and say I must go home for a family emergency. My mother is very sick."

"Did he buy it?"

"Oh, yeah—he say, 'Go be with your family, Alberto. I understand.' We are out of the race, man, so it don't matter."

If they could find Jefe by nightfall on Friday, maybe they could still keep a lid on everything, Sam thought. But it was beginning to look like a long shot. Miranda's friends were their only hope. Without them, finding Elena in the shanties would be like looking for a specific blade of grass in the outfield at Fenway Park.

Sam woke up several hours into the flight and glanced to his left. Miranda had his arm around Heather's shoulders, and her head was nestled into his chest. A blanket covered both of them from the neck down. Sam put his head back on his pillow against the window and thought, They're good for each other. He soon fell asleep again.

They landed at Maiquetia Airport at about three in the afternoon. They retrieved their bags from the carousel and walked out to the street in front of the terminal to hail a cab. The cabbie who pulled up and got out to help with their luggage had a black armband on his short-sleeved white shirt. He immediately recognized Miranda; he smiled, shook the ballplayer's hand, and they conversed for several minutes in Spanish. At one point, Miranda pointed to the armband, and the cabbie became serious as he spoke. Then they all got in the cab and headed for Caracas.

"What's with the armband?" Sam asked Alberto.

"One of the airport cab drivers was murdered last month," Alberto said. "He was our driver's cousin."

"Was anybody arrested?"

"No. But our driver thinks it was the police who shot him."

"The police?"

"We are not in America anymore."

That became obvious when the cab emerged from the tunnels and entered metro Caracas. Sam was stunned to look at the smog-shrouded hillsides surrounding the city and see the endless shanties, stacked to the sky like discarded birdhouses. The squalor of those dwellings could be felt from the freeway that cut through the floor of the valley, miles from the hillsides. Yet the modern glass and steel buildings of the central city seemed impervious to the encroaching shanties. The scope of the poverty represented by those shanties made Sam wonder how human beings could live that way—or let others live that way.

Heather was unable to take her eyes off the shanties. She was the first to collect her thoughts and overcome her speechless amazement.

"Alberto, how long has Caracas been like this?" she said.

"As long as I have been here," he said. "My mother and father tell me the shanties began in the '60s. My own home, when I was a boy, was not much better. They are made of tin, of brick, scrap wood, anything the people can find. When the heavy rains come, many wash down the hills in landslides. In the dry season, many are destroyed by fire. Chavez has promised 100,000 new housing units each year, but they build maybe 25,000. Meanwhile, more babies, more people...more shanties."

All three fell silent while the cab made its way into the central city. Alberto asked the cab driver to wait while they checked into the Gran Melia, a modern high-rise hotel that was apparently the favorite of most rich visitors to Caracas. Heather changed into a pair of shorts and a sweater, and then they returned to the cab. Alberto asked the driver to take them to Parque del Este, a public park in central Caracas. When they arrived, Alberto gave the driver a huge tip, for which the cabbie began crying in gratitude.

Parque del Este was a series of gardens, lakes, and open spaces, shaded by deciduous trees and punctuated by palms. It reminded Sam of a tropical version of the Public Garden in Boston. They passed a small zoo, an aviary with exotic birds, a planetarium, and a cactus garden. Thousands of locals and tourists wandered among the gardens and reflecting pools; many recognized Alberto and pointed him out to their companions. Some walked close to him and patted him on the shoulder; others just smiled and said, *"Hola, Alberto!"*

The shanties weren't visible from the park, but there was a spectacular view of the Avila Mountains to the north. Between the hotel and the park, it was possible to think of Caracas as successful and modern, with all the comforts of an American city, rather than the landfill it appeared to be during the drive into town.

They came to a fifty-foot replica of Columbus' Santa Maria floating in an artificial lake. Four young men in light-colored short-sleeve shirts and blue jeans waved to Alberto from the dock near the ship and walked quickly through the crowds to reach him. Though not well dressed, they looked strong, healthy, and capable of hurting someone. Finally, Sam thought, we have guys, too.

One of the young men, who had a goatee and a thick bush of black hair, reached out to his old friend and put him in a playful headlock, saying "Albertito!" The five men bantered in Spanish for a few moments, but there was an underlying look of determination in the eyes of Miranda's friends. Soon the talk turned serious. Miranda introduced Sam and Heather to his friends. Something about the way Miranda introduced Heather, and the body language they both projected as they stood close to each other, sent a signal to his friends that Heather was to be treated with respect.

Another of the young men, who had dark hair parted in the middle and hanging below his cheekbones, said in English, "We have a car. Come with us."

"Can we all fit?" Alberto asked.

"*Si,*" his friend replied.

"*Adonde vas?*"

Once again the group began conversing in Spanish. Miranda listened intently, asked a few questions, and then turned to Sam.

"They think they know where my mother is," Miranda said. "Pedro here knows many Caracas police officers. He found out the station where Guillermo Llenas works—the man called Jefe. Pedro and Eduardo waited for him to leave the station this afternoon and followed him to a hillside barrio called Antimano. Jefe went to a house owned by another man—people in the neighborhood say the man is named Hector. They see Jefe come and go—he brings food and other supplies. Pedro can take us there."

Sam looked at Miranda and his friends, slapping each other's backs and grasping hands as though headed onto the field for an important game. They'd grown up together, all products of the Caracas slums, now separated by Miranda's supreme athletic gifts and his residence in another country, where he lived in luxury that these young men couldn't imagine. Yet there was a palpable bond between them, a blood-brother relationship forged when none of them had anything but the shirts on their backs and, perhaps, some old baseball equipment to share. Sam could see it in the eyes of Miranda's friends: They loved him, idolized him, and would give their lives for him. Miranda would no doubt do the same for them.

Sam knew it would be almost impossible to control what happened when they found Jefe. Would Miranda's friends be any use in a fight with a trained police officer, who also happened to be a kidnapper, probably a murderer, and who stood to gain $1,000,000 if Kenwood paid the extortion money? Miranda's friends were vigilantes, ready to storm the house in their righteous anger, but not the kind of force Sam wanted with him if things got complicated. They had no training, no discipline—and their loyalty was to Miranda, not to Sam and Heather. If he wasn't able to direct them, and perhaps give them a short lesson in SWAT procedures, they could all end up dead.

"What do your friends have for weapons?" Sam asked Miranda. Miranda asked them in Spanish, and Sam understood the answer.

"*Machetes.*"

"That's it?"

Sam had his Glock 23, but he didn't want to use it. He wouldn't be able to get back to Boston any time soon—or ever—if he shot a local police officer. It was a stretch to believe an untrained bunch of machete-toting Venezuelan street punks would be enough to do the job, but he had to find a way to work with what he had.

"Maybe they could find a handgun or a rifle," Miranda said.

"No time," Sam said. "We have to go."

It was nearing six, and the sun was descending over the western shoulder of Mount Avila. Sam would have preferred to wait for nightfall to attempt the rescue, but the deadline for Kenwood to transfer the money had passed. Jefe might be willing to wait a few more hours to hear from Bruce, but Sam couldn't count on that. They had to find Elena now.

They followed Pedro, the young man with the goatee, to the eastern edge of the park, where his dented delivery van was parked on the street. There was a back bench seat, and behind that the floor of the van was covered with old newspapers, sacks, ropes, and a half-dozen machetes with two-foot-long blades. Sam and Heather sat down on the floor behind the back seat, while Miranda got in front with Pedro, and Eduardo and the two others sat in the bench seat.

"Alberto, we can't just rush the house," Sam said. "We need a plan, so no one gets hurt."

"Jefe will get hurt," Pedro said over his shoulder. The others nodded.

"Listen to me," Sam said. "When we get to the house, drive past, come around again, then park the van down the block. When I see what the layout is, I'll decide what we'll do. No one goes running in unless I say so."

Sam assumed that Eduardo and the other two on the bench seat didn't understand much English. He asked Alberto to repeat his instructions in Spanish.

"I want you to stay in the van," Sam said to Heather.

"Hey, look, cowboy, how many times do we have to go through this?" she said. "I go where you go. We're a team."

"Not anymore," Sam said. "I can't afford to have Alberto worrying about you once this thing starts. I know you can take care of yourself, but he's likely to get himself hurt trying to protect you. You want this to go well? You want Alberto and his mother to come out of this alive? Stay in the van."

Sam expected an argument, but Heather looked toward the front seat, and saw Alberto looking back at them. He nodded at her.

"All right," she said quietly.

Sam had never seen Heather show fear, but he thought he'd caught a glimpse of it in her eyes this time—and the fear seemed to be for Alberto, not for herself.

The van began a gentle climb at the edge of the city, and then a steeper ascent as the road became rougher. Soon they were beyond the pavement, and the dirt street wound narrowly through two- and three-story houses, duplexes, and apartments with adjoining walls, some with slivers of sidewalks, most right up against the road. Second-floor windows and small balconies hung just above the passing van. Many of the windows were covered by wrought-iron bars to keep out intruders, even on the second floors.

The crumbling houses were all slightly different—broken brick fronts or cracked concrete, some painted burnt red or blue-green, many left unpainted—and yet indistinguishable from each other in their relentless neglect. People milled around outside, mostly women and children, with little evident purpose.

"This is the good part of the barrio," Miranda said. He turned to look at Sam and Heather. "The shanties are far worse."

Pedro drove on for several miles, continuing to climb the hill until they could see downtown Caracas below them through the occasional gaps between the buildings. At one point, where the road curved up the hill to the right, they had to drive around a public works crew with a cement mixer, wheelbarrows, picks, shovels, and a gravel truck, attempting to put a surface over the dirt.

"Chavez promises to pave all the streets," Miranda said. "At this rate, it will take a thousand years."

Pedro slowed down just past the crew, pointed to his right and said, "*Eso es la casa*" to Miranda. It was a white concrete building with a second-floor apartment that extended several feet over the sidewalk. To the left was a two-story brick building with a three-by-six-foot hole in the exterior, which someone had attempted to patch using larger bricks and mortar; to the right of the house was a one-story entranceway, covered by scrap lumber for a roof, and next to that was a two-story house with a façade made of small, painstakingly laid stone—which would have been an elegant look, had the three street-level windows not been covered with plywood, while the three second-story windows were covered with iron grates.

The houses were fortresses, Sam realized, though it was hard to imagine what the occupants owned that was worth stealing. Except in Jefe's case—he was protecting something worth $50,000,000.

"Drive around again," Sam said to Pedro. Pedro maneuvered through the street repair crew, accelerated up the road and turned around at the next crossroad, while Sam looked over the buildings on the block for any ideas on how to get at Jefe without costing Elena Miranda her life.

"What would happen if you just knocked on the door?" Heather asked.

Sam thought about that, but before he could answer, Pedro said, "If he expecting no one, he not answer. Or he shoot."

"Well, that's no good," Sam said, mostly for Miranda's benefit. He knew the ballplayer was getting nervous, scared, and angrier with each passing moment. Sam needed to keep him calm. An enraged son tearing a house apart to find his kidnapped mother would be of no help.

By the time they had driven back down the block and approached the house again, Sam had an idea.

# Chapter Thirty

*Señor* Bruce had not called.

It was past seven now, two hours beyond the deadline. Jefe could understand if Kenwood wanted to wait until the last possible minute to transfer the money; it would take a bit of time for the transaction to go through and the money to show up in the account Bruce had created. That could take a half-hour, perhaps. But two hours? Something had gone wrong. Jefe tried to call Bruce, but Bruce did not answer his phone. Jefe was not supposed to call Bruce—ever—but now he had to know. Had the plan fallen apart? Was Bruce in jail? Was he dead? Did Kenwood refuse to pay? Did Miranda talk? What about Frankie Navarro—where was he?

Two hours—that was too long. The agreement was always very clear: Bruce would call immediately after the deadline. When the money was paid, kill Elena Miranda. If Bruce told him the plot had fallen apart, kill her. If Bruce said Miranda was going to "confess" to throwing the World Series, wait for the public statement—then kill her.

It would almost be unnecessary. Elena now lay limp on the bed in Hector's second-floor duplex. Her breathing came in shallow spurts, she could no longer eat, and her collarbone protruded like that of a starved corpse. Even Hector seemed to have lost interest in her. Now that Elena was a sack of listless bones, he thought only of the money.

It was time to get rid of him.

They sat in the upstairs room together, Jefe and Hector. The house was a pig sty, with dirty clothes, dishes, and garbage everywhere. Hector had not so much as picked up a sock or scraped a plate since his wife, Gloria, had taken their children and left. He told Jefe that once he got his money, he was going to walk away from this house and never come back. Let the squatters take it, as they had taken so many of the houses in the barrio.

"But things will be better here, now that Chavez is firmly in power," Jefe said to him, less from conviction than as a way to fill the idle time with conversation while Elena slept. "Look outside. They are fixing your street. A little paint, some patching, a new front door, and once again *su casa es muy bien*. Gloria, she will come back. You'll see."

Hector didn't want her back. She could have the kids. He wanted his money, and he wanted to go as far from Caracas as possible.

In the meantime, Hector drank. He was drunk now. Jefe would not have permitted that while Hector was watching over Elena, but now it served Jefe's purpose. In fact, Jefe poured Hector's last three glasses of rum for him. Celebrate, Jefe told him. It's almost over. The money will soon be ours.

"To Elena Miranda, the whore who thought she was too good for me," Hector said, raising his glass. "Soon she'll be dead, and the worms can have her."

"*Si*," Jefe said. The thought made him a little sad—but not as sad as he was about the very real possibility that he was not going to get his money.

"I want to do it, Jefe. Let me shoot the *puta*."

"Of course," Jefe said, shrugging. "I always intended for you to shoot her. We became friends, Elena and I—as much as ones such as she and I could become friends. It would not feel right for me to kill her. I'd rather you do it."

Hector smiled and poured himself another drink while Jefe drew his pistol from its holster and attached the silencer, the one he'd used in the tunnel to shoot the cabbie. He wore a pair of blue gloves, something Hector neither noticed nor would have cared about.

The silencer was hardly necessary, with all the noise from the jackhammer, the cement mixer, and the dump truck in the street below. Yet Jefe was a careful man, so he waited until the tailgate of the dump truck began banging after depositing a load of rock. He timed the bangs, and on the third one, he put the gun to Hector's left temple and pulled the trigger.

Hector's body crumpled off his chair and onto the floor. Jefe stood up quickly, bent over and put Hector's fingers around the butt and trigger of the gun. He had wiped it down carefully; there would be no fingerprints but Hector's on the gun. Jefe pulled out an envelope that he'd kept for this very purpose, and scrawled in a sloppy hand, "Life means nothing to me without Gloria."

Jefe put the note on a half-eaten plate of frijoles. Now, to attend to Elena.

He could not bring himself to shoot her. Bullets were for men who could fight back. Firing a bullet into Elena's head would be like using a grenade to kill a dog. A pillow over the face was sufficient—a decent, civilized death for a woman who had done nothing to bring this upon herself, except to give birth to an exceptional baseball player.

Jefe stood over Elena's bed, listening to her shallow breathing, and wondered if he ought to wake her up, to talk to her one more time, to explain. It would be the honorable thing to do before sending her to her permanent rest. Yet, in the end, Jefe knew he was too much the coward to look her in the eye before killing her. All the rest of his life, whenever he watched Alberto Miranda play baseball on television, he would have to see her eyes. He had to kill her, but he didn't need to have her look at him. That much, he could spare himself.

Part of him was angry with her, too. He had risked and sacrificed so much the past few weeks to watch over her, all in the certainty that it would make him a rich man. Now? Maybe it had all been for nothing. It was not her fault, but it made Jefe bitter to think of the pains he had taken to keep this secret, to keep Elena alive, to keep her from escaping. He was owed much, and someone had to pay. For now, it would be Elena.

Hector's linens were as filthy as the rest of the house. The two pillows on Elena's bed were spotted and gray, and Jefe was glad he had the gloves on when he picked up one of the pillows and held it over Elena's face.

At that moment, he heard someone pounding furiously on the door downstairs.

"Out! Out! Everyone out of the house!" the male voice yelled in Spanish. "We hit a gas line! This house is going to explode! Get out!"

Jefe panicked. The street crew had provided convenient background noise, but now their stupid digging was going to kill them all. He dropped the pillow and was about to run for the door, but then he thought: If I evacuate, and the house does not blow up, they will not let me back in until the house is searched. They'll find Hector's body, and they'll find Elena.

He couldn't let that happen. She could not be found alive, able to identify him.

What could he do? Shoot her? Then put the gun back in Hector's hand? They might hear the shot, and how could he explain escaping such a tragedy? But wait—a fire. Even if the house did not blow up, who was to say the work crew didn't accidentally start Hector's house on fire? Yes, that was it. Jefe could set the blaze, walk out the door, and never look back.

He found a book of matches by the stove and hastily lit a pile of newspapers under the sink, where Hector's wife had kept a few bottles of household fluids and some rags. Then he lit the curtains. The house was a tinderbox, Jefe knew. It would be ablaze within minutes.

He ran down the stairs and out into the street, expecting to find the work crew frantically running up and down the block, warning people to evacuate. But the workers were standing across the street, shovels and picks in hand, watching him come out the front door and into the arms of five strong young men, none of whom was wearing a hard hat.

"Where is she?" the largest of the men demanded. The other four held Jefe by his arms.

"Where…who?" Jefe stammered, though he knew who the large man was. He'd seen him on television dozens of times, pitching and hitting for the Cardinals and Dodgers. He'd seen Alberto Miranda with a bat or a glove, but never before with a machete.

"Are you the one called Jefe?" Miranda shouted. His friends jostled Jefe and waved their own machetes close to his face.

"No! No! I don't know what you're talking about! Run, you fools! The house is going to explode!"

Some of the young men grinned, and Pedro—who had pounded on the door and screamed about hitting the gas line— took an exaggerated bow. Jefe looked across the street at the work crew, most of whom were laughing. It had been a trick—how could he have been so stupid? Could he somehow keep them from going into the house until the fire consumed it?

"She is not here," Jefe said.

"Who?" Miranda demanded.

"Your mother. I've been looking for her everywhere. I found her in a shanty—I was going to her when you began banging on the door. Come on—there isn't much time. She is dying."

Jefe could see in Miranda's eyes that he wanted to believe the story—that if they moved quickly enough to this other location, he could save his mother. Jefe could lead Miranda and his friends back to the empty shanty where they'd kept Elena for nearly a month. Forensic evidence could prove she'd been there. By then, Hector's house would have burned down, and perhaps many would be killed. In the chaos and confusion, he might be able to escape. Perhaps Elena's body would not be identified. At any rate, Elena would never be able to identify him.

Sam stood across the street, his hand on his holstered gun. Pedro had carried out his role to perfection, and the street crew had been more than happy to back off and watch after they recognized Alberto Miranda, heard the story about his mother, and received $500 in cash, apiece. Sam didn't want to risk getting detained by the local police, so he allowed Miranda's friends to jump Jefe when he emerged from the house. But now the Venezuelans were exchanging a flurry of Spanish, and both Jefe and Miranda were looking up the street, as though they were about to go somewhere else.

Then Sam saw Heather sprinting from the van, which had been parked down the street. She dodged between parked cars and ran to the entrance of the house Jefe had come from, pointing up to the second floor windows as she entered.

"Fire!" she screamed.

She raced into the house and up the stairs. Sam ran across the street and started to go up after her, but then turned to Miranda and said, "Don't let him go! All of you, stay here and keep that man from leaving!"

Then he took the steps two at a time, reaching the door that led to the second-floor room that Jefe had just left. Black smoke billowed out, and Sam pulled his jacket over his mouth, trying to keep the acrid air from overwhelming him. Heather was somewhere in that small house, trying to find Elena, but he couldn't see two feet in front of his face.

"Heather!" he called out.

"Back here!" she called, her voice choking.

Sam followed the sound, and tripped over something that felt like a body. He fell to his knees, where the air was somewhat easier to breathe and he could see a bit better. He was afraid the body belonged to Elena, but after grabbing an arm and rolling the body over, Sam could tell it was a man, with a gaping bullet wound to the side of his head. There was fresh blood on the floor, and the man was clutching a pistol.

Heather uttered a choking scream somewhere ahead of him.

"Get down on the floor and crawl to my voice!" Sam yelled, and then he crawled forward. They bumped into each other as the smoke got darker, and Sam could tell that Heather was trying to drag the small, wilted body of Elena Miranda along with her. He managed to get an arm around Heather's waist, the other arm around Elena, and they crawled together toward the door. They all became smeared with Hector's blood as they passed his body. Sam took the gun out of Hector's hand and tucked it into his pants.

The air improved as they stumbled down the stairs, and once they emerged from the smoky entrance, they were able to carry Elena across the street from the building and lay her down on the cracked sidewalk. Miranda rushed to them, crying, "Mama! Mama!" Elena opened her eyes at the sound of her son's voice. She was coughing and streaked with blood and soot, but she was trying to smile.

"Albertito," she said softly. "*Te amo.*"

Sam drew himself away and tried to cough the smoke out of his lungs. Heather was coughing, too, but she had no intention of leaving Elena and Alberto.

Jefe had other ideas, but he was still being held by Pedro and his friends, and could not break away.

"I am an officer of the law," Jefe said, playing his last card. "I demand that you release me at once."

Pedro looked at Alberto, kneeling next to his stricken mother, looked at the smoke pouring through the bars over the second-floor windows, and then looked back at Jefe.

"You are a murdering pig," Pedro said.

He raised his machete and brought it down violently on Jefe's upper arm, slicing through the policeman's blue shirt and causing blood to spatter onto the others. Eduardo was next, hacking Jefe's leg as he writhed and screamed. They each took turns, three holding Jefe while one furiously slashed at him with a big blade. Blood poured from Jefe's gaping wounds and he could no longer stand. The street workers were now somber as they watched the assault, but they did nothing to try to help Jefe. Neither did the many neighborhood residents who had come out onto the street when the commotion began. Twenty-foot flames now leaped toward the sky from the roof of Hector's house, but as yet there were no sirens, and no one seemed to be concerned about saving the house. Instead, all eyes were riveted on the drama of the bloody police officer, and the young men who were in the process of killing him.

"Alberto!" Pedro called. "Finish him!"

Pedro held a machete at arm's length, blood dripping from the blade onto his fingers and arm. Miranda put his fingers to his lips, touched them to his mother's lips, then rose from the sidewalk. He walked slowly across the street and joined his friends in their circle around the fallen Jefe.

Jefe's eyes were open and he was trying to speak, but he struggled to form the words that were in his head.

"Alberto," Jefe managed to say, looking up into the eyes of the Venezuelan hero. "Do not do this. You are a great ballplayer, not a murderer."

Miranda glanced back at Heather, who had his mother's head cradled in her lap. If he was looking for a sign from her suggesting what he should do, he didn't receive it. Heather simply held his gaze, then looked back into the eyes of his mother. She stroked Elena's hair and said, "You're going to be all right. Alberto's here now."

Miranda looked back at Jefe, whose wild, desperate eyes pleaded for mercy. Then he held his empty hand out to Pedro, who gave him the bloody machete. With the power that allowed him to hit a baseball 500 feet and throw it 97 miles per hour, Alberto Miranda swung the machete down into Jefe's skull, slicing his face open. The machete was embedded so deep into Jefe's brain that it did not easily come out, so Miranda left it there.

He turned again to look at Heather, who gave him a reassuring nod.

# Chapter Thirty-one

The American Airlines flight from Caracas to Boston made a stop in Miami, and was scheduled to land at Logan at 10:40 Sunday morning. The Sox—who had won again on Friday night and Saturday afternoon, and now were just a game out of first place—were scheduled to play the Yankees at seven p.m. on ESPN's "Sunday Night Baseball." That would give Sam the afternoon to meet with Lou Kenwood and fill him in on what had happened.

Most of it was good news. Best of all, Elena Miranda was alive, her kidnappers were dead, and Lou would not have to pay the extortion demand because Alberto Miranda had no intention of claiming he'd thrown the Series. Miranda had stayed behind in Caracas to support his friend Pedro, who'd been arrested for murder, but the local attorney who represented Miranda was certain the case would be quickly dismissed, thanks partly to Alberto's influence, but primarily because of the gun that was found in Jefe's ungloved right hand—the same gun that had fired the bullet that killed Hector—when the police and firefighters eventually arrived at the scene.

With a little bit of luck, they could keep the story out of the news. If it looked like someone in the media was getting wind of part of the story, Sam could call on Russ Daly of the L.A. Times, who would verify the crucial details and make sure what did become public was accurate.

There was bad news, too. Sam didn't know where Bruce Kenwood was, or what had happened to Frankie Navarro. Maybe they'd been killed by Mink's gang. More likely, the cops had arrived in time to interrupt the gunfight. Perhaps they were all in jail, including Mink; or maybe they were all on the loose, still gunning for each other. During the stopover in Miami, Sam hadn't been able to reach anyone in L.A. who knew what had happened in Palos Verdes on Friday night. He'd try again when they got to Boston.

But there was more bad news for Lou.

Shortly after their flight lifted off from Maiquetia Airport in Caracas, Sam had turned to Heather and said, "Alberto is in love with you."

"I know," Heather replied quietly.

"And I think you're in love with him, too."

"I am."

"What are you going to do?"

Heather didn't immediately reply. Sam knew she'd had her life planned out for years. No doubt she'd realized Lou Kenwood's interest in her from the first week she'd worked for him. It was not hard to believe that she had come to love the man as they worked closely together in one of the most exciting businesses in America. Why wouldn't she marry him? He was rich, still attractive, a hero to Red Sox Nation, and a guaranteed ticket to a lifetime of fame and glamour after she inherited his empire. What 28-year-old business whiz wouldn't take that deal?

If she wasn't conscience-stricken about stealing another woman's husband, it was understandable. Katherine would be dead soon, so there was no need for Lou to walk out on her. Besides, she'd had her own turn living the glamour life as Mrs. Lou Kenwood—and she had fallen into it the same way Heather had. When Lou Kenwood decided he wanted someone younger and prettier, he acquired her—just as he'd go out and get a right-fielder or a pitcher.

"I'm not going to tell you what to do, but I will mention a couple of facts," Sam said.

"Go ahead."

She was looking at a magazine on her tray table and didn't glance at Sam, but he knew she wasn't paying any attention to the article.

"Alberto is a good man. He made a mistake getting mixed up with HGH, but it says something about his character that he wasn't willing to throw the Series to keep it quiet."

"I know," Heather said. She still didn't look at him.

"He is also a hell of a player, and he hasn't been caught doing anything illegal—yet. You could help get him off that stuff, and he could play another ten years. He ought to be more, uh, capable, too."

Heather smiled, but said nothing.

"Players are going to be caught, suspended, and maybe even banned from baseball, but Alberto doesn't have to be one of them," Sam said. "And when it comes to money, he may not be Lou Kenwood, but he's already got more than the two of you will ever need. If he plays another ten years, you can live any way you want, for the rest of your lives."

"I thought I loved Lou," Heather said after a while. "I really did. But now…Now all I can think about is Alberto."

"I'll point out one other fact, and then leave you alone," Sam said. "Alberto is going to outlive Lou by fifty years. After Lou's dead, Alberto is the kind of man you're going to be looking for anyway. I don't know if you think he's worth more than owning a major league baseball team, but I do know this: The Red Sox are going to give you way more heartaches than Alberto would."

Heather smiled, and finally looked at Sam.

"You're right. I can't marry Lou. I've known that almost from the moment I laid eyes on Alberto. I'll have to tell Lou as soon as we get back to Boston."

Heather was one of the most gorgeous women he'd ever met, but at that moment—despite the wearying travel, the lack of sleep, the lack of attention to grooming and attire, the poor lighting in the plane—Sam was sure he saw something blossom within her that heightened all of her exquisite features. For the first time, he saw real beauty in her, rather than just good looks. He was now more than attracted to her or entertained by her; he liked her. And in that moment, he felt sorry for Lou Kenwood.

"He'll be devastated."

"I know," Heather said. "And I'm sorry. But maybe it's for the best. At least he's still got Katherine."

Sam did not reply.

◇◇◇

Despite the gloom of another rainy day, Boston was in the familiar throes of pennant race frenzy when they got off the plane at Logan. The Sox had been given up for dead just ten days ago, but as Sam and Heather were walking through the terminal to the baggage level, signs of the team's resurrection were everywhere. The local papers had given their front pages over to previews of that night's battle for first place in the A.L. East: "Sox can catch Yanks tonight," screamed the banner headline in the Globe; "Babe to Yanks: 'Curse this'" said the Herald. Sox hats, sweatshirts and pennants were being sold at the bookstores, gift shops, newsstands, and from impromptu novelty stands and carts. The TV monitors in the terminal were all tuned to NESN, which was showing highlights of the team's improbable comeback from near-elimination to the brink of the playoffs.

The cab that Sam and Heather got into had a soggy Sox pennant hanging from a plastic holder attached to the left rear window. As the cab splashed out of the airport parking lot, Heather called Kenwood's office, but he wasn't there. When she told Sam she'd try him at Fenway, their turbaned driver, whose license identified him as Abrar Sohrab, turned his head to look at them.

"You know Red Sox people?" the driver said. "Can get tickets tonight? Abrar pay very high dollar."

"Sorry," Sam said. "We can't help you."

"Aghhh," the driver said. "Never tickets for Abrar."

Heather dialed Fenway, and Lou answered the phone in his suite.

"Hi, Lou, we're back," she said. "We've got a lot to talk about."

Sam watched Heather's face turn from almost apologetically happy to concerned as she listened to the owner's voice. She said, "Just a minute—talk to Sam," and held out her phone.

"What is it?" Sam asked.

"I got a call from Bruce this morning," Kenwood said. "He's in Boston. He wants me to meet him at noon in the Monster Seats. He says he's going to kill Katherine."

"Did you call her?"

"She's not home."

Sam went over the jumble of events from the past few days. They'd gone to Bruce's house on Thursday night; that would have left Bruce the rest of that night, and maybe Friday, to explain his way out of the shootout, and, possibly, to make bail. He could have caught a plane to Boston on Saturday, while Sam and Heather were in Venezuela. He should have realized that Bruce wasn't going to let this go. All he had ever really wanted was to hurt his father in a deep and lasting way. If he couldn't disgrace the Red Sox and besmirch their first World Series victory in 86 years, he could still inflict a mortal wound on his father.

"Don't meet him," Sam said.

"I have to."

"Call the cops, and stay put till we get there. We're just leaving Logan in a cab."

"I'm not afraid of that sniveling little punk. I'll meet him anytime, anyplace. And I don't want the police involved in this. I told you that."

"Don't be stupid, Lou." Sam raised his voice. "Your kid was willing to fake his own death and hire mobsters to hurt you. I think he's dangerous—and I know he's nuts."

"He's a sissy. I've known that since he was kicked out of college for...molesting his roommate."

So that was why Kenwood had disowned his son.

"Okay, Lou, don't call the cops, but stay in your suite and lock it till we get there. If Bruce does show up, let me handle it. You're paying me for that, remember?"

"This is family stuff now, Skarda. It's personal. I can handle it."

He hung up. Sam gave the phone back to Heather and said, "Driver, get to Fenway Park as fast as you can."

"Now maybe tickets for Abrar?" the driver said.

"Yes, tickets for Abrar. Now, move it."

They reached Yawkey Way a little past noon. The first pitch was not due for almost seven hours, yet Kenmore Square had already begun the game-day conversion from busy metropolitan crossroads to baseball-themed street carnival, with food and merchandise vendors setting up shop under dripping umbrellas, while ticket scalpers and buyers huddled in groups under eaves and in shop doorways. Every few feet, someone had a radio tuned in to WEEI, where Sox talk had passed irrational and was now tending to the surreal. It created a stereo effect with the radio in Abrar's cab.

"Ben from Framingham, think we're gonna get tonight's game in?"

"We have to. We can't lose our momentum now. We're gonna run the table. The Yankees SUCK!"

"Okay, I think we all agree that the Yankees suck. But gimme your best shot on Hurtado. Do we sign him after the week he's had?"

"Oh, geez, yeah. He's homered in, what, six of the last seven games? It's like Yaz in '67. I always said Hurtado was a gamer. I love the guy."

"So sign him to a four-year deal?"

"Whatever he wants. Whatever it takes."

Abrar pulled the cab up to the corner of Yawkey and Brookline, got out of the car and opened the trunk, holding an umbrella over Sam and Heather as they removed their luggage. Heather paid him and gave him her card.

"Call my office later today, and I'll see that you get tickets for tonight," she said.

"Oh, bless you," Abrar said. "Four, please."

They hurried down Yawkey Way to the entrance to the Red Sox offices. A security guard opened the door for them.

"Morning, Ms. Canby," the guard said. "Nasty day."

"Who's come in today, Fred?" Heather asked.

"Mr. Kenwood's here. And Mrs. Kenwood came in about a half hour ago with someone I didn't recognize."

"Man or a woman?" Sam asked.

"Woman, I think. She was using an umbrella, and I didn't get a good look at her."

Sam glanced at Heather, then looked quickly at Fred's belt. He was not wearing a firearm, but he did have a radio clipped to his belt.

"Do we call the police?" Sam asked Heather.

"Why would you want the police?" the guard said, suddenly looking worried.

Heather pulled Sam into a secretary's cubicle off the main lobby, put her bags down and pulled him close to her.

"Lou said no police," she said, quiet enough that Fred would not hear her. "No reporters. The other employees can't know about this. We've got to do this his way."

"I don't agree," Sam said. "This is getting out of hand. That was Bruce who came in with Katherine."

"You don't know that."

"One way to find out. Let's go up."

They took the elevator up to the top level, and walked down the concourse to the entrance to the Kenwoods' suite. The door was open, but no one was inside. Sam walked into the suite and picked up a pair of binoculars from an end table. He fixed them on the Monster Seats atop the left-field wall, and spotted two figures, one slowly lowering the other's wheelchair, one step at a time, down to the first row of Monster Seats. When they reached the bottom row, next to the light standard that held up the giant Coke bottles, the one walking held an umbrella over the head of the woman in the wheelchair, who was wearing a Nor'easter rain hat and was covered in a brightly colored blanket. They both appeared to be gazing out over the sodden, empty ballpark and the tarp-covered field as though waiting for the game to begin.

Sam turned the binoculars to the left, and saw Lou Kenwood walking toward them from the left-field foul pole. He was bareheaded with no umbrella or topcoat.

"Lou's out there," Sam said.

"Who's that sitting right above the wall?" Heather asked.

"Bruce and Katherine." Sam put the glasses down. "We've got to get out there."

"It doesn't make any sense. Bruce loathes Katherine. She hated him."

"Doesn't matter now. Come on."

Sam took Heather by the elbow and pulled her out into the concourse. They ran as fast as they could to the Green Monster.

# Chapter Thirty-two

The rain had become a steady downpour, and puddles had formed in the green-painted rows and aisles when Sam and Heather exited the concourse and crossed the short metal bridge onto the Monster Seats section. Low-hanging rain clouds obscured the Prudential and John Hancock buildings beyond the stadium walls; to the right, they saw Lou Kenwood four rows below them, engaged in an angry conversation with his son.

Bruce noticed Sam and Heather as they approached, but didn't seem concerned about their presence. He handed the umbrella to Katherine, who held it aloft with her right hand while she pulled her patterned blanket closer to her chin with her left hand. Kenwood was now standing between his son and his wife, gripping the wheelchair and looking protective of Katherine. A row of green metal swivel chairs was separated from the edge of the wall by a short beverage counter, which came up to Kenwood's waist. Aside from a six-inch backsplash on the rain-soaked beverage counter, there was no other barrier between the seats and the field, thirty-seven feet two inches below.

"I'm glad you're here, Skarda," Bruce said in a cheerful, almost sing-song voice. "You too, Heather. You should both see this."

"See what?" Sam said. He and Heather slowly moved closer.

Bruce was definitely out of his mind. He was dressed in a Burberry raincoat, his neck protected by a purple scarf, with a short, blond wig covered by a broad-brimmed rain hat. He wore pants, but Sam noticed that his shoes were a pair of purple pumps that matched his scarf. His makeup was garishly applied, with purple eye shadow above his left eye, and green above his right. His lipstick was bright red and smeared hideously all around his mouth. The raindrops that hit his face caused mascara to streak down his face. Bruce looked like a man—or a woman—prepared to act upon the first insane idea that flashed across his tortured mind. Sam's gun was still in his suitcase, in the secretary's cubicle off the lobby, and he was kicking himself for not getting it out before they'd gone up to Lou's suite.

"He said he was going to push Katherine off the top of the wall," Lou Kenwood said. "That's why I had to come out here. I couldn't let him do that."

"He's not going to do that, Lou," Sam said. "Get away from him."

"What do you mean?" Kenwood said. He held his position between Bruce and Katherine.

"If he intended to toss Katherine over the wall, why did he wait for you to come out here and try to stop him?"

"Because he's a crazy fuck-up who's never done anything right in his whole goddamned life," Kenwood said, barking the words into Bruce's grotesquely painted face. "Look at him. Look at him!"

"Yes, look at me," Bruce said, laughing. "Don't you think I'm pretty, Father?"

"Shut up, you sick freak," Kenwood said.

"Get away from him, Lou." Sam took a slow step down the aisle toward them, hoping not to panic Bruce. "Back away."

"Why? And let him hurt Katherine?"

"As if…you'd do anything…to stop him," Katherine said, speaking for the first time in her halting, exhausted voice.

"You don't get it, Lou." Sam took another step down the aisle. "You're the one Bruce wants to hurt. So does Katherine. They've been in this thing together from the start."

Kenwood released his grip on the wheel of Katherine's chair and stared blankly at Sam as the rain splashed and dripped off his face.

"What?" Heather said. She grabbed Sam's sleeve and turned him toward her. "You never told me that."

"It just hit me on the plane," Sam said. "They both want to hurt Lou. That scam took money, planning, connections, and brains. They've been at it for over a year. You and I both realized that a punk like Frankie Navarro couldn't have put it together. But the more I knew about Bruce, the more sure I was that he couldn't do it, either. You saw his house—he didn't have enough money to keep the place from falling apart. He needed help, a lot of it, to pull this off. We figured he was getting tipped off by somebody close to Lou, but we assumed it was Paul."

"I fired Paul when you told me to," Kenwood said.

"You owe him an apology." Sam took another step down the aisle. He was about four long strides from Bruce now. "So do I."

"But Bruce said Paul was his inside source," Heather said.

"Sure he did. But it wasn't Paul, was it, Bruce?"

Bruce cackled, as though Sam had told a tremendously funny joke.

"No, no, no," he said, shoulders heaving. "God, I wouldn't work with some street scum from Southie. Are you out of your tree?"

"But you would work with one of the richest women in America, even if you hated her. Somebody who sent you off to prep school, and summer camp, and then to college, keeping you away from your dad. Never letting you get close to the Red Sox."

"Is this true, Katherine?" Kenwood said.

Katherine nodded. Lou sagged to one side, grabbing a seat back for support.

"Whose idea was it?" Kenwood said.

"Mine," Katherine said. "I needed Bruce's...mobility."

"I thought of the kidnapping," Bruce said. He appeared indignant that his stepmother wasn't sharing the credit. It was clear that there was still no affection between them.

"Who decided to try to have me killed?" Sam asked.

"Nothing personal, Sam," Katherine said. She managed a wan smile. "I didn't want Lou to...hire a private investigator...but Heather talked him into it. You were...inconvenient."

"The guy on the boat was almost too good, wasn't he?" Sam said. He took another step closer. Bruce was beginning to look at him warily. "You got hit."

"I did that...to myself," Katherine said. "Down below...with my little gun. It didn't hurt much...and it threw you off...didn't it?"

"For a while."

"How...where did you get the money?" Kenwood said to his wife. "It must have cost a fortune to put this thing together. I'd have noticed if you were spending that kind of money. So would Heather."

"You did," Katherine said. "But you thought it was...going for my treatments. I stopped. What was the point? It's emphysema, Lou. I was going to die anyway. I had more important things to do."

"I don't understand, Katherine...why?" Kenwood asked.

"Because I wanted our life...to be about something more... than winning trophies," Katherine said. "How many times... did I ask you about setting up a trust...a foundation in our names?"

"I wasn't ready," Kenwood said.

"It might have escaped your attention...but I didn't have much time to wait. Each year you became more hesitant. There was always something the team needed...a free agent...a new section of seats...new suites...an outdoor mall...something that would add to your legacy...as the Curse Killer.

"You were going to get all the credit...there was nothing for me. I had no children...I gave all my time to you and the team...yet 100 years from now, there would be nothing bearing my name. It would be all Lou Kenwood."

Rainwater flowed from the corners of her yellow hat, but Katherine was oblivious to the steady downpour.

"I begged you to establish...the Louis and Katherine Kenwood Charitable Trust. Eventually, I realized you would never do it...All you cared about was...beating the Yankees every year."

"Katherine, a charitable foundation is a lovely idea for after we're gone," Lou said. "But I have to think about the future of the club."

"I worked as hard as you did…to make the Red Sox great again," Katherine said. "I did the Jimmy Fund…I organized the reunions…I took care of Ted Williams when he visited…You got all the credit…but I deserved…my legacy, too."

"So you blackmailed me?"

"If you paid the money, my half…would set up a foundation in my name…after we both died," Katherine said. "I wasn't going to be…the forgotten second wife…of the great…the immortal…Lucky Louie."

"And if I didn't pay?"

Katherine looked at Heather, but said nothing.

Still in a daze, Kenwood put his hand up to wipe away the rain that was plastering his silver hair to his forehead. At that moment, Bruce grabbed his father in a choke hold around the neck and pulled him between two of the swivel seats at the edge of the Green Monster. Kenwood fell back into the rainwater that had pooled on the beverage counter.

"Get back, Skarda," Bruce screamed. "Get back! He's going over!"

Bruce was not a physically imposing man, but his stunned, elderly father was no competition for him in a wrestling match. Kenwood's feet left the ground as Bruce pushed him backward, his shoulders extending over the edge of the wall and the warning track below. Bruce stood up on one of the swivel chairs, then braced one of his purple pumps against the back of the chair and kneeled on the beverage counter for the leverage he needed to push his father all the way over the edge, while Sam struggled to get past Katherine's wheelchair and grab Bruce's leg. Bruce saw Sam lunging for him, and tried to tuck his legs underneath him while he pushed his father closer to the edge of the wall. But the counter was slick and wet from the heavy rainfall, and as Sam finally got his hand around a bare ankle, Bruce's other leg slipped out from under him and his weight pitched forward.

Sam switched his grasp to Lou's leg just as Bruce let go of his father and tried desperately to grasp the low backsplash on top of the wall. There wasn't enough surface to hold on to, and the momentum taking Bruce over the edge was too great. His pumps scissored furiously but got no traction on the wet counter, and in an instant he had disappeared over the edge, screaming all the way down.

Sam pulled Lou Kenwood to safety, then both men peered cautiously over the edge of the Green Monster. Bruce's twisted body lay far below them on the wet warning track, face up, the neck bent in an impossible angle. His purple shoes had both come off on impact and lay a few feet away. Sam turned back toward the seats, but Lou kept staring at his son's body.

"I didn't want it to be like this," Kenwood said, his voice choking as he finally turned away. "I thought he was dead. I'd made my peace with that."

And now it was going to get worse for Lou Kenwood.

Sam glanced at Heather, wondering when she intended to tell Kenwood about Alberto Miranda. She had not gone to the edge of the wall to look down at Bruce's body; instead, she merely stood in place a few feet away and hung her head in silence. Sam knew that in every way, Heather must be feeling like an outsider now to this family that she had once hoped to join—the cause of much of their pain, and the bearer of even more bad news for one of them.

No, this was not the time for Heather to tell Lou that she was leaving him. Anyone could see that.

"I need…a cigarette," Katherine said.

Her hands and her head were visibly shaking. Sam watched as she put her hands under her blanket. The beauty he'd thought he'd seen in her just a few days ago seemed to have vanished. Before him now was a wet, withered, bitter woman with nothing on earth to live for.

He watched her pull out her cigarettes, and then reach under her blanket again for a lighter.

"What do we do now, Lou?" Sam said, looking at the owner.

Kenwood just shook his head. He glanced back at the field behind him, knowing that he had no idea how to explain to the press why his son had fallen from the top of the Green Monster to his death.

"I don't know," he finally said. "Heather?"

Both turned to look at her just as they heard the crack from Katherine's Beretta Bobcat and saw Heather crumple to the ground from the bullet that tore through her heart.

Sam lunged toward Katherine's chair, afraid she might shoot again. Instead, she held out the gun and handed it to Sam.

"You were right, Sam," Katherine said. There was a hard, satisfied glint in her eye and a wet, unlit cigarette dangling from her lips. "If you put it…in the right place…it only takes one."

Sam turned away from her and joined Kenwood at Heather's side. Blood had seeped out of Heather's chest wound, and he knew even without checking her pulse that she was dead.

"Get an ambulance," Kenwood said. "Call 9-1-1. Sam, call the police!"

Sam pulled out his cell phone and dialed 9-1-1. When the dispatcher said an ambulance was on the way, Sam took the phone away from his face and said, "Lou, are you sure you want the police now?"

"Yes," Kenwood said. He stood up, looking at his wife in stupefied disbelief. "Yes, call the police."

Sam's call was routed by an emergency dispatcher to the Boston cops. There was nothing else to do but wait for the squad cars and ambulances to arrive.

"I'm not sorry, Lou," Katherine said.

Kenwood sat down in one of the swivel seats with his back to Heather, hanging his head and holding his temples.

"Why, Katherine? Why?"

"Because she was going to end up…with everything," Katherine said. "The house, the boat, the team…you. You ignored my idea…my legacy…you were going to give it all to her."

"I don't understand," Kenwood said.

"She was willing to ruin you before you married Heather," Sam said.

Kenwood looked up slowly, staring first at Sam, then at Katherine.

"What are you talking about?"

"You and Heather would sink every dime...back into the team," Katherine said. "Then someday you would be gone...and Heather would have what I never had...The chance to run the best team in baseball...A dynasty...She'd spend all the revenues on the Sox...pleasing the fans...improving her image...

"Sooner or later...she'd marry some slick hunk in a suit... they'd have kids...and God knows who'd end up with the team...Meanwhile, I'd be totally forgotten...nothing to say I'd ever been a part of it...nothing of me..."

Lou walked up to Katherine, put his hands on either side of her wheelchair, and lowered his face close to hers. She flinched as though expecting Lou to strike her, or scream at her, but instead he spoke to her with the quiet sadness of a bewildered old man.

"Where'd you get the idea I was going to marry Heather?"

"Heather told me you promised to marry her after Katherine died," Sam said.

"I knew it all along," Katherine said.

"Never," Kenwood said. "May God strike me dead if I ever told her that."

It was Sam's turn to be stunned.

"Then where did she get that idea?" Sam said.

"God rest her soul, she was brilliant and beautiful, but I think she must have been a little crazy," Kenwood said. "Yeah, we had a fling. That wasn't hard to guess. But marry her? All in her imagination. I've been married twice. That's enough."

He looked at Katherine. The streaks running down both of their faces were tears mixed with the rain.

"I'd already found the love of my life."

# Chapter Thirty-three

The clouds parted well before game time that Sunday, but the Red Sox-Yankees showdown was postponed anyway. It would be made up the day after the regular season, if necessary. The Sox went on to sweep the following series with the Rays, while the Yankees were losing two of three to the Orioles, and Boston had a one-game lead with three, or at most four, games to play.

Katherine Kenwood was arrested for murder and was released from the Suffolk County jail when Lucky Louie paid her $500,000 bail. He wanted to take her home, but she was too frail. She died at Mass General two days later. Lou Kenwood scheduled a memorial ceremony for her prior to that night's Rays game at Fenway Park, and was persuaded by his staff to include Heather, too. Katherine's video tribute lasted five minutes, and included the announcement of the establishment of the Katherine Kenwood Foundation. Heather was mentioned once.

Sam called the L.A. police and learned that Frankie Navarro and a Kimberly Ryan had been detained after the Palos Verdes shootout, and eventually released. Joey "Icebox" Mattaliano had been found unconscious on Ryan's back deck, and was still in custody. No arrests had been made in the Laswell Gym murders; Sid Mink was seen in his oversized Dodger Stadium box seat Sunday afternoon. No one seemed to know where Frankie Navarro was, but his girlfriend Fawna had been found shot to death at the home Frankie owned. Frankie was the prime suspect in a presumed domestic dispute, but Sam knew otherwise. Sid Mink's boys had gone back to Frankie's house after the car wreck, forced Fawna to tell them where Bruce lived, and then killed her. She had been acting when she told Sam and Heather she didn't know who Bruce was. She'd actually been damn good.

Acting was not in Frankie's future, at least not in L.A.

Sam remained in Boston until Thursday, answering questions about the case for the police, the press, and the Commissioner's office. Lou Kenwood was convinced that it was safe to talk about the plot now, with Miranda willing to refute the allegations and no other proof ever having been brought forward. To deal with the increasing crush of worldwide media attention the story had gathered, Lucky Louie scheduled a press conference at Fenway Park for Thursday at one p.m.

Russ Daly flew in from Los Angeles on Wednesday for the press conference, and called Sam at the Taj Boston. Sam invited him up for a drink. He had a bottle of Woodford Reserve, which Daly gladly helped him finish.

"You owe me, Skarda." Daly eased his bulky frame into one of the stuffed armchairs by the fireplace. "I could have blown this story open last week."

"I know," Sam said. "That's why I decided to call you in L.A. I knew you wouldn't."

"I think I deserve something for my remarkable discretion."

"What do you want?"

"Something other than the B.S. Kenwood's been feeding the Boston writers."

So Sam told Daly the whole story, starting with the call he got from Heather in Minneapolis, the shooting outside the Boom Boom Room, and almost everything else right up to the moment that Katherine pulled the trigger on the gun Sam had helped her learn how to use.

He did hold back on a few details. He didn't tell Daly that the hitman in the boat was somewhere at the bottom of the Atlantic off Marblehead Neck, and he didn't tell him that the fatal blow to Guillermo "Jefe" Llenas had been struck by Alberto

Miranda; nor did he tell Daly that he'd placed the gun in Jefe's hand before the Caracas police arrived.

"Use whatever you want," Sam said when he was finished. "As long as you get the lead right: Alberto Miranda did not throw the World Series. The Sox won it."

"Some people will never believe that now," Daly said.

"Do you believe it?"

"Doesn't matter what I believe."

"Yeah, but I'm curious."

Daly took a long sip of his bourbon and then put his glass down on the table next to him.

"I believe it. That's the trouble with being a sportswriter. With all the shit I've seen, I'm still too fuckin' gullible. I want the fairy-tale ending."

"Not much of a fairy tale," Sam said. He swallowed some of his own bourbon and felt its effects moving like sorrow through his system. "Heather's dead, Katherine's dead, Bruce is dead…Fawna's dead, and Lou's going to be dead, too, before too long."

"I'll tell you one thing," Daly said. "If I was a beautiful blonde with office skills, I'd be applying for a job with the Red Sox tomorrow morning. Could end up owning the team."

Sam thought about hanging around through the weekend to see how the Sox did in their season-ending series with the Orioles—Lou had almost begged him to watch the games with him in his owner's suite—but he knew he needed to get away from Fenway, the Green Monster, and the Red Sox. He would watch the Sox in the playoffs, if they made it that far.

Sam placed two calls before leaving Boston. One was to Caroline, assuring her that he was still in one piece. Caroline had read about the Green Monster deaths in the paper, and asked if the woman who was killed was the same woman she'd helped fly to Caracas with Sam. Sam said it was.

"Sam, come to Tucson as soon as you get a chance," she said in a soft voice. "We need to be with each other for a while."

The other phone call was to Alberto Miranda. His elation at saving his mother's life had turned to despair at the news of Heather's death.

"She loved you, Alberto," Sam said. "She knew you were a good man."

"I loved her," Miranda said. He sounded much farther away than the 2,200 miles between Boston and Caracas.

"Honor her memory. Play the game the right way. Play it clean. That's all she would have asked of you."

"I know, man. I know."

◇◇◇

Kenwood sent a car to the hotel Thursday afternoon to take Sam to the airport, and Sam was happy to see Paul O'Brien get out of the driver's seat and greet him in front of the hotel.

"Afternoon, Mr. Skarda," Paul said. "Let me help you with your luggage."

Once they'd pulled away from the hotel, Sam said, "Paul, I want you to know how sorry I am for what happened."

"Don't worry about it." Paul looked back at Sam in his rear-view mirror. "It was a bad deal, but it wasn't your fault. You risked your life."

"I got you fired."

"No harm done," Paul said. The accent was creeping back into his voice, the "r" disappearing from "harm." "Mr. Kenwood explained what happened. I got a nice raise, too."

"How's your dad?"

"Hanging in there. Thanks for asking."

For the rest of the ride to the airport, Sam and Paul did what guys do: They talked baseball. Hurtado had agreed to a new four-year contract at $20,000,000 per season. He'd be 36 years old at the end of the deal, and Paul didn't think he'd be worth that kind of money in two more seasons, but how could you let him go after what he'd done in the last week? The pitching staff—especially the bullpen—was worn out after the furious effort it had taken to string together the 11-game win streak that had put them in first place. But the Yankees' pitching was in even worse shape; their bullpen was in tatters, and they'd had to call up a starting pitcher off their Scranton roster to start Friday's game in place of their 18-game winner, who had a sore elbow.

"I gotta say, it looks good for the Sox this weekend," Sam said.

They had emerged from the Ted Williams Tunnel near Logan Airport. Paul glanced back at Sam in the mirror, and Sam saw it in his eyes: the eternal battle between faith and despair that was the birthright of every Red Sox fan.

"I only know one thing for sure about the Red Sox," Paul said. "Sooner or later, they're gonna find a way to break your heart."

To receive a free catalog of Poisoned Pen Press titles, please contact us in one of the following ways:

Phone: 1-800-421-3976
Facsimile: 1-480-949-1707
Email: info@poisonedpenpress.com
Website: www.poisonedpenpress.com

Poisoned Pen Press
6962 E. First Ave. Ste. 103
Scottsdale, AZ 85251